TREADING WATER

THE TREADING WATER SERIES, BOOK 1

MARIE FORCE

Published by HTJB, Inc.
Copyright 2011. HTJB, Inc.
Cover by Courtney Lopes

ISBN: 978-1-942295-25-9

All characters in this book are fiction and figments of the author's imagination.

marieforce.com

The Treading Water Series

For my dear friends Julie Cupp, Chris Camara and Lisa Ridder, who loved this book from the beginning and never let me give up on it. And for Jack Harrington and the house we've built together—you were the first and the best.

AUTHOR'S NOTE

A mother isn't supposed to have favorites among her children, right? Neither should an author, but I bet we all have one. This is mine—my first book, the ultimate book of my heart and the first character to live inside my mind as a real, live person. It is also the only book of mine that my late mother was able to read, albeit a much earlier and rougher version. This book has taken me on a nearly eight-year journey from inception to publication. I'm delighted to now bring *Treading Water*, and its three sequels—*Marking Time, Starting Over* and *Coming Home*—to my readers.

A special thank you to the many friends who read this book, loved this book, believed in this book—and asked for the story that became *Marking Time,* which then led to *Starting Over* and *Coming Home.* Thank you also to my agent, Kevan Lyon, and her partner, Jill Marsal, who helped to make it a much better book. Read more about "The House That Jack Built" on my website at marieforce.com/marie/about-writing/24-the-house-that-jack-built.

As always, I love to hear from readers, so please let me know what you think of Jack's story. You can reach me at marie@marieforce.com.

PART I

*Treading Water: Using the feet and hands
to keep the head above water.*

CHAPTER 1

Jack gauged the impossible twelve-foot putt.

Jamie Booth, his best friend and business partner, sighed with exasperation. "There's *no way*, Jack, so just putt, will you?"

"Stop rushing me." Jack took a deep calming breath and aligned his putter as a warm spring breeze blew in off Rhode Island's Narragansett Bay. He tapped the ball, watched in amazement as it dropped into the hole, and pumped his arm like a professional golfer.

While their clients congratulated Jack, Jamie moaned and groaned. "I'll be hearing about this for *weeks*."

"Watch and learn, my friend," Jack said with a grin. "*Watch. And. Learn.*"

His cell phone vibrated in his pocket as the foursome moved to the fifteenth tee. Jack checked the caller ID and saw it was his wife, Clare. After the terrible fight they'd had that morning, he was relieved to hear from her.

"*Dad?*"

The frantic tone of his oldest daughter's voice stopped his heart. "What's the matter?"

"It's Mom."

"What? *What, Jill?*"

"She was hit by a car." Jill was crying so hard, he had trouble understanding her. "They're taking her to Newport Hospital."

Her words sent a jolt of icy fear straight through him. "I'm coming, honey," he managed to say. "I'll be right there."

Abandoning his clubs and his clients, he took off running across the golf course.

In the parking lot, Jamie pried Jack's keys out of his hand. "What's wrong, Jack?"

"It's Clare." Jack told him the news in a flat, shocked tone as they peeled out of the parking lot.

"Oh my God," Jamie muttered.

During the brief ride, a series of images flashed through Jack's mind, spanning the nearly twenty years he'd spent with Clare. His stomach ached when he remembered their angry words that morning. *She has to be all right. She has to be.*

"Talk to me," Jamie said.

"We fought." Jack felt detached from the moment, as if he was watching a movie of someone else's life.

"When?"

"This morning."

"I didn't think you guys ever fought."

"We never used to, but lately…Seems to be all we do." Jack hadn't even realized it until that moment, until it was possible he could lose her.

"What happened this morning?"

"She…pushed me away. In bed. Again. I can't remember the last time she *didn't* push me away. It's been months."

"You never said anything was wrong."

"I was afraid to say it out loud until I heard she might be hurt." He ached with worry and fear over what he'd find at the hospital. "Or worse." Forcing himself to breathe, he said, "God, what if she's dead? What if the last thing I said to her was 'if you want out of this marriage, just let me know?'"

"You'll work it out. You two are solid, man. Whatever's wrong, you'll get through it."

Provided she isn't dead, Jack thought. *Please don't let her be dead.*

They pulled up to the emergency entrance, and Jack leaped from the car. Inside he found his daughters in the care of a nurse and a police officer. Jill, Kate, and Maggie were crying as they flew into Jack's arms.

Jack held them for a long time, his heart racing as their gut-wrenching sobs ramped up his already out-of-control anxiety. "Can you tell me what happened?"

Jamie put an arm around Maggie and led her away so her older sisters could talk to their father.

"We were leaving the mall," Jill said, swiping at tears. "And this car came right at us. We jumped out of the way, but she just stood there, and the car hit her." A sob hiccupped through her. "She went right over the top and landed on the pavement."

"Okay, honey," he said, comforting his daughter while he tried to process what she'd said. As he imagined the scene, his chest tightened. "Maybe she just couldn't get out of the way in time."

Kate shook her head. "She didn't move. It was like she wanted the car to hit her or something."

"I'm sure it was so scary, but you must've seen it wrong," Jack insisted. "Mom would never do that."

A young doctor came through swinging doors to the waiting room. "Mr. Harrington? I'm Dr. Rooney." He led Jack away from the girls.

Jamie left Maggie in the care of her sisters and walked over to hear what the doctor had to say.

"Your wife is in extremely critical condition with a significant head injury," Dr. Rooney said. "She also has multiple fractures and a lacerated liver. When we get her stabilized, we'll be taking her up to surgery to remove her spleen and repair her liver."

Shocked, Jack said, "But she'll be all right, won't she?"

"The head injury is a big concern. We're inducing a coma to allow the swelling in her brain to subside. The next twenty-four to forty-eight hours will be critical."

Jack's hands were trembling, so he jammed them into his pockets. "How long will you keep her in the coma?"

"Hopefully, only a few days," Dr. Rooney said. "We'll have to wait and see what happens when we take her off the sedation."

"What could happen?" Jack had never experienced such raw fear. "She'll wake up then, right?"

"I can't say for certain. The head injury is severe. I wish I could tell you more, but it's a wait-and-see thing at this point. I'm sorry."

"I want to be with her."

"I'll come and find you when we get her settled after surgery," the doctor said as he walked away.

"A coma," Jack said, incredulous.

Jamie squeezed Jack's shoulder. "Why don't you call your mother and ask her to come help with the girls?"

"I just can't believe this. She's never been sick a day in her life. Remember how she was after having the girls?"

"I remember. She's superwoman, so there's nothing to worry about. I'm sure she'll be asking for you in no time."

"Yeah," Jack said. "Definitely."

The surgeons removed Clare's spleen, mended her liver, and set her badly broken arm and leg. After a week, her doctors were relieved that she was able to breathe on her own when they took her off the respirator. Encouraged, they also weaned her from the sedation. Jack, the girls, his sister, Clare's mother, brother, and sister kept up a round-the-clock vigil by her bedside. They sang to her, played her favorite music, cried, begged, and pleaded until they were hoarse, but she didn't regain consciousness.

At the end of the third week, Dr. Blake, the neurologist, asked to speak with Jack. Worried about what he might hear, Jack asked his sister, Frannie, to come, too.

"I'm afraid there's nothing more we can do for your wife. The blow to her head was tremendous, and we believe her coma is irreversible."

Jack and Frannie gasped as the doctor snatched away their last shred of hope.

"So what does that mean?" Jack asked. "What're you saying?"

"You have choices. Difficult choices."

"Such as?"

"Since she has no advanced directive, you can make decisions for her as her next of kin."

"Are you suggesting I end her life?"

"It's an option you may need to consider at some point down the road."

"I want to hear the others, because that's not on the table."

"Mr. Harrington, she's forty-three years old. She could live in this condition for decades."

Jack held up his hand to stop the doctor. "Is she brain dead?"

"Not technically—"

"Then I don't want to hear another word about ending her life. As long as there's activity in her brain I want her treated as if she's going to recover."

"We don't believe she will."

"As long as there's any chance at all—"

"There's less than a one percent chance."

"That's not zero," Jack said with a look that all but dared the doctor to argue with him.

The doctor seemed to realize the conversation was pointless. "We'll discharge her in a few days. I suggest you investigate long-term care for her. I can get you the names of some places, if that would help."

Left alone with his sister, Jack tried to absorb what the doctor had told him.

"I'll move here, Jack," Frannie said decisively. She lived in New York, where she worked as an artist, and had recently ended a brief second marriage. "I'll help with the girls and whatever else you need."

"I can't ask you to do that."

"You didn't ask. I want to." She gripped his hand as her hazel eyes heated with emotion. "What's more important than making sure the girls are well cared for right now?"

"Nothing," Jack said, resigned to the fact that he needed what his sister was offering. Besides, he was too drained to argue with her. "Thanks, Fran."

When Frannie left to pick up Maggie at a friend's house, Jack went back to Clare's room, where he'd spent most of the last three weeks. Despite the feeding tube, yellowing bruises, and casts on her arm and leg, she looked so much like herself that he ached with yearning to have her back, to have her turn those brilliant blue eyes his way and flash that special smile she used to save just for him, back when things were right between them.

Taking her hand, he held it against his face, and smoothed the blonde hair off her forehead with his other hand. "I know you can hear me," he said softly. "The things I said that day…I didn't mean them. You know I didn't. Whatever's bothering you, we can fix it. I need you to come back to me. Please, Clare. Don't give up."

How could this have happened to her? To them? If the girls were to be believed, she'd let the car hit her. But why? The questions tortured him through sleepless nights and agonizing days. Since her accident, he'd run through every minute he could remember from the last few months. Something had definitely been off between them. In place of her usually sunny, upbeat disposition, she'd been prone to long silences and bad dreams she thought he didn't know about. But every time he'd tried to broach the subject with her, he'd been rebuffed.

Their usually passionate and satisfying sex life had all but disappeared. Was it possible she'd met someone else? Had she decided to end a marriage that ranked as one of the proudest accomplishments in his life? Had she been waiting for the right time to tell him?

No. Not Clare. She loved him. They'd loved each other from the start and had a marriage and family others envied. She'd never leave him. But looking down at the battered woman in the hospital bed and remembering how she'd gotten there, suddenly he wasn't so sure.

Jill stepped into the room, and Jack forced a smile for his oldest daughter.

"Hi, honey."

"Hey." She stared at her mother with gray-blue eyes that were just like his. "No change?"

Since he couldn't bear to tell her what the neurologist had said, he shook his head. "Could I ask you something?"

Jill moved to the other side of the bed and rested a hand on her mother's arm. At fifteen, she moved with the poise of a woman twice her age. "Sure."

"Before this happened, did you notice anything…you know…different about Mom?"

"Well, *yeah.*" Her sarcastic reply surprised him.

"Like what?"

"That she was totally distracted, disorganized, scattered? And she was always forgetting stuff—like getting Maggie from school. That happened a bunch of times. They'd call the house, and I'd have to go get her because we couldn't reach Mom."

Astounded, Jack stared at her. "Why didn't you tell me?"

Her shrug was full of teenage insolence. "We didn't think you'd care."

"Why in the world would you think that?"

"Because! All you care about is work! And making money! You don't care about us."

Jack stared at her, his heart aching. "Everything I do is for you and your sisters." He glanced down at Clare. "And your mother."

"When was the last time you came to one of my lacrosse games or watched Maggie play soccer? Do you even *know* that Maggie plays soccer now?"

Where was this coming from? How long had she wanted to say this to him? "I'm sorry you think I don't care about you. I love you more than anything. I've always tried to show you that."

The cold, hard look she sent his way let him know he'd failed miserably.

"I tried to talk to her about what was bothering her, but she refused to tell me," he said.

"I wonder if we'll ever know."

Jack couldn't bring himself to tell her that the doctor had said her mother would probably never recover.

Frannie held back the tears until she reached the parking lot and couldn't contain them any longer.

"Fran," Jamie called from the next row. As he jogged over to her, tall, blond, and so handsome, she brushed frantically at the dampness on her face.

He stopped short in front of her. "Hey," he said, cupping her face and forcing her to meet his gaze. "What's wrong?"

Telling him what the doctor had said brought new tears to her eyes.

"Shit," he muttered as he gathered her into his arms.

Frannie relaxed against his muscular chest, wishing she could stay there forever. "Why'd this have to happen to her? To them?"

"I wish I knew." His ragged sigh told her he was upset, too. As Jack's best friend and business partner as well as the girls' godfather, he'd always been close with Clare. Telling herself this embrace was all about comfort, Frannie put her arms around his waist.

"Are you going to be okay?" he asked after they'd held each other for a long time.

"What choice do I have?" Reluctantly, she released him and took a step back. "My brother needs me."

He reached for her hand. "I'm here if you need me. You know that, don't you?"

She wished she had the nerve to tell him all the ways she needed him, but she never had before, and now was certainly not the time. "Thanks. I may take you up on that. I'm moving in with Jack and the girls."

"Really?" He seemed to brighten at that news.

"I can't keep running back and forth between here and New York, and the girls need someone they can count on."

"They're lucky to have you." Tucking a lock of her hair behind her ear, he surprised her when he pressed a lingering kiss to her forehead. "Whatever you need, whenever you need it. I'm here."

His softly spoken words nearly reduced her once again to tears. "I'd better go. Maggie's waiting for me."

"Take care, Fran." He opened the car door and held it for her as she got in.

She waved to him as she drove past him. Glancing in the mirror, she saw that he was still watching her. Now what did that mean?

Frannie moved in lock, stock, and easel to care for the girls while Jack made phone calls, searched the Internet, and consulted with doctors around the country. They all said the same thing—the longer the coma lasted, the less likely it became that Clare would recover.

Since he refused to put Clare in a nursing home, Jack brought her home to the large contemporary house he'd designed and built as a surprise for her five years earlier. He had the first-floor dining room converted to accommodate a hospital bed and the equipment needed by the team of round-the-clock nurses. Most nights he slept on a sofa he'd dragged into the room so she'd never be alone.

A week after Clare came home from the hospital, Jack received a call from Sergeant Curtis, the Newport police officer who'd investigated the accident. The driver had suffered a fatal heart attack, which explained why the car had been so out of control in the mall parking lot. Jack had thought the case was closed as far as the police were concerned.

"I was wondering if I could come by for a few minutes," Curtis said.

"Is there something new with the case?"

"I have something you need to see."

Fifteen minutes later, Jack opened the door to the tall, blond cop, and they shook hands.

"What've you got there?" He nodded at the disk in Curtis's hand.

"I was finally able to get a copy of the security video from the mall parking lot. I think you need to see it, but I have to warn you, it's tough to watch."

Jack swallowed hard and gestured for Curtis to follow him into the family room. He fed the disk into the DVD player, turned on the television, and watched in stunned silence as his daughters jumped out of the way of the speeding car and then turned to scream at their mother to do the same. They'd had time to turn and scream. Clare had time to move, but she didn't. She stood there and let the car hit her as her horrified daughters looked on.

"I just don't understand," Jack whispered as he watched it a second time. "Why in the world would she do that?"

"Can you, um, think of any reason why she'd want to end her life?"

"Of course not," he said, but after his conversation with Jill he wasn't so sure anymore. "She'd never do that, especially in front of her children. They were her whole world."

"I'm sorry. I don't mean to imply—"

"That my wife was suicidal?"

"It's just, well... Why didn't she move?"

Crushed by yet another wave of helpless despair, Jack shook his head. "I don't know."

CHAPTER 2

The video of Clare's accident haunted Jack for months. He'd wake up in the middle of the night, drenched in sweat and breathing hard because he had once again relived the horror of it in a dream. It was the same thing every time—he saw the car coming toward her but couldn't get to her in time to push her out of the way. He was equally plagued by the questions of why she hadn't moved and what she'd been thinking in that final life-changing instant before the car hit her.

After more than a year of waiting and hoping for some change in Clare's condition, Frannie clued him in that the girls never brought their friends home anymore because their house had become a hospital staffed by round-the-clock nurses. In light of this revelation, he'd made the unbearable decision to move Clare into a nearby place of her own, her care overseen by the same team of nurses.

Jack had taken the day after the move to wallow in his grief, but now he had no choice but to pull himself together. Jamie had been running the architectural firm they owned for more than a year on his own, the girls needed their father, and he had to figure out what to do with the rest of his life. While he'd much prefer to ignore all these pressing issues, he couldn't do that any longer.

Standing in front of the mirror, he dragged a razor over his face for the first time in several days. He went through the rote motions the way he did everything lately—out of necessity. His face seemed a little thinner than it had been the last time he'd looked closely. On the inside, he was totally numb. Would it always be this way? From now on, would he go through life without feeling anything? Without experiencing joy? Was that his fate?

As he started the water in the shower, his thoughts turned once again to Clare. Since memories were all he had left of her, he allowed himself to revisit them often. He vividly remembered the first time he ever saw her. She'd been tending bar at the National Hotel on Block Island. In constant motion, she'd been a whirling dervish of activity and banter and wit as she made drinks, washed glasses, talked to customers, rang up sales, and carried on a good-natured sparring match with the other two bartenders.

She'd looked then much as she did twenty years later: petite with unruly blonde hair and the most amazing blue eyes he'd ever seen.

From across the bar, she'd glared at him. "You got a problem, buddy?"

"I'm sorry. I didn't mean to stare. I've just never seen anyone get so much done in as little time as you do."

Collecting abandoned glasses, she worked her way to his end of the bar. "I don't let any grass grow. That's why they ask me back every year."

"You've worked here before? I don't remember you."

"This is my fifth summer. I bussed tables until I was old enough to bartend. Ready for a refill?"

He pushed his mug forward. "Heineken, please. Funny, I'm sure I'd remember you."

"I'll bet you say that to all the girls." She winked and moved on to other customers.

Jack continued to watch her—without staring—while he ate dinner and drank another beer. The bar got busier, and though he'd planned to hit some of the island's other hot spots, he was still there at last call.

"One more for the road?" she asked as she cleaned up discarded glasses and dishes.

Since he wasn't driving, he said, "Sure, thanks."

When she brought him the beer, he asked what she did the rest of the year.

"I teach third grade in Mystic."

"I had you pegged as a college kid."

She laughed. "Everyone always thinks I'm too young to be the teacher, but I'm going into my third year. What about you?" While they talked, she cleared off the bar, washed dishes, and ran credit cards.

"I'm an architect. Just finished graduate school last week. I'm taking a break before I go back to work."

"I love architecture. I've always been interested in how buildings are designed and put together. It sounds like it would be a lot of fun."

"It is." He sipped the beer, trying to make it last so she would keep talking to him. "I've had the opportunity to work on some great projects, and I've got a couple of others waiting for me when I get back."

She crooked a skeptical eyebrow. "If you just graduated, how is it you've already worked on such great stuff? Doesn't that usually come *after* school?"

"I worked for a Boston firm while I was in grad school."

"Where'd you go?"

"Berkeley and Harvard."

She let out a low whistle. "Oh, well, don't mind me, Harvard boy. La-di-da."

"It's just a school."

"Yeah, right. Just a school we mere mortals couldn't begin to aspire to. So what've you worked on? Anything I might've heard about?" Her pace slowed as the crowd filtered out to find after-hours fun elsewhere.

"The new symphony hall in Boston, for one."

"Didn't Neil Booth design that?"

Impressed, he looked at her with new appreciation. "You do pay attention. I work for Neil. My friend Jamie is his son." He wasn't sure why he told her that. He usually didn't mention it since Jamie was sensitive about the advantages that came from being Neil's son in their profession.

"Well, well. This just gets more and more interesting, doesn't it?"

"Neil is a terrific guy. Very normal despite the fame."

"I took an architecture class in college. I read a lot about his work." She scooped up Jack's empty glass.

As he got up to leave, he tried to recall the last time he'd enjoyed a conversation with a woman this much. Most of the women he met were either not interested in his work or totally self-absorbed. The tiny dynamo with the blonde hair and startling blue eyes was different.

"Could I walk you home, or do you have other plans?"

She studied him for a long time before she answered. "I don't have any plans, but how do I know you aren't a freak? We get a lot of freaks around here in the summer," she said with a teasing grin. "Besides, I don't even know your name."

"It's Jack Harrington."

She made him suffer through a seemingly endless minute before she said, "I'll go with you, Jack Harrington, but I still have another half hour or so here."

"I'll wait." His heart skipped a beat, and somehow he knew everything was about to change.

The sting of shampoo in his eyes interrupted Jack's remembrances. Rinsing off the soap, he realized he'd been in there a long time and shut off the shower.

He got dressed and straightened the messy room. Stripping the sheets from the bed, he tossed them into the washer along with the clothes that had piled up the last few days. After he remade the bed, he wandered outside to the deck. With only the relentless pounding of the ocean below for company, Jack sat there until the sun began to dip toward the horizon, thinking about his daughters, the huge job his company had been awarded to build the Infinity Group's Newport hotel, and the staggering list of things he needed to do to get his life in order. First on the list was reconnecting with his kids.

He eventually wandered downstairs, where Frannie and the girls were about to sit down for dinner.

Frannie offered him a warm smile. "It's good to see you."

"I'm sorry I punched out yesterday. I just needed a little time."

"I understand. We're glad to see you, aren't we, girls?"

Their replies were mostly mumbles: uh-huh, sure, I guess.

"Are you hungry?" Frannie asked.

"I could eat."

"Great. Maggie, set another place, please."

Jack felt like a visitor in the home he'd built largely with his own hands. Since the girls seemed to have nothing to say to him, he took the opportunity to study them, to really *look* at them for the first time in longer than he could remember.

Each of them had healthy tans from long days at the beach. While he hadn't been paying attention, Jill and Kate had become young women, and Maggie had lost the baby fat in her cheeks.

Jill was sixteen and the image of him—tall and dark-haired with gray-blue eyes. Kate, at fifteen, had Clare's blonde hair and her shocking blue eyes, but was tall like him. Ten-year-old Maggie was a combination of the two of them: Jack's dark hair and Clare's eyes. He and Clare had always joked that they each had a "mini-me" and then, as a surprise, along came a "mini-we."

He hadn't thought about that in a long time, and the memory made him yearn for her.

His attempts to make conversation with the girls were greeted with one-word answers. Only Frannie seemed glad to have him there. Clearly, he had his work cut out for him.

"I'd like to go out to the island this weekend," he said as they were finishing up.

"Have fun," Jill said.

"I want you girls to come with me."

They all spoke at once.

"I have plans."

"Meghan's sleepover is this weekend."

"I'm babysitting."

"I want you to come with me." Making eye contact with each of them, he added, "It's important." He had no idea what he'd do if they refused.

His mother owned Haven Hill, a house on the island, and some of their happiest times together as a family had been spent there. Jack was counting on the house to work its magic and help him reconnect with his daughters.

"I think that's a great idea, Jack," Frannie said with a meaningful look at each girl. "Some time away together will be great for all of you."

They never came right out and said they'd go, but they stopped protesting when Frannie weighed in.

Jack sent her a grateful smile.

After dinner, the girls scattered. Jack helped Frannie clean up the kitchen and then set out for a walk on the beach. Usually, he ran at this time of day, but today he didn't feel like it. Taking in the soft late spring air and relieved to be out of the house, he walked for miles and visited with Clare for a short time. He returned home well after dark and took a moment to stare into the dining room, which once again boasted a table and chairs where a hospital bed had been for more than a year. Even though he knew he'd done the right thing for his kids, it would take some time to get used to not having Clare close by.

He trudged upstairs, halting when he heard sniffling in Maggie's room.

He peeked in to find her tucked into bed with her favorite sleeping buddy, Froggie. She looked so cute in her yellow pajamas with her cheeks pink from the day at the beach and her dark hair shining.

"Maggie? Are you are all right?" When she scrambled to wipe her face on the sheet, his heart began to ache.

"Uh-huh."

Stepping into the room, he moved hesitantly toward the bed, not sure if he'd be welcome. "Can I get you anything? Some water, maybe?"

"No, thanks. I'm fine."

"Okay." As he turned to leave, something stopped him. He wasn't sure if it was Clare looking down on him from wherever she was just then or what, but he couldn't bring himself to leave his child crying in her bed. Summoning courage, he sat on the edge of the bed. "You want to talk about it?"

She bit her lip, and his heart broke all over again when her eyes filled with new tears. "Is Mommy ever coming back?" The small voice was so unlike her. Apparently, he wasn't the only one adjusting to yet another change in their lives.

"Oh, honey, I don't think so."

She sat up and reached for him. "Why did Mommy let that car hit her?" she asked with a sob as she clung to him.

How long had she waited to ask him these questions? "Baby, she didn't do it on purpose. She froze because she was scared. The accident hurt something in her brain, so she can't be with us. But inside, where her heart is, she still loves you and Kate and Jill and me very, very much. You have to believe that." He settled her back onto the pillow and tucked her in again.

"I do," she said, wiping her face.

"Good, because as long as you believe it, then you'll feel Mommy's love, no matter where she is." He wished *he* could believe it.

"Will you be here when I wake up?"

The question tugged at his already raw emotions. "You bet. I'll even make my famous chocolate chip pancakes." It was the only thing they allowed him to cook.

"Awesome!" she said, sounding more like herself again.

"See you in the morning."

He walked out to find Frannie waiting for him in the hallway. She had gathered her long auburn hair into a ponytail and was dressed for bed in a T-shirt and sweats.

Spent, he rubbed the back of his neck. "How much did you hear?"

"Enough. You said all the right things."

"I'm so tired," he said, anxious to get upstairs where he could be alone.

"Go to bed. I'll wait up for Jill."

"Where is she?"

"On a date."

"With who?"

"A boy in her class named Kyle. I've met him. Seems nice."

Jack realized that *he* should've met the boy his daughter was out with. Next time, he'd make sure he did. "Well, if you don't mind waiting up…"

"I've got a movie to watch. Go to bed."

"Thanks, Frannie. For everything."

"My pleasure." She kissed his cheek and headed downstairs.

Jack went up the spiral stairs to his room and wandered again to the deck overlooking the pool and ocean farther below. He waited to crawl into bed until he was certain he was tired enough to drift off to sleep without being tortured by unpleasant thoughts. Just as sleep overtook him, the phone rang, jarring him awake.

He waited, hoping Frannie would answer it. On the third ring, he grabbed it.

"Dad?" Jill sounded a bit frantic. "Can you get Frannie?"

"She must've fallen asleep downstairs. She didn't pick up."

"I need to talk to her."

Something about Jill's tone and the slight slur to her speech caught his attention. "What's wrong?"

"I need a ride home."

"What happened to your date?"

"Can you just get Frannie? Please?"

"I'll come get you. Where are you?"

"That's all right. I'll find a ride."

"Jill. Tell me where you are. Right now."

Reluctantly, or so it seemed to him, she gave him the address.

"I'll be right there. Don't move."

He threw on clothes, grabbed his keys and cell phone, and went downstairs, where Frannie was curled up on the sofa sound asleep. Not at all sure of what he would find when he got there, he drove into downtown Newport. At the address Jill had given him, several police officers were attempting to break up a raging party. His heart in his throat, he called Jill's cell. "Hurry up and get out here. The place is crawling with cops."

Jack watched the police drag one teenager away in handcuffs while another puked in the empty lot across the street before Jill materialized out of the darkness.

She slid into the car and slammed the door.

"What're you doing here? Have you been drinking?"

"Spare me the fatherly concern, will you?"

"Fine, then let me get one of the cops to take you for a sleepover at the city jail." He reached for the door handle.

"Yes! I had a couple of beers. Who cares?"

Punching the gas to get out of there, he couldn't believe what he was hearing. "I care! You're *sixteen*, Jill!"

"I know how old I am."

Under the glow of the streetlights he could see her eyes were glassy and deduced that she'd had more than a couple of beers. Jack's mind raced with things he wanted to say, but he kept his mouth shut until he figured out what he *should* say.

Jill stayed quiet on the way home.

"What happened to the guy you were with?" Jack finally asked.

"I don't know. We got separated."

"What were you even doing there?"

"They're friends of his. We were just going for a little while."

"How much did you have to drink?"

She shrugged. "I told you. A couple."

"Really, Jill. I just can't believe you'd—"

"Relax, Dad! It's no big deal. Everyone does it."

Jack bit back the urge to snap at her. "You're not everyone, and don't tell me to relax."

"Whatever." Her cell phone rang as they pulled into the driveway. "Where'd you go?" She glanced at her father. "I got a ride. All right. Yeah, I'll talk to you tomorrow."

Jack waited for her and watched her teeter on the way into the house.

Frannie sat up as they came in. "Hey, what's going on?"

"Someone had a few too many at a party and got separated from her date."

Frannie frowned at her niece. "Jill…"

"Can we save this Hallmark moment until tomorrow? I'm tired."

"Sit down," Jack said.

Releasing a dramatic sigh, she dropped into a chair.

"Is this what you do with your friend Kyle?" Jack asked. "Go to out-of-control parties and get drunk?"

"I've never been to an out-of-control party *or* gotten drunk with Kyle before."

"You might want to lose the sarcasm, Jill," Frannie warned.

"You're not my mother! You can't tell me what to do."

"That's enough, Jill! You'll not talk to your aunt—or me—like that, do you hear me?"

Just as Jill started to reply, she turned green. Clasping her hand over her mouth, she bolted for the bathroom.

Jack glanced at Frannie before he got up to follow his daughter. Standing at the open door to the bathroom, he watched helplessly as she wretched.

Frannie came up behind him. "Go," she whispered. "Go to her."

Hesitating for another second, he ventured into the bathroom and gathered Jill's long dark hair into a ponytail.

"Go away," she moaned. "Leave me alone."

"You're stuck with me." He stayed with her through another vicious bout of vomiting as well as the dry heaves that followed. When it was over, he wiped her face with a cool washcloth and sat down next to her on the bathroom floor.

"I'm never drinking again."

Laughing softly, Jack remembered once making the same vow after a similar incident. "Good." He put his arm around her, brought her to rest against him, and was relieved when she didn't resist. "Think it's over?"

"For now, but there could be more."

"Then we'll wait."

"Why are you being so nice to me?"

"Because you're sick."

"So I'm not grounded?"

"I never said that."

She mulled that over for a few minutes. "How long?"

He hadn't the foggiest idea. "What would Mom say?"

"Um, forever?"

"That sounds about right."

Jill moaned. "Seriously. How long?"

"How does a month sound?"

"Like forever."

"But fair in light of the crime?"

"I guess."

He held out his hand. "I'll take your phone and keep it safe for the next month."

"Oh come on!"

"As I recall, cell phone surrender was a key part of Mom's grounding program."

"Why does it have to be part of yours?"

"Cough it up."

She dug it out of her back pocket and slapped it into his hand.

They sat on the bathroom floor until she sagged against him, asleep. Somehow, he managed to lift her off the floor and carry her to the sofa in the family room. Covering her with a blanket, he kissed her forehead. Then he got comfortable on the other sofa.

Just in case she needed him again during the night.

Leaving the port of Point Judith on the Friday night ferry, Jack stood on the bow and watched the ship sluice through the foamy water. He took a drink from his cup of coffee, wishing for a shot of whiskey instead. "Here goes nothing," he whispered as he turned away from the rail to join the girls inside.

As usual, Kate sat by herself, strumming the guitar she never left home without these days. Maggie was attached to her iPod, and Jill had curled up with a book on one of the benches. An obnoxiously large pile of duffel bags sat on the floor next to them. Jack had been so glad they were coming with him that he'd chosen not to make an issue of how much stuff they'd brought for one weekend.

He had no plan, per se, for when they got to the island. All he knew was that he had to do *something* to get their attention, to reconnect with daughters he'd somehow managed to grow estranged from while living under the same roof.

The ferry backed into Block Island's Old Harbor just after six. Disembarking with their two tons of luggage, Jack and the girls piled into the old station wagon he kept on the island. Their silence during the short ride to the south end grated on his already frayed nerves.

"Another busy weekend on the Block," he said, feeling stupid and desperate as the words came out of his mouth.

More silence.

"What do you guys want for dinner?"

"Pizza from Aldo's," Maggie said.

"Aldo's it is," Jack said, smiling at her in the mirror.

It was just pizza, but it was a start.

By Saturday afternoon, Jack was ready to shoot himself. With each of them immersed in some form of technology—iPods, computers, cell phones, televisions—they were doing an excellent job of ignoring him. The cowardly part of him wanted to go up to his room and kill time until they could go home the next day. However, the coward was overruled by the inner voice telling him he'd already squandered too much time with them.

Bracing himself for outrage, he stepped into the huge living room that over-looked the ocean. "Hey, guys." He waved a hand at Kate to get her attention, since she had her earbuds in. "Let's go for a ride."

"I'm watching something," Maggie said.

"I was just about to take a shower," Jill added. She'd been only slightly friend-lier to him since their interlude on the bathroom floor. He took the progress where he could get it.

"We're going for a ride," he said more forcefully this time. "And Kate, bring your guitar, will you?"

Sending him a quizzical look, Kate did as he asked. Though they grumbled all the way, they found shoes and coats and trooped out to the car.

As Jack drove toward the bluffs on the island's north end, he so hoped he was doing the right thing. He got them as close as he could in the car. They'd have to walk the rest of the way.

"Am I bringing the guitar?" Kate asked with a wary glance at the rugged trail.

"Yes, please."

As Jack watched them exchange puzzled looks, his gut clenched with nerves. "Listen, guys, I know I haven't given you much reason to trust me or to believe in me, but I'm asking for thirty minutes."

Silence.

"I need half an hour with no attitudes, no anger, no dispositions. Can you give me that?"

"What're we going to do?" Maggie asked, her expression open and accepting.

Jack smiled and tugged on her ponytail. "Come with me, and I'll show you."

He led them up the rocky trail to the place where he and Clare first made love, where they'd first talked of marriage, and where they'd come to make the big-gest decisions of their married life. Here he'd convinced her the time was right for him and Jamie to leave Neil Booth's firm and start their own company, to move their growing family from Boston to Newport and begin a whole new life. Later, she'd brought him here to tell him about their unplanned third child who turned out to be one of the best surprises of his life.

At the top of the path, the Atlantic stretched out before them. Jack could think of no better place for Clare's daughters to say good-bye to their mother.

"This was your place with Mom," Jill said quietly, taking in the view of the ocean.

"Yes."

"I remember coming here once with you, when I was really young," Jill said. "Mom told me it was your special place."

Jack gestured to a grassy patch. "Sit with me?" He waited until they were settled and dropped down next to Kate. "Whenever we were out here on the island, Mom and I would try to get up here to have a chat. Sometimes we talked about serious stuff; other times we just chilled and watched the water for a while. Often we talked about you guys." He looked up to find them hanging on his every word and could see the hunger on their faces. They were desperate for any part of their mother they could still hang on to.

Forcing himself to press on, Jack took a deep breath and tried to get it together. He'd been unprepared for the wallop of emotion that came with returning to this place. "Before the accident, when I knew something was wrong, I should've brought her here. She wouldn't talk to me about it at home, but perhaps…if we'd come here…"

"Maybe it was something she needed to work out on her own," Kate said.

"That's possible," Jack conceded, wanting so badly to believe it. "But I need you to know that I wish I'd tried harder to figure out what was bothering her."

"We wish we'd tried harder, too," Jill said.

Her sisters nodded in agreement.

Touched by their confession, he turned to Kate. "Will you play something for us? Something that reminds you of Mom?"

"I know just the thing." She launched into a familiar tune that made her father and sisters smile. "Remember her singing *so loud*?"

"*And so bad!*" the others chimed in, laughing at the memory.

Kate played *Landslide*, and Jack couldn't believe how very good she'd gotten since the last time he heard her play. Clare had loved the Stevie Nicks song, and he wished she could've heard their daughter sing it. Kate had chosen the perfect song. The last year had been just like standing at the bottom of a landslide.

She played the last note and glanced at him, a shy smile gracing her pretty face. "That was beautiful, honey. Your voice is so lovely."

"Thank you."

"Can I say something?" Jill asked.

"Of course," he said, pleased that they had picked up on the reason he'd brought them here.

"I had to memorize a poem for school recently. We could pick anything we wanted, so I chose Mom's favorite."

"Tennyson," Jack said.

She nodded. "It reminded me of her and of what our family has been through in the last year:

Though much is taken, much abides; and though
We are not now that strength which in old days
Moved heaven and earth, that which we are, we are—
One equal temper of heroic hearts,
Made weak by time and fate, but strong in will
To strive, to seek, to find, and not to yield."

Watching his beautiful, brave daughter so eloquently speak the words her mother had loved moved Jack to tears. He cleared his throat and hoped he could say what they needed to hear. "That's exactly what we have to do, you know? We have to continue to be a family."

"Everything's different now," Maggie said sadly.

"Yes, it is. And as much as we wish it wasn't, we have to find a way to go on without Mom."

"I really wish we didn't have to," Maggie said.

"So do I, honey. But here's the thing… Mom always took care of you guys, and I let her. It was easier for me to hang back and let her do the heavy lifting than it was for me to get in there and get my hands dirty with you guys."

They giggled at the words he used, but he had their attention. "That's not the kind of father I want to be anymore. I know this is another big change on top of so many others, but from now on, I'm in charge at home. Frannie's there to help us out, but she's not responsible for you guys. I am. If you want to go somewhere or do something, you ask me. When I'm at work or out of town, of course you can check in with her, but I always want to know where you are and who you're with. Agreed?"

Their mumbled replies indicated their agreement.

"I know I haven't been the world's best father, but I really want to fix that. I hope you'll let me try."

Maggie moved closer to him and rested her head on his shoulder.

He slipped an arm around her.

"Can I sing a song that reminds me of Mom?" she asked.

"Absolutely."

In a small voice, she sang the theme song from *Barney*.

The others smiled, remembering Clare singing the happy-family song to mend hurt feelings after dustups between sisters.

"We were a happy family," Maggie said, her voice catching.

"We will be again." Jack brushed a kiss over her silky dark hair. "I promise. We will be again."

For the first time in a long time, he had reason to hope. They'd taken the first, most important step on what would no doubt be a long journey. But they'd taken the step, and he was filled with relief.

CHAPTER 3

When Jack walked into the well-appointed offices of Harrington Booth Associates for the first time in fourteen months, he was hit with a familiar surge of pride.

He and Jamie started HBA after learning everything they could from Neil Booth during their seven years with him. Neil had been disappointed when they declined his offer to take over his firm as he contemplated retirement. They'd longed for something simpler than the fast-paced, high-profile positions they held in Neil's firm. Over time, though, HBA had grown a reputation to rival even Neil's.

Spotting the framed silver dollar under the company's name on the inside wall, Jack smiled at the memory of flipping it with Jamie to determine which one of them would come first in the company name. Only when Jack won for the third time did Jamie concede defeat.

Before Clare's accident, Jack wouldn't have dreamed of taking more than a week of vacation at a time. *Proves no one is indispensable*, he thought with a small smile as several of his employees welcomed him back.

His longtime assistant, Quinn Jeffries, greeted him with a fierce hug. Hired as his secretary more than twelve years earlier, she'd long since become his right hand and close friend.

"So good to see you here," she said as she released him from her warm embrace.

"It's good to be back." His corner office boasted two full glass walls with an exquisite view of the beach and rocky shore. Jamie's office occupied the other corner on the same side with a shared bathroom in the middle.

"Come in," Jack said to Quinn.

He dropped his leather bag on his desktop where the lack of clutter was a stark reminder of how long he'd been gone. "So bring me up to speed," he said when he'd recovered his bearings. "What's going on?"

"Jamie said you'll be heading up the next phase of the Infinity project."

"That's right."

"You've got a conference call with their team at eleven to get acquainted and set the schedule for the next few months." She rattled off the list of HBA staff members Jamie had assigned to work with Jack on the hotel.

"What's everyone else got going?"

"Four houses, a shopping center, a new auto dealership, and the sailing museum renovations."

"Wow."

"Yeah, everyone's pretty stretched. You and Jamie may need to talk about hiring a few more people."

Jack loved that Quinn didn't hold back opinions that were usually astute and right on the mark.

"Did Jamie tell you he's been asked to consult on a job in Tokyo?" she asked.

"No, but I'm sure he'll tell me about it when he gets a chance."

"Here are the preliminary files on the hotel. You can look them over before the call. Oh, and Jamie called a staff meeting at ten."

"Sounds good. I have a standing dinner date at six with the girls every night from now on. I'll probably need your help getting out of here on time. "

"You got it."

"Thanks for everything, Quinn. I know you managed a lot more than your own job over the last year. I appreciate everything you did to help Jamie."

"We're just glad to have you back." She left him with a smile and closed the door.

He turned in his chair to inspect the shore as it emerged from morning fog to the kind of glorious early summer day Clare had loved. The beach was alive with joggers, dogs on leashes, and lifeguards meandering out to their posts. It was all so normal, a scene he'd witnessed many times before, and yet nothing was normal anymore because Clare wouldn't be waiting for him at the end of the day.

Since the day on the bluffs with the girls, emotions that had lain dormant for so many months of numbness were once again raw. Thinking of Clare and all they'd lost brought tears to his eyes. He'd been a regular waterworks lately, as if all the feelings he'd fought so hard to suppress during the long year since the accident were suddenly trying to get out. But then he remembered promising the girls he would get their lives back on track. He wiped his eyes on the sleeve of his shirt and turned to the files Quinn had left.

"I can do this," he whispered. "I *will* do this."

By ten o'clock, he'd caught up on the project that would take over his life for the next year and a half. Stopping to grab a fresh cup of coffee, he headed into the conference room for the meeting.

"Surprise!" The entire staff greeted him, and a huge banner hung on the back wall that said *Welcome Home, Jack*. They offered hugs as he absorbed the emotional outpouring from his coworkers.

"Wow," he said once the uproar had died down. "You really surprised me. Thanks for the warm welcome. It's great to be back."

"Speech!" someone called.

Cornered, Jack had no idea what to say. "I…ah… Thank you for the overwhelming support this past year and for all you did to help Jamie." He paused to collect himself. "It was comforting to know you were taking care of HBA so I could take care of my family. I guess today is the first day of the rest of my life. I'm glad to be spending it here."

His coworkers' applause embarrassed him.

"Welcome back, bud." Jamie grinned and clapped Jack on the back.

"Thanks." The animated group dug into the coffee and bagels on the conference room table. "I'd forgotten how much fun it is to be here."

"I need to remind you of *all* the fun you used to have."

Jack raised an eyebrow. "Speaking of fun, what's this I hear about you and Tokyo?"

"Word travels fast. It's an office being modeled after one of my dad's buildings in New York. They asked him to consult, but since he'd rather be playing golf, he sent them to me."

"Are you interested?"

"Sort of. I've never been to Japan, so that part intrigues me. But I wasn't sure the time was right to take on something overseas."

"Quinn thinks we need to hire some more hands. Then maybe you could do it."

"Even with the hotel?"

"I don't see why not. What if we made Quinn our very first vice president and gave her responsibility for managing the office? She's more or less doing it now. We could make it official and get it off my plate."

"That would allow me to be gone for a week or two every now and then if I need to be in Tokyo." Jamie rubbed his chin and mulled it over. "How much more should we pay her?"

"Twenty-five thousand?"

"Done."

"Great, I'll tell her today. Let's hit up the Crimson for a couple of new grads," Jack said, referring to their alma mater.

"I'll take care of that," Jamie said as they wandered over to join the party. "I'll let you know what unfolds with Tokyo. I was waiting until you came back to decide."

The rest of the day flew by as Jack consulted on a variety of ongoing projects, participated in the conference call with the Infinity Group's Chicago headquarters team, and began preliminary planning for the next phase of the hotel project.

Infinity had chosen HBA's design over seven other New England firms. In designing the one-hundred-and-fifty-room resort, the challenge had been to create an old-fashioned New England beach "cottage" with all the modern amenities. As part of the first phase of building the hotel, Jack would work with the interior design team to ensure their décor choices brought HBA's design to life.

He stood, stretched, and checked the beach, which was almost deserted. Fog hung off the coast, waiting for the sun to give up for the day and reminding him of the dinner date with the girls. He buzzed Quinn and asked her to come in.

She came through the door a minute later and laughed at the scene on his desk. "I love what you've done with the place." His messiness and her obsessive neatness was a running joke between them. "How's it going?"

"I got more done today than I thought I would. I made a list of ideas for the interior designers' research trip for the last week in August. Do you mind taking it from here and setting up accommodations?"

"No problem."

"None of them have ever been here before, so we'll send them to Cape Cod, Martha's Vineyard, Nantucket, and Boston the first week, plus they'll do a second full week in Newport. Let's go the bed-and-breakfast route, since we're aiming for an inn feel with the Newport hotel. Get tickets for a Red Sox game, too. They can't be in Boston and not go to Fenway."

"Them or you?"

"Them, of course," he said, smiling.

"I'll get on it in the morning." She scanned his list. "You're not taking them to Block Island?"

"Not this time. Nantucket will take care of the 'resort island' theme." After the emotional trip with the girls, he wasn't ready to go back to Block Island just yet.

She checked her watch. "You'd better think about wrapping it up. You don't want to keep your ladies waiting."

"There's one other thing before I go."

"What's that?"

"Jamie and I would like to offer you a promotion."

Her brows knitted with confusion. "What kind of promotion?"

"How about vice president, in charge of running the office. Are you interested?"

"That's always been your thing."

"I need to focus on the hotel, and Jamie's got the Tokyo job brewing."

"I'd love to do it, and I appreciate the new title."

"Great. Thank you."

"I should probably mention that I'm getting married."

Startled, Jack said, "Is that so?"

Her warm, green eyes danced with amusement. "You *have* been gone a while, Jack. Things have happened."

"Who's the lucky guy?"

"Brian. You met him a long time ago."

"Ah, our friend from Down Under?"

She smiled. "That's him. We're planning a small wedding this fall."

He stood to give her a congratulatory hug. "I'm very happy for you. And I'm sure you'll both be glad to hear your promotion comes with a twenty-five-thousand-dollar raise."

She gasped. "*Are you serious?*"

Laughing at her reaction, he said, "You're extremely valuable to us, and you've shown us again how much you're capable of during this past year. We appreciate it, and we want to reward you for it."

She flung her arms around him. "Thank you, Jack! I love working for you guys, and I appreciate your vote of confidence."

"We couldn't run this place without you," he said as another thought occurred to him. "If you want Haven Hill for the wedding, it's all yours."

"Oh my God! That'd be fantastic!"

"It's nothing." Jack shrugged. "Just let me know the date, and I'll tell the family it's yours that weekend."

"I can't wait to tell Brian about all of this. I'm so glad you're back. It just wasn't the same without you."

"Get out of here. I'll see you in the morning."

She hurried away as Jamie came in through the door that connected their offices.

"Who lit a fire under her?"

Jack dropped files into his briefcase and turned off his computer. "I told her about the promotion and the raise. Did you know she's getting married?"

"I've heard some talk about that. Brian's a nice guy. They've been out on the boat a few times."

"It's funny how life went on without me. I feel like everything stopped fourteen months ago." He paused and shook it off, not wanting the negative thoughts to intrude on the best day he'd had in longer than he could remember. "I offered her Haven Hill for the wedding."

"That's really nice of you."

"So I had a really interesting chat with Infinity's chief designer today. Andrea Walsh?"

"She goes by Andi," Jamie said. "Wait 'til you meet her. Amazingly talented."

"She seemed really sharp on the phone. She's got some great ideas. They're looking forward to the visit."

"You're sure you're up to handling so much right out of the gate?"

"It'll be good to think about something other than my own problems for a change."

"How're things going with the girls?"

"Much better. They seem to have accepted that their old man is in charge and paying attention. I'll tell you, though. Their social lives exhaust me. I need a color-coded spreadsheet to track their comings and goings. I have no idea how Clare managed to make it look so easy."

"She was one hell of a mother," Jamie said.

"That she was, and now they have me. The sorry substitute."

"When they're all grown up with kids of their own, they'll remember what you did for them, and they'll appreciate it."

Jack eyed him skeptically as they walked to the parking lot together. "You sure about that, oh wise one?"

"Positive."

"Day one went better than I thought it would. Thanks again for the party."

"We're glad to have you back. Say hi to the girls for me."

"Will do. See ya."

Jack unlocked his silver BMW convertible, got in, and sat for a long time before he could make himself move. *Clare won't be there.* "But the girls will be," he said as he started the car and drove home to them.

PART II

Freestyle: Using a swimming stroke of one's choice instead of a specified style.

CHAPTER 4

On the last Sunday in August, Jack rode the airport escalator and wondered how he would pick out Andrea Walsh from the crowd arriving on the Chicago flight. As he approached the top, he spotted a gorgeous brunette with long curls walking toward him. Based on Jamie's description, Jack realized it was her. *Well, that was easier than expected.*

When her brown eyes scanned the crowd and connected with his, her stunning smile left him staggered as he was hit with an odd sense of recognition. Had they met before? Not that he could recall.

"Andrea?"

"Hi, Jack." She shifted her briefcase so she could shake hands with him. "Please call me Andi. Thanks so much for meeting me."

"No problem." He took her bag and ushered her down the escalator to retrieve her luggage. "You picked a great day to arrive. Rhode Island at her finest."

"The view from the air was amazing."

"I never get tired of it."

"I'm sorry to drag you away from your family on a day like this," she said as they arrived at the baggage area.

"I blocked two weeks for your team's visit, so they understand. They might join us later to go sailing if you're interested."

"I'd love to."

When she glanced up to find him studying her, her cheeks heated with color. "What?"

"I keep feeling like I've met you before, but I'm sure I haven't. You seem so familiar."

"I think I'd remember you," she said and then quickly looked away as if embarrassed by her frank reply.

"Hmmm," he said, flustered. He grabbed her two bags off the carousel and led her to the door.

She put on a pair of Jackie O-style sunglasses and followed him to his car. "Oh, a convertible! Can we take the top down?"

"Sure," he said, relieved that the awkward moment at the carousel had passed.

She gathered up her long hair into a ponytail for the ride.

"I enjoyed your colleagues," he said once they were heading south on Interstate 95. He had accompanied her team to Cape Cod, Martha's Vineyard, and Nantucket before sending them on their own to Boston. They were due back in Newport late the next day.

"That's nice to hear."

"Your coworker Michael is quite the character," Jack said, grinning.

"He sure is, but he knows his stuff, so I put up with his eccentricities. I hope he didn't drive you crazy."

"Nah, he kept me laughing. They had me out until one in the morning, and then they were up at seven, ready to hit the streets again. I haven't done anything like that in years, and it's official: I'm getting far too old for it. I was *dead* the next day."

"You have to say no to them. They know better than to ask me, but I'm sure they took full advantage of you."

He laughed and stole a glance at her. She had her face tipped into the warm sun, and he was struck once again by how stunning she was. Jamie had failed to mention that. Jack wondered if the oversight had been intentional.

"So what's our plan for today?" she asked.

"I thought we'd drop your bags at the hotel and then run by HBA where I've set aside an office for you. After that, I'll take you to see the site."

"I appreciate the office space. I hate working in hotel rooms."

"So do I." They crested the hill that led to the Jamestown Bridge. "This is where the view gets spectacular."

Andi took it all in. "I thought Lake Michigan was pretty, but this is something else. Do people live on all the islands?"

"Some of the larger ones are inhabited. We're heading onto an island up ahead known as Conanicut Island. Locals call it Jamestown." They crossed the first of two bridges. "Newport is also on an island, called Aquidneck."

"I saw this one from the air," she said of the Newport Bridge.

"You'll have a great view of Newport in a minute. If you look to the right when we get to the top, you might be able to see Block Island on the horizon."

"Yet another island?"

"Popular spot about twenty miles from here." A stab of pain cut through him when he thought of being there with the girls.

"I've never seen so many boats!"

"The City by the Sea is the sailing capital of the world, and I guess you can see why from up here." He pointed out the Naval War College on the north side of the bridge, and told her about the navy's long history in Newport.

"You could be a tour guide. Are you from here?"

He shook his head. "I'm what's known as a carpetbagger. According the locals, you can't be 'from' Newport unless you're born inside the city limits. I'm originally from Connecticut."

"What brought you here?"

"Jamie and I came here when we were in graduate school and fell in love with the place. We both love to sail, so when we started HBA, we decided to locate it here. On a day like this, you can see why."

"I wouldn't get anything done if I lived here."

"We take a lot of half days in the summer," he said. "Have you lived long in Chicago?"

"All my life except for college in New York. I guess I'm pretty boring, but I love the city. I can't imagine living anywhere else."

After she checked into her downtown Newport hotel, he drove her through the city. She marveled at the rows of colonial homes, cobblestone streets, and gas-powered lantern streetlights. The streets teemed with tourists as they poured in and out of restaurants, shops, and bars.

On the way to the office, he drove past the crowded town beach and merry-go-round. In HBA's parking lot, he walked around to open her door.

"Another amazing view," she said when they reached his office. "I have a great view of the lake from my office, but I hardly notice it anymore. You can't help but notice yours. And I love this building."

"This was our first collaboration. We'd worked for the same company but not on any projects together. The way this place came together boosted our confidence about going out on our own."

"Where were you before?"

"We did seven years with Neil Booth in Boston."

Andi's eyes widened. "*The* Neil Booth?"

"The one and only. He's Jamie's father."

"Oh my God, of course! I didn't make the connection, and Jamie never mentioned it."

"He doesn't make a big production about it, so don't let on I told you," Jack said, smiling.

She wandered over to look at his framed degrees on the wall. "Well, look at you: Berkeley, Harvard, *and* a Roman numeral. John Joseph Harrington the *third*. Very impressive."

Sadness descended upon him when he remembered Clare teasing him about being a Harvard graduate. "Yes, terribly impressive," he forced himself to say, "and that's the only place in my world you'll ever see that Roman numeral. Let me show you to your office. Then we'll grab some lunch and head out to the site."

"Sounds great, John the third," she teased, smiling at his playful scowl.

After lunch and a tour of the Infinity site, Jack flipped open his cell phone. "Let me check with Jamie about sailing and at home to see who wants to come along."

"I need to call home, too."

He pulled into a gourmet deli to pick up the picnic dinner he had ordered.

"Tell him I love him," Andi was saying when Jack returned to the car.

"Who's the lucky guy?" Jack asked after she ended the call.

"My son. He's five and sound asleep at the moment."

"I love that age," he said wistfully as he drove to the marina. "They're still so cute and funny. Teenagers can be anything but cute *or* funny. Although I'm lucky—mine aren't as bad as some."

"I'm sure they aren't."

Her cell phone rang as they arrived at the marina.

"Sorry, I have to take this. It's my deputy director calling from Juneau." She rolled her eyes. "*Lots* of issues out there."

"Take your time. I'll unload the car and come back for you."

While Andi took her call, Jack walked down the dock with an armload of bags. He unlocked the large navy blue sailboat he and Jamie had named *Blueprint*. When he was greeted by a blast of heat from the cabin, he opened the hatches to let in the cool sea breeze.

Glancing up at the parking lot, he saw Andi laughing and talking with animated hands. *God, she's beautiful.* An ache formed in his gut that he was startled to recognize as desire. It'd been so long, he'd almost forgotten the sensation of wanting a woman. Acknowledging that he'd been attracted to her from the first moment he saw her, Jack felt as if he was awakening from a long slumber and had to remind himself not to stare as he watched her.

A few minutes later, she strolled down the dock to join him. "I like the name of the boat. Very clever."

"Thanks. Come aboard. The others will be here soon." He offered her a hand. "What can I get you to drink?"

"Do you have white wine?"

"Sure do. Everything all right in Juneau?" he asked from the galley as he uncorked the bottle.

"It is now. We've had one disaster after another out there, and we're getting down to the wire with the opening." She sighed. "Why is it some jobs are so smooth and others are a total mess from the get-go?"

"I wish I knew. We've had our share of disaster jobs, but most of the time we can find a way to blame it on someone else."

She laughed. "I like that strategy. Fortunately, Bill, my deputy, was able to straighten things out. He's on his way back to Chicago with a new artist commissioned to fill in for the one we all *loved* until she got pregnant with triplets and had to quit."

Smiling at her dismay, he handed her a glass of wine.

"He told me the funniest story about an old man and a dog-sled team. One of those 'you had to be there' things, but it was comical."

Jack gestured at the picturesque marina. "I'd say you got the better end of the deal." The sun was a ball of fire in the late afternoon sky with hours yet to go until sunset.

"No kidding! I didn't dare tell him where I was when he called."

"Here they come." Jack gestured to the rowdy group pouring out of Frannie's Range Rover. Jack had bought the car for her to run the kids around in. He never let anyone use Clare's Volvo wagon, which still sat in the garage. "You remember Jamie, right? Well, he's got my sister, Frannie, and my daughters, Kate and Maggie, with him."

Jack made hasty introductions as the group boarded.

"Hey, Andi, nice to see you again." Jamie shook her hand. "I hope Jack is showing you a good time so far."

"Nice to see you, too. We've had a great day. I can't wait to get out on the water."

Jamie rubbed his hands together. "Then let's do it."

Jack handed out beers and sodas to the crew and told Andi to relax and leave the work to them.

Jack joined Andi on the bow to watch the sunset. Sitting next to her, he said, "Can I get you anything?"

"No way! I haven't eaten this much in one day, well, ever. Dinner was great. Thank you."

"My pleasure." He nodded to the colorful sunset. "Pretty, isn't it?"

"I feel kind of guilty calling this work." She wrapped her arms around her knees and turned to him. "Your girls are lovely. You must be so proud of them."

"I am. They amaze me in some new way just about every day."

"It's fun to watch you all together. You're obviously very close to Jamie and Frannie."

"Jamie is the brother I never had, and Frannie is much more than a sister. She's always been one of my best friends, too."

"You're lucky to have them," she said wistfully. "I'm an only child."

"Sometimes when Frannie was trying to dress me up or get me to play tea party, I used to *dream* about being an only child," he said, and they laughed at the visual.

Frannie stood next to Jamie at the helm.

"Is my brother *laughing* up there?" she whispered.

"Nice to see him so relaxed."

"She's a knock-out."

Jamie leaned down to kiss her forehead. "So are you."

Startled, Frannie looked up at him. "Are you *flirting* with me, Jamie Booth?"

"Maybe."

Flustered, she turned the conversation back to Jack and Andi, who sat close to each other on the bow, engrossed in conversation.

"He's attracted to her," Frannie said.

Jamie took a long swig from his beer. "You're seeing things."

"What's her deal anyway?"

"I'm not sure. I didn't spend much time with her outside the office in Chicago."

"She was *so* nice to the girls and genuinely interested in them."

"I know what you're thinking, Fran."

"And what's that?"

"He might look, but he won't touch. You know how devoted he is to Clare."

"So he's supposed to spend the rest of his life alone?"

"That's the bitch of this whole situation. Who knows what the rules are?" He glanced down at her. "What about you? How do you plan to spend the rest of your life?"

Stunned, she could only stare at him—tall, blond, and devastatingly handsome. She'd loved him her entire adult life but had never acted on it because of his friendship with Jack, not to mention the groupies who followed him around like useless fools. She had no desire to join the parade. "What are you up to?"

He shrugged. "I think about you. A lot."

A lump formed in her throat, and her heart pounded when she looked up to find his blue eyes trained on her. "I think about you, too. Far too much." The craziness of this sudden shift in their relationship filled her with nervous laughter.

He hooked an arm around her to pull her close to him and kissed her cheek. "We'll have to talk about this at a more appropriate time." Calling to Jack and Andi, Jamie said, "Hey, you guys, we need to come about, and you'll get wet on this tack."

Jack held Andi's elbow to steady her as they made their way to the boat's spacious cockpit.

Frannie tossed a look to Jamie to draw his attention to the gentle way Jack handled Andi. As Jamie rolled his eyes at her, Frannie held a hand out to help Andi down to the sitting area.

"Thanks, Frannie. How about that sunset?"

"We ordered it just for you," Jamie said.

Jack refilled everyone's drinks before he joined them on deck. He caught Andi stifling a yawn. "Did I run you ragged today?" he asked with a grin.

"No, not at all, but my flight was early, and I'm turning into a pumpkin. Will your wife mind the long day alone with the baby?"

The three of them stared at her in stunned silence.

Andi's face radiated with embarrassment. "What?"

"Maggie is my baby."

"Oh God, Jack, I'm sorry. I thought when they said you were on family leave…I thought you'd had a new baby. I have no idea how I leapt to that conclusion."

"It's an obvious conclusion," Jamie said. "You shouldn't feel bad."

"I've really put my foot in it. I apologize."

"That's not necessary," Jack said.

"Hey, girls, we're about to dock," Jamie called to Kate and Maggie in the cabin. "Can you come give us a hand?"

"Sure." Kate avoided eye contact with the adults when she came up the stairs to help her father lower the sails.

Awkward silence hung over the group as they docked, cleaned up, and prepared to head home.

"I can do the rest," Jack said.

Jamie gave Andi's shoulder an affectionate squeeze. Then he put a hand on Jack's arm, and their eyes met.

Jack nodded, and Jamie left with the others.

"I've obviously upset everyone," Andi said. "I'm so sorry."

She was so distressed that Jack couldn't help but reach out to her. He took her hand. "It's my fault. I assumed everyone knew what happened. You did nothing wrong, so please don't be upset." He guided her to sit next to him. To ward off the sudden chill, he tossed his jacket over her shoulders and took her hand again. "Look at me."

The impact of her soft brown eyes meeting his was like a punch to the gut.

"You didn't know, okay?"

She nodded.

"Just over a year ago, my wife was hit by a car. She's in a coma and, well, she's lost to us."

Andi gasped and clutched his hand. "*Oh!* What I said! The girls, they heard me… I made such a big assumption!"

"They're much better than they were. We all are."

"Where is she now?"

"In a home of her own with twenty-four-hour nursing care." He braced himself for the blast of pain that never materialized. At some point, he'd apparently gotten used to the new arrangement.

"I'm so sorry. You're all heartbroken."

"We're resigned now. There were months and months of heartbreak. I didn't work for more than a year and just went back almost two months ago. I had to get things back to some sense of normal for my girls. My oldest daughter, Jill, will turn seventeen soon."

"You adore them," she said, squeezing his hand.

"Yes," he said, "and I had no choice but to get on with it for their sake. Frannie's also been a godsend. She moved in with us right after it happened, and she helps me with everything."

"That's amazing. I liked her right away."

"We've always been close, but now we're on a whole other level. It was so incredible of her to put her life on hold when we needed her."

Andi rested her hand on his arm. "You've had quite a time of it, haven't you? All of you."

"It's been rough." As he watched her hand gently caress his arm, the urge to kiss her overtook him. Alarmed, he sat up straighter and broke the spell. "I'd better get you back to your hotel. It's been quite a day, and we've got a big week ahead of us."

"Yes, you're right." She stood to gather her things. "Thank you for today. I've had a lovely time."

"Me, too."

CHAPTER 5

A shaft of light slicing through the hotel curtains woke Andi the next morning. When she remembered the night before, a fresh wave of embarrassment hit her. She groaned and buried her head under the pillow.

How could I have made such a huge assumption?

Recalling the stricken expressions on the faces of Jack and his family had her burrowing deeper under the pillow, where she planned to stay forever.

Until the phone rang.

"Ugh!" She pushed the mass of curls off her face and reached for the receiver. "Hello?"

"Good morning, Andi. Hope you slept well."

Her face flushing with heat at the sound of Jack's voice, she sat up and tugged at the blanket. "Yes, I did. Thanks."

"Okay if I come by to pick you up in about an hour? We can grab a bite to eat and head out to see some sights. Your group won't be back in town until late this afternoon, so we have all day."

"That sounds good. I'll meet you downstairs." She paused, wincing once again at the awkward memory. "Jack, I feel awful about last night."

"I told you, it's fine. Don't give it another thought, okay?"

"Ah, yeah, sure," she said with a laugh. "No chance of *that*."

He laughed softly, and she was startled when her skin tingled with anticipation. She couldn't wait to see him again. *Stop it right now, Andrea. He's a colleague—a* married *colleague.* She thought of Tony, the very nice man she'd recently begun seeing in Chicago. *And you're…well…involved…*

"It's already eighty degrees, so plan for a hot day."

"See you soon."

After she hung up the phone, she lay there for a time thinking about Jack and Tony and her son. Eric's father had hurt her deeply, and she'd kept her distance from men ever since—until recently. Tony, the father of one of Eric's friends, had asked her out repeatedly before Andi finally gave in and said yes. They'd been to dinner a few times over the last couple of weeks and were taking it slowly. She enjoyed his company, but as she thought of Jack's phone call, she realized her skin had never tingled in anticipation of seeing Tony.

"You're being ridiculous," she said out loud. Nothing good could come from allowing herself to become infatuated with Jack. He lived more than a thousand miles from her and was married with children of his own. *One broken heart per lifetime,* she thought as she dragged herself out of bed. *That's more than enough.*

Wearing a long sundress and a wide-brimmed straw hat, she met Jack in front of the hotel.

He came around to open her door. "You look lovely."

"Thank you." Her heart tripped into overdrive at the sight of him. "You weren't kidding when you said it was hot."

"I can put the top up and crank on the AC if you'd like."

"No, it's fine. I love having the top down. That's why I brought the hat. So where're we headed today?" She stole a glance at him and noticed how handsome he was in a pale blue silk shirt and khakis. *Stop it.*

"I've arranged for us to have private tours at the Breakers and Marble House."

"I can't wait to see them. I read the material your office sent about the 'summer cottages.' That's a laugh."

"When you see how enormous they are, you'll find that even harder to believe. I have a couple of books in the office that show where the Astors and Vanderbilts and their ilk lived the rest of the year. Those houses put the summer cottages to shame."

The gilded rooms and period furnishings captivated Andi's imagination and started her thinking about how she could bring the early twentieth century to the hotel.

Jack seemed to enjoy watching her delight at every new discovery as they wound their way through hallways and stairwells within the mansions. She pointed out one feature after another that only a decorator would notice. In turn, he focused her attention on the architectural aspects that made each house unique.

Next, he took her to Hammersmith Farm, the Kennedy family's summer White House. Even though the house was no longer open to the public, Jack told her the new owner was a friend who'd permitted the tour. The estate, which had been owned by Jackie Kennedy's stepfather, Hugh Auchincloss, was located on the Ten Mile Ocean Drive.

Andi especially liked the tour guide's story about President Kennedy's helicopter landing on the expansive front lawn that abutted the shores of Narragansett Bay. The president, bad back and all, would bound up the lawn and hop through the bay window to sit down for lunch. Andi decided to feature the Kennedy connection to Newport in one of the hotel's suites.

"This was wonderful, Jack, simply amazing," she said, thrilled to have experienced a small slice of Camelot.

"I have one more thing to show you before lunch."

They stopped at St. Mary's Church where President and Mrs. Kennedy exchanged wedding vows in September of 1953. "The reception was held on the lawn of Hammersmith Farm."

"We have to make sure the rest of the team gets the Kennedy tour," she said as they were seated for lunch.

"We'll get Hammersmith on their itinerary. While you were in the ladies' room, Frannie called to invite you all for a cookout at the house tonight."

"That's too much of an imposition. They're a crazy bunch."

"We have teenagers. We're used to crazy. Frannie and the girls are excited to have you."

After they ordered a late lunch, he sat back in his chair and studied her with gray-blue eyes that drew her right in. Once again her skin tingled, and once again she reminded herself to proceed with caution.

"You said you have a son. What's his name?"

"Eric. I know all mothers think their kids are adorable, but in his case, it's true."

He laughed. "So your house is probably loud and raucous like mine. Are you married?"

"Not anymore," she said with a sigh. "And I wish my house was loud, but Eric was born profoundly deaf and can't speak. He's a world-class sign language champ and is getting better at lip reading, but it's far too quiet."

"That must be hard for you on your own."

"My mother lives with us, and she's been such a help to me. Eric doesn't let his handicap hold him back. He's a typical five-year-old. His school has done wonders for him, so we're doing much better these days."

"Does his dad help out?"

Shaking her head, she struggled to find the words, even all these years later. "He...couldn't handle the idea of a 'damaged' child. He left us ten days after Eric was diagnosed, and we haven't seen him since. That was more than four years ago."

Jack stared at her, clearly shocked. "Who does that?"

Touched by his outrage, she smiled. "I made my peace with it a long time ago. Eric hasn't asked me where his father is, so I've been able to put it behind me for now, anyway. I'm sure the questions are coming."

"I'm so sorry. It must've been a terrible time for you."

"It was, but we survived. Everything was much harder when he was younger, and I was panicked all the time about him being hurt by what he couldn't hear. I've gotten better about that."

"There was nothing they could do for him?"

"He wasn't a candidate for a cochlear implant. I hope maybe someday there'll be other options." She reached into her bag for a photo of a gorgeous blond towhead with huge blue eyes.

"He looks just like you," Jack teased as he handed the photo back to her. "Beautiful."

"Thanks for that, but he's *all* Alec."

"That must be tough in light of how things ended with him."

"It doesn't bother me. Eric is a constant reminder that even though life sometimes doesn't work out like you'd hoped, good things can come from disappointment. My life would be so much less without him at the center of it."

"That's a great way of looking at it. You're amazing. A lot of people would've been destroyed by that kind of betrayal."

"Just like you, I didn't have the luxury of allowing it to destroy me. I had a child to think about, and believe me, it's Alec's loss. He's missed out on a wonderful kid."

"We've both been through the wars, haven't we?" he asked as their lunch was served.

She smiled at his choice of words. "You could say that, but we're lucky, too. We have great kids and fun, interesting jobs. Things could be worse, right?"

"I've spent an awful lot of time the last sixteen months feeling sorry for myself."

"You seem to have done an admirable job of handling an unimaginable situation."

"That's nice of you to say, but I did a pretty crappy job of taking care of my kids for a long time. I was so focused on Clare that I neglected them. Thank

God Frannie and Jamie and a lot of other people were there for them when I wasn't."

"It sounds like you did everything you could for your wife. That's why you were able to go back to being a dad to your girls and get back to work—because you know you did everything you possibly could for her."

"I usually find it hard to talk about, but you make it easy."

"I'm still recovering from my foot-in-mouth incident last night," she said, enjoying her lobster salad as the conversation went in a less intense direction.

"I thought we were past that."

His wry grin made her heart skip a beat. He was so magnetic and everything she'd ever wanted in a man. But she reminded herself—and her galloping heart—that he belonged to someone else. Thinking of Tony and their fledgling relationship, she experienced a pang of guilt over all the feelings she suddenly had for Jack.

"What is it?" he asked.

She ventured a glance at him. "Nothing, why?"

"You just had this look…in your eyes, like something upset you."

Rattled, she put down her fork and took a sip of her wine. "You're a very nice guy, Jack Harrington."

As a muscle in his cheek pulsed with tension, he glanced down at the table and then at her. "May I ask you something that might seem wildly inappropriate coming from a professional colleague?"

Releasing a nervous laugh, she said, "Sure. Go for it."

"Are you seeing anyone at home?"

A flush of heat worked its way through her, settling in her face. Andi put her hands on her cheeks, hoping he wouldn't see how his question had affected her.

"I'm sorry," he said. "I've embarrassed you."

"No, it's fine. It's just kind of warm in here."

"It's none of my business. I don't even know why I asked."

He looked so befuddled that Andi's heart went out to him. *Danger!* "We'll be working together very closely for the next year and a half. I'd like to think we could be friends as well as colleagues."

His face lifted into a small smile that sent arrows of desire darting through her. *Big trouble.*

"I'd like that," he said.

"In that case, I can tell my *friend* who is also my colleague that I recently started seeing the father of one of Eric's friends."

Was that disappointment she saw on his face?

"And how's that going?"

"It's…ah…interesting, I guess you could say, to be back in the dating world after so many years of being married and then single during my 'I'll never date again' phase."

"I can't imagine ever dating or anything like that. I mean who'd want to take on a situation like mine? Married but not really… How would that be fair?"

"You don't have to decide that for someone else. If a woman chooses to get involved with you, she'd do so knowing your situation."

"I still can't see it ever happening. I'd feel so disloyal to Clare, you know?"

"I can see what you mean." She paused for a moment. "I didn't know her, but I can't imagine she'd expect you to be alone the rest of your life. Wouldn't she want you to be happy?"

Laughing, he said, "Not if being happy included other women. She was a little territorial where I was concerned." He fiddled absently with an extra napkin on the table. "I've been so caught up in trying to mend fences with the girls and get back in a groove at work that I haven't given my own future the first thought." His eyes shifted up to meet hers. "Until recently."

The statement hung in the air between them.

Andi cleared her throat and got busy finishing her salad.

"I've made you uncomfortable again. I'm sorry."

"Nothing to be sorry about." She forced a bright smile as her heart hammered in her chest. "What time are we meeting everyone at your house?"

He studied her for a long, breathless moment. "Six."

Since they had some time to kill, he took her to the Cliff Walk that ran along the backyards of the mansions they'd toured that morning. The ocean crashed against the jagged rocks below, sending huge streams of mist into the air.

Jack stopped her to point out his house across the wide span of water. "It's between the two white ones, lots of glass. See it?"

"Wow, I can't wait to see it up close." She looked up at him, a teasing grin on her pretty face. "Is it a Jack Harrington original?"

"As a matter of fact, it is."

"Was it difficult to build right on the coast like that?"

"It was a bit of a challenge but well worth it. I love living so close to the water."

She took a good look at the view. "I can see why."

Making a studious effort to stay away from the personal topics they'd strayed into over lunch, Jack kept the discussion focused on the plans for the hotel, decorating ideas, and design highlights. But despite his best intentions, he was captivated as she talked with animated gestures about the ideas the day in Newport had generated.

He'd embarrassed her over lunch by asking personal questions he had no right to ask. Not only was she a colleague, but she was involved with someone else. Why that information had filled him with such unreasonable jealousy would be something he could stew over later when he was alone. For now, he was delighted to simply be with her.

She was so caught up in what she was telling him that she missed a small dip in the path and lost her footing.

Jack reached for her and stopped her from falling.

Gasping, she looked up at him with chocolate brown eyes gone wide with surprise.

Jack kept his arms around her as she regained her balance. "Are you all right?"

She glanced at the rocky shoreline below the path and tightened her grip on his arms. "That would've been quite a fall."

"Someone goes over at least once a year." When she looked up at him, the impact once again hit him like a punch to the gut. "Andi…"

"Yes?"

"I…" He wanted to kiss her. After more than a year of feeling nothing at all, the desire was so fierce, he could barely breathe. Then all the reasons why he couldn't kiss her or anyone else came flooding back to remind him he needed to let go of her.

But damn it, he didn't want to.

He finally released her.

"Jack? What is it? What's wrong?"

Rattled, he shook his head. "Nothing. Let's get going, shall we?"

CHAPTER 6

At Jack's house, a game of Marco Polo was going on in the pool. Andi waved hello to her coworkers and to Frannie and Jamie, who were working the grill.

"We'll be back in a minute," Jack called to them. "Andi wants to see the house."

"Take your time," Frannie shouted over Jimmy Buffett on the stereo.

After Jack introduced them, Jill got up to offer Andi a drink.

Andi waved to Kate and Maggie in the pool as she accepted the glass of wine from Jill.

"It's *unreal!*" Andi said as she and Jack went into the house. "She's you all over again!"

"So I've been told. She gets sick of hearing it from everyone."

"I'm glad I didn't say anything to her, then."

"She's used to it. But what sixteen-year-old girl wants to look just like her dad?" he asked, grinning. "Clare and Kate, same story—uncanny resemblance. Then there's Maggie."

"A bit of both of you?" she asked as she followed him through the kitchen.

"Exactly. You can probably tell by how much younger Maggie is that we didn't plan her. And believe me, we were taken aback by the idea of another baby when Jill and Kate were in elementary school. But Maggie completes us. I'm so glad she came along when she did."

Listening to him talk about his kids made Andi sad that Eric didn't have a father like Jack in his life. Pushing that depressing thought away, she focused on the incredible house he'd built for his family. It featured hardwood floors and lots of glass to take full advantage of the magnificent ocean view.

He led her upstairs to the girls' floor and then up the spiral stairs to the master suite.

"I've lost count," she said. "Four bathrooms?"

"Six," he said with a sheepish grin. "Seven bedrooms."

A casual photo of Jack and his pretty blonde wife sat on a table, and Andi could tell it had been taken on the boat. She followed him to the balcony that hung over the pool area with the ocean farther below.

"This was Clare's favorite spot. She used to come out here every morning for a few minutes no matter what the weather."

"I can see why she loved it so much. It's an amazing house, Jack. Truly."

"Thanks." He seemed embarrassed by her effusiveness. "I surprised Clare with it at Christmas six years ago in one of my finer moments, if I do say so myself."

"She knew nothing about it?"

"Not a thing."

"And how'd you pull that off?"

"There was a lot of lying involved," he said with a grin. "For which I was forgiven when she saw this place the first time."

"She's lucky to have you."

"I was lucky to have her," he said, hesitating, as if he wanted to say something else.

"Jack? What is it?"

His face tightened with tension, and all at once, he seemed far away. "There was more to Clare's accident than I told you last night." It seemed to cost him something vital to talk about Clare standing in front of the speeding car, her failure to move, and how he now had to live with the gnawing uncertainty that perhaps she'd done it on purpose.

"You don't really think that, though, do you?" Andi asked, deeply moved by his story and the pain that radiated from him. In that moment, she was startled to realize there was almost nothing she wouldn't do to make him smile again.

"I didn't believe it was even remotely possible until I saw the video from the mall security. She had time to get out of the way."

"After meeting you and the girls and seeing the home you built for her, it would seem to me that Clare had everything in the world to live for."

"That's what I always assumed, but who knows if that's how she felt. We had a fight on the morning of the accident, and when I look back over the months preceding it, I can see now that something was off. You know what they say about hindsight…"

"You can't do that to yourself, Jack."

"That's what everyone tells me, but the image of her standing there when the car was coming at her haunts me. I wake up a lot of nights in a cold sweat, even all these months later, because I've been dreaming about it and can't stop the car from hitting her. I run for her, but I'm always too late."

Blinking back tears, she reached for his hand. If not for the patio full of people below them, she would've hugged him.

"Anyway, I'll probably never know for sure what really happened." She watched him make a supreme effort to shake off his grief. "I'm sorry. I didn't mean to drag down our day."

Andi squeezed his hand. "You didn't. I'm glad you told me."

"I appreciate you listening."

Frannie looked up at Jack and Andi on the balcony, talking with their heads close together. "Something's up."

"You might be right," Jamie said as he flipped the burgers and sneaked a peek.

Frannie smacked his arm. "Stop looking!"

"You were looking, too! Before they come back, I want to ask you something."

"What?" She made an effort to sound casual despite the strange hum of tension between them since the night before on the boat.

"Will you have dinner with me tomorrow night?"

"Like a *date?*" She pretended to be horrified, but her heart was banging around in her chest.

"*Yes*, like a date," he said, laughing.

"That's not such a good idea."

"What do you mean? It's the best idea I've ever had. In fact, I should've had it years ago."

"If we start something that doesn't work out, it'd be a mess. For everyone." She gestured to the pool where the girls swam with their friends and Jack's guests.

Spinning a lock of her hair around his finger, Jamie brought his face down close to hers. "*When* we start something, it's going to work out because we already love each other."

Her mouth hung open in surprise as he handed her the spatula and walked away.

"You and Jamie were looking pretty intense," Jack said when he joined her a few minutes later. "Everything all right?"

"Of course it is." Frannie returned her attention to the grill. "You were looking pretty intense yourself up there with Andi."

"I *was?*" He sounded panicked. "*Really?*"

Frannie watched her brother seek out Andi, who was on the other side of the pool with her coworkers. "Relax," she said. "No one noticed."

"You did."

"What's going on, Jack?"

He hesitated before he said, "I wasn't expecting to meet someone who'd make me want more."

His helpless shrug made Frannie ache for him. "There's nothing wrong with wanting more, Jack. You can't be alone the rest of your life. Clare wouldn't want that for you."

"Get real. She would've flipped out if I so much as looked at another woman."

"That was then."

"So you're giving me permission, little sister?" he asked with a small smile.

"You need to give *yourself* permission." She squeezed his arm. "Permission to live, Jack. What else can you do?"

"I can't see anything happening with her."

"Why not?"

"For one thing, we're professional colleagues, and nothing good ever comes of getting involved with someone you work with."

"I hate to point out the obvious, but you don't actually work *with* her."

"You know what I mean. She's a client."

"She's the *employee* of a client."

He scowled playfully at her. "She also lives a thousand miles from me and is dating someone at home."

"Oh," Frannie said, grinning. "So you asked, huh?"

"It came up."

"Is it serious?"

"Apparently, it's new."

"I'm still not hearing a convincing argument of why you can't see her."

"How about this then: what woman in her right mind would want to take on the mess that comes with me?"

"Um, maybe the one who's been sneaking peeks at you the entire time you've been talking to me?"

Jack's eyes darted to the other side of the pool, and sure enough, Andi was watching them. He smiled at her, and she smiled back.

Frannie laughed watching the exchange. "Got yourself a little crush going on, do you?"

"I don't know," he said, flustered as he ran his fingers through his hair. "Maybe."

"Go for it, Jack. What've you got to lose?"

"I've already lost so much. I'm not sure I could take that kind of risk again." His face clouded with tension that he made a valiant effort to shake off. "Anyway, what's up with you and JB?"

"I have no idea what you mean."

"He said something that left your mouth hanging open."

She rolled her eyes and started to walk away. "What*ever*."

Taking her arm, he stopped her and raised a questioning eyebrow.

"If you must know, he asked me to have dinner with him tomorrow night." She pulled her arm free.

"Well, isn't that interesting? Are you going?"

"I haven't decided. I have no interest in joining his harem."

"He's been over his Barbie phase for a while now. In fact, I can't remember the last time I saw him with *any* woman. Our boy might just be growing up. Maybe he's looking for a woman of substance."

"Is that what I am? A woman of *substance?*" She pretended to be offended as she scooped the burgers onto a plate. "Burgers are ready," she called out and handed the plate to Jill.

"Go out with him. See what happens."

"What if it doesn't work out? He's your best friend and one of my best friends, and he has been for *years.*"

"I see what you mean, but look at it this way: what if this is what you've both been looking for, and all these years it's been right under your noses?" He tweaked her nose. "It's just dinner. Go with him. If you don't, you'll always wonder what might've happened."

Her eyes narrowed with suspicion. "Did he pay you to plead his case?"

Laughing, Jack raised his hands to fend her off. "He hasn't said a word to me about this. Honest."

"Okay, okay, I'll go, but if it turns into a mess, remember I tried to tell you it would."

"That's a great way to start something, looking for a mess. Good strategy, Fran." He patted her head and went to join the others.

Frannie watched him go, her heart soaring as she watched Andi smile when she saw him coming. Things were definitely looking up.

After dinner Jack lit the poolside fireplace, and Andi sat next to him on a double-sized lounge chair to watch the fire. Her coworkers entertained his daughters with stories about some of their bigger design challenges. The girls were hooked on the decorating shows on HGTV and chatted about their favorites with the eccentric interior designers.

Jack laughed at Maggie charming Andi's coworker, Michael, into taking "just a quick look" at her room. She had totally bamboozled the comical designer.

"Watch out for her in a few years," Andi whispered.

Jack groaned. "She'll be the one to give me gray hairs. Jill and Kate have had boys flocking around for years, but neither of them has really singled one out. They usually prefer to hang out in groups, which is fine with me. Maggie, on the other hand, terrifies me."

"She's adorable," Andi said, laughing at his distress. "So what were you badgering Frannie about earlier?"

"Me? Badger? I don't know what you mean."

"Let's hear it."

"You're awfully bossy," he said with a teasing smile. "It seems my best friend and my sister may have a thing for each other—only twenty-five years after they first met. She's been married twice, both times to guys who disappointed her. I'd love to see her with someone solid like Jamie."

"You approve. That's good. It would matter to her."

He was once again surprised—and delighted—by her insight. "I approve, but I'd still have to make sure his intentions are honorable."

She arched an eyebrow in disapproval. "You're kidding, right?"

"Hell no! That's my little sister we're talking about."

Andi leaned around him to study Frannie. "She looks all grown up from where I'm sitting."

"You mean I can't interrogate him and threaten to have his fingernails removed if he hurts her?"

"You need to stay out of it."

"I'm beginning to wonder if I like you as much as I thought I did," he joked.

She chuckled. "Maybe that's better for both of us."

"No, it isn't."

Across the patio on another lounge chair, Jamie was doing some badgering of his own under the guise of "convincing."

"So did your brother give you permission to go out with me?" he asked Frannie.

"Aren't you arrogant? Your name never came up."

"Yeah, *right*!" he said with a hoot. "I know how you two operate. Give me a break. So is he going to let me take you out?"

"You need to be wondering if *I'm* going to let you take me out."

"You drive a tough bargain, Frances Harrington."

"You think calling me that is going to help your chances? Think again."

He took her hand and kissed each finger as the firelight danced on her astonished face. "So," he asked between kisses, never taking his eyes off hers, "what *would* help my chances?"

"That's helping," she said breathlessly. "That's definitely helping."

He grinned and kissed her hand again.

"Can I ask you something?"

"Of course," he said, starting over with her thumb.

In danger of losing control of the conversation, she tugged her hand out of his grip. "How come you suddenly want to go out with me?"

He sat up. "It's *not* sudden, Frannie."

"It's not? You could have anyone—"

Taking her hand again, he said, "But I *want* you. I've *always* wanted you."

"You have *not*. Don't lie to me." She frowned as she got up, stormed into the house, and slammed around the kitchen, cleaning up.

Jamie came up behind her and put his arms around her. "Stop." He buried his face in her hair. "Stop thinking I'm toying with you."

Frannie had to force air to her lungs. "Aren't you?"

He turned her to face him, lifted her chin, compelling her to meet his gaze. "I've loved you since the first time you came to visit us in California. I was blown away by you, but we were just kids. And then the timing was never right. You got married—*twice*—and then everything happened with Clare. I thought I'd *die* when Jack told me you'd gotten married." He leaned in to kiss her. "Both times, I wanted to die, Frannie."

Tears rolled down her face. "Why didn't you ever say anything?"

He brushed her tears away. "I don't know, but I wish I had. Is there any chance you might, you know, love me, too?"

Clinging to him, she tried to catch her breath. "I've always loved you," she said in a hoarse whisper. "*Always.*" She risked a glance at the face she had adored for more than half her life and saw his love for her.

Finally.

"Will you do something for me?" she asked.

"Anything."

She curled her fingers around his. "Take me home with you?"

He closed his eyes for a brief moment, took her hand, and led her to the front door.

Jack and Andi came into the kitchen a few minutes later with cups and plates from the patio. He looked around the corner to the family room but didn't see Jamie or Frannie. Peering out the front door, he discovered Jamie's car was gone.

"Interesting," Jack said when he returned to the kitchen. "They left."

Kate and Maggie came in with more items from the cookout. Jill had left earlier to catch a late movie with her friends.

"Where's Frannie?" Kate asked.

"I think she went somewhere with Uncle Jamie," Jack said.

"She seemed mad," Kate said.

"I'm sure they'll work it out—whatever it is."

"Dad, why do we call Frannie, who's our aunt, just Frannie, but we call Uncle Jamie, who's not really our uncle, Uncle Jamie?" Maggie asked with a serious expression.

The others cracked up.

"That's a good question, Maggie, and I have absolutely no idea why we do that," Jack said, ruffling her hair.

"It's weird," Maggie decided.

"Yes, it is," he agreed. "And now it's your bedtime, Miss Priss."

"No way! I want to go work on my room. Michael told me just what to do. Plus, it's summer vacation. I can stay up late."

"Nice try, but it's almost eleven. That's late enough."

"Come on, brat, I'll tuck you in," Kate said, herding her sister along.

"Thanks, Kate. I'm going to run Andi over to her hotel. I'll be back soon."

"Okay." Kate chased her sister up the stairs, tickling her as they went.

"Kate's good with her," Andi said.

"They used to fight like wombats," Jack said, "but since everything happened… They're a lot closer now."

"You don't have to drive me. I can go with the others."

"Are you sure?"

"Of course. There's no need for you to make a special trip."

"Okay," he said, disappointed that he wouldn't get more time with her.

A few minutes later, Andi and her team left with a burst of "thank yous" to Jack and compliments on his daughters and his home.

Watching her leave with the others, he thought about how much he'd enjoyed the day with her—and how badly he wished he could spend the night with her. Sick with guilt, he felt as if he'd *already* been unfaithful to Clare. The quiet ache he'd carried inside for so long resurfaced with a sudden, powerful intensity. He closed the door and leaned his head against it.

Two steps forward, one step back.

Frannie and Jamie were quiet on the short ride to his downtown condo. The whole way, her heart beat a wild staccato that left her breathless. She couldn't believe this was actually happening.

Seeming to sense her out-of-control nerves, Jamie reached over to put his hand on top of hers, and just like that, her heart rate slowed to a more normal speed.

Frannie watched the city lights whiz by as he drove his vintage Porsche faster than he probably should have. What if it was weird between them? What if they'd been friends too long to take this leap? What if it was every bit the disaster she'd feared it would be?

"Frannie?"

His voice jostled her out of the pensive state she'd slipped into, and she realized they'd arrived at his place.

When she went to release her seat belt, she was all thumbs.

Once again, he stopped her and took care of the task himself. "Come here." He reached across the console for her.

As he wrapped his arms around her, his enormously appealing scent surrounded and calmed her. "Tell me we're not crazy to be messing with a good thing," she said after a long moment of charged silence.

"We've been crazy to wait this long to mess with a good thing."

"But what if—"

His fingers slipped into her hair and held her still as he kissed the words off her lips. He used his tongue to coax her mouth open, making her burn from head to toe. No other kiss had ever had such an effect on her.

As she sent her tongue to tangle with his, she wanted to cry from the sweet relief that came with being in his arms. This was Jamie. *Her* Jamie. The man she'd loved forever.

The kiss went on so long that Frannie lost track of time and place.

By the time he finally shifted his attention to her neck, her heart was racing again, but for different reasons this time.

"Let's go in," he whispered, sending goose bumps skirting down her spine.

Frannie released her hold on him and was hit with a fit of laughter when she noticed they'd steamed up the windows of his car.

"Just like a couple of teenagers." His grin was so sexy and so compelling that it was all she could do to let him go long enough to get out of the car and come around to retrieve her. Standing next to her door, he held out a hand to her.

Frannie reached up to put her hand in his.

He kept a firm grip on her hand as he led her inside and up the stairs to his second-floor condo. The faint glow of streetlights made it so they could barely see each other in the darkness. She expected him to turn on a light, but the minute he closed the door, he drew her into his arms and devoured her with more passionate kisses.

"God, Frannie," he whispered as he dropped kisses from her jaw to her neck to her throat. "Do you have any idea how long I've wanted you? How many times I've sat across a table from you and wondered what it would be like to do this?" His hands moved from her hips to cup her breasts. He tweaked her nipples, and she cried out from the sensations that darted through her. "Sometimes I'd get hard, right there at your brother's table, imagining pushing you against a wall and taking you." His teeth clamped down on her earlobe as he backed her up to the wall and pressed his erection into the V of her legs. "I wanted you so badly. Every minute I've spent with you since the day I met you, I've wanted you."

Inflamed and astounded by his words, Frannie gripped a handful of his hair and urged him into another deep kiss. "Do it," she said when they came up for air. "Just like you imagined." No longer concerned about implications or potential for disaster, she pushed back against him, telling him exactly what she wanted.

His blue eyes heated as he tugged at the button to her shorts. He undressed her reverently, until she stood naked before him. His gaze devoured her, sending heat zipping into sharp desire between her legs.

She pulled at his shirt, wanting to see him and touch him.

Reaching over his shoulder, he shed the shirt in one quick move.

Frannie unbuttoned and unzipped his shorts, pushing them and his boxers down over his hips. When his erection sprang free, long and thick and hard, her mouth went dry. She wrapped her hand around him, stroking, as his hands found her breasts.

Groaning from what she was doing to him, he dipped his head and drew her nipple into his mouth, sucking and licking until she wondered how much longer her legs would support her. Seeming to sense her concern, he tightened his arm around her waist and shifted his attention to her other breast.

"Jamie," she gasped.

"What, baby? Tell me."

She squeezed him and felt him pulse against her hand. "Now. Please."

"Do we need protection?"

She shook her head. She hadn't had a period in more than a year, not that she'd ruin this moment by sharing that unsavory detail with him.

He ran his hands over her back and down to cup her bottom. Lifting her, he propped her back against the wall and stepped between her legs. As he brought her down on him, Frannie cried out from the sensations taking her over. Nothing had ever felt so good, so right, so meant to be.

"Okay?" he asked, sounding as breathless as she felt.

"So far beyond okay."

He smiled against her lips as he captured her mouth again.

Frannie held on tight as he took her hard and fast against the wall.

All at once, he tore his lips free of hers and threw his head back as he pushed deep, triggering an orgasm that she felt in every cell of her body.

He surged into her, lost in his own release.

For a long time afterward, they held each other, breathing hard and recovering their bearings.

Jamie tightened his hold on her and walked them to the sofa, coming down on top of her without losing their connection.

Frannie combed her fingers through his hair, wiping away the dampness on his forehead. "I thought it would be weird," she said after an extended period of silence.

"What?" he asked, his lips brushing against her neck.

"You. Me. This."

"What's weird is that we haven't been doing this for years."

"I can't believe you never said anything."

"Neither did you," he reminded her.

"Stupid."

"So stupid." He pushed his hips against her as his reawakened erection made its presence known. "You know what would be really stupid?"

"What's that?"

"If either of us ever does this with anyone else."

Frannie smiled up at him. "I'd like to think I'm done being stupid."

He brushed a sweet kiss over her lips. "Me, too."

CHAPTER 7

Jack ran on the beach where the sun was rising on another hot summer day and returned home to shower before anyone else was up.

He checked Frannie's room and found her bed empty. While he was delighted for her and Jamie, the idea of them as a couple still surprised him, even though it probably shouldn't. They'd shared a special friendship since she first came to visit them in California, and he'd always wondered if she felt more for Jamie than she let on. Even Clare had had her suspicions.

Well, I guess now we know. Jack wished he could talk to Clare about it.

After leaving Jill and Kate a note asking them to keep an eye on Maggie until Frannie got home, he headed out to his car.

He drove along the beach and stopped at the florist to pick up a dozen yellow roses before continuing down the block to a row of oceanfront condos. Using his key, he let himself in and walked into the kitchen, where Clare's head nurse, Sally, was having a cup of coffee. She was a stout grandmother with gray hair and warm blue eyes. Jack had liked her the instant he met her, and she'd been a godsend to him since the accident.

She greeted him with a smile. "Morning."

"Hi, there. How are things?"

"Pretty good. You?"

"I've been keeping busy since I went back to work."

She took the roses from him and reached into a cabinet for a vase. "It's good for you to be working."

He shrugged. "Life goes on, right?"

"It sure does," Sally said as she trimmed the roses. "Go on in and say hello. I'll get these gorgeous flowers ready for Clare."

"Thanks." Jack took a moment to prepare himself and walked into Clare's bedroom, which was still dark even as sunlight beamed faintly through the closed blinds. He ran his hand over her blonde hair and down her soft cheek. The other physical signs of the accident were long gone, and she looked just as she had on all the mornings over nearly two decades when he'd awakened to her next to him.

Flipping a lock of her hair around his finger, he leaned in to kiss her forehead. The unfamiliar scent of her hair saddened him. He needed to stop by the salon she'd frequented to buy some of the shampoo she liked.

"I love you, sweetheart," he said with a last look at her in the narrow hospital bed. For better or worse, she was still his wife. *What am I doing even thinking about another woman?* A fresh wave of guilt struck him as he stepped out of the room.

"I'm leaving, Sally."

She emerged from the kitchen. "Okay, I'll be starting her therapy soon. Don't worry about anything here."

"Thanks."

Frannie eased herself from under Jamie's arm and watched him sleep, still amazed by what'd happened the night before. She stretched, exhausted from making love with him all night long, pulled on the discarded T-shirt that bore his scent, and went in search of coffee.

Rummaging around his kitchen, she found coffee and filters and started the coffeemaker. She ran her hands through unruly curls and stretched again as a big yawn rippled through her.

Jamie's condo occupied the top floor of a building that housed shops and restaurants in the heart of downtown Newport. The small balcony off his living room faced the busy harbor. She leaned with her coffee over the railing as a small truck pulled up below with lobsters for one of the restaurants. Farther down the street, she was mesmerized by a trash truck lifting a Dumpster to empty it.

Everything seems magical this morning, even a garbage truck, she thought with a snicker.

Jamie crept up behind her and nuzzled her neck. "Mmm. There you are. I was worried when I woke up and you were gone."

When she turned to face him, he captured her mouth in a long, searing kiss that made her want him all over again.

"Good morning." He walked her backward into the condo, took her coffee cup, put it down, and led her back to bed.

"Don't you have to work? It's Monday."

He tugged her down on top of him and held her tight against him with one arm as he reached for the bedside phone with the other. His eyes never left hers as he dialed the phone and kissed her again while he waited for someone to answer.

"Hey, it's Jamie. I won't be in today."

Frannie gasped.

"Ask Jack to reschedule it for me."

She hid her face at the mention of her brother's name.

Jamie poked her ribs. "Tell him I'll call him later. Okay, thanks." He clicked the off button, tossed the phone aside, and rolled them over in one smooth move. "Now, you were saying?"

She had forgotten what she was going to say.

Jack was greeted by a melee of voices when he walked into the office. Andi and her team had commandeered the conference room, and they all seemed to be talking at once.

Quinn handed him his messages. "Quite a ruckus, huh?"

"I guess all that energy bodes well for the hotel." As he read through his messages, one caught his attention. "What'd Jamie say when he called?"

"He asked if you could reschedule his conference call with Tokyo because he has something to take care of today."

Yeah, my sister, Jack thought on the way into his office. Not that Jamie hadn't earned a day off after running the business on his own for more than a year. It was *how* he was spending the day that put Jack on edge. Maybe he should've taken Frannie's concerns more seriously last night. She was right—it *would* be awful for everyone if things didn't work out between her and Jamie.

Andi knocked a few minutes later while Jack was on the phone rescheduling Jamie's meeting. He waved her in and signaled for her to close the door.

"Did you sleep well?" he asked after he finished the call.

"I worked for a couple of hours and then slept like a dead woman. Must be the sea air."

Jack smiled but didn't tell her that he'd tossed and turned for most of the night, thinking about her and his conflicted feelings.

Quinn buzzed in on the intercom to let him know his coastal resources people had arrived for their meeting.

"I guess that's my cue." Andi got up to leave. "We're off to the Redwood Library today."

"That'll be a blast."

"All in the name of research."

He wished they could spend another day together. "Don't let me keep you. Call me if you need anything."

"Thanks, I'll see you later." She left him with a dazzling smile on her way out.

After she'd gone, he sat down and released a long, tortured sigh. He'd spent ten minutes with her, and she'd left him breathless with yearning. He was getting in deep and felt as if he was outside himself watching someone else. A minute or two later, he couldn't have said how long, Quinn buzzed him again to remind him his guests were waiting.

Getting up, he ran a hand through his hair and gathered the drawings he needed for the meeting. When he opened the door, Quinn shot him an inquisitive look.

He walked by her without a word.

The day dragged as Jack and his staff went round and round with the coastal engineers who were looking to ensure the hotel's drainage and septic systems had been designed to protect the fragile environment. They worked through lunch and into the afternoon to address the engineers' lengthy list of requests. Jack made one design concession after another to clear this all-important hurdle in the permitting process. But more than once, his mind wandered elsewhere.

When all the items on the list had been addressed, Jack stood to shake hands with the engineers.

"We should be ready to put the final proposal before the coastal council at its next meeting," the lead engineer said.

"I'll be there," Jack assured them.

After he had seen them out, he went back to his office. "My God, I thought it would never end," he groaned to Quinn. "It was like a day-long colonoscopy."

She laughed. "Thanks for the visual, Jack. That part should be done after today, right?"

"We have to take it before the full council next month, but it looks good for approval." He stretched out the stiffness of the all-day meeting.

She cocked that eyebrow of hers at him.

"What?"

"What's going on with you?"

"Nothing."

"All righty, if you say so."

"I say so," he retorted on his way into his office where a pile of messages awaited him. He flipped through them and put aside those that could wait until tomorrow. After he returned the calls that needed immediate attention, he gave his email the same quick glance.

Jack had just returned his attention to the hotel plans when Jamie walked in with a sheepish grin on his face.

He leaned against the closed door. "How much trouble am I in?"

Jack crooked his head to give Jamie the once over. His friend looked happy and dopey at the same time. "How much trouble should you be in?"

"Quite a lot, I suspect."

Jack held up a hand. "Do *not* tell me."

Jamie grinned and pushed off the door to flop in Jack's chair. "I love her, Jack. I really do. I think I always have."

"*Seriously?*"

"I swear to God."

"Wow… After all the crap you've both been through with other people, especially her."

"I hate to even think about all the time we've wasted, but the timing was never right. She was married and then everything with Clare…"

"Of course I have to give you the 'if you hurt her, you're dead' speech." Jack lightly punched Jamie's shoulder on his way past him to close windows he had opened that morning.

"No, you don't, because I'm going to marry her."

Jack spun around to gape at him. "Did Jamie Booth just use the '*m*' word? Get the hell out of here! Just like that?"

Jamie laughed. "It's been 'just like that' for years. We've spent a lot of time together since she moved in with you, and I guess something I've always suspected was there just finally clicked into focus."

"She said she'd never get married again after the last disaster," Jack warned him.

"I'll get her to change her mind."

Jack grinned. "If anyone can do it, you can."

"Before I ask her, though, I need to know… Is it okay with you?"

Jack considered making him suffer and then thought better of it. He had never seen such vulnerability on Jamie's face, and he had certainly never heard him use the "m" word before. "You're already my brother. Why not brother-in-law, too?" Jack offered his hand.

The relief showed on Jamie's face as he shook Jack's hand. "Thank you."

"I just can't believe this," Jack said, amazed by the turn of events.

"It's crazy, but it feels good."

"I'm glad for you—both of you."

"Best thing to ever happen to me, that's for sure. What's going on around here?"

"Nothing much. Just tweaking the hotel plans a bit."

Jamie had headed for his office when another thought stopped him. "I forgot to ask if you got a chance to talk to Tokyo today?"

Jack rolled his eyes. "It's all set. I convinced them your personal emergency was unavoidable."

Jamie winked. "Thanks, I owe you one."

"No, you don't. Five years from now I'll still be paying you back for all you did around here when I was gone."

"No, you won't."

When he was alone, Jack picked up the business card Andi had given him and flipped it back and forth between his fingers, debating whether he should call her for dinner.

But then he thought of Clare and how she'd looked that morning in the hospital bed. Tossing the business card on his desk, he left the office and went home to have dinner with his daughters.

CHAPTER 8

Jack was bent over the hotel plans on his drafting table the next afternoon when Andi tapped him on the shoulder.

"How goes it?"

Ridiculously happy to see her, he smiled. "Hey, I didn't hear you come in."

"I was spying on you. I like watching you work. You're very intense," she said, making a serious face. "What're you doing?"

"Some fine-tuning, nothing major. What've you been up to?"

"We just went through the Tennis Hall of Fame. It was wonderful. What a city this is! There's so much history to draw from. The suites will be *amazing*."

"I'll bet you can already picture them."

"But of course. I sent the others on to Hammersmith and St. Mary's for the Kennedy tour."

"I thought you'd like the Hall of Fame. Was anyone playing on the grass courts?"

"We watched two matches before we dragged ourselves back to work." She consulted her watch. "I have meetings with some artists today. Commissioning local art is a big part of our site visits."

"I remember the lady in Alaska with the triplets."

She groaned. "Don't remind me."

"After we talked about that, I was thinking you might want to look at some of Frannie's stuff. She's an amazing artist, and since she moved here, she's done a lot of local work."

"I had no idea! I'd love to see her work. Can we do it now? I have about ninety minutes until my next meeting."

"Sure, I'm done here." He rolled up the plans that were scattered about on his drafting table. "At this point, I'm just obsessing anyway. Let's go."

"Oh, Frannie, these are amazing!" Andi declared as she flipped through the stack of canvases propped against the wall in the former tool shed Jack had converted into a studio for his sister.

"You've been busy, Fran." Jack leaned over Andi's shoulder to get a look at some of his sister's recent work for the first time. "They're great."

"Thanks. I've had more time with the girls on vacation, so it's been a productive summer."

"I'll say!" Andi went through the canvases again. There were scenes of boats under sail in Narragansett Bay, a few of the mansions at unique angles, tennis players at the Hall of Fame, and children frolicking in the surf. "What're you planning to do with them?"

Frannie shrugged. "I haven't gotten that far. I've been meaning to talk to some of the local galleries about a show, but I've been so busy."

Jack felt a pang of guilt over how much she'd sacrificed to help his family.

"What if I told you I'll take them all for the hotel?" Andi stood to face Frannie and named a high six-figure price that made the siblings gasp.

Frannie's mouth fell open in shock. "For real?"

"Your work is magnificent and brings just the local flavor we seek for our hotels. I can't imagine why I'd look any further."

Jack hugged Frannie. "Congratulations!"

"Who represents you?" Andi asked.

"Um, I do."

"That makes things much simpler. I'll take everything here and will commission about ten more specific pieces. I'll talk to you about them once I get back to Chicago and we confirm the final plans for the suites."

"I can do that," Frannie said.

"You two sure have artistic genes, don't you?" Andi asked.

"Just don't ask our father about that," Jack said. "He has no idea where the two of us came from."

Frannie smiled in agreement.

After they cemented their plans, Frannie hugged Andi. "I can't thank you enough for this."

"I should be thanking you—I've stumbled upon the best there is on my first stop. Which reminds me, I need to cancel my afternoon appointments." Andi started to go but turned back. "You aren't planning on having triplets in the near future are you?"

Jack laughed.

Frannie looked at Andi like she was crazy. "Ah, no plans for triplets."

"Excellent, you're hired," Andi said and went to the pool deck to make her calls.

After she walked away, Frannie jumped up and down with a whoop and threw herself into her brother's arms. "Oh my *God*, Jack, isn't this crazy?"

"I'm so happy for you, Fran. You deserve it."

"I can't wait to tell Jamie. Oh, and what'd she mean by triplets? I don't get it."

"They lost the last artist they hired to pregnancy with triplets."

Frannie shuddered at the thought.

"Go celebrate. Have a good time."

"You, too." Frannie looked over at Andi, curled up on a lounge chair as she talked on her cell phone. She had kicked off her sandals and appeared relaxed in the late afternoon sunshine. "We need to talk one of these days. A lot's happened."

"Yeah, but not today." He nudged his sister toward the house. "Go tell Jamie your news."

The rest of the week flew by in a flurry of brainstorming sessions and planning meetings. Most of the advance decorating work would be done from Chicago until about two months before the opening when a headquarters team would be dispatched to Newport to put the guest rooms and suites together. Andi told Jack she didn't relocate for final setup at new properties anymore because it required too much time away from her son. However, she expected to make frequent short trips to keep tabs on the work.

Knowing he was unlikely to see her again for quite some time, Jack experienced a growing sense of desperation as her departure time drew near. Over the course of the week, they'd worked closely together, shared many confidences, and forged the start of a promising friendship. Every time he was with her, he walked away craving more, and he had a sinking suspicion he'd regret letting her leave without trying to find out if she felt the same way.

Before he could chicken out, he ventured into the office they'd given her to use for the week.

"Need any help?" Jack asked from the doorway.

Looking up, she flashed the smile that made his knees go weak. "I'm just about done."

Now or never. Stepping into the room, he closed the door and leaned back against it. "I was just wondering…"

She sifted through a pile of folders and jammed them into her already over-stuffed briefcase. "About?"

While he waited for her to look at him again, he lost his nerve. "I was going to ask if you need a ride to the airport."

As she came around the desk, her lips quirked with amusement. "If that's all you wanted, why'd you close the door?"

"I, um…"

She folded her arms and looked up at him with those gorgeous eyes. "What're you wondering?"

"Just, ah…" His heart pounded like a jackhammer, and his mouth went dry as dust. "Well, I wanted to know if it's, you know…serious…with the guy you're seeing in Chicago."

"I don't know yet."

"Could be?"

"I suppose, down the road, maybe."

"Oh."

"Why do you ask?"

"If you're happy with him, then it doesn't matter."

She took a step closer, until only a foot separated them. "What if it matters to me? I'd like to know why you asked."

Swallowing hard, he forced himself to continue. "If you were unattached—hypothetically speaking, of course."

"Of course."

"I might've asked if you'd consider coming back some time."

"To work on the hotel?" she asked with a coy smile.

Exasperated, he said, "You're enjoying this far too much."

"I'm sorry." He watched her make a futile attempt to curb her amusement. "You were saying?"

"Would you? Consider coming back? To, um, see me? If you were unattached. Hypothetically."

Taking the final step to close the distance between them, she reached up to caress his face.

"Andi…"

"Yes, Jack?"

Suddenly, he couldn't seem to get air to his lungs. "What're you doing?"

She wound her arms around his neck to draw him down to her. "This."

At the instant his lips connected with hers, he was lost.

The sensation of her tongue caressing his made Jack feel light-headed and empowered at the same time. Leaning back against the door, he put his arms around her and lifted her for a better angle. "This is so crazy, but I can't resist you." He tipped his head and went back for more, nearly imploding from the heat of the sensual kiss.

In desperate need of air and searching for sanity, he nuzzled her neck, breathing in the scent that was so uniquely hers.

"Jack—"

"Come back," he whispered. "Not for work but because you want to see me. Come back, Andi."

"When?" She sounded as breathless as he felt.

"Soon. Next weekend?"

"I don't know." Her hands moved to his chest. "I'll have to see what's going on at home."

"I want to see you again."

A knock on the door startled them.

"Ready to go, boss?" Andi's colleague, Michael, asked from the hallway.

She rubbed a trembling hand over her swollen lips. "I'll be right there." Looking up at Jack, she studied him for a long moment. "I need to think about it."

"Okay." Jack rested his hand on the doorknob while she collected her briefcase and belongings. All the while, he watched her, memorizing every detail.

As he was about to open the door, she stopped him. Going up on tiptoes, she pressed her lips to his cheek. "I've never kissed him," she whispered.

Somehow he managed to open the door. Somehow he managed to let her walk away. Somehow he managed to start breathing again.

Jack thought endlessly about that kiss. He replayed every nuance of his last minutes with her. When he was supposed to be working, he thought about the kiss. When he was supposed to be paying attention in meetings, he replayed the kiss and pondered the meaning of her parting words. When he was supposed to be sleeping, he thought about how it had felt to hold her. He'd kissed his share of women, but no other encounter had ever rocked his world quite the way this one had—a realization that filled him with giddy hope and crushing guilt. What was wrong with him that he was thinking so much about another woman while his wife lay comatose and helpless?

Quinn stepped into the office and cleared her throat to get his attention.

"Hey," he said. "What's up?"

"I might ask you the same thing. Where the heck *are* you this week?"

"Nowhere. Here."

"Is something wrong? Is it Clare?"

"No," he said, once again filled with guilt. *No, he wasn't obsessing over his sick wife—not anymore.* "Nothing's wrong."

She studied him for a second or two and then handed him several files. "The weekly conference call with Infinity is in twenty minutes. Do you want me to reschedule?"

His heart beat faster at the reminder that he'd get to speak to Andi again. Soon. "No need."

"All righty, then. I'll let you get to it."

"Thanks."

In preparation for the meeting, Jack forced himself to take note of the files Quinn had given him, while trying to stop thinking about Andi and THE KISS. That damned kiss! By the time he dialed into the call, he was almost mad with her for twisting him into knots and then leaving him hanging without a word for two days.

But then he heard her voice on the phone, and a burst of wild desire chased away the anger. He tried to focus on the call and not on the memory of how it had felt to hold her, to kiss her, to be engulfed by her alluring scent. When he tuned back in to the meeting, ten minutes had gone by, and Jack had no idea what he'd missed. They wrapped up a short time later, and Andi asked him to stay on the line. While she waited on her end for the others to leave, he suffered in silence.

"How are you?" she finally said.

"Great. You?"

"I'm good. It's always nice to get home to Eric."

"I'm sure." *What're we doing?* he wanted to shout. *What're you doing to me?*

After a long, pregnant pause, she said, "So, I've been thinking…"

"About?"

"Coming back to visit."

Jack sat up straighter in his chair. "And?" *Please don't let her say no. Please.*

"How does the weekend after next sound?"

Thrilled, he gave the calendar a quick scan and found the second weekend in September wide open. "That sounds good."

She released a long deep breath that told him this conversation was making her as nervous as it was making him. "So I'll send you my flight info?"

"I'll pick you up. Do you think…"

"What?"

Feeling like an awkward teenager, he said, "Could I maybe call you before then? Ten days is a long time."

Her soft laughter rippled through the phone and stirred emotions he hadn't experienced in far too long. "Sure. I'd like that."

"So, um, what about the guy you've been dating?"

"I told him last night we couldn't see each other anymore."

Overwhelmed with relief, Jack wanted to rest his head on the desk. "What did you tell him?"

"That some things had changed, and it wasn't going to work out."

"What's changed?" he asked in a teasing tone, needing to hear her say it, to confirm he wasn't the only one who felt the magnetic pull.

"I'm not quite sure yet, but I couldn't come visit you as long as he thought we were together."

Jack released a deep breath he hadn't even realized he was holding. "Andi?"

"Yes?"

"Are you scared? Of whatever this is?"

"I'm petrified."

Laughing, he said, "That makes two of us. How am I supposed to wait ten days to see you again?"

"You could come here…"

"I can't," he said, groaning with frustration. "Jill has a lacrosse game, and Maggie's playing soccer."

"It's only ten days. You'll survive."

"I'm not sure I will. How do you feel about spending the weekend on the boat?" In a rush of words, he added, "There're plenty of beds and a shower and everything we need."

"That sounds great. Perfect, in fact."

"All right, then. It's a date."

"I can't wait."

CHAPTER 9

Jack and Andi fell into the habit of talking late at night, sometimes for hours, about the kids, work, friends, places they'd been, people they knew. Jack lived for that time with her at the end of every hectic day. The night before she was due to arrive, he got home late from a dinner meeting with clients and found Frannie in the family room, watching a movie.

"Where is everyone?" he asked, plopping down next to her on the sofa.

"Finishing homework and taking showers."

"I'll run up to see them in a minute."

"Everything all set for this weekend?"

Resting his head back on the sofa, he glanced at her. "I guess."

"What's wrong? You're not having second thoughts, are you?"

"Not about wanting to see her. I can't wait for her to get here. I just feel kind of…"

"Guilty."

Nodding, he said, "I went to see Clare today, and it was so weird knowing I'd be spending the weekend with someone else."

Frannie reached out to rest her hand on his arm. "There's nothing you could do for Clare that you haven't already done or tried. It's time to move on."

"You're sure I'm doing the right thing by not telling the girls I'm seeing Andi?"

"I can't see any reason to involve them until you know where it's going."

"I suppose you're right." Jack didn't like keeping things from them but didn't want to upset them when they were finally getting back to some semblance of normalcy.

"I'm going to head over to Jamie's now that you're home, but we'll be here this weekend."

"Thanks, Fran, for everything. I don't know what I'd do without you."

"Have a great time, and don't worry about anything."

The flight was thirty minutes late. After waiting ten torturous days, the extra half hour was unbearable. Jack paced the waiting area at the bottom of the escalator, keeping an eye on the passengers descending from the second-floor arrival area. Just when he thought he'd go mad if he had to wait another second, he caught sight of those curls, those eyes, that smile. *Oh, that smile gets to me.*

She signaled for him to stay put rather than fight his way through the crowd. The metaphor wasn't lost on Jack as he watched her come toward him, knowing exactly what she could expect from him—and what she couldn't. In that moment, he realized with clarity he couldn't easily understand or explain—even to himself—that he loved her. At some point over the last two weeks of talking to her and sharing confidences he had fallen hard.

Before he had time to process the startling discovery, she was standing in front of him, and he couldn't decide whether he wanted to hug her or kiss her or maybe both. Reaching out to frame her face with his hands, he bent his head and brushed a light kiss over her lips. "I thought you'd never get here."

Her eyes flittered shut as she dropped her bag and stepped into his embrace.

He held her for a long time, breathing her in and wanting her more than he'd wanted anything in longer than he could remember. They held each other for several minutes before he released her, reached for her bag, and walked with his arm around her to the parking lot.

In the car, he turned to her. "I'm so glad to see you."

Her face flushed with a slight blush that he found charming. "All the way here," she said, "I kept thinking, what am I *doing*? But I wanted to see you again. So badly."

"I wanted to see you just as badly." He cupped her cheek and brought her close enough to kiss. Skimming his tongue over her bottom lip, he fought the urge to devour. "Mmm," he whispered against her lips, "all I've thought about since that amazing kiss in the office was doing it again."

Her fingers combed through his hair, encouraging him to take more. "Me, too."

He kissed her again, this time holding nothing back. Her slick lips and teasing tongue made him want her naked and horizontal under him with a fierce urgency he wouldn't have thought himself capable of anymore before he met her.

Breathing hard, he rested his forehead against hers and gazed into her soft brown eyes. "I told myself I wouldn't do this."

"Kiss me?" she asked with that teasing smile he so adored. "I would've been disappointed if you hadn't."

"Jump all over you like a hormonal teenager the minute you got here."

"We jumped all over each other."

"I can't remember the last time I made out in a parked car," he said with a smile as he reluctantly pulled himself away from her to drive them to Newport. "I'd forgotten how fun it can be."

The ride was punctuated by small talk and comfortable stretches of silence. On the way, Jack struggled to process the strong reaction he'd had to seeing her again as well as the discovery that he'd fallen in love with her.

"What're you thinking about over there?"

Startled out of his thoughts, Jack glanced at her. "A lot of things."

Reaching over, she linked her fingers with his. "Care to share any of them?"

"Maybe," he said with a coy smile. "Eventually."

"Are you feeling okay about…well…everything?"

"I'm conflicted. I won't lie to you about that."

"I wouldn't want you to."

"This feels like it has the potential to be a very big deal. And it'd be one thing if we had only ourselves to think about, but there're so many other people to consider."

"May I make a suggestion?"

"Of course."

"How about we take this weekend just for us? No worries or talk about the future, the kids, the logistics, or any of the other issues standing in the way. Just us."

Overwhelmed by the relief of having her and her thoughtful sensibility with him for the next few days, he brought their joined hands to his lips. "That could very well be the best idea you've ever had."

Laughing, she said, "Oh, I've got a few others you'll like just as much—if not more."

Jack groaned and pressed harder on the accelerator.

When they arrived at the marina, Jack was relieved to find it oddly deserted. He wasn't prepared to explain Andi to people he and Clare had known for years, nor did he want rumors reaching the girls before he was able to talk to them himself. But remembering their vow to keep this weekend all about them, he pushed those thoughts aside and took her bag down to the cabin.

Turning to go back outside, he discovered she'd followed him.

"Hey," he said, his heart racing.

"Hey, yourself."

They stared at each other for an emotion-packed moment before she was back in his arms, clinging to him as he plundered. He pulled her in tight against his instant erection.

A mewling sound erupted from her throat.

When he lifted her, she wrapped her arms and legs around him without breaking the intense kiss. Pressing her against the wall freed his hands to cup her breasts, and he ran his thumbs over pebbled nipples.

Gasping, she tore her lips free. "Jack…"

"What, honey?" He dropped soft kisses on her neck. "Tell me."

A tremble rippled through her. "I want you."

Her softly spoken words went right to his heart—and a few other places. "Let's get out of here and go someplace where we can be alone."

"All right." She slid down the aroused front of him until her feet were back on the floor.

A few minutes later, Jack cast off the last of the lines and backed the boat out of its slip.

She watched him maneuver the big boat in the small space. "You're good at that."

"Lots of practice. It used to scare the hell out of me," he said with a grin as he guided the boat into the channel that circled Newport Harbor. He steered the boat into the bay so they could see the hotel site from the water.

Zeroing in on the construction site, she said, "It's going to be spectacular." The dreamy expression on her face caught his attention.

"Tell me what you see."

"The rolling lawn is sprinkled with umbrellas and Adirondack chairs filled with guests enjoying the view of the bay. Sunday brunch is being served on the veranda. Green-and-white-striped awnings and huge terra cotta pots filled with lush flowers."

"Wow, I can picture it. How do you do that?"

She grinned and shrugged.

"I added a second veranda to the plans on the south side, right about there." He pointed. "I can't take too much credit for the initial design, but I'm very pleased with what our gang came up with. I wouldn't have done it much differently myself."

"They've learned from the best."

"So did I." Jack steered the boat toward Mackerel Cove to anchor for the night. "Working for Neil was so important. It made everything else possible."

"I'd love to meet him."

"You'd be surprised at how normal he is. He's not at all affected by the attention he's received. It hasn't spoiled him."

"Sounds like you learned more than just architecture from him. You could be describing yourself."

"Thank you for that, but my career certainly doesn't warrant the same attention his did."

"You've gotten your share. I knew about your firm for years before we hired you."

"It still amuses me to hear that. We had no intention of working at the level we are now. We just wanted to keep it simple. That's why we left Neil's company, but it hasn't worked out quite the way we planned."

"You know what John Lennon said about life? It's what happens when you're busy making other plans."

"Ain't that the truth? If my father had his way, I would've been a banker."

Andi grimaced. "I can't picture that."

"Neither could I. My grandfather started the bank, and my father took it over when his father retired. It was assumed I'd follow in their footsteps."

"What bank?"

"Bank Atlantic."

"I had an account there when I was in college!"

Jack grinned. "Thank you for your business. Anyway, after I told him I was forgoing business school at Yale—his alma mater—to go to architecture school at Berkeley, he flipped his lid and didn't speak to me for years." He'd carried the pain of his father's unreasonable anger with him for years. "I've never regretted my choice, but I always wished that I could've had the career I wanted and made him proud of me, too." Shrugging it off, he added, "But that's neither here nor there now."

"It must still hurt a little."

"I never think about it anymore."

"He has to be proud of you, Jack. How could he not be? Look at all you've accomplished."

"I hope he is, but I really don't know. It stopped mattering to me years ago. For a long time, I wondered if anything could ever bridge the awful gap between us. Then I brought Clare home to Greenwich to meet them. Since he can be a world-class snob, I figured he'd disapprove of me marrying a schoolteacher from working-class Hartford, but he loved her from the minute he met her. She helped to smooth out a lot of the rough edges. After Jill was born, we let go of the anger and got over it."

"Kids have a way of putting things into perspective."

"True, but we've never talked about what happened."

"At least you talk. That's something."

He smiled at her, marveling at how easy it was to tell her things he never spoke of to anyone else. "Also true."

Once they'd anchored in the quiet cove, he opened a bottle of wine and turned on the CD player. Sinatra roared to life on the boat's sound system. Jack turned it down and went up on deck to join her. They sat together on the wide bench seat as the sunset over Jamestown faded into darkness.

He drew her closer so her head rested on his chest.

She wrapped her arm around him.

"Are you hungry?" he asked, rubbing his cheek against her soft curls.

"Not really."

He tipped her chin and studied her face for a long, intense moment, as if there was still a decision to be made. Who was he kidding? Taking her wineglass, he put it on the table next to his.

"Every time I kiss you," he said, gliding his lips over hers, "all I can think is how long I have to wait until I can do it again."

"I seem to have the same problem." She sighed. Her arms tightened around him as she met the ardent thrusts of his tongue with her own.

He slipped his hand under her T-shirt and pushed up her bra to free her breasts. Groaning against her lips, he teased her with his fingers until her nipples were hard and tight. Suddenly in a rush, he tore his lips free, pulled the T-shirt over her head, and kissed his way to her breasts. He reached behind her to unhook her bra. Tugging on one nipple with his lips, he gave the other the same treatment with his fingers.

Andi took a deep breath of the salty sea air as the water lapped against the hull and his hot, hungry mouth fed on her breasts. She opened her eyes to a sky sprinkled with stars and a moon that might've been hung just for them. Arching her hips, she found him hard and ready for her. She reached for his shirt and tugged it off to discover his chest was muscular but not bulky. The light dusting of dark hair was soft under her hands, his nipples firm against her palms.

He unbuttoned her shorts and skimmed them down her legs until only a thin strip of lace covered her. Taking a long, leisurely look at what he'd uncovered, he got rid of his own shorts and lay on his side next to her on the narrow bench seat.

Breast to chest, hip to hip, hard pressed to soft, he kissed her gently, patiently, with easy thrusts of his tongue. He slid a hand into her panties and groaned when he found her damp with desire.

She gasped as his fingers parted her and delved deeper.

"Andi, honey, I want you so much," he whispered against her lips.

She replied with the lift of her hips against his fingers and cried out when he eased them into her, reducing her world to the throbbing need between her legs.

Suddenly impatient, he got rid of the panties and hooked her leg over his hips. Kissing her with deep thrusts of his tongue, he moved his fingers over her and into her, in a steady, relentless rhythm that quickly sent her flying.

"Jack! *Oh!*"

He kept it up until she came a second time, trembling and gasping. Nothing had ever been quite like this.

"You're so beautiful," he whispered, shifting so he was between her legs. "I love you, Andi. I can't offer you anything else, but I do love you—"

She stopped him with a finger to his lips. "That's all I need."

Resting on top of her, he leaned down to kiss her. "Do we need protection?"

She shook her head. "I'm on the pill."

He made her crazy with hot kisses to her neck and breasts, but he surprised her when he suddenly stopped and rested his forehead on her chest.

"Jack? What is it?"

Breathing heavily, he said, "I just…I need a minute, honey."

Putting her arms around him, she brought him up with her.

"I'm sorry."

"Don't be." She caressed his back with gentle strokes.

"I was so sure I could do this."

The pain she heard in his voice made her ache for him. "You're just not ready. I understand."

"Maybe I could've figured that out before we were naked and desperate."

She smiled and brushed her lips over his hair. "It's all right."

He brought her closer to him, and they were quiet for a long time. "Do you think maybe we could try again?"

"We don't have to. I'm happy just to be here with you."

"I know we don't have to, but I really, really *want* to make love with you. Give me another chance?"

She ran her fingers through his hair and kissed him, a gentle undemanding kiss. Finally, she sat up, took his hand, and led him inside. "Which one's yours?" she asked of the two closed doors.

He pointed to the one on the left.

In the small cabin, they lay down together on the bed. Their lips met in another soft kiss.

Without breaking the kiss, Andi stretched out on top of him.

His hands coasted over her back, making her tremble with desire.

She slid down, dragging her lips along his chest and belly.

He sighed and tangled his fingers in her hair.

When she took him into her mouth, he gasped. "*Andi…*"

With her hand, lips, and tongue, she loved him until he was panting and sweating. Then she moved over him, and without giving him time to think or prepare, she sank down onto his hard length. With her hands resting on his chest, she let her head fall back in surrender. The feeling of completion overwhelmed her. *Here* was what she'd always wanted—right here, right now, this man, this love. For a long moment, she didn't move, she just held still and reveled in the intense pleasure of having him deep inside her.

He laced his fingers through hers.

She raised their joined hands and brought them down on either side of his head as she lifted and lowered her hips in small, delicate movements. Sliding her lips over his, she gazed down at him. His eyes were closed, and she watched the tension drain from his face.

"It's okay, Jack," she whispered. "I love you."

His eyes flew open to meet her gaze. He squeezed her hands and let himself go.

CHAPTER 10

They lay facing each other, listening to the symphony of crickets on the near-by shore and the soft music. He twirled one of her curls around his finger as he whispered along with Sinatra singing "The Way You Look Tonight."

She closed her eyes to hold back tears that threatened to ruin the loveliest moment of her life. He was everything—*everything* she had ever wanted and so much more.

"Are you sad, Andi?"

"How could I be? It was so... I've never..."

He leaned over to quiet her with a kiss. "I know."

She ran her fingers up and down his back, wanting to savor every minute with him.

"I'm starving," he said, his voice muffled against her breasts.

She laughed and hugged him for another minute before she let him go.

He pulled on a pair of shorts he unearthed from a drawer below the bed. "Don't move."

They stayed in bed and devoured the dinner he'd brought. He fed her crackers loaded with brie and thin slices of prosciutto ham.

"Mmmm," she said. "That's heavenly."

The CD player flipped to the next disk, and Andi giggled when Sammy Davis Jr.'s "Candy Man" came on. "I'm sensing a theme."

"Jamie loves all things Rat Pack. He's even got a stash of Cuban cigars around here somewhere. Want one for dessert?"

"I think I'll pass." She leaned over to kiss him and refilled the wineglass they were sharing. Taking another handful of grapes, she fed him several and kissed the juice off his lips. "Speaking of Jamie, I meant to ask, how're things with him and Frannie?"

"Apparently, he's planning to propose."

"Wow, how do you feel about that?"

"I'm thrilled. I love them both, and it's funny how what would've seemed crazy a couple of weeks ago suddenly makes perfect sense."

"I know what you mean," she said with a coy smile.

He grinned. "I guess you do, don't you?"

"The girls will be excited about Frannie and Jamie getting married, won't they?"

"For sure, but you know who would've really loved it?"

"Clare."

He looked up at the ceiling. "She was always fixing them up with friends of hers, trying to get them settled. She would've found this very ironic, to say the least."

Andi rested her head on his shoulder. "I'm glad it's worked out for them. It's such a sweet story, how it's taken them decades to find something that was always there."

"It's amazing."

She reached up to play with his hair. "What're you thinking?"

"It's important that you know I was never unfaithful to Clare. I never even thought about it."

Caressing his face, she said, "You've been so faithful to her, Jack."

"Everyone's been urging me to get back to living, and I thought I was doing that by reconnecting with the girls and going back to work." He ran his fingers through her silky curls. "But it took meeting you to make me feel truly alive again."

"You've been through an awful thing, but it hasn't destroyed you."

"I never would've gone looking for this, even though I'm so glad I found you." He kissed her softly. "But I worry I'm dragging you into a no-win situation."

"I've stepped into your life with my eyes wide open. We've asked nothing more from each other than what we have right now. You've got so many things to worry about. Don't add me to the list."

"Thank you for what you did…before. Somehow you knew just what I needed. I don't think I could've done this with anyone but you."

She hugged him close to her.

He trailed kisses up her neck. "Had it been a long time for you, too?"

"Since Alec."

"Then why are you still on the pill, or is that none of my business?"

"To keep my periods regular. I get all out of whack without it."

"Mmm," he said, "we can't have that. You taste so good, like wine and…" Taking another taste, he added, "Sweetness. I could very easily get addicted to you." He flicked his tongue in a teasing stroke over her lips before traveling to her neck and breasts.

The feel of her fingers combing through his hair seemed to fuel his desire as he pressed his lips to her belly. Parting her legs with his shoulders, he trailed a finger through her dampness.

"Jack," she whispered, arching her back.

He dipped his head and added his tongue.

She cried out.

Dropping soft, openmouthed kisses on her inner thigh, he kissed his way to her core and took her right over.

"Oh, God," she said, gasping for air and looking up at him with wide eyes.

He kissed his way to her mouth. "I love you," he whispered as he entered her. "I love you so much."

She brushed the hair back from his forehead and kissed him. "I love you, too."

Jack awoke next to Andi on Monday morning after a desperate last night of lovemaking.

He experienced a horrible, sinking sensation every time he imagined going back to the lonely existence he'd led before she swooped in and changed everything. She'd helped him see that, despite how it seemed, his life wasn't over. Altered? Yes. But over? No.

The weekend had been one of the best of his life. They'd sailed and fished and gone swimming and exhausted themselves making love into the wee hours of each morning. But with her departure time creeping closer, Jack had sensed her withdrawal, as if she was preparing herself to leave him. Her quiet introspection had begun to worry him as the sun rose on their final morning together.

He hugged her tight against him, and she stirred.

She pushed her hair back and turned to face him. "Are you all right? What is it?"

He stroked her cheek. "No, I'm not all right. I don't want you to go."

"I have to go. You know that."

"What happens now?" he asked.

She studied him for a long time. "I don't know," she finally said. "Maybe we go about our lives with a lovely memory of a once-in-a-lifetime weekend."

His stomach dropped. "You can't be serious. You expect me to pretend this never happened?"

"We have to be realistic, Jack." As she said the words, her lips quivered and her eyes filled. "We live more than a thousand miles apart. We have established lives and children who can't be uprooted. How can we put ourselves through a long-distance relationship that can't go anywhere? It'll just get more difficult every time we see each other."

"Isn't an occasional weekend or vacation better than nothing?"

"You can't do that to your girls, Jack. How will you ever explain me to them?"

Frustrated and panic-stricken, he stared at her. "If you felt this way, why did you come this weekend?"

"I almost didn't, but I needed to see you. I needed to know—"

He sat up and moved away from her. "What? What did you need to know? That you're walking away from what could be the love of your life?"

A sob hiccupped through her. "I have no doubt that's exactly what I'm doing. I'm so sorry, Jack. I wish things could be different, but I feel like my heart is being ripped out of my chest after one weekend with you. How can I keep putting myself through this when I know we can never really be together?"

Jack rubbed his eyes as despair crept back in. He hadn't missed that feeling this weekend. "There has to be a way. I can't lose you now that I've found you—now that we've found each other. I love you, Andi. I've loved only one other woman in my life, and I knew it just as quickly then as I do now. This is right between us. I can't tell you how I know. I just do."

"I love you, too." Her voice caught with emotion as she cradled his face in her hands and turned him to her. "I love you so much. I'd like nothing more than to have the rest of my life to show you just how much. I've never admired anyone more than I do you, the way you've survived in spite of everything. I wish things were different, that we'd met at a different time in our lives."

He held her close enough to drink in the scent that was so uniquely hers, knowing she was right. But he couldn't imagine going back to the bleakness he'd been living with before. When everything in his world turned to black and white, she'd brought back the color.

"I'm not sorry," she whispered. "I wouldn't have missed this for the world."

"Me either." He kissed her gently at first and then with more passion as her enthusiastic response fed his desire. Knowing they were short on time, he entered her with a quick thrust of his hips and then gave her a moment to adjust. He gazed down at the lovely face that would haunt him forever.

She reached for him and fused her mouth to his.

"How can we let go of this?" he asked, filling her and then withdrawing, leaving her bereft.

When he went deep again, she wrapped her legs around him to keep him there and rocked against him.

The end, when it came, was more powerful and consuming than any other time.

"How am I supposed to let you go?"

"Please, Jack," she whispered. "Please."

He shifted off her but kept his eyes fixed on her when she got up to take a shower.

Two hours later, they drove over the bridge on the way out of town, and Andi took a last look back at the harbor.

When they reached the airport, Jack parked to walk her in. At security, he took her hands. "Thank you," he said, his voice heavy with emotion.

Her long lashes sparkled with tears. "I had the best time, Jack. I'll never forget it—or you."

He hugged her and whispered, "This is not the end, Andi. It's not over."

They held each other for a long time before she backed away. "Bye."

He said nothing as he watched her go.

Those who knew Jack best agreed that the recent healing they'd witnessed had suffered a serious setback in the aftermath of Andi's departure.

"I'm so worried about him," Frannie said to Jamie late one night when they were in his bed. "It's almost worse this time because he had a second chance at happiness, and now that's gone, too. He looks devastated again."

"He's been trying to hide it, but he's a mess. Do you think he's in love with her?"

"I'm sure of it."

"Maybe he could convince her to move here."

"She won't do that. He told me she has a hearing-impaired son, and she won't want to move him away from his school. She's got a great job and a life in Chicago. Besides, it's not like he can marry her."

"It's not fair. He's already been through enough." Jamie kissed her hand and then her lips. "It makes me appreciate how very lucky we are."

"I still want to pinch myself sometimes to make sure I'm not dreaming."

"I guarantee you're not dreaming. As a matter of fact, stay right there and don't look." He jumped up, left the room, and came back a minute later holding something behind his back. "I was waiting for the right moment, and it just occurred to me that this is it."

She gasped when he knelt beside the bed and reached for her hand.

"Frannie, I love you. I've always loved you, and I always will. So will you do me the great honor of being my wife?" From behind his back, he produced a diamond ring and slipped it on her finger.

She threw her arms around his neck. "Yes, yes, *yes!*"

Jamie and Frannie's engagement was the talk of the town, or so it seemed to Jack. He was thrilled for them and tried to share in their excitement as they planned a New Year's Eve wedding. Jack teased Frannie about "the rock," but no amount of teasing could detract from her happiness in finally getting what she now admitted she'd always wanted.

Jack struggled to hide his inner turmoil and was determined not to let it affect his girls this time. He'd respected Andi's wishes by not calling her since she left, but he missed everything about her. And while he yearned for her soft skin and alluring scent, he especially missed their late-night phone calls.

Somehow he managed to get through the workweek, not that he accomplished a damned thing. The weekend stretched out before him desolate and empty after the one he'd spent with Andi.

A knock on his office door startled him out of his thoughts. "Come in."

"Hello, darling."

Surprised to see his mother, Jack got up to greet her with a hug and kiss. "What're you doing here?"

Madeline smiled at him. She had white hair and the same gray eyes as her son. "Does a mother need a reason to visit her children and grandchildren?"

"Of course not. The girls will be thrilled to see you."

"Gorgeous day out there. Got time for a walk on the beach?"

Since the day was a wash anyway, he said, "Sure." He told Quinn he was leaving and escorted his mother down the path to the shore.

They walked along the water's edge for a long while in silence.

"So how about your sister and Jamie?" Madeline said. "I'm still trying to decide if I saw this one coming or not."

Jack laughed. "I'm with them both all the time, and even *I* didn't see it coming. But I'm thrilled for them. I hope you are, too."

"Oh, I am, Jack. You know I've always adored Jamie. He's not exactly tough on the eyes, either."

"Mother!"

"Well, there may be snow on the roof—"

"All right already," he said with a grin.

"So what's new with you?"

Suspicious, Jack glanced at her. "What do you already know?"

"A mother never reveals her secrets."

"Frannie told you about Andi."

"She said you seemed happy again for a while, but she's been worried about you this week."

A rush of emotion caught him off guard. Afraid of the secrets he might be revealing, he looked down at the wet sand.

His mother squeezed his arm. "Sweetheart? You want to talk about it?"

"There's not much to say." His heart ached when he thought of Andi and how hopeless she'd made their situation seem. "It's not going to work out."

"Why's that?"

"We've decided it's too complicated. She lives a thousand miles away where she has a son, a job, a life. With the girls in high school and Clare, there's no way I can relocate. So what's the point?"

"I'm sorry you've learned nothing from all you've been through."

Startled, he stopped to look at her. "What's that supposed to mean?"

"Jack, my darling boy, life is so short, and when you have a chance to be happy, you have to take hold of it with both hands and never let go. It doesn't come along every day."

"She has a great job in Chicago. Her mother is there, her son's school. How do I ask her to give all that up to come here when I can't promise her a damned thing? That's too much to ask of anyone."

"It's more than either of you has now. The older girls will be in college soon, and Maggie won't be far behind them. What's left for you, then? You've got a lot of years still to live, and I hate the idea of you spending them alone."

He held up his left hand where he still wore Clare's ring. "What about this?"

"You have to carve out a life for yourself without Clare." Madeline's eyes filled as she said the words. "Somehow."

"I think I've finally accepted that she's really gone. For so long, I didn't believe it, you know? But now... It's been such a long time."

"I so admire that despite *everything* you still honor the vows you took with her, but nothing can change what's happened." She took his hand and looked into his eyes. "*Live*, Jack. That's all you can do, my love."

He remembered Frannie saying almost the same thing. "I know what I need to do. Thanks, Mom."

"Any time, darling. Want to take your mother sailing this weekend?"

"I'd love to." He hugged her and walked the rest of the way back to the office with his arm around her shoulders.

CHAPTER 11

Jack brought Quinn in on his plan, and she helped with the details. Her contagious excitement helped to dispel any final doubts he had. With many of the most important people in his life urging him forward, Jack couldn't help but be swept up.

When he got to Chicago, he hoped to meet with Infinity's CEO David Johnson to go over the latest set of plans for the hotel, but not until after he saw Andi. He didn't want anyone to spoil his surprise.

Late on Monday afternoon, Jack cut through their shared bathroom to Jamie's office. "Are you busy?"

Jamie waved him in. "Not at the moment. Come in."

"Quinn told you I'll be in Chicago for a few days?"

"She did, but I didn't think we were due to meet with them again for another month or two."

"I'm going to see Andi, and you know it."

Jamie grinned. "So what's the strategy when you get there?"

"I have some tricks up my sleeve. I've learned a few things from watching you in action over the years."

"Oh, to be a fly on the wall…" Jamie laughed. "You've been off the market a long time. You're aware a few things have changed, right?"

"Spare me the details, killer. Don't forget you're engaged to my sister. I don't want to hear about your 'moves.' I'll stick to my own plan, thank you very much."

"So what changed? I thought you guys had decided to cool it."

"Would you believe I listened to my mother? She basically said I'd be a fool to let Andi go."

"I've always loved Madeline's voice of reason. You seem a little better lately."

"Maybe," Jack said with a shrug, "but I wouldn't want anyone to think I've forgotten Clare or left her behind or anything."

Jamie got up and came around the desk to lean against it. "No one who knows what you've been through would ever think that, Jack."

Jack nodded, overwhelmed by Jamie's unwavering support. "Do you know what I wonder about sometimes?"

"What's that?"

"This thing with Andi happened so fast, you know? It was like being hit by lightning or something. I wonder what I would've felt for her if Clare had never gotten hurt. I still would've met Andi…"

"You were the most solidly married person I ever knew. You might've had a few thoughts about Andi, but you *never* would've acted on them."

"That's what I hoped you'd say," Jack said, relieved. "You know what I think about a lot? That putt. Remember?"

Jamie chuckled. "Yeah."

Standing, Jack said, "The last moment of normal life."

"Before you go, there's a favor I need to ask of you."

"Sure, anything."

"Will you be my best man?"

"Of course I will." Jack stood to hug Jamie. "I'd love to."

"I know it's got to be kind of weird for you—me marrying your sister after all these years."

"It's terrific, and Clare would've loved it, too."

"Especially after all her failed matchmaking efforts on my behalf—and Frannie's." Jamie smiled. "I'm sorry she won't be able to share it with us."

"So am I. Have you told your parents yet?"

"I asked them to come up this week without telling them why. I wanted to give them the news in person, and I can't get away right now."

"I'm sure they'll be thrilled. Make sure they see the girls, will you?"

"As if my mother would be here and not see them." He checked his watch. "I need to get out of here and meet Frannie. Have a good trip. I hope you get whatever it is you want."

"Thanks. I guess I've gotta get busy planning a bachelor party." Jack stroked his chin, feigning deep thought. "I wonder if that stripper you had at mine is still in the business."

Jamie blanched. "Don't you *dare*!"

Hired sight unseen, the woman had been old enough back then to be their mother. With a shudder and a laugh, Jack went to his office to clear off his desk.

Jack flew to Chicago early the next morning, unsure of how he would be received but prepared to do battle—if that's what it took—to keep Andi in his life. On his way into the city in the limo Quinn had hired for him, all he could think about was seeing Andi again.

He checked into a suite at the Infinity flagship property. In the lavish lobby as well as the suite, he got an impressive first glimpse at Andi's work. The hotel was gorgeous, among the nicest he'd ever seen, and he knew the Newport property would be equally amazing.

His fifteenth floor suite overlooked Lake Michigan, and he took a few minutes to appreciate the view and calm his nerves before he rode the elevator to the top-floor executive suite. He wore tan dress pants, a navy blue cashmere blazer with a light blue silk shirt, and Italian wingtips. When he got to the top floor, he asked for Andi at reception. They sent him down a long hallway to a large corner office.

Andi's assistant, Jen Brooks, looked up from her desk to greet him. Quinn had let her know he was coming.

He asked if Andi was in, but when Jen reached for her phone, he held up a hand to stop her. Gesturing toward the closed door, he asked, "May I?"

"Of course." With an intrigued look on her face, she waved him in.

Andi's large office had a marvelous view of Lake Michigan as well as Chicago's famous Lake Shore Drive.

She sat with her back to the door, looking out at the lake. "What is it, Jen?"

"It's not Jen."

She swiveled around, her face slack with shock. "What're you doing here?"

"I couldn't stay away."

She stood up and circled the desk. "I thought we agreed…"

Jack took in her cranberry-colored suit and heels so high she almost met him eye to eye.

"Wow, look at you," she sighed, her gaze skipping over him.

"Look at *you*." It was all he could to resist the urge to haul her into his arms and show her just how much he'd missed her.

"What're you doing here, Jack?"

"Let me quote someone near and dear to me: life is short. When you have the chance to be happy, you have to go for it."

"But nothing's changed. We're setting ourselves up for so much pain. I can't," she whispered, shaking her head. "I just *can't*."

Unable to wait another second to touch her, he closed the distance between them and took her in his arms. "And I can't let you go. I can't forget about you and what we have together. Somehow we'll figure it out. I love you, Andi." He kissed her. "I *love* you."

Her resolve seemed to melt away as she put her arms around him.

When he felt her surrender, he kissed her again, weak with relief that part one of his plan had succeeded brilliantly.

Andi got home two hours before Jack was due to pick her up. He hadn't said where they were going, just that she needed to get dressed up. *What'll I wear?*

Her mother, Betty, wiped her hands on a dishtowel as she came out to greet Andi. "Hi, honey."

Andi rushed by with a quick kiss to her mother's cheek. "Hi, Mom. Would you mind watching Eric tonight? A friend of mine is in town unexpectedly, and he's invited me to dinner."

"Must be a pretty good friend."

Andi stopped short. "Why do you say that?"

Betty nodded to the front hall table. "Look."

Andi turned to find a huge box from Sak's Fifth Avenue sitting on the table. She gasped, and her hand shot up to cover her mouth. "What is it?"

"I don't know, honey. It didn't have my name on it." Betty laughed when Andi approached the box as if it might be filled with explosives.

She lifted the top off and pushed aside tissue paper to reveal an exquisite ivory silk dress. Gingerly, she lifted it out of the box. She couldn't believe he had done this. The card said, *Even Cinderella had something new to wear. See you soon. Love, Jack.*

Under the dress, she found a gorgeous pair of high-heeled, beaded sandals she would have chosen for herself. He had left her office saying he had things to do, but she couldn't have imagined this.

"It's beautiful, Andi. It'll be lovely on you. You never did say too much about what happened in Rhode Island, and I didn't want to pry, but I have to admit I'm curious."

"I didn't say anything because I had ended it with him."

Betty followed Andi into the bedroom, where she laid the dress on her bed.

"I didn't know he was coming today," Andi continued. "He's asked me to give him a chance, and that's what I'm going to do."

"You definitely haven't been yourself since you came home from the weekend in Newport. Why did you feel like you had to end it with him? There couldn't have been much to end. You only spent a short time with him."

"I spent just long enough with him." Andi sighed and sat on her bed. "It's complicated."

Betty sat next to her. "How so? Other than the obvious geography problem."

"He owns a business and has three daughters—two in high school—so it's not like he can move. Eric's in such a great school, and you're here. Then there's my job. It's such a mess." Andi's earlier excitement faded as she revisited all the reasons their relationship was such a bad idea. "I just didn't see the point of getting into something so impossible."

"I can see what you mean, but do you love him?"

"I do," Andi said, smiling. That was the easy part. "I love him so much. I know you're thinking that I hardly know him, but I already know him better than I ever knew Alec. He's a wonderful father, and he's smart, talented, and *so* handsome." Her belly fluttered with excitement as she thought of how sexy he'd looked earlier. "He's everything I've ever wanted. I've been sick with missing him since I got home."

"He sounds lovely."

Andi bit her bottom lip. "There's one other thing."

"What's that?"

"He's married."

"*Oh my God*, Andrea! Tell me you're kidding me!"

Andi held up her hands. "Let me explain." She told her mother about what had happened to Clare and everything Jack went through before she met him. "Believe me, he wasn't looking for this any more than I was. It just happened. To both of us. Please try to understand."

"You can't change the fact that he's married."

"I'm not asking him to change it. That's just one of the reasons why I told him we couldn't see each other anymore. But he flew out here today and asked me to give it a chance…" Andi shrugged.

"You're far too old for me to tell you how to live your life, but you were right when you told him this is a no-win situation. I can't bear to see you hurt again like you were with Alec. You're setting yourself up for a terrible disappointment."

Her mother's words hurt, and Andi knew there was some truth to them. But as she ran her fingers over the exquisite dress, she decided he was a risk she was willing to take.

"What's Eric doing?" Andi got up from the bed. "I want to spend some time with him before Jack gets here."

"Is he your boyfriend?" Eric signed as Andi helped him into his favorite Spiderman pajamas. He smelled so sweet from his bath, and she held him close for a minute before he squiggled away.

Andi was glad now that she'd never told him about the few dates she'd had with his friend's father. She'd hate to have to explain the change in direction to a five-year-old. She could barely explain it to her mother—or herself. "Sort of." Checking her watch, she saw she had only forty-five minutes.

"Can I meet him?"

"Of course you can. He wants to meet you, too. Mommy's going to get dressed while you have your dessert, okay?"

"Okay."

She kissed him and left him eating his ice cream in the kitchen.

After a quick shower, she pinned up her long dark hair in an elegant French twist. When she couldn't keep a few curls from springing free, she gave up trying. She realized she was nervous when her hand trembled as she applied mascara.

Her mother's somber warning ran through her mind, but she chased those thoughts away when it was time to put on the gorgeous dress and shoes, which fit as if they'd been made just for her. She wondered how he'd managed such a wonderful surprise.

Cinderella indeed, she thought, checking the complete ensemble in a full-length mirror. She couldn't have done better herself. As she walked out of her room, the doorman rang to announce her visitor. She asked him to send Jack up and called for her mother to bring Eric.

Andi opened the door, and her mouth went dry at the sight of Jack in a tuxedo.

He handed her a single red rose and kissed her cheek. "Magnificent."

Wiggling a finger to bring him closer, she kissed him back and whispered, "You, too." She took him by the hand to lead him into the living room where her mother and Eric waited. "Jack, this is my mother, Betty Franklin. Mom, Jack Harrington."

He shook Betty's hand. "Pleased to meet you, Mrs. Franklin."

"Likewise." Andi heard the hint of reserve in her mother's tone but didn't think Jack tuned into it.

"Who's that cute guy behind you?" He crouched down and signed, "Hello, Eric, my name is Jack."

Andi's heart swelled with love as she watched him communicate with her child.

Eric's big blue eyes sized up the stranger in the funny clothes as he signed, "Hi."

Jack turned to Andi. "I might need your help here." He spoke slowly and signed, "Do you like baseball, Eric?"

Eric looked at his mother, and she signed baseball correctly.

Jack watched and mimicked her signs.

Eric nodded enthusiastically.

Jack reached for his inside jacket pocket and withdrew four tickets to the next day's Chicago Cubs game.

Eric's eyes lit up when Jack handed him the tickets.

"Do you want to go?" Jack signed.

Eric looked at his mother, who nodded and signed rapidly to remind her son of his manners.

"Thank you," Eric signed and scampered from the room with the tickets and his grandmother in pursuit.

"Have a nice evening," Betty called over her shoulder.

"How did you learn sign language?" Andi asked, astonished.

"Don't be too impressed. That's about the extent of it. Kate's friend Miranda has a sister who's deaf. She gave me a few pointers last night."

"It must've taken you hours to learn that much!"

"Just a few," he confessed as he walked her to the front door. "I was a good student. Miranda said so."

"Thank you for doing that and the dress and the tickets. How did you manage all this?" she asked in the elevator.

"I'll never tell my secrets." He led her to the limo he had waiting at the curb. "I'll admit to having had just a tiny bit of help, but that's all I'm saying."

"I'll get it out of you," she said confidently.

He laughed. "I'll look forward to that."

"So where are we going?"

"You'll just have to wait and see." He slipped an arm around her, drew her close, and kissed her. "I've needed that since the minute you opened the door. You look stunning."

"Thanks to my secret shopper." She reached up to caress his face. "I didn't think I could love you any more, but what you did with Eric... Thank you, Jack."

He kissed her again, this time more intently, and after a few minutes they were both breathless with longing.

"Ever done it in a limo?" he asked, nibbling his way up her neck.

She laughed. "Nope."

"We'll have to fix that later." He kissed her again. "Hey, I forgot to tell you before that Frannie and Jamie got engaged last week."

"That's wonderful! You must be delighted."

"We all are. Jamie asked me to be his best man."

"Of course he did. When's the big day?"

"New Year's Eve."

"I like that—a new year and a new start."

He kissed her hand. "I hope you'll be there with me."

"Maybe," she said wistfully, still finding it hard to believe they could have a future together.

The limo slowed to a stop, and Jack helped her from the car onto a pier. A uniformed man waited to welcome them aboard the *Esmeralda*, a classic eighty-foot Trumpy yacht.

"Oh, Jack, it's gorgeous!" She turned to him as a steward escorted them up the gangway. "Whose is it?"

"It belongs to a former client who was happy to loan it to us for the evening."

The steward led them into a large dining room where a single table was set for two. A trio in the corner provided background music.

She gazed at the extravagant surroundings while the steward told them the boat, built in 1966 in Annapolis, Maryland, was considered the "Rolls Royce of American motor yachts."

Andi walked around the elegant, candlelit dining room. When she turned to Jack, he shrugged, as if it'd been nothing to arrange this fairy-tale evening.

They dined on one exquisite course after another. The musicians kept up a quiet tempo while they ate the delicious food and enjoyed the exceptional wine. After they shared a chocolate soufflé for dessert, Jack held out his hand to her.

He escorted her to the small dance floor at the front of the room and pulled her close as the musicians swung into a different tune. One of them stepped to the microphone and to sing "The Way You Look Tonight."

"Jack," she gasped when she heard the familiar song.

"I wanted to be sure you'd remember all our first times," he whispered, brushing his lips over hers.

The band played one love song after another as they danced close together. After a while she looked up to study his handsome face.

"What is it?"

"Just admiring the view."

He smiled. "Happy?"

"Mmmm." She rested her face against his chest. His heart beat against her cheek as she played with the hair that curled above his collar.

"Let's get some air," he said, leading her off the dance floor with a wave of thanks to the musicians.

Jack dropped his tuxedo jacket over her shoulders, and they leaned on the rail to watch the water rush by below as the sleek yacht sluiced through the vast lake.

"I can't believe you did this, Jack. I'm overwhelmed." She reached for him and could tell she surprised him with a deep, searching kiss.

His hands moved with tantalizing slowness on her back under the jacket he'd put around her.

Her skin tingled from his touch.

The kiss went on forever, or so it seemed, before he pulled back to kiss her cheeks, her forehead, and the end of her nose. "I can't get enough of you," he said, his voice hoarse as he kissed her again. "I need you so much, Andi. Tell me you'll give us a chance."

"I want to so badly. More than anything."

"But?"

"I'm so afraid of getting hurt again. It nearly killed me once before. I don't know if I'd survive it again—not when it's so much bigger this time."

Jack leaned his forehead against hers. "As much as I wish I could offer you guarantees, that's one thing I don't have to give. All I can do is tell you again how much I love you and how much I want to be with you—if you'll have me. That's all I've got right now."

She reached up to caress his face. "It's far more than I've ever had before."

He reached for her hand and pressed a kiss to her palm.

A tremble rippled through Andi. She'd never wanted anything more than she wanted him.

"There's a very cozy stateroom down below that's ours for the evening." Tilting his head in invitation, he extended a hand.

Aware that she was agreeing to far more than a few hours in a cozy stateroom, Andi met his gaze and sealed her fate by wrapping her fingers around his.

He led her down a small flight of stairs and through a narrow hallway. The moment he closed the cabin door behind him, he reached for her.

Their kiss quickly became urgent.

She pushed his tuxedo jacket off her shoulders, and it fell to the floor. Reaching for his collar, she removed the bow tie and went to work on the onyx studs lining his shirt.

He unzipped her dress. With a soft flutter, it billowed into a cloud at her feet. "Oh my *God*," he whispered, gawking at the ivory lace corset that boosted her full breasts to overflowing.

Pushing his shirt aside, Andi rested her hands on his hips and pressed her lips to his chest. Flicking her tongue over his nipple, she was thrilled by the deep groan that rumbled through him.

He surprised her when he filled his hands with her bottom, lifted her off her feet, and devoured her mouth.

Andi wrapped her arms and legs around him and pushed her core tight against his erection.

Their tongues mated frantically.

"Andi," he gasped. "I want you so badly."

"I'm yours, Jack. Take me."

He eased her down to the bed and fumbled with the corset. "How do I get you out of this damned thing?"

Laughing at him, she rolled over so she was facedown, showing him the clasp on the back.

He unhooked her, his lips worshiping each new bit of soft skin as he uncovered it. When she would've turned over, he held her still. "Wait."

Her heart pounded with desire and anticipation as he unzipped his pants and let them fall to the floor.

He reached for the pins in her hair and tugged at them to free her curls. Bringing a handful of her hair to his face, he took a long deep breath. "You smell like heaven, Andi." He moved her hair to one side to leave hot, wet kisses on her neck.

Under him, Andi squirmed with impatience.

"Relax, honey," he whispered. "We've got all night."

"I need you, Jack. I've missed you so much."

He kissed her cheek, her neck, her shoulder, the middle of her back. "I missed you, too. So very much." He ran his hands over her bottom, and her breath got caught in her throat. Lifting her to her hands and knees, he moved behind her.

He held her open with his fingers, tormenting her with his tongue until her legs shook and her heart raced.

As she teetered on the edge, he drove himself into her and sent her flying.

Holding her hips still and pumping into her, he rode wave after wave of her orgasm. "Do you like it this way?" he asked, sounding breathless.

Out of her mind and unable to form a single coherent thought, she said, "*Mmm.*"

Increasing the pace, he reached around to stroke her to another shattering climax and then cried out with his own.

Without losing their connection, they fell into a heaving pile on the bed. For a long time, they were quiet as they struggled to catch their breath.

"Jack?"

His cheek pressed to her back, he muttered, "Hmm?"

"What made you decide to do this? To come here?"

He withdrew from her and shifted onto his back. "You'll laugh if I tell you."

She turned so she could see him in the faint light. "Now you *have* to tell me."

"Well, first, my mother gave me a not-so-subtle kick in the ass and told me I'd be an idiot to let you go," he admitted with a sheepish grin.

"Remind me to thank her someday."

"And I missed you so much after you left. I never want to feel that way again."

"I was sick with missing you."

"Why am I secretly glad to hear that?" he asked with a smile.

"Ha! So you've wined and dined me and somehow managed to get me back in bed. What's your next move, Romeo?" She crooked her elbow and propped her head on her hand.

Trailing a finger between her breasts, he said, "I won't divulge my plan, except to say it seems to be working quite well so far." He ducked when she swatted at him.

She scooted over so she was on top of him and pinned him down. "I want some answers, mister. Tell me how you knew my dress and shoe sizes."

He flipped them so he was back on top. "I'll answer three questions and not one more."

"How did you know my shoe and dress sizes?"

"That's two."

She rolled her eyes. "Fine! How did you know my shoe size?" When he nibbled on her neck and ear, she pushed him back. "Stop trying to change the subject."

"Okay, busybody, if you must know, Quinn called Jen."

"*Jen was in on this and didn't tell me?* I'll kill her!"

"She didn't know why I wanted to know."

"But she knew you were coming?"

"Is that your second question?"

"*Jaaaaack!*"

He laughed. "Yes, she knew I was coming, but Quinn swore her to secrecy."

"I'll still kill her."

He kissed the end of her nose. "No, you won't. It was fun to surprise you, and you had a good time."

"That's true, but I get one more question," she reminded him when he tried to kiss her more seriously.

"What's that?" he asked against her lips.

With her hands on his shoulders, she held him off because this one mattered. "What happens now?"

"I have a few ideas, but we don't need to talk about it right now, do we?" he asked as he cupped her breasts and ran his thumbs over her nipples.

She shuddered with pleasure. "I suppose it can wait."

CHAPTER 12

Andi dragged herself out of a sound sleep to go home in the middle of the night, since she knew her mother wouldn't approve of an all-nighter. *I'm thirty-seven years old and still worried about my mother's approval,* she thought as they rode the elevator to her top-floor apartment. Andi hadn't mentioned her mother's disapproval to Jack and didn't plan to.

She hugged him at her front door. "Thank you for the most amazing evening."

"It was entirely my pleasure. I'll see you at your office later this morning after my meeting with David. Will you be able to leave around noon for the game?"

She stifled a yawn. "Mmm, but I'll probably fall asleep in the third inning."

"Go get some rest. I'll see you in few hours," he said with one last kiss.

Jack let the car go so he could walk the short distance to the hotel. Even though it was still dark, the sky was shot with the first traces of sunrise. After the evening with Andi, he was more convinced than ever that they had a future together if they could figure out a way to make it happen.

Back at the hotel, he managed a few hours of sleep before his meeting with David Johnson. Waiting in the conference room, Jack stretched out the kinks of the nearly sleepless night.

A burst of energy preceded David into the room.

Jack stood to shake hands with the youthful-looking man with the bright red hair who presided over Infinity.

"It's such a pleasure to finally meet you, Jack."

"Likewise," Jack said, withstanding the scrutiny of one of Andi's closest friends. "I'm sorry I've been unable to get out here to meet you before now."

"We've enjoyed working with your team. They've done an outstanding job of capturing just what we were looking for in the Newport property."

"I'm glad you're pleased with it."

"I don't know if Jamie told you that I once had secret ambitions to be an architect myself, but when the family business called..." David shrugged and smiled.

"Ah, that explains why the CEO himself is involved with the building plans."

"I've overseen the design of all the properties we've built since I took over the helm. It's my way of having my cake and eating it, too, if you will."

"Maybe we could put you to work on some of our projects."

"Don't tempt me," David said with a chuckle as they rolled out the latest plans for the hotel.

Jack pointed out the recent updates, most of which had been made to appease the coastal resources council. "We should be set now with the coastal requirements, but we'll know for sure next week. If everything goes according to plan and the weather cooperates, we should be on schedule to open a year from December."

"That's good. I wanted a winter opening, so we could work out any kinks before the high season. I particularly like the new veranda on the south side. I can't wait to see it finished." David rolled up the plans. "Andi and her team were very impressed with Newport."

Jack sat down across from him. "We enjoyed having them."

David leaned forward to rest his arms on the table. "Jack, may I be frank?"

"Of course."

"I know you didn't come to Chicago to show me these plans."

"Guilty as charged."

"Andi hasn't said much about what's going on, but I've heard a few rumors. Let me just say this—Andi and Eric mean a lot to me. They're family." He signed the word "family," to make it clear he spent a lot of time with the boy.

"I appreciate your concern, and I'm aware of what she's been through. I hope it makes you feel better to know I love her."

"It does. She deserves some happiness. That bastard she was married to left some serious wreckage behind. I don't want to see her hurt like that again."

"I'll never hurt her intentionally, David. I can promise you that."

"I guess that'll have to be good enough."

Jen was away from her desk when Jack arrived at Andi's office. Through the open door, he could see her working at her desk, lost in concentration as she pored over fabric swatches. He watched her smother a yawn and then cleared his throat to let her know he was there.

"Hey," she said, welcoming him with a warm smile.

"Am I disturbing you?"

"Please come disturb me." She got up to close the door. "How do you manage to look so good with no sleep? I'm a wreck."

He sat and drew her onto his lap. "If that's what you look like when you're a wreck, I can't wait to get you really tired."

Today she wore a fashionable black pantsuit with a fuchsia silk blouse. She'd left her hair down the way he liked it. When he put his arms around her, she rested her head on his shoulder.

"I couldn't wait to see you this morning," she whispered in his ear.

"Me either." He kissed her forehead. "I just had an interesting conversation with your friend David."

She raised her head to look at him. "Interesting how?"

"He more or less asked my intentions."

Groaning, she said, "I'm sorry. He's very protective. We go back to college, and he and his wife Lauren were so good to me after Alec left."

"I'm glad you have someone like him looking out for you. I like him."

"I thought you would. You two have a lot in common." She paused, dropped her eyes, and added, "So what *are* your intentions?"

He raised her chin to compel her to look at him. "I'll tell you the same thing I told him. I love you, and I'll never hurt you on purpose."

"When will we see each other?"

"Weekends, holidays, whenever we can. For now."

"For now?"

"Let's just take it a week at a time and see how it goes, okay?"

"I suppose that'll work. For now." She pressed her lips to his. "When do you have to leave?"

"Tomorrow afternoon."

"*So soon?*"

"I want to stay longer, but Jill's playing in a big lacrosse tournament this week, and I need be there. I missed too much last year."

She stood up and went over to her desk to check her calendar. "What about next weekend?"

They went back and forth and ended up at Columbus Day—the weekend of Quinn's wedding.

"Why don't you and Eric come with us?"

"Are you sure she won't mind?"

"I'm positive."

"What about the girls?"

"I'll talk to them before you come. Don't worry. We'll take the boat, since I gave Quinn the Block Island house for the wedding."

"You're a good guy, Jack Harrington." Andi returned to his lap. "But now that you've come and swept me off my feet, how am I supposed to live without you for almost a month?"

"I was just wondering the same thing." He checked his watch and found it was five after noon. "We need to leave soon to see a boy about a ballgame."

She got up, straightened her desk, and shut off her computer.

He took her briefcase and put his arm around her. "There's a defect in my suite I wanted to bring to your attention," he said in a serious tone. "It's something the chief decorator should probably tend to personally."

She laughed. "You're shameless."

"I have no idea what you're talking about." He held her close during the elevator ride to the fifteenth floor. "Ever done it in an elevator?"

"Shame*ful*."

Flashing her a dirty grin, he pulled off his tie and released his top button.

The elevator doors opened, and he led her to his suite where they spent an hour checking the "defects" before the game.

After the game and dinner, they rode the elevator to Andi's apartment. Eric was asleep on Jack's shoulder, clutching a new Cubs pennant in one hand, his baseball glove in the other. Jack helped Andi undress the boy and get him into bed.

"Whew," she said as they tiptoed out of Eric's room and closed the door halfway. "He's done for."

Jack yawned and followed her to the living room. "I know how he feels."

"He had a wonderful time, Jack. Thanks again for getting the tickets."

"I loved it when he crawled into my lap at the game. He's adorable."

"I've decided to keep him."

Jack stretched out on the sofa and invited her to join him. "Are you still upset about your mom? She seemed pretty pissed."

Andi snuggled into his embrace. "I'm disappointed. It's not like her to be so rude."

"She's worried about you. I can understand that."

"It's funny, really, because she *loved* Alec, and look at how that worked out."

"She doesn't want you hurt like that again."

"This is different." She turned to face him. "It's *different*."

With his hands on her face, he kissed her gently, a charge of excitement coursing through him as it did every time he touched her. It *was* different. He felt it, too. "Are you sure your mother is staying at her sister's?"

"Yep."

He worked his way free of the sofa, held out a hand to help her up, and swept her into his arms. "Which way to your room?"

She laughed and pointed the way.

CHAPTER 13

A few days before Andi and Eric arrived for Quinn's wedding, Jack asked the girls if he could talk to them after dinner.

"What's up, Dad?" Jill plopped down next to him on the sofa. She looked more like a woman than a girl these days, and his heart ached at the thought that this time next year, she'd be in college. He wasn't ready.

While he attempted to collect his thoughts, Kate and Maggie landed on the other sofa.

"You remember Andi, who was here this summer from Chicago?"

"Sure," Kate said. "She was nice."

"And *so* pretty," Maggie added.

He smiled. "Yes, she's nice *and* pretty. I've invited her and her son, Eric, to go to Quinn's wedding with us."

"Is she a friend of Quinn's?" Jill asked. She spun her long dark hair around a finger tipped with hot pink polish.

"Not exactly." He swallowed hard. "It's more like she's a friend of mine."

Kate's eyes widened. "Like a *girlfriend*?"

He had promised himself he'd be honest with them. "Yes, like a girlfriend. How do you feel about that?"

They were silent until Jill finally said, "I hadn't thought about you having a girlfriend."

"I hadn't either. You know I wasn't looking for one."

Biting her lip, Maggie looked worried. "Are you going to marry her?"

"No, sweetie. I'm still married to Mom, and that's not going to change. I promise you." He reached out to bring her onto his lap and put his arms around her.

"I want you to be happy, Dad," Kate said. "If Andi makes you happy, I'm glad she's your girlfriend."

"Thank you," he said softly. She reminded him so much of Clare that it sometimes took his breath away. "I mentioned her son Eric's coming, too. Remember when I went to Chicago, and Miranda taught me some sign language because I was going to meet a hearing-impaired boy when I was there? That's Andi's son. You guys will love him. He's five, and he's *so* cute."

"Not cuter than me?" Maggie asked with an arched eyebrow.

He laughed and tickled her. "No way. No one's cuter than you, Mags."

Jill and Kate rolled their eyes at Maggie's baby-of-the-family act. Maggie and Kate kissed him good night and went upstairs.

He reached for Jill's hand when she lingered a moment longer. "Are you okay with this, hon?"

"I want it to be as simple as Kate made it out to be, but it's not, is it?"

"No, baby, it isn't. But she makes me happy. That's all I can say."

"I still miss Mom."

"I do, too, and I always will. I hope you believe me."

She nodded and kissed him before she went upstairs.

He sat there a long time thinking about them and hoping he was doing the right thing by bringing two new people into their lives.

Jack stood in the same spot where he first met Andi the summer before to watch the stream of people coming off the Chicago flight but didn't see her or Eric among them. He was starting to worry they'd missed the flight when he saw Eric come around the corner, dragging Andi behind him.

Jack held out his arms, and Eric ran to him. He swung the boy up and around. When Andi caught up to them, he pulled her to him with his spare arm, and the three of them held each other for a long moment.

"It's Friday," Andi whispered in his ear.

Jack leaned in to kiss her and had to remind himself to show some restraint in front of Eric. "Thank God. Let's get this show on the road."

They arrived in Newport as the girls were settling into the boat for the sail to Block Island. Since they had only about three hours of daylight left, they hurried to get under way.

The girls showed Eric where to put his things and where he would be sleeping. Kate's friend Miranda had taught them some basic sign language, and they were like three mother hens with the little boy.

Jack kept an arm around Andi as they watched the kids together. "They're going to smother him," he said.

"He loves the attention. I can't believe they learned some sign language for him. That's so sweet."

"They wanted to be able to talk to him and figured if they learned a few things, they could work together. If they hit a snag, they know you're here."

"Looks like they're doing fine so far."

Jack looked down at her, burning with the need to kiss and touch her. Somehow he managed to curb the urge in deference to their children.

"Stop looking at me that way," she whispered. "This is a G-rated weekend."

"*What?* No way."

She gave him a gentle nudge. "Yes, way."

"We'll see about that…" He glanced into the cabin and noticed Jill watching them with a blank expression on her face. Realizing how strange it must be for her to see her father with another woman, he stepped back from Andi.

"It'll take some time," Andi whispered.

"I know."

Frannie and Jamie arrived and greeted Andi with hugs.

"We're so glad you could come this weekend," Frannie said.

"I understand congratulations are in order for you two," Andi said.

Jamie hooked an arm around Frannie as she showed Andi her engagement ring.

"It's gorgeous, Frannie. I'm so happy for you."

"If you're done with your female bonding ritual, we ought to get going," Jack said dryly.

"You be quiet," Andi said.

Jack rolled his eyes at Jamie as the women continued to oooh and ahhh over Frannie's ring. She told Andi about wedding plans while Jack and Jamie eased the boat out of the dock and prepared the sails. Jack motioned Eric over to him so he could outfit him with a life jacket and handed another to Maggie.

The brisk westerly wind gave them a quick, easy sail to the island. Jamie was at the helm when they arrived in New Harbor on the island's north end. After securing the boat and visiting with their friends at Payne's Dock, they piled into the old station wagon Jack kept on the island to drive to Haven Hill. The girls brought their bags to stay at the house with Quinn, who had invited them to hang out with the bridal party the next day.

Andi let out a gasp when she saw Haven Hill for the first time. The rambling twenty-room "cottage" with the sweeping front porch stood high on a hill, its shingles weather-beaten from more than half a century of fending off the elements on the island's south end.

The noisy group fell out of the overcrowded car and charged inside. Eric followed close on Maggie's heels while Andi stood back to get a better look at the house that bustled with workers making final preparations for the wedding.

"It's beautiful, Jack. I can't wait to see inside."

With the kids inside, he slipped an arm around her. "I love it here. This house made me want to be an architect. It's inspired every house I've ever designed."

"I can see why." They walked along the driveway so Andi could get a better look at the widow's walk that faced the Atlantic Ocean. "It's amazing. How did it come to be in your family?"

"My grandfather bought it right after World War II for two hundred thousand, if you can believe that. The guy who built it died just as construction was being completed, so his estate needed to sell it. When my grandfather died, he left it to my mother. We spent summers out here when we were growing up, and Clare always brought the girls out, too."

He walked her in to show her around, and she exclaimed over the comfortable yet elegant furnishings that gave it the atmosphere of a beach house but with classic touches like the grandfather clock that stood in the front hall next to a winding staircase.

"I *love* it," she said when he led her to the large back porch outfitted with comfortable wicker furniture and a hammock that overlooked the ocean. "I can imagine whiling away an entire summer on this porch." They watched the kids disappear down the steep stairs to the beach. "Show me the rest."

He took her through the large open rooms downstairs that would be used for Quinn's wedding.

"I want to show you the upstairs." Jack steered her to the second floor.

"Which one's yours?" she asked with a coy smile after he had shown her several rooms.

He grinned and led her into one of the house's two master suites, where he pressed her against the wall to kiss her the way he'd longed to for hours. Ten passionate minutes later, he groaned with frustration and tore himself away to check his watch. "The ferry will be in soon. I need to send Jill to get Quinn and her family." He leaned his forehead against Andi's in an effort to cool off. "We'll continue this conversation later."

"I'll look forward to that."

After dinner with Quinn, her fiancé, and parents, Jack, Andi, Eric, Frannie, and Jamie headed back to the boat. Eric was out cold by the time they arrived at the marina.

"This is getting to be a habit," Jack said as he carried her sleeping child to the boat.

"One I could get used to."

"Oh, yeah?" He cocked an eyebrow at her as they boarded the boat. Frannie and Jamie had gone to the marina bar to have a nightcap.

After they tucked Eric into his bunk, Jack opened a bottle of wine, and they took it up on deck with a heavy blanket.

"Look at the stars!" Andi said.

The night sky over the Great Salt Pond was alive in the total darkness. The pond, which was packed with boats in the summer, had thinned to just a few hardy souls. After the long weekend, the island would all but shut down until spring.

"It's the best stargazing in the world," Jack said.

"I can see why you love it here."

"I met Clare out here." He shared the story of how they met the summer after he graduated from Harvard.

"That's right, you went to *Harvard*," she said in a mocking tone.

"Oh, God, don't start on that. Clare never got over teasing me about it. I went there for graduate school with Jamie after Berkeley. Where'd you go?"

"Parsons. I lived in an apartment across the hall from David while he was at NYU. That's how we met. His father founded Infinity. David went to work there right out of school and hired me. Three years ago, his dad retired, and David became the CEO."

"Funny how your career ended up being decided by the apartment you rented in New York. Mine has revolved around the friend I met the first day at Berkeley."

"It's worked out well."

He had seen her office and apartment and knew it had worked out better than well for her. Holding her close to him, he pulled the blanket up around them. "I missed you so much," he whispered in her ear. "A month apart is far too long."

She leaned her head back on his shoulder. "I hate to say it, but it looks like it might be six weeks before I have another free weekend. Things are nuts at work. I have to go to Juneau for at least a week early next month, so it could be Thanksgiving before I have enough time to get away again."

"I should be able to come out for a weekend before then. Do you think you can come here for Thanksgiving?"

"I'd hate to leave my mother, but she's been spending more time at her sister's anyway. I suppose we could probably come."

"I'm sorry it's so complicated, honey."

She tipped her head back to kiss him. "Me, too."

"Could I ask you something?"

She shifted to study his face in the dark. The dim cabin light cast a faint glow on them. "Sure."

"Would you ever consider moving here to live with me? With us?"

Her eyes widened. "Seriously?"

"Very seriously."

"I don't know, Jack," she said, her voice infected with a stammer. "I can't imagine how I could... There's Eric and his school, my job, my mother..."

"It's messy. I know it is. And it's terribly unfair that you'd have to be the one to move. I'd be out there in a minute if I could, but I just can't. Not now anyway."

"I know."

"We haven't known each other that long, but everything about us feels right to me. I want so much more than occasional weekends together."

"I want more than that, too. You know I do. But I can't imagine leaving my whole life in Chicago."

"I promised myself I wouldn't even mention this to you until after Frannie and Jamie's wedding. I wanted to give us more time to get to know each other, but this last month has shown me I don't need it. I know I'm asking so much, and all I have to offer in return is my love for you and Eric."

"And that's no small thing," she said, caressing his face. "As much as I want what you're offering, it's an enormous step for me. I don't know if I have it in me after what happened with Alec."

A flash of anger took him by surprise. "You can't *possibly* be comparing me to him."

"No, love, never." With her hands on his face she touched her lips to his. "I don't know if I trust *myself* anymore. You've made me a lovely offer, and I don't take it lightly. I know what you've been through, what your family's been through, so I get that it's a big deal for you, too. Can I have some time to think about it?"

"I guess that's not too much to ask," he said.

"And can we put it on the back burner, so we don't spoil this wonderful weekend together?"

"That's not too much to ask either." He leaned in to kiss her. "Let's talk about it again after Frannie and Jamie's wedding. That gives us more than two months, okay?"

"Okay."

He wrapped his arms around her. "I love you, Andi. I love you so much."

"I know you do."

"My whole world had tipped upside down until you came along and made everything right again."

"Jack," she said with a sigh. "I love you, too. If I had only myself to consider, I'd move today. Right now."

He tilted her chin up to kiss her again. "I'll do my best not to pressure you."

Andi laughed. "And you're known for your patience?"

"I'm working on that."

Frannie and Jamie boarded the boat wearing grim expressions.

"What's wrong?" Jack asked.

"That tropical storm has taken a turn away from the Carolinas and is headed due north," Jamie said.

"The new track puts Block Island right in the path," Frannie added.

"Shit," Jack said, thinking of Quinn and the wedding. "When will it be here?"

"Monday night."

The Sunday wedding went off smoothly despite the frantic work going on around the island to prepare for the direct hit of a significant tropical storm. Jack and his group did what they could to help get Haven Hill buttoned down before they sailed back to Newport early on Monday, ahead of the storm.

At home, Maggie, who'd tended to Eric's every need all weekend, insisted he stay in her room and pulled out the trundle from under her bed for him. Jack wondered how she would ever let Eric go back to Chicago. After putting the younger two kids to bed, he called to check on Clare and her nurses, who reported being tucked in to ride out the storm.

While the wind howled outside, Jack spent most of the night making love with Andi in the guest room. Suffering through an attack of guilt over being with another woman in Clare's house, he left Andi's room before dawn. If she agreed to come live with them, there'd be adjustments for everyone—including him. He hoped the extra days they'd get thanks to the storm would convince her they could make it work.

The slow-moving hurricane continued well into Tuesday, and after the storm finally ended, Jack was relieved to hear that Clare was fine and there was hardly any damage to his property.

With the power out on Aquidneck Island, Jamie and Frannie came over to spend the evening with them. Frannie was all but living with Jamie these days, but she still helped Jack with the girls.

The fireplace cast an amber glow over the family room as Eric and Maggie played a card game.

Jill used the firelight to read by, and Kate played her guitar. She tended to be the more introverted of the three girls, so Jack had been surprised and amazed when she led them in a sing-along earlier. He was again taken aback by how very good she had gotten.

As the fire burned down, Frannie and Jamie sat together on one sofa, Jack and Andi on another as they worked on a second bottle of wine. He had a generator for the refrigerator but had told the girls they could do without power for one night. After some grumbling they'd been good sports overall.

Andi stretched and yawned. "This was the most relaxing day I've had in years."

Jack grinned at her, thrilled to have their time together extended. "Did you ever get through to the airline?"

"I tried, but they left me on hold forever. I didn't want to waste the power on my phone waiting, so I hung up."

"Oh, too bad," Jack said.

Frannie laughed. "You're all broken up, Jack."

He put his arm around Andi. "It's not funny, Fran. Andi's missing work, and Eric is out of school. It's terrible how they're stuck here with us."

Jamie made a barfing noise that made the others laugh.

Frannie and Jamie left a short time later.

Jack and Andi hustled the kids off to bed, walking them through the dark house with flashlights and candles.

After he tucked Maggie in, Jack went back downstairs to make sure all the candles were out and found Andi watching the last of the fire. "Hey, I thought you were upstairs." He sat next to her on the sofa and reached out to stroke her hair. "What're you thinking about?"

She smiled. "Nothing. Everything."

"Hmm, which is it?"

"I loved the storm. Isn't that crazy? I should've been scared, but it was exhilarating. And I loved being here with you and our kids."

He smiled. "You said *our* kids."

She rested her head on his chest. "Are you sure you didn't manufacture the storm to keep us here longer?"

Laughing, he ran his fingers through her silky curls. "It was kind of tricky getting it to move in the right direction, but I was able to pull it off."

"I'm beginning to sense that you usually get what you want."

"Oh, I sure hope so." He took her hand to lead her up to bed. "I really hope so."

The hurricane disrupted travel along the entire east coast, and they learned on Wednesday that it would be several days before the airlines got back on schedule.

"Any luck?" Jack asked when Andi hung up the phone in the study. He'd been pretending to stay busy in the kitchen while he waited to hear how she made out.

"The best they could do was stand-by on Saturday afternoon," she said as she joined him in the kitchen.

He tried to hide a smile.

"Oh, stop it! I can see you grinning."

He swept her into his arms and nibbled on her neck. "Who's grinning?"

When she squealed and tried to get away from him, he lifted her off her feet.

"I didn't take that Saturday flight."

"No?"

"I went for the sure thing on Sunday evening."

He let out a whoop, swung her around, and kissed her. "Is this going to screw you up at work?" he asked as he set her down.

She raised an eyebrow. "Do you really care?"

He pretended to think about it. "Not really."

"I didn't think so."

Once the girls were off to school on Thursday, Jack went to the office. He'd wanted to stay home with Andi and Eric, but he needed to get some work done. With Quinn on her honeymoon, he knew things would be hectic.

Jamie poked his head in at noon to see how Jack was doing.

"Why did I agree to give her *three weeks* off?"

"Because you're a sucker," Jamie said with a smile. "Anything I can do to help?"

"No, I've got it."

"Were you out at the hotel site this morning?"

"Yeah. The storm didn't really hurt us, so we're right on schedule. The foundation will be finished within the month."

"That's good news. How are things at home?"

"Great. The airlines are a mess, so they're staying until Sunday."

"Bonus."

"I wasn't exactly heartbroken over it." Jack sat back in his chair and motioned for Jamie to come in and shut the door. "I asked her to move here to live with us."

Jamie seemed stunned. "What'd she say?"

"She wants some time to think about it, so we've agreed to talk about it again after your wedding."

"I can see why she's hesitant. Can you?"

"Sure, I can. But I don't want to be doing this every month or two long-distance thing forever. I want her with me, but I don't want to push her into doing something either of us will regret. I'm also worried about how the girls will take it. I haven't mentioned it to them because she hasn't said yes yet."

"You've got to look at it from her perspective. She's got an established life out there, a career, and a son to think about."

"I worry it'll be too much for her to give up, that what we have won't be enough to replace it all." Verbalizing his greatest fear made Jack ache with worry.

"I've seen the two of you together—this comes down to logistics, not feelings."

"I guess we'll see what happens."

"You've got four more days to show her what domestic tranquility Harrington-style would be like," Jamie said with a grin.

"Believe me, I know."

CHAPTER 14

Watching Andi's plane lift off, Jack already yearned to have her back. They'd had such a wonderful week together. He'd noticed the girls beginning to appreciate Andi's gentle sweetness as much as he did. One night he came home from work to find her at the table, helping Maggie with long division. When Andi looked up to find him watching them, her smile had stopped his heart.

This time, saying good-bye to Andi had also meant saying good-bye to the boy who'd become so dear to him.

Jack replayed their long visit as he drove home from the airport and remembered all the moments that added up to one simple truth for him—he loved her and needed her more all the time. He could only hope she would reach the same conclusion.

She'd promised to come to Rhode Island for Thanksgiving, but that was five long weeks away. In the meantime, they were back to phone calls and the online video chats the girls had suggested they try.

He got home from the airport and came in through the kitchen, where Jill was getting a glass of water.

"Did they get off okay?" she asked.

"Right on time. Shouldn't you be in bed?"

"I'm going now. I had some homework to finish."

He kissed her cheek. "See you in the morning."

She walked toward the stairs but turned back. "Dad?"

"Yeah, hon?"

"I like her. I didn't want to, but I do."

"I'm glad. Thanks for telling me."

"Good night."

"Night."

Andi called at twelve thirty to let him know they'd arrived in Chicago.

"Next time I might not let you go," he said.

"Is that so?"

"You know it is."

After a long pause, she said, "I'm thinking about it, Jack."

He'd thought of hardly anything else in days. "Good."

"I'll talk to you tomorrow."

"I can't wait."

At the end of her first day back to work, Andi wandered over to David's office. His secretary was away from her desk, so Andi looked in to see if he was busy. "Knock, knock…"

"Hey, come on in. You look like you could use a drink." At the minibar he kept stocked in his office, he fixed them glasses of wine and invited her to join him in the sitting area facing Lake Michigan. "Of course, you know that means I could use one, too."

Laughing, she flopped down, kicked off her heels, and put her feet up on the glass table just like she used to when he lived across the hall from her in New York.

"Hard day?" he asked, handing her a glass.

"My unscheduled week off caught up to me the minute I walked in this morning. Of course all hell breaks loose when I'm stranded without a phone for a few days. Bill did a great job covering for me, but it's been a crazy day."

"We're just glad you survived the storm. The pictures on the news were unreal."

"It looked worse than it was. We were never in any danger."

"So you had a good time?"

"The best. I highly recommend being marooned for a few days with great company, no phones, no power. It was good for the soul."

"When will you see him again?"

"Thanksgiving and again over the holidays. Get this—his sister is marrying Jamie Booth on New Year's Eve."

"Huh. I'd pegged him as bit of a player."

"I guess he was, but he and Frannie have been friends for years—decades, in fact—and suddenly everything clicked for them. It's a great story."

"Sounds like it. What about you? You've gotten yourself into a complicated situation."

She put her drink down and looked at him. "Jack asked me to move there to live with him."

"What're you going to do?"

"I don't know. Like you said, it's complicated. I'd have to leave Infinity, Eric's school, my mother…" She shrugged.

"There's a lot to consider, no doubt. What does your heart say?"

"Go," she said so softly it was almost a whisper.

"How about your gut?"

"The other day, Jack took Eric to the park. I saw them through the window when they were coming home. He had Eric on his shoulders. Their cheeks were flushed from playing in the cold. Jack was bouncing him all around, and Eric was laughing so hard. Right in that moment, I started to think seriously about moving."

"Then what's the problem?"

"Just like that?"

"Why not?"

She eyed him suspiciously. "Why are you making this so easy for me? I figured you'd have a fit and tell me I can't go."

"Is that what you want me to do?"

"I want you to tell me I'd be doing the right thing."

"No one can tell you that, but I can make one part of it easier for you."

"What do you mean?"

"You wouldn't have to leave Infinity."

"I don't get it."

"I believe you're aware we're building a hotel in the very town you wish to move to. I don't see why you couldn't manage it for us."

Andi gasped. "But I'm not a hotel manager!"

"Come on, Andi." David got up to refill his glass. "You've been an executive with us for fifteen years. You're tuned in to every aspect of our operation. On top of that, you're one of my closest advisers and know almost everything I do about running a hotel. There's no reason you couldn't move to a different job within the company. That said, don't think I *want* you to go." He looked over at her. "I'd miss you and Eric terribly. We all would. But if this is what you want, and I think it is, let me make it easier for you."

She sat back, stunned by what he'd said. Running the Newport property would be a huge responsibility, and she knew he'd been looking for someone within the company to take the job.

"I don't know what to say."

"Don't say anything now." He returned to the sofa. "Think about it for a few weeks and see how the idea feels. We're only just now beginning construction, so I'm not in any rush to fill the job. I'll need someone in place within six months to manage the final setup and to handle the local hiring. You know what has to be done for an opening."

She nodded, trying to process it all. "You're so good to me," she said. "Everything I have, I owe to you."

"No, Andi, everything you have you owe to *yourself*. If I didn't think this was a good business decision, I wouldn't have mentioned it. Newport is the biggest property we've built on my watch. I've got a lot invested. I want someone I can trust there, and if it helps you on a personal level, all the better."

She slid her shoes back on and stood up. "Thank you," she said, humbled by the faith he had in her.

He got up and folded her into a hug.

"I'll let you know what I decide."

"Take your time."

Andi didn't immediately tell Jack about David's offer because she wanted to decide on her own what was best for her and Eric. Jack would see it as a sign that her move was meant to be, a point she would have a hard time debating. So she sat on it for a few weeks and tried to consider the many ways her life—and Eric's—would change if they moved. The one thing she knew for certain was that in the three weeks since she'd last seen Jack, her longing for him had only grown more intense.

One Friday afternoon, she left work early after her mother called to say Eric had come home from school with a stomachache.

When Andi walked into Eric's room, he was sleeping fitfully. She ran her hand over his forehead and discovered he was hot with fever.

Her mother looked on with concern.

"We should call the doctor," Andi said.

"I'll stay with him while you call," Betty said.

After consulting with the doctor, Andi returned to Eric's room. "He wants us to bring him in. He's meeting us at the ER." She tried to hide the sudden tremble in her hands from her mother.

They bundled the sleeping boy into a cab and rushed him to the hospital. Eric woke up on the way, crying out in pain as he clutched his stomach.

Andi exchanged worried glances with her mother.

Dr. Porter, Eric's pediatrician, walked in just after they arrived. He led them to an exam room where he performed a few quick tests. "I think it's appendicitis," the doctor said. "I'll order blood work and a scan to confirm it, but I'm fairly certain he'll need an appendectomy."

Andi's hands began to tremble again at the thought of her baby undergoing surgery.

"Try not to worry. You got him here very quickly, and it should be routine," Dr. Porter said. He went to find a nurse to draw the blood.

Eric was so miserable that the blood test hardly registered, but Andi was relieved when it was done. Her cell phone rang, and when she saw it was Jack, she walked out to the hallway to take the call.

"Hi, honey, how are you?" he asked.

"Not so good. I'm at Mercy Hospital with Eric. They think he has appendicitis."

"Oh no. Is he okay? Are you?"

Her voice broke. "He's really sick."

"I'm sure he'll be just fine," Jack assured her. "Is there anything I can do for you?"

"I don't think so. I've got to go. The doctor is coming back. I'll call you when I can."

"Okay, honey, hang in there."

Andi was pacing the hallway outside the surgical suite when Jack came off the elevator a couple of hours later.

At first she thought she'd wanted him so badly that her imagination had produced him. "Oh my God! I can't believe you're here!"

"How could I *not* be here?" He hugged her tight against him. "How is he?" he asked, wiping tears from her cheeks.

"Still in surgery." Her voice hitched, and her heart ached from the hours of worry. "I can't believe how fast it happened."

Jack took her hand and led her to a row of chairs. Holding her close, he offered what comfort he could while they waited.

Andi's mother returned with coffee and stopped short when she saw him there. "Hello, Jack. What a surprise."

"Hi, Betty."

"It was good of you to come."

David and his wife Lauren rushed into the waiting room.

"We got here as soon as we could get a sitter for the girls," Lauren said as she hugged Andi. "How is he?"

"Still in surgery," Andi reported and introduced her to Jack.

"Nice to see you again, Jack," David said as he squatted in front of Andi. "Sorry about the circumstances, though. You doing okay, kid?"

"I'll be better when I hear Eric's all right," Andi said, grateful to all of them for coming to be with her.

Jack squeezed one of her hands in reassurance while David took her other.

After an interminable wait, Dr. Porter returned, still in the surgical scrubs he had worn to assist in the surgery.

Andi jumped up when she saw him coming.

"He did just fine, Andi. No perforation."

She sagged against Jack as her legs threatened to give out.

Jack kept both arms around her. "When can we see him?"

"He's in recovery. I don't expect him to be awake for a few hours, so you might want to go home for a while. The nurses will call you when he starts to come around."

"Thank you, Dr. Porter," Andi said.

David and Lauren had to get home to their four daughters. They promised to check in later. Andi and Betty wanted to stay, but Jack talked them into going home to rest. After he left Andi's phone number with the charge nurse, he took them home and whipped up some eggs and toast for them.

When they'd finished eating, Andi called the nurse's station. Eric was still asleep, so she let Jack talk her into trying to take a nap on the sofa before they went back to the hospital.

"I'm going to bed," Betty said. "You'll wake me if you hear anything?"

"Of course. Good night, Mom," Andi said.

"Thanks for your help, Jack," Betty said. "I'll see you both in the morning."

After she left the room, Jack stretched out on the sofa next to Andi and put his arms around her.

"Your approval rating seems to have gone up a bit with Mom," Andi whispered, thrilled to feel his arms around her even if the circumstances were less than ideal.

He chuckled. "Remind me to thank Eric for that."

As she studied his handsome face, she could honestly say she'd never loved him more. "I still can't believe you're here. You were such a rock. Thank you."

"It felt like my own child was in that operating room."

"Nothing you could say would mean more to me."

"I love you, sweetheart, and I love Eric, too." He kissed her forehead. "Why don't you get some rest?"

"I'll try."

He covered her with a blanket and went into the kitchen to call home to check on the girls. She dozed off to the comforting sound of his voice, relieved to know he was there to share some of the burden with her.

Jack was alone with Eric when he woke up late on Saturday afternoon. He'd closed his tired eyes for a few minutes, and now he rubbed his hand over the stubble on his face as he tried to force himself to wake up. Being in a hospital had brought back memories he'd rather not revisit, but he'd pushed them aside so he could focus on Andi and Eric.

The boy smiled and signed, "Hi, Jack."

"Hi, buddy." Jack's sign language had improved during the week they spent together earlier in the month.

Eric asked for his mother, and Jack held up five fingers to let him know she would be back soon. Eric squeezed Jack's hand and drifted back to sleep.

Andi came in a few minutes later to find them holding hands. "Did he wake up?"

"Just for a minute."

"I'm sorry I missed it."

Jack tucked Eric's hand under the blanket. "I told him you'd be right back."

"I know it has to be hard for you to be hanging out in a hospital," she said, surprising him as she often did with her insight.

"I'm okay, honey." He reached out to run his fingers through Eric's soft blond hair. "He's so little in that big bed. I hate seeing him in there."

"I know. Thank God it was *only* appendicitis, and he'll be able to come home in a day or two."

"Yes."

She leaned over Jack's chair to hug him from behind. "What're you thinking about?"

He hesitated for a moment, not sure this was the time to be dredging up the past, but he wanted to be honest with her. "Being here and seeing him so sick has brought back all kinds of memories. I remember thinking, after Clare's accident, that as bad as it was to lose her like that, it would've been so much worse if the car had hit one of the girls. I have to think Clare would agree."

"Oh, Jack, of course she would. I'm so sorry that being here is hard for you."

Reaching for her hand, he brought it to his lips. "Being with you is never hard for me. Don't worry about me."

Betty joined them a few minutes later. "How is he?" she asked.

"About the same," Andi replied. "Still sleeping a lot. They'll lower the pain medication tomorrow to keep him awake. He'll be getting up, too."

"Did the doctor say when he could go home?"

"A couple of days. He should be back to normal in two to three weeks."

"Well, the worst part is over," Betty said with relief. "Why don't you two take a break? It's nice outside."

"Are you sure you don't mind staying?" Andi asked.

"I'm fine. I have my book and my knitting. Go on along for a while."

Andi kissed Eric's forehead. "We'll be back in a few hours. Call my cell if he wakes up or if you need me."

"I will. Don't worry."

Jack held the door for Andi and kept his arm around her while they walked to the elevator. Outside, the city bustled with limousines headed to the theater district and people venturing out for dinner. The crisp air held the promise of a chilly evening as they walked hand in hand along the busy street.

"Are you hungry?" he asked after they'd gone a few blocks.

"Not really, are you?"

"I'm good for now."

"I hope you're not missing anything important at home. I haven't even thought to ask you."

"It's a good weekend for me to be gone. Jill had a lacrosse game, but they've already clinched a playoff berth, so the game was a formality. We have some clients in town, and Jamie's taking care of them. Don't worry, honey. I'm right where I need to be."

They wandered into a small park, and he steered her to a bench where they sat to watch an older couple with two young girls who had to be their granddaughters. The girls giggled as they fed the pigeons. When the birds chased after them, the girls shrieked with delight.

"They remind me of Jill and Kate at that age," he said as he caressed Andi's fingers absently.

"Jack…"

"Hmm?"

"I've been doing a lot of thinking."

That got his attention. "Oh, yeah?" He'd gone out of his way not to mention "the question" to her.

She looked down at their joined hands. "David offered me the Newport property."

"What do you mean?"

"Managing the hotel. The job is mine if I want it."

Jack sat up straight, his grin stretching from ear to ear. "Are you *serious*?"

She nodded, smiling at his reaction. "I'm glad I waited to tell you in person."

"Oh my *God*! This is fabulous! When did it happen?"

She focused again on the girls and the pigeons. "A couple of weeks ago."

"You weren't going to tell me?" Jack asked, surprised and hurt that she'd kept such big news from him.

Turning her attention back to him, she brushed the hair off his forehead and ran a finger over his cheek. "I was thinking about the big picture, trying to decide what's best for Eric and me. And what's best for you and your girls."

"I've told you what's best for me—and the girls." He hoped they'd agree if it happened, but he'd seen no point in broaching the subject with them until Andi decided.

"You've been so patient about giving me time to think, and I appreciate that."

"Do you want the Newport job?"

"I think I do," she said sounding almost surprised. "I love what I'm doing now, but I'm ready for a new challenge and less travel now that Eric is getting older."

He could feel her edging toward a decision and had to resist the urge to push. "Let's get going."

"Good evening, Ms. Walsh," the uniformed doorman said as they stepped into her building. "How's Eric?"

"Much better, Joseph, thank you."

"That's real good news. You have a nice evening."

"You, too."

In her apartment, Jack stopped her when she reached for a light. He took her hand and kissed it as he brought her into his arms, kissing her neck and working his way up to her lips.

She pulled him closer, desperate with need after so many weeks without him. Pushing his jacket off his shoulders, she unbuttoned his shirt and kissed his chest and neck, while her fingers caressed his back, making him tremble.

He startled her when he suddenly lifted her and headed for the bedroom.

He set her down, worked fast to get rid of their clothes, and brought her down so she faced him on the bed.

Sighs became moans, arms and legs became tangled, two became one. Cupping her bottom, he held her tight against him as he slid slowly into her.

Only when she needed to breathe did she pull her lips free.

Jack shifted so he was over her and picked up the pace. Hooking his arm under her leg, he pushed it up to her chest and sank deeper than he had ever been before.

"*Jack!*"

He opened his eyes to find hers glistening with tears and froze. "Honey, what is it? Does it hurt?"

"No." She arched her back and fought to absorb the staggering array of emotions and sensations. The sorrow he'd shown her earlier had touched her deeply, and she wanted so badly to help him forget his pain, even if the relief was only temporary. "Nothing…"

He brushed his lips over her face. "What? Tell me."

"Nothing has ever been like this. Ever." She reached for him to bring his mouth back to hers. The thrusts of his tongue matched the motion of his hips. He filled his hand with her breast and rolled her nipple between his fingers.

She cried out when the climax hit, her hips surging up to meet him, and her hands clutching his shoulders.

"*Andi.*" He trembled as he pushed hard against her and groaned with his own release. They lay panting in the darkness for several minutes afterward.

"You can turn the light on now."

Laughing, she said, "What was *that?*" She had never before felt such a fierce need and was almost frightened to accept that she'd never again feel it for anyone but him.

"That," he said, kissing each of her fingers, "was you and me and our love. Something comes over me when I'm with you."

"The same thing comes over me."

"Whatever it is, I love it, and I love you." He gazed at her. "You're all I want in the world, all I'll ever want."

She caressed his face. "Ask me again, Jack."

It took a second for him to understand, and then he seemed to know. "Andrea," he said, his voice heavy as he gazed into her eyes, "will you come live with me and be my love?"

"Yes," she whispered.

He closed his eyes and rested his forehead on hers. "Thank you."

CHAPTER 15

"So when did you decide?" Jack asked on the walk back to the hospital.

"I think it was the minute you stepped off the elevator when Eric was in surgery. I was so upset, but everything became crystal clear in that moment."

"That's not why I came, you know."

"I know that." She tucked her hand into the crook of his arm. "I already told you if I hadn't had Eric and my job to think about, I would've said yes the first time you asked me." She reached up to kiss him. "I've never doubted us. Not for one minute."

"Neither have I."

"What would've happened if I just couldn't do it?"

He thought about that for a minute. "I guess we would've kept doing what we're doing until Kate graduates next year. Then Maggie and I would've moved out here."

Startled, she said, "But Clare and your business…"

"I would've figured it out."

"Now you don't have to."

He leaned down to kiss her as they walked. "I think we should keep this to ourselves until after Frannie and Jamie's wedding."

"I agree. This is their moment—and they've certainly waited long enough for it."

"That doesn't mean I wouldn't like to shout it from the rooftops," Jack said with a devilish grin as he stopped to look around at the people on the street. "Matter of fact, I don't see anyone I know…"

"Jack…"

He smiled and restrained himself. "She loves me." Against her lips he whispered what he wanted to shout. "She loves me, and she's coming home with me."

"Oh, yes, she loves you. Even though you're crazy, she loves you."

When Andi and Eric arrived in Rhode Island for Thanksgiving, everyone was relieved to see him fully recovered from his surgery. Andi got to meet Jack's parents and Jamie's parents, who had flown up from Palm Beach for the holiday.

On Thanksgiving morning, Jack and the girls left for an hour to visit Clare.

"How'd it go?" Andi asked him when they got home.

"It was okay. They were good," he said, referring to the girls.

With her hand on his cheek, she asked, "How about you?"

"I'm fine." He kissed the palm of her hand and smiled, but it didn't reach his eyes the way his smile normally did. "Let's eat."

As everyone sat down for dinner, Jack proposed a toast.

Jill folded her arms and scooted down in her chair. "Get comfortable. Here comes the annual speech."

He swatted at her with his napkin while the rest of them laughed. "That'll be quite enough out of you." In that moment, he realized how far they'd come from the somber holiday they'd observed a year ago. "I'm thankful for my girls, even the bratty one," Jack said, raising an amused eyebrow at Jill.

She stuck her tongue out at him.

"There'll be no speech except to say I'm thankful to everyone at this table who helped me through the worst time in my life. Better days are ahead for all of us, so let's drink to that." Glancing at Andi, he raised his glass.

The others followed suit.

Neil barked out "Hear, hear!"

After dinner Frannie corralled the women into the study to look at the books she'd brought from the dress shop so the girls could pick their bridesmaid dresses.

"Are they gone?" Jamie peeked around the corner and reached into the pocket of his tweed jacket. He pulled out a fistful of cigars and passed them around.

"Let's enjoy them while we can," Neil said in what he considered to be a whisper. The others shushed him.

Jack rounded up ashtrays and poured brandy as the others lit up.

"When do you leave for Tokyo, son?" Neil asked Jamie.

"Monday. I'll be back Friday night, though. I tried to put it off until after the wedding, but the account needs some attention."

"You'll need two full days' sleep after doing it that fast," Jack said, taking a deep drag on his cigar. Clare never would have allowed them to smoke in her house, a thought that gave him a pang of guilt, so he opened the sliding door to let out the smoke.

The gorgeous day was unseasonably warm for late November in Rhode Island, and the yard was littered with large yellow leaves dancing in the sea breeze.

"I'm going to get some air," Jack said. "It's so nice out." The mild November had put them ahead of schedule on the hotel, and the foundation had been poured earlier in the week.

Jack walked past the now covered pool to the edge of his property to look down at the shoreline. Light seas hit the rocks, launching salty spray into the air but not high enough to reach him. He was enjoying the roar of the ocean and his cigar when his father walked out to join him.

"Beautiful day," John Harrington said.

"Sure is. Won't be many more like it before winter."

"So how are you, Jack?" John puffed on his cigar and placed a hand on Jack's shoulder.

Jack looked down at the hand and then up at his father with surprise. His hair was now all silver, and his brown eyes were filled with unusual warmth. "I'm much better. We all are."

"I'm so glad to hear it—and to see it. Much different than last year."

"We still miss Clare very much, but life goes on."

His father nodded in agreement. "I like Andi. She's a beautiful girl. I never could fault your taste in women."

"Well, at least there's something," Jack said dryly.

"That's not all."

Jack stared at his father as if he had never seen him before.

"Don't look at me like that. I'm trying here… You shouldn't have had to wait almost forty-five years to hear this, but I'm proud of you, son."

Jack's mouth almost fell open with shock, but when he saw the effort his father was making, he kept his expression neutral.

"You've done all this yourself." John waved a hand to encompass Jack's home. "You never touched a dime of the money I gave you. You built a business from the ground up, whereas everything I have was handed to me. I've, uh, I've read every word of what's been written about your work and, well, I'm proud."

"I appreciate that, Dad. I'm…I don't know what I am." He was flabbergasted but couldn't say that.

"You were right to stand up to me all those years ago. I wish I had it to do over again, because I made a big mistake. I've wanted to say this to you for a long time, for years, in fact, but somehow we let all this distance get between us, and there never seemed to be a good time."

"Thank you for saying it now," Jack said, trying desperately to absorb it all.

"I also admire the way you took care of Clare after the accident and yet, I'm glad to see you moving forward with Andi. Quite a spark between the two of you."

Jack smiled. That "spark" had all but consumed him.

"Chicago's an awful long way from Rhode Island," John said.

"I've discovered that over the last few months," Jack said with a touch of sarcasm that made the older man laugh. Jack had almost forgotten the music of his dad's laughter, a sound that softened years of curt conversations and silences when so much went unsaid. In that split second, Jack decided to take a risk. "Want to be in on a secret?"

"Absolutely."

"I'll tell you something I haven't told anyone else, not the girls or even Jamie or Frannie."

John let out a low whistle. "This ought to be good."

"After the wedding, Andi and Eric are moving here to live with us. We're waiting until after the wedding to tell the kids."

"Wow, that's a big step, Jack. Are you sure you're ready for that?"

Jack looked out to the ocean. "If someone had told me six months ago that this would be happening, I would've said they were crazy." His gaze drifted back to his father. "All I can say is I feel like myself again when I'm with her, and as you pointed out, Chicago's pretty far from here."

"You've weathered a storm that would've brought a lesser man to his knees and kept him there. Your instincts have served you well so far. I can't imagine they'd fail you now."

Andi walked up to join them and put an arm around Jack from behind. "Are you giving away our secrets, love?"

John laughed. "Uh-oh, we're busted, Jack."

"Yes, you are," she said with a smile. "Can we trust you to keep it quiet until after the wedding? This is Frannie and Jamie's moment, not ours."

"No one will hear it from me—well, except maybe your mother, but she won't tell," John assured them. "I'm happy for both of you, and I wish you well." Clapping Jack on the shoulder, he said, "I love you, son." He kissed Andi's cheek and went inside.

"Okay, what just happened here?" Jack asked in amazement after his father had walked away.

"You tell me."

"I think he just said he's proud of me, he was wrong to fight my career choice, he admires me, and he loves me," Jack said, counting off the compliments on his fingers, still stunned by it all.

"Wow, all that in ten minutes?"

"Yeah," Jack said, still reeling.

"I'm happy for you, Jack. You've waited a long time to hear that."

"Only my whole life. I hope you don't mind that I told him our news."

"Of course not. I all but told David yesterday when I accepted the new job. I didn't say anything else, but he knows."

"No second thoughts?"

"Not a one. How about you?"

"None."

They spent Christmas Eve putting the finishing touches on the enormous tree Jack had brought home. Since Christmas had always been Clare's favorite holiday, they hadn't bothered with a tree the year before because no one had been in the mood. A year later, the girls enjoyed getting out the decorations, even if they stirred up a lot of emotions and brought back memories of Christmases past.

Jack spent most of the evening on a ladder with Andi and the girls directing the placement of every item. Andi had brought a box of Eric's favorite ornaments from home, and he hung them on the lower branches while Maggie arranged and rearranged the presents under the tree until she was satisfied with how they looked.

"Okay, that's it," Jack said. "I'm coming down. I'm getting a nosebleed up here."

Andi laughed and took his arm to check his watch. "It's almost eleven thirty. We'd better hurry if we're going to make midnight mass."

Jack sat close to Andi in church, feeling the pointed looks directed at them from people he knew through church and the girls' school. Tongues would wag after their appearance together, and Jack felt a twinge of anxiety over that, even though he knew he couldn't prevent it. Halfway through mass, Eric crawled into Jack's lap. He shared a smile with Andi when the boy dozed off on his shoulder.

Once the kids were in bed, Jack and Andi snuggled on the sofa with the tree and the fire providing the only light in the family room.

"I can't wait to give Eric the bike," Jack said.

"He'll love it."

Jack reached behind a pillow. "Santa brought something special for you, too."

"Are we doing this now? I thought we'd wait until tomorrow."

"I have others for you, but this one's just between us." He handed her a tiny, elegantly wrapped box.

Her hands trembled when she removed the paper covering a jeweler's box. "What did you do?"

He took the box to help her open it. "I hope you'll wear this as a reminder of how very much I love you and Eric." Even though he was confident they were moving in the right direction, he couldn't help the pang of guilt that stole some of the joy from this moment. At times like this, the fact that he was still married to another woman was hard to forget.

Nestled inside the box was a spectacular ring with a large sapphire gleaming in the center of a circle of diamonds.

She gasped. "*Oh*, it's beautiful!"

He slipped it on her right hand and kissed it.

She hugged him and held out her hand to look at the ring again. The Christmas tree lights reflected off the stone, giving the illusion of fire.

"Do you like it?"

"I love it, and I love you, very much." She kissed him. "You think of everything, don't you?"

"If I can't stand up in front of a room full of the people we love and tell them I'll cherish you for the rest of my life, then I can tell you and hope it's enough."

"It's more than enough."

CHAPTER 16

Jack came upon Frannie boxing up the last of her things a few days before the wedding. Andi had helped her all morning, but he was glad to catch his sister alone. She was moving into Jamie's condo while they built a house a few miles down the road from Jack's house.

"Need any help?"

She sat on the bed. "Actually, I think I'm done."

He came in to sit next to her. "I've been meaning to tell you, I had the most amazing conversation with Dad on Thanksgiving."

"I did, too! He told me how glad he is that I'm marrying Jamie and how proud he is of my painting. It was crazy."

Jack smiled. "He said the same things to me. I guess he's finally mellowed. He also told me he was wrong to fight my career choice."

"That must've been nice to hear."

"Better late than never," Jack said. "I'm going to miss having you here."

"I'll miss you, too, but I'm not going far."

"I don't know what I ever would've done without you, Fran. In a million years, I'd never be able to properly thank you."

"I should be thanking you."

"How's that?"

"Well, if I hadn't come here to help you, Jamie and I never would've gotten together, and look at what I would've missed. Also, being here gave me new inspiration for my painting, and you know how that's worked out."

Smiling at her logic, he put an arm around her. "You and JB… Who knew? I still can't get over it."

"Sometimes I can't believe it myself."

"I'm so glad you're happy. No one deserves it more."

"It's nice to see you happy again, too. I love Andi."

"I'm glad to hear that, because she and Eric are moving here."

"When?"

"Six weeks."

"Wow."

"How do you think the girls will take it? I've held off on telling them until I was sure it was going to happen."

Frannie thought about it for a moment. "Andi's too smart to come in here and try to replace their mother. There'll be some adjustments, but in the end it'll be fine."

"I hope you're right. I'll talk to them about it after the wedding. If there's any drama over it, I didn't want it to upset your big day."

"Let me know how it goes when you tell them."

"You'll be on your honeymoon."

"I'll still want to know."

Jack kissed her cheek and hugged her. "You'll be the second to know."

Jack peeked in at the room set up for the wedding service and watched the last of the guests arrive. Bathed in candlelight, the room was fragrant with floral arrangements, and chairs had been arranged in a semicircle around an arbor of red roses. A string quartet played as the last traces of sunset lit the sky over the bay.

Jack turned back to the oh-so-cool-and-collected Jamie and remembered his own wedding day. The butterflies in his stomach had felt more like bats by the time he said, "I do." Jamie, on the other hand, had been calm all day.

He straightened Jamie's bow tie one last time and brushed some imaginary lint off his jacket.

"Will you stop fussing over me?" Jamie's eyes twinkled with amusement.

"Sorry," Jack mumbled.

The officiating judge signaled to Jack.

"Ready?" Jack asked his friend.

"I've never been more ready for anything in my life." Jamie reached out to shake Jack's hand. "Thank you for being my best man—not just today but every day."

The comment undid what was left of Jack's composure, and he blinked back tears. "You really had to do that, huh?"

Jamie laughed and hugged his friend. "Sorry."

"Let's get you married," Jack said, and they walked together into the adjoining room.

Just as they turned to face the back of the room Andi scooted in with Eric after spending the day getting the girls ready. She wore a stunning long black dress that clung to every curve. Her hair fell in soft curls around her shoulders the way he liked it. Eric was decked out in a dark suit and bow tie.

Jack caught Andi's eye and feigned a whistle.

She smiled at him as they took their seats.

When Jamie's parents were settled in the front row, Jack walked to the back of the room to escort his mother to her seat. He left her with a kiss on the cheek and returned to stand beside Jamie. He was unprepared for the vision in red that appeared then at the top of the stairway.

Maggie looked far too sophisticated with her hair twisted into an elegant style. Wearing a long red silk sleeveless dress and impossibly high heels, she made her way down the stairs and the aisle, carrying an elaborate bouquet of red and white roses. She had turned eleven the week before Christmas and fought back a nervous giggle when she made eye contact with her astonished father.

Next came Kate, wearing the same red silk dress and hairstyle.

Jack's chest tightened, and for a second, he wondered if he was having a heart attack as he watched his daughters.

Jamie laughed out loud when Jack whispered, "Holy Moses" as Jill came down the stairs.

Jack would never forget Jamie's reaction when he caught the first glimpse of Frannie at the top of the stairs. Her long auburn hair had been contained in the same elaborate style as the girls', but hers included a diamond tiara that had been her maternal grandmother's. She wore no veil, just a simple white silk dress. Like the girls' dresses, it was sleeveless but was followed by an embroidered five-foot train. Frannie had said that since this was her one and only real wedding, she was wearing white. No one had dreamed of arguing with her.

After more than half a lifetime spent wishing for this very moment, Frannie never took her eyes off her groom as her father delivered her to him.

Watching his father join her hand with Jamie's, Jack decided his sister had never looked more radiant.

"You're gorgeous," Jamie whispered to his bride.

"And you're dashing."

Listening to them, Jack swallowed a lump in his throat, and the ceremony hadn't even started yet.

"Dearly beloved, we're gathered this evening to join this man and this woman in matrimony…" The judge said a few words about the bonds of marriage and then cut to the chase. "I think these two have waited long enough for this, don't you?" He asked Jamie and Frannie to face each other.

Frannie handed her bouquet of white roses to Jill and took hold of Jamie's hands.

The judge turned to the groom. "Jamie?"

"I was all set until I saw you." Jamie leaned his forehead against Frannie's for a moment to collect himself. He released a long deep breath. "My mother waited forty-four years to get her only child married off, so I can't blow it," he said to laughter. "I met the girl of my dreams twenty-six years ago, and today I finally get to marry her.

"I've spent my whole life running, and now I just want to be still. I want to be still with you, Frannie. I take you to be my wife, to be mine for the rest of my life, and I'll spend every day making sure you're never sorry you married a confirmed bachelor."

Frannie laughed through her tears. "I was seventeen when I met the boy of my dreams, and every man I've met since then has had the unfortunate luck to be measured against him and found lacking." She squeezed Jamie's hands. "It was always you, and it always will be. I take you as my husband, to be mine for the rest of my life, and I *know* I'll never be sorry I married *this* confirmed bachelor."

A wave of laughter and tears swept through their guests.

"Jack, may we have the rings, please?" the judge asked.

Watching them exchange rings, Jack remembered his own wedding day nearly twenty years earlier. He thought of the vows he'd taken and never once broken— until recently. A cold sweat descended upon him. The wedding ceremony was a taunting reminder that he'd been unfaithful to his wife. He remembered Andi saying that he'd been so faithful to Clare, and even knowing the circumstances were extraordinary, he still felt sick. Scanning the audience, he found Andi watching him with concern etched into her pretty face, and he forced a smile for her.

After the exchange of rings, Kate handed her bouquet to Maggie. She walked to where her guitar had been set up earlier next to a stool and microphone stand.

If she was nervous, Jack couldn't tell. Her voice was angelic as she sang John Lennon's "Grow Old Along with Me." By the time she sang the final note, there wasn't a dry eye in the room.

After Kate returned to her place between her sisters, the judge said, "By the power vested in me by the State of Rhode Island and Providence Plantations, I pronounce you husband and wife. Jamie, you may kiss your bride."

He proceeded to do just that as the guests applauded.

"Ladies and gentlemen, I'm pleased to introduce for the first time, Mr. and Mrs. Jamie Booth." The judge began another round of applause.

Jamie took Frannie's hand to lead her down the aisle.

Jack escorted his daughters. "You guys look *amazing*."

"You were cracking us up with the faces you were making when we came in," Jill said.

"What faces?" he asked, making them laugh. "And Kate, I'm stunned. When did you get so good?"

"I've been practicing."

"I guess so!"

When they reached the back of the room, Kate was bombarded with compliments from her grandparents and other friends. Jamie and Frannie stood nearby to greet their guests as the crowd moved across the hall to the reception room.

Jack spotted Andi and went over to her. "You're beautiful," he said with a kiss to her cheek.

"So are you." She reached up to smooth his hair and seemed to be curbing the urge to kiss him in front of everyone. "Everything all right? You went pale up there for a minute."

Amazed by how tuned in to him she always was, he smiled. "Everything's fine." He'd done all he could—and then some—for his wife. This was his time with Andi, and somehow he had to make peace with the past.

"Are you sure?"

"Positive." He reached down to scoop up Eric before the boy became lost in the sea of wedding guests. As one person after another said hello to Jack, he held Eric in his arms and introduced them.

"I guess this is our grand debut," he whispered to Andi.

"Looks that way. Are you worried what people will think?"

He shifted Eric to his hip and cocked an eyebrow at her. "Do I look worried?"

Jamie had hired a band that played all the old standards, and the newlyweds danced to Sinatra's "For Once in My Life."

The bandleader called the best man to the stage as the waiters circulated with another round of champagne.

Jack took a glass and made his way to the front of the large room. He reached the microphone as a hush fell over the room. "I've got to be the luckiest guy in the world tonight," he said. "My sister just married my best friend. What could be better than that?"

The question received a thunderous round of applause.

Jack cleared the emotion from his throat, hoping he could get through this without losing his composure. "I never could've imagined how a chance meeting in a dormitory stairwell in California would change my life and now my sister's life, as well. You all know Jamie's been our friend for more than twenty-five years. Since their engagement, a lot of you have asked if I saw this coming, and honestly, I've had to say no, I didn't. But with hindsight, I should have. Jamie Booth is the best friend anyone could ever hope to have, and I've been so very lucky to call him *my* best friend for all these years. And Frannie, well…" Jack looked down for a moment when emotion threatened to derail him. "Frannie was my first best friend, and she always will be. Two of the finest people I know have taken the long way home to each other, and I couldn't be more delighted that they've finally arrived. So please join me in raising your glasses to Jamie and Frannie."

"To Jamie and Frannie," the guests chimed in with applause.

Frannie was still dabbing at her eyes when Jack returned to their table.

He kissed the bride and groom and then sat next to Andi, who was also wiping her eyes.

"Perfect," she said.

He squeezed her hand under the table.

After dinner, Jack was dancing with Andi when the bride and groom bumped into them.

"Hey, get a room, will ya?" Jamie teased.

"Look who's talking," Jack said. "You're hogging the bride." He held out a hand to his sister.

"Go ahead, you two," Andi said. "I'll take care of the groom."

Jamie pouted as his wife made off with her brother.

Jack kissed Frannie's cheek. "You look stunning."

"You don't look too bad yourself. Your toast was wonderful. Thank you."

"It's a wonderful occasion—a once-in-a-lifetime kind of night."

She tilted her head back to look up at him. "I really missed Clare today."

"I've thought about her a lot lately, too. She would've loved this." He shook his head. "Hard to believe our twentieth anniversary is next week."

"She's always with us."

"Yes, she is," Jack said. "Kate was amazing, wasn't she?"

"I couldn't believe it! How did she sneak that by us?"

"I guess we've both been a bit preoccupied lately."

They looked over to where Andi laughed as she danced with Jamie.

"Just a bit. Andi looks gorgeous."

"She sure does, but no one can hold a candle to you tonight, Fran." He hugged her when the song ended, and Jamie came to reclaim his wife.

The wait staff circulated another round of champagne while Maggie and Eric passed out noisemakers and hats as the group counted down to midnight.

At the stroke of midnight, the band launched into "Auld Lang Syne."

Jack lifted Andi off her feet as he kissed her. Noisemakers and confetti filled the air around them, but he heard none of it as he welcomed in the New Year with a new love and renewed hope for the future.

Next to them, Jamie kissed his bride. "Let's get the hell out of here," he said. They were leaving the next morning for two weeks in Fiji.

They left in a vintage car Jack and the girls had decorated with "Just Married" signs and tin cans.

Back inside, Jack was talking with the senior Booths when he heard the first notes of what had become his song with Andi. "Excuse me," he said to Neil and Mary and went to find her.

She was seated at a table with the three girls and Eric. They all had their shoes off, and Maggie had let her hair down at some point during the evening. Andi heard the song at the same instant Jack did and turned to look for him.

He held out a hand to her, his heart racing as their eyes met and held. The guilt he'd experienced earlier was no match for the overwhelming love he felt for her.

With a smile for the girls, who watched them intently, Andi reached out and took his hand.

CHAPTER 17

Knowing he couldn't put off telling the girls his news any longer, Jack let them pick the breakfast place. That's how he ended up at IHOP, which was, in fact, hopping on New Year's Day.

"I'll miss you guys," he said as they dug into four different kinds of pancakes. Clare's mother, sister, brother, and their families were taking the girls on a weeklong cruise to the Caribbean. They'd invited Jack to go, but he couldn't be away while Jamie was on his honeymoon.

"We'll miss you, too, Dad," Maggie said, her mouth full of chocolate chip pancakes. "But it's only a week."

"That's a long time," he said with a pout that made her giggle.

"You've got Andi and Eric to keep you company for a few more days," Kate said. She looked far too grown up sipping a cup of coffee.

"That's true." Anxiety zipped through him when Kate gave him the perfect opening for what he needed to tell them. "Listen guys, about Andi and Eric…" He searched for the words he needed.

"What about them?" Jill asked.

"Well, you know Andi and I are very close."

"She's your girlfriend," Maggie said.

"Yes, but she's more than that." He noticed Jill had stopped eating and was staring at him from across the table where she sat with Maggie. "I love her very much, and I want to be with her more than just every few weeks."

"Don't even *tell me* we're moving to Chicago," Jill said, looking frantic.

"No, *no*," he said when the other two looked at him with equally panicked expressions. "We're not moving. They are."

Maggie's face lit up with what appeared to be delight.

Jill looked down at her unfinished blueberry pancakes.

"So would Eric be like our brother?" Maggie asked.

"Don't be such a dork, Maggie," Jill snapped. "Dad's not marrying her. He's not going to be our *brother*."

"There's no need to get mean about it, Jill," Jack said. Looking at Maggie, he added, "Jill's right, honey. I'm not marrying Andi, but she's wrong about Eric. It *will* be like he's your brother in some ways. I'm sure he'd like you to treat him that way."

"So they'd live with us?" Kate asked.

"Yes. I'm hoping you girls will be okay with that."

Jill scowled. "Why do they have to live with us? Why can't they just move close to us?"

"Because I don't want to be torn between two homes, and I don't want to spend any more time than I have to away from you guys." He paused to give them a moment to absorb that. "Andi and I talked about whether it would be better to move everyone to a new home and start fresh together, but we didn't want to take you out of your home—the home where you lived with your mother."

"I'm glad we're not moving," Kate said. "I love our house."

"I do, too," Maggie said.

Jill maintained a stony silence that worked on his already frazzled nerves.

"I want you to know something Andi said to me this morning." He stopped to make sure he had their full attention. "She very much wants to be a friend to all of you if you'd like her to be, but she has no intention of taking your mother's place, because no one ever could."

When Kate seemed to struggle with her emotions, he put an arm around her.

He held out his other hand to Maggie and Jill, who put theirs on top of his. "No one ever could," he said again softly.

Jill appeared to be fighting her own private battle.

"Where will everyone sleep?" Maggie asked.

Thank God for Maggie, Jack thought. "Since Frannie is moving in with Jamie, I was thinking we'd give Eric her old room. We could have some fun fixing it up for him. Andi will stay with me in my room."

Jill looked up at him. "In Mom's room? But all her things are there—"

"And we'd have to deal with that eventually, even if they weren't moving in. I was thinking we could box up Mom's stuff and keep it in the attic. That way if any of you ever want anything of hers, it'll be there for you. What do you think?"

With her head still resting on his shoulder, Kate nodded.

"Okay," Maggie agreed with a sad expression on her face.

"Jill?"

Her eyes flashed with anger. "Does it really matter what we think? They're moving in with us whether we like it or not. That's what you're telling us, right? You're already sleeping with her in the guest room, but we're not supposed to know that. We're not stupid."

"Watch yourself, Jill." It took everything he had to stay cool. "I'm hoping you can find it in your hearts to welcome Andi and Eric into our family and to help me find some happiness after all we've been through."

"We want you to be happy, Dad," Kate said with a pointed look at her sister. "We can give it a try."

"When are they coming?" Maggie asked with excitement.

He smiled at her as he paid the bill. "They have to pack up their house, and Andi has some things to settle at work, so it'll be a month or two. You know the hotel we're building in Newport?"

Kate and Maggie nodded while Jill continued to sulk.

"Her company asked her to manage it when it opens."

"That's cool," Kate said.

The girls were quiet on the way home. When they pulled into the driveway, he stopped them before they got out of the car. "I love the three of you so much, and nothing will ever change that. I promise."

Jill got out of the car and went into the house.

Kate and Maggie nodded and followed their sister.

Watching them go, Jack prayed he was doing the right thing for all of them, but Jill's emotional outburst had him questioning everything.

Andi had left a note to say she'd walked to the park with Eric.

Jack looked in on each of the girls as they finished packing for their trip. They were excited to be going with their grandmother and Clare's family on the cruise. Jack carried bags downstairs for Kate and Maggie before he went back up to check on Jill. He found her lying on her bed with her packed suitcase sitting by the door.

He was glad that she had straightened up her room, which was usually a disaster area. One whole wall was covered with pictures of her with her friends. As his time with her at home dwindled, he hated the idea of tension between them. "Honey?"

He sat on her bed and caressed her hair. She'd been like a grown woman last night, but today she was once again his little girl, and she was hurting.

"I'm sorry you're upset. I hope you'll think about it while you're away and maybe decide to give it a chance."

She turned away from him.

Resigned to her silence, he got up and took her suitcase downstairs.

When Clare's mother arrived, Jack pulled on a coat and went out to meet her.

Anna Richardson was an older version of Clare—petite with short gray hair and bright blue eyes. She greeted him with a warm hug.

"How are you, Anna?" He hadn't seen her in a while, but the girls saw her whenever she came from Hartford to visit Clare.

"I'm doing well. How about you?"

"Tired today. Big day yesterday with Frannie and Jamie's wedding." They'd invited her to come, but she'd chosen to spend some time with Clare before the trip.

"Everything went well?"

"It was amazing. The girls looked gorgeous. I'll make sure you get pictures."

"I'd love to see them."

"You've been to Clare's?"

"I stayed there last night." She shook her head ruefully. "It's so hard. Nothing ever changes."

"I know what you mean." He kicked at the gravel driveway. "Listen, Anna…"

"What is it?"

"I've, um…I've been seeing someone."

"I wondered if you would eventually."

Surprised to hear that, he had no idea what to say.

"It's been a year and a half, Jack. You can't be alone forever."

"I told the girls this morning that Andi and her son, Eric, will be moving from Chicago next month to live with us." He released a choppy laugh. "It's almost harder to tell you."

"I can see that you're happy," she said, her smile tinged with sadness. "I'm glad for you. I really am."

"I want you to know I'll never stop taking care of Clare, and I have no intention of divorcing her."

"I know that, Jack. You don't have to say it. How'd the girls take the news?"

"Kate and Maggie were pretty good about it, but Jill…" He shook his head and shrugged.

"I'll talk to her while we're gone and see what I can do. She'll come around, don't worry."

Despite her reassurances, he had his doubts as Andi and Eric came into the yard, their cheeks red from playing in the cold air.

He gestured them over. "Andi, this is Clare's mother, Anna Richardson."

The women shook hands.

"Pleased to meet you, Mrs. Richardson."

"Likewise. And this must be Eric."

Andi used sign language to introduce him to the girls' grandmother. He waved before he scampered off, probably to find Maggie before she left.

"I'd better go see where he's headed," Andi said. "It was a pleasure to meet you. I hope you have a wonderful time on your trip."

"Thank you." After Andi went inside, Anna turned back to Jack. "She's lovely."

"I hope you understand it just happened—"

Anna rested her hand on his arm. "Clare loved you so much. You were her whole world, and you were always so good to her—before *and* after the accident. I have no doubt she'd want you to be happy."

"Thank you," he said, his voice gruff with emotion as he hugged her. "The girls are ready to go." With an arm around her shoulders, he walked her inside to collect the kids.

They left a few minutes later in a flurry of hugs, chaos, and promises to send postcards.

Jill hugged Jack before she left, but she didn't say anything.

Jack, Andi, and Eric waved good-bye from the front porch. Back inside, Andi held out her arms to Jack as Eric wandered off to play with the trucks he'd gotten for Christmas.

"How was it? I was on pins and needles at the park."

"Not too bad," he said, absorbing the comfort of her embrace. "Kate and Maggie were great, and Anna really surprised me. She was very understanding."

"And Jill?"

"She was upset, but not about you. She's still dealing with losing her mother, and it's hard for her to face more change. I hope you won't take it personally."

"I expected Jill and maybe Kate might be upset about it. I had a feeling Maggie would be happy to have Eric here, and if I'm part of the deal, she'll put up with me."

"Can we tell Eric later? I'm totally drained."

She hugged him. "Of course we can. Let's go watch a movie and be lazy."

"Sign me up."

Jack awoke to the blare of the TV with Andi and Eric asleep next to him on the sofa. He moved slowly, trying not to disturb them as he retrieved the arm that'd gone numb under them.

Andi stirred, and when she saw the pickle he was in, she lifted her head to let him up. She giggled when he shook his arm, grimacing as the blood flowed into the limb.

He stretched and yawned. "That was, without a doubt, the best nap I've ever had."

"This one will be up all night," she said, running a finger around on Eric's cheek.

His eyes fluttered open, and he swatted at his mother's hand. He pushed her away when she continued to nudge him awake.

"Uh-oh, he's grumpy."

Jack sat on the sofa and tickled Eric's feet.

Eric's eyes flew open again, but this time he smiled when he saw who was tickling him.

"That's so not fair!" Andi said, laughing. "You're becoming his favorite!"

Jack shrugged, but he was thrilled by his burgeoning relationship with the little boy.

Eric sat up, stretched, and rubbed his eyes.

"Feel better after a snooze?" Andi signed.

He nodded and moved closer to Jack, who put an arm around him.

Andi looked at Jack, and he nodded.

"Honey, Jack and I have something we want to tell you."

"Are you getting married?"

"No, sweetie, but Jack has asked us to come here to live with him and the girls."

Eric's eyes brightened. "Really?" He turned to look at Jack. "Would you be my dad, then?"

Jack's heart skipped a beat. "Would you like that?"

Eric nodded.

Andi blinked back tears.

"I'd love to be your dad," Jack signed and then pulled Eric into his arms. He reached out to include Andi and held them close, filled with contentment as the sun set and darkness fell upon the room.

After dinner, the three of them played two rounds of Candy Land. Eric won both times, giggling at Jack's agony when he got stuck in the Molasses Swamp for the third time.

Andi signed to Eric that it was bedtime.

Jack stopped her when she started to get up. "Let me." He picked Eric up and slung him over his shoulder. Jack held the squirming boy so he could give his mother an upside-down kiss.

Andi watched them go upstairs, thrilled that Eric had such a wonderful man in his life. She was giddy with happiness as she went into the study to put away the game.

On the way back, she paused to look at the family portrait hanging in the hallway off the kitchen. Judging by the ages of the girls, she figured it had been taken about a year before Clare's accident. They were casually dressed, and Jack's arm was around Clare. He and the girls were missing the hint of sadness in their eyes that Andi still caught occasional glimpses of in each of them.

Although she'd seen many photos of Clare, for some reason she felt drawn in this time. She shuddered at the chill that went through her when Clare's startling blue eyes seemed to issue a challenge. Andi shook it off, straightened the photo on the wall, and went to finish cleaning up the kitchen.

Upstairs, Jack wrestled Eric into his pajamas, helped him brush his teeth, and tucked him into bed with the stuffed dog he slept with. He pulled the covers up, tickling him as he went.

Eric giggled and crooked his finger to bring Jack closer.

He lowered his face.

Eric kissed his cheek and signed, "I love you."

Overwhelmed, Jack kissed Eric and signed, "I love you, too, buddy. Good night." Flipping the light off, he blew a kiss from the doorway and went downstairs.

He slid his arms around Andi from behind. "Your son is awesome."

She had been wiping the countertop and loading the dishwasher. Turning to him, she put her hands on his shoulders. "What happened?"

"He told me he loves me."

"Oh, Jack, of course he does. You're so good to him."

"He knocked the wind out of me when he asked if I'd be his dad. I'll never forget that. I can't wait to get you both here for good."

She went up on tiptoes to kiss him. "Me, too."

He wrapped his arms tight around her as he kissed her. When they came up for air, he hoisted her over his shoulder—just as he had done to Eric—and carried her upstairs.

They fell onto the guest bed laughing. He kissed her without breaking the intense eye contact between them. "I love you, Andi," he whispered. "I love you so much."

"I love you, too. Happy New Year."

Andi and Eric flew back to Chicago for the last time before their move. Now it was her turn to tell the people in her life about their plans, but as worried as she was about how her mother would react, she was relieved their children now knew. She and Jack had taken Eric to tour the Rhode Island School for the Deaf. He'd met the woman who would be his teacher, and she'd signed that she couldn't wait to have him in her class. The director also put Andi in touch with a carpool from Newport.

Andi decided to tell her mother about the move the next evening and asked Eric not to mention it to his grandmother before she could. He was sad when Andi told him his grandmother probably wouldn't move with them, but he promised he wouldn't tell her.

After breaking the news to her coworkers during an emotional day at work, Andi tucked Eric into bed and worked up the courage for what she needed to do next. She found her mother in her room watching one of her favorite TV shows.

"I can come back later," Andi said when she saw what was on.

"Come in. It's a rerun." Betty clicked off the television and looked at her daughter. "Everything all right?"

"I need to talk to you."

"Oh?"

Andi sat on the edge of her mother's bed and hesitated for a moment. *Here we go.* "Jack has asked us to live with him in Rhode Island."

"You're going."

Andi nodded.

"How can you uproot your whole life for a man who can't even marry you?"

Andi struggled to keep the anger out of her voice. "Because I have more of a life with him in five minutes than I do in a whole year here, and that's enough for me."

"I've told you how I feel about this."

"You're welcome to come with us. We'd all love that, and there's plenty of room."

"Thank you anyway, but I'll be staying right here in Chicago. This is my home, and I won't be leaving it."

"I'm sorry you feel that way. I wish you could be happy for me."

"How can I when I see you setting up yourself—and Eric—for disaster? He's *married*, Andrea. I'm deeply disappointed in you—and in him. I appreciated his kindness when Eric was sick, but it doesn't change anything."

Andi got up to walk to the door. "We're leaving on the eighth of next month. I'll help you move in with Auntie Lou before then, if that's what you'd like."

"That's fine."

Saddened, Andi went back to her room. The conversation had gone pretty much as she'd expected, but she had hoped her mother might've changed her mind about Jack—especially after everything he did for them when Eric was sick. She knew that if his situation had been different, Betty would've been delighted to see her daughter with a man like him. Just like Jack had said about Jill, it wasn't personal. But knowing that didn't take the sting out of her mother's words. Before she called Jack, Andi decided to take a shower and try to get her emotions under control.

In Rhode Island, Jack faced a daunting task of his own. He'd decided to pack up Clare's things while he was alone in the house, which was eerily quiet with the girls away, Andi and Eric back in Chicago, and Frannie on her honeymoon. Jack couldn't remember the last time he'd been so alone, and it seemed like a good time to face the dreaded task.

Starting with Clare's large walk-in closet, he folded her clothes and placed them in boxes. He made a separate pile of things he was certain the girls would never want, which he would donate. Working fast, he tried to think about anything other than what he was doing.

Once he'd finished with the hanging clothes, he moved to the closet shelf, packing away sweaters and purses. When he reached up to grab the next item, his hand hit a large envelope, hidden beneath a pile of sweaters.

He spilled the contents on the bed and froze when he realized he was looking at every card he'd ever given Clare—Valentine's Day, Mother's Day, birthdays, anniversaries, and all the silly notes he'd written her over the years.

Staring at the pile on the bed, he felt like he'd been gut punched. He opened one card, a Valentine, dated 1994, in which he'd written, "I love you today, I'll love you tomorrow, I'll love you forever."

The magnitude of the loss roared through him as if it had only just happened. He sat on the floor next to the bed as the sharp pain of it assailed him all over again. He heard the phone ring and knew it would be Andi but couldn't make himself move to get it. Only the sound of the phone ringing a second time jogged him out of his stupor. It was after ten, and he realized he'd been sitting there for almost an hour.

He reached for the phone. "Hello."

"Jack? What's wrong?"

"Nothing. Can I talk to you in the morning?"

"You're scaring me. Are you sure you're okay?"

"I'm fine. I'll call you in the morning."

"All right. I love—"

Clicking off the phone, he lay awake all night next to the pile of paper on the other side of the bed. He knew Andi would be worried about him but couldn't bring himself to call her back. Not yet. He just couldn't believe Clare had kept *everything*, and the sheer size of the pile on the bed said volumes about the years they'd spent loving each other so completely.

He studied the small mountain of paper Clare had saved and let his thoughts wander again to the night he met her on Block Island.

CHAPTER 18

Jack waited for her while she finished at work and then walked with her down the stairs from the National Hotel's porch.

She called good night to her coworkers on the way out. A few seemed concerned when they saw her leaving with a customer, but she just smiled and waved.

Jack had always envied the camaraderie he saw among the young people who worked in the island's tourist industry. They lived in places that pulsed with music, teemed with people, were cluttered with laundry hanging off decks and had bikes lying on lawns. It'd always seemed like the ideal way to spend a summer.

"Do you live in the employee housing?" Jack asked Clare.

"Hell no." She laughed as they walked along the waterfront, which was still crowded even after the bars closed. "I did that the first three years, and it was really fun. Then I grew up a bit, and the idea of spending another summer living like that lost its appeal. I rent a place with a college friend. She works at Aldo's."

"Where'd you go to school?"

"UConn. I grew up in Hartford, and a lot of my friends went there. They have a good education program. I know it's not Harvard, but I liked it."

"Am I ever going to hear the end of that?"

"Probably not," she said with a saucy grin. "A friend is having a party on the beach tonight. Want to go?"

Not wanting to appear too eager, Jack pondered the offer. "Is he your boyfriend?"

"Are you fishing?"

"Maybe," he said, amazed at how easy it was to talk to her.

"No, he's not my boyfriend and neither is anyone else. I haven't been too lucky in that department."

"I can't believe that."

"Believe it. What about you? Where's your girlfriend?"

"Going to school full time and working for Neil has left me with just enough time to eat and sleep a few hours a day. What girl wants to be around that?"

"Oh, come on, a handsome Harvard boy like you must have all the girlfriends he can handle," she said, giggling at his playful scowl.

He shook his head with regret even as he delighted in the compliment. "I never should've told you that."

"No, you shouldn't have. So do you want to come to the party?"

They stopped walking. She seemed tiny and almost vulnerable despite her sassiness, and he couldn't believe how drawn he was to her after just meeting her. "I'll go if you behave and not tell everyone I went to Harvard."

"Wow, that's a tall order," she said with a twinkle in her eye as she rubbed her chin. "Not sure I can do that."

He folded his arms and contemplated the impish look on her face. "Well, I need assurances or all bets are off."

"If you're going to be a total pain about it, I'll keep your pedigree a secret."

He laughed to himself, thinking that she didn't know the half of his pedigree. He'd be in for it when she found out about his father's banks.

They arrived at the beach where the party was in full swing with a raging bonfire and two kegs of beer in ice buckets on the sand—just the kind of party Jack used to watch from a distance when he was with his family. His father had never approved of the partying the summer kids did every chance they got.

Clare greeted her friends and introduced Jack. She got them beers beforethey walked down to the water's edge, ducking around a glow-in-the-dark Frisbee football game. People called out greetings to her as they walked along.

"Do you know everyone here, or does it just seem like it?" Jack asked.

"Not *everyone*. I've been out here for years with some of them. There's a group that works here in the summer and in Vail during ski season."

"That sounds so cool."

"You think so? I only come back every year because the money's great. I make more out here in three months than I do all year teaching."

"Seriously?"

"Yup, it's an awesome gig. My mother freaks every year when I tell her I'm coming back. But I love it. Even though we work really hard, we have a lot of fun, too."

He looked around at the party going strong at damned near two in the morning. "I can see what you mean. I always wanted to do this," he said, gesturing to the party. "But my old man wouldn't hear of it. When I was old enough to work, I had to go with him during the week, and then we came back out on the weekends."

The spark of interest in her eyes told him he'd said too much.

"Your family spent summers out here?"

"Uh-huh. So where in Hartford did you live?"

"No, you don't. Back up. Do you still have a place out here?"

"Maybe," he said with a sheepish grin.

"Oh, this is going to be good." She tossed her head back and laughed. "How bad is it?"

"Pretty bad." When he looked down into those magnificent blue eyes and leaned in to kiss her, he felt the connection go through him like an electrical current. The smell of sand and rotting seaweed would always remind him of that moment.

He felt her hand encircle the back of his neck, and they kissed for a long moment as the water lapped at their feet and the party went on around them.

She pulled away after a minute. "That's one way to change the subject."

He laughed. "Did it work?"

"Not on your life, buddy. Now spill it." She put her hands on her hips and crooked that eyebrow at him again.

"Haven Hill," he said, bracing for her reaction.

A look of disbelief crossed her expressive face. "No way."

He smiled.

"I *love* that house. I've always wondered what it's like inside."

"You can see it whenever you want to." He ran a finger along her cheek and drew her into another kiss.

"I'm off tomorrow," she said. "We can go to the beach or something if you want."

"I want to. I really want to."

He walked her home that night and every night all week. They went to the beach and to Haven Hill, grabbed meals at odd hours between her shifts and hung out with some of her friends at other parties. And they talked about everything. He'd never told anyone how much his father's rejection had hurt him, but one night while he held her on the sofa in her tiny apartment, he told her about it. Of course, she handed out some major abuse when he mentioned the estate where he'd grown up in Greenwich.

He heard about her happy middle-class upbringing with a younger brother and sister in Hartford. She shared with him the agony of losing her beloved father to cancer during her senior year of college. They talked late into one night about what they wanted out of life and who their friends were. And on the last night before he went back to Boston, Clare called in sick to work, and they took a picnic out to the bluffs to watch the sunset.

The family's longtime Block Island chef provided caviar, lobster salad, fresh-baked croissants, white wine, and chocolate-covered strawberries for dessert.

"I think you're trying to impress me," Clare said as they polished off the picnic. She gave him the impish look he'd grown to love during the week they'd spent together.

He smiled and took another sip of his wine. "Is it working?"

"I haven't decided yet. You know, I love that smile of yours. You could've skipped the lobster if you were going to look at me like that."

He took her wineglass, and set it down next to his in the sand. Pulling her to him, he rained kisses over her face and down her neck, whispering, "Let me know when you're impressed, okay?"

She giggled. "Not quite there yet."

They rolled in the sand, kissing again, more seriously this time. After a few intense minutes, he pulled away, sat up, ran his hands through his hair, and took a deep breath.

"Jack? What is it?" She put an arm around him. "Did I do something wrong?"

"No, honey." He realized he had upset her. "I'm sorry, I didn't mean to do that. It's just I feel so much for you so soon. It's caught me off guard."

"I feel the same things," she said with a wide-eyed expression. "I can't imagine you leaving here tomorrow and having to figure out what to do with myself without you. How crazy is that? I just met you a week ago."

"It *is* crazy, but I've been looking for you everywhere, and now here you are." He held her close as the sun set in brilliant pinks and oranges, and he felt a peace come over him that he'd never known before. Looking into her amazing eyes, he had no doubt she was the one for him. "I love you, Clare. I've never said that to anyone before, and I mean it. I don't ever want to be without you again."

"I love you, too. I can't believe it, but it's true."

He kissed her with a kind of passion he hadn't known he was capable of, and there on the bluffs at sunset, he made love with her for the first time.

They were married six months later. She left her job in Mystic to live with him in Boston, where they'd had a great apartment on Beacon Hill. He remembered how happy they'd been during those first years together. While he put in long hours for Neil, she worked part time for the city's school system until they were expecting Jill, and Jack insisted she take it easy.

The estate she'd admired from afar on Block Island became her summer home. She and the girls moved out there as soon as school got out each summer, and Jack commuted back and forth on weekends. Clare didn't work again until Maggie went to first grade, when she began a successful new career in real estate. By then they'd settled in Rhode Island, and he was busy getting HBA established with Jamie. They adored their girls and spent countless hours at dance recitals and soccer games as the girls and their friends grew up.

Until the months before the accident, he'd never known a moment of discontent with her, which had made losing her so agonizing. As the sun peeked through the drapes, he forced himself to get up and put the pile of paper back in the envelope. He was unable to bring himself to look at anything other than the one card he'd opened the night before. When he was done, he tucked the envelope away in his own closet.

That's when it hit him that today was their twentieth anniversary. Staggered anew by the realization, he sagged against the door frame and had to summon the will to finish the job he'd begun the night before.

Moving fast, he finished going through the rest of her clothes, cleaned out her dresser and her half of their bathroom. Suddenly, it was critical to have it all gone. When everything was in boxes, he took them to a corner of the attic until they were stacked together, Clare's life reduced to a group of boxes under the dusty eaves of the house he'd built for her.

He went back to the bedroom, shutting the door to the now empty closet and the dresser drawers he'd left open in his haste. Changing into warm running clothes, he left the house a minute later to run on the beach. He needed to move, to sweat, to flee from the fresh pain of an old wound reopening.

When he'd run the length of the deserted beach, he turned back, breathing hard and sweating. One of Kate's favorite songs, "Sand and Water," came on his iPod as he watched the gulls dive for fish in the frigid surf. He slowed his pace and tuned into the song's haunting refrain about how we come into this world alone and leave alone. Despite all the people and love in his life, in that moment Jack felt utterly and completely alone.

As he listened to the song's final notes, he realized he'd stopped in front of Clare's condo. He stood there, breathing hard for a long time, until he looked up to find Sally watching him from the window.

She waved to him, gesturing him inside.

He walked up the beach and over the dunes.

CHAPTER 19

Sally met him at the door. "You're out early today, Jack. Are you all right?"

Nodding, he wiped the sweat off his face.

"Is everything okay with the girls?"

"Yeah, they're on the cruise with Clare's mother."

"Oh, good. Anna was here before they left, and she was excited about the trip." Sally led him into the kitchen where she had brewed a fresh pot of coffee. She poured him a cup and studied him. "You want to talk about it?"

Surprised that she'd seen right through him, he looked down at his coffee. "I was packing up some things last night, some things of Clare's. It was a lot harder than I thought it would be. I don't know what I was expecting, but…"

"I'm sure it was very difficult for you, Jack. I know it doesn't feel like it right now but you've probably taken another step in your recovery. One of the key stages of grief is acceptance."

"Is that what I'm doing? Accepting all this?" He gestured angrily at the condo.

"I don't know. Are you?"

"Well, my girlfriend and her son are moving here from Chicago to live with me, so I guess I am." When he saw that he'd failed to shock the older woman, he set down the mug, feeling ashamed. "I'm sorry."

"You must love her very much to make that kind of commitment to her."

"I do," he whispered, all the fight draining out of him. He sat down hard on one of the kitchen chairs, and held his head between his hands.

Sally sat next to him.

"I'm so sorry," he said. "I have no idea what's wrong with me. I'm thrilled to have Andi and Eric coming."

Sally squeezed his shoulder. "Please don't apologize to me. I'm glad I was here when you needed a friendly ear."

"Clare and I were married twenty years ago today."

"It's all piling up on you, isn't it?" She paused. "Want my take?"

He nodded. "Please."

"You're about to take a big step forward with Andi by making room for her in your home and your heart. You're leaving Clare behind—much more so than you have already."

"I never wanted to leave Clare behind."

"I know." She rested a hand on top of his. "But it's probably time, don't you think?"

"I guess so. I'm sorry to show up here in this condition."

"I told you not to apologize to me," she said in her stern mother's voice.

He gave her a weak smile as he got up. "I'd like to spend some time with Clare, if that's all right."

"Of course. Take your time."

He went into Clare's room and sat in the chair next to her bed, thinking about the stack of cards she'd saved and wondering once again what could've happened to drive her away from him in the months before the accident. As he stared at the diminished woman in the hospital bed, hundreds of memories from twenty years flooded him, culminating with her standing in front of a speeding car. He still couldn't believe the Clare he'd known and loved would do such a thing, and even after all this time he couldn't accept that she'd done it on purpose.

"I like to think you can hear me," he whispered. Rising, he bent over the bedrail to press a kiss to her forehead. "Twenty years ago today was one of the best days of my life. Happy anniversary, Clare. I love you." Overcome by a flood of happier memories, he stood by her bed for a long time, brushing his fingers through her hair, before he turned to leave the room.

On the way out, he thanked Sally again.

"I hope it all works out for you and your Andi," she said as she saw him out the door.

He reached out to squeeze her hand. "Thanks."

The refrain from the song he had listened to earlier ran through his head during the short jog home, reminding him that, despite the painful loss, he had every reason to be thankful for the life he had now.

Between the awful scene with her mother and the odd conversation with Jack, Andi had tossed and turned all night. At four in the morning, she finally got up, knowing it was pointless to try to sleep until she was sure he was okay. She'd never heard him sound that way before, and she knew something was very wrong.

By seven she couldn't wait another minute to talk to him but got the answering machine at home and voice mail on his cell phone. His voice on the message made her yearn for him while she waited to hear from him.

She was thinking about calling the airlines by the time he rang her cell phone at nine. "Jack? Are you all right? I've been so worried."

"I'm sorry, hon."

"What's wrong?"

"I, um, I cleaned out Clare's stuff last night. It was a lot harder than I'd expected it to be. I'm sorry you were worried."

Andi ached for him. "You did that all by yourself? Why didn't you wait to let someone help you?"

"I wanted to get it done, and it seemed like a good idea at the time," he said with a wry chuckle.

"I'm so sorry it was tough for you." She swallowed hard. "Do you want to put our plans on hold for a while to give yourself some more time?"

"I don't want more time, Andi," he said with a desperate edge to his voice. "I want you here. I *need* you here."

"If you're sure…"

"I'm sure. Nothing's changed. So how did it go with your mother?"

"Just as I thought it would," she said with a sigh. "She's 'very disappointed' in both of us."

"I'd hoped she'd be more supportive of you."

"It was more or less what I expected, but it did hurt a little."

"I'm sorry, hon. I wish you were already here."

"Me, too. Are you lonely in that big house by yourself?"

"Kind of. It's way too quiet."

"I can imagine. Where are you now?"

"On my way to the office."

"Will you be okay?"

"I'm better now that I've talked to you. I'm sorry you were worried."

"I love you, Jack. You know I'm here if you need me, right?"

"I know. I love you, too. Have a good day. I'll call you tonight."

"Talk to you then." She hung up but still felt anxious. Something wasn't right. She thought about it for a few minutes and then picked up the phone again.

As Jack opened a beer and put a frozen pizza in the oven, the doorbell rang, startling him. He wondered who was there at that hour.

He opened the front door and was stunned to find Andi on his doorstep. Her long dark hair was in a ponytail and she wore jeans with a black leather jacket. He'd never been so happy to see her. "What're you doing here?"

"You were lonely," she said with a casual shrug. "You gonna let me in?"

He stepped aside. "Of course."

She dropped her bag in the front hall and reached up to brush the hair back from his brow, the loving gesture so familiar that he nearly swooned with need as she drew him into her arms.

"How'd you know I needed you?" He rested his forehead on her shoulder and breathed in the scent he would recognize anywhere.

"The same way you knew I needed you when Eric was sick."

He lifted his head to find her eyes. "How'd you get here?"

"The slowest cab in all of Rhode Island. What's burning?"

"Shit!" He grabbed her hand and pulled her along with him to the kitchen where he retrieved the pizza just before it turned black. "Hungry?"

"That's what you're eating?" She took in his old T-shirt and ratty sweats. "The situation's worse than I thought."

He smiled and shrugged. "It was here, and it looked good."

"Don't let me stand between you and your fine cuisine."

"Want some?"

"I'll pass." She opened a bottle of wine and poured a glass as he ate the whole pizza. "That's really gross."

"I ran six miles today," he said as he finished the pizza and drained his bottle of beer.

She got him another beer, opened it for him, and joined him at the table. "What's wrong, Jack?"

He took her hand and kissed it. "Nothing now."

"What was wrong earlier, then?"

Standing to put his plate in the sink, he took a sip of his beer and turned back to her. "Let's go in by the fire."

The temperature outside had dipped well below freezing, and the fire cast some welcome extra heat upon the family room as they sat together on the sofa. Waiting to hear what he had to say, Andi fought back panic. She realized she'd never seen him so disheveled or so undone. Whatever had happened the night before had clearly shaken him. His dark hair stood on end, as if he'd been running his fingers through it all day, and his face was scruffy with whiskers. It was the despondency she saw in his eyes, however, that was the most disconcerting. Loving him so much she ached with it, she had no idea what she'd do if he'd changed his mind about them.

"I can't believe you came all this way." He twirled a curl around his finger. "Where's Eric?"

"My mom was happy to watch him. Her time with him will be limited, so she was glad to have him to herself for a little while."

"Just a little while?"

"As long as you need me."

"You'd better get comfortable."

"Are you going to talk to me?"

"I am talking to you."

She raised an eyebrow.

He released a jagged deep breath. "I found some things of Clare's, stuff I never knew she kept, old cards and letters... It just, I don't know...it hurt," he whispered.

She held her arms out to him.

"It was a pile of paper, but it brought it all back again," he said, resting against her.

She tightened her hold on him. "And you were all alone."

"I'm glad I was. I don't want the girls to see me like that anymore."

Choking back the fear that lodged in her throat, Andi closed her eyes and breathed in his familiar scent. "It was pretty bad?"

He nodded.

She ran her fingers through his thick dark hair.

When he looked up at her, the shattered look in his eyes brought tears to hers.

"It scares the hell out of me to think there may be other things around here that could set it off. I can't promise it won't happen again."

"You don't have to." She guided his head back to where it had been resting against her chest and continued to caress his hair as a tear rolled down her cheek. "If it happens again, I'll be right here with you, and we'll get through it together."

"I'm so tired, Andi."

"I know, love." She took him up to bed and held him close until he drifted into peaceful sleep, but she lay awake for a long time hoping she wasn't about to make another huge mistake.

The phone woke them early the next morning. Jack fumbled to pick up the bedside extension.

"Jack?"

"Fran? What's the matter?"

"Nothing. What's the matter with you?"

"Other than it being six in the morning?"

"Oh, crap. I can't figure out the time thing. Sorry. Is everything okay there?"

He was finally awake. "Everything's fine. Are you already bored with your new husband?"

Andi smiled at his question, and he wrapped his free arm around her.

"I heard that," Jamie said.

Frannie laughed. "I'm definitely *not* bored."

"Spare me the details. How's Fiji?"

"What I've seen of it seems pretty nice."

"I told you to spare me the details."

"Are you sure everything's okay, Jack? I had the strangest dream about you, and it really bothered me, so Jamie told me to call you."

"I'm fine," he assured her as Andi's hair brushed against his cheek. "Enjoy yourself and don't worry about anything here."

"Okay. I'll see you next weekend."

"See you then." He clicked off the phone, ran his hand through his hair, and yawned.

"Everything all right in Fiji?" Andi asked.

"Sounds like it. She said she had a crazy dream about me and needed to call. My heart almost stopped when the phone rang. I thought of the girls on that cruise ship."

"Funny that she sensed something was up with you." Andi turned to study him. "You look better."

He rolled over so he was on top of her. "I was having an amazing dream myself, and I woke up to find it wasn't a dream at all," he said, kissing her lightly at first and then more intently. "You know what I want to do?"

"I have an idea," she said with a dry chuckle as she lifted her hips against his erection.

"Well, that, too." Laughing, he left a trail of hot kisses from her ear to her collarbone. "But you know what we've never gotten to do?"

"What's that?"

"Stay in bed all day."

"And pretend we're in Fiji?"

"Why not? How many times will we find ourselves without any kids underfoot for a whole day?"

"I can't argue with you there. Don't you have to work?"

"Don't you?"

"You got me again."

"Hearing no objections… All in favor? Aye and aye, and the motion passes." He kissed her before she could render an objection. "Unanimously."

"This is utter decadence," Andi whispered hours later after they'd devoured a box of leftover Christmas chocolates, taken a bubble bath, and made love again. "I've never been so lazy in my life."

"We should make this a monthly event. One day a month, Jack and Andi will be absent from life—definitely on a day when the kids are in school. All in favor?"

"Aye," they said together.

"And another motion passes unanimously," he said. "I love this governing system we've established."

"It goes back to you getting your way all the time, which, I've come to realize, is one of your many gifts."

"So, if I'd let you be in charge—only for this one day, mind you—what would you have changed about it?"

"Not a damned thing."

"I have to go home tomorrow, you know," she said as they ate Chinese take-out in front of the fire downstairs.

"You are home," he reminded her.

"Let me correct that. I need to wrap things up in Chicago, so I can get back home to you."

"Much better." He fed her some of his lo mein. "I'm still coming on moving day, right?"

"You don't have to."

"I want to. One more month…"

Gazing into the fire, she said, "I know."

"What's wrong?"

She turned to him. "Are you sure, Jack? Really sure you're ready for all this? It's not too late to put it on hold for a while—" The expression on his face stopped her.

He put the Chinese carton on the table and reached for her hand. "Andrea, you've saved me in every possible way. I thought my life was over, and then there you were. Remember when you said you were worried I was upset yesterday and everyone was gone?"

She nodded. It was the first time all day he'd mentioned it.

"No one else could've helped me the way you did. You're my first thought in the morning and my last thought at night. I can no longer imagine my life with out you or Eric. I don't want you to have a single doubt about my love for both of you or my commitment to you."

She caressed his face. "I don't."

He leaned in to kiss her and gathered her close. "I won't let you down."

She closed her eyes and rested her head against his chest to listen to the strong beat of his heart, knowing for certain it belonged to her.

Jack flew to Chicago two days after the moving van pulled away with the last of the things Andi and Eric were taking to Rhode Island. The rest of her furniture was in storage, and her new tenant was moving in next week. With the apartment empty, she reserved a suite at Infinity for their final night in the city. Eric was at his last day of school when Andi took one of the company cars out to O'Hare to meet Jack. Buying a car was first on her to-do list when she got to Rhode Island.

She was leaning against the limo when he emerged from a lower-level door into a freezing, gray February day.

"Hey, sailor, need a ride?" She smiled as he came toward her, looking sexy in jeans and a black wool coat.

He dropped his small bag on the curb and swept her into his arms, lifting her off her feet and kissing her as he brought her slowly back down.

"Well, hello to you, too," she said, thrilled to see him after a long month apart.

He leaned her back against the limo. "You know what my first thought was this morning?"

"Hmm, was it 'damn, I have to get my butt out of bed early to make this flight'?"

"No, you're way off. That was my second thought. Want to guess again?"

She pulled him close enough to kiss again. "I'm stumped."

"My first thought was that *last night* was the *last night* I'll ever spend without you." He kissed her as a policeman blew his whistle, warning them to move the limo.

They didn't hear a thing.

CHAPTER 20

David invited Andi, Jack, and Eric to dinner at the hotel, and they were stunned to find the room filled with her colleagues and friends, some of whom Jack met for the first time. David even thought to invite several of Eric's school friends. Andi was disappointed that her mother wasn't among the well-wishers.

She and Jack finally made it to bed at midnight after they tucked Eric into the suite's other bedroom.

"How're you feeling?" he asked, drawing her in close to him.

"Kind of sad. I'll miss them very much."

"I don't know if I've said this to you enough, but I appreciate all you're doing, all you're giving up."

"Do you know what I said to my mother when I told her we were moving?"

"What's that?"

She turned to face him. "That I have more of a life with you in five minutes than I have here in a whole year. I'm not giving up *anything* compared to what I'm getting in return."

He kissed her softly. "That's good to hear."

She snuggled into him, peppering his chest with kisses. "I'm so glad you're here. I hate sleeping alone."

"I can't believe we can sleep together every night now."

Trailing a finger over his belly, she wrapped her hand around his erection. "That's not all we can do every night," she said with a saucy smile.

He shifted so he was on top of her. "Mmm, every night, huh? Promise?"

"We have a lot of time to make up for."

He slid into her and sucked in a sharp deep breath. "*God*, is there anything better than this?"

"Not that I can think of." Her fingers caressing his back made him tremble. "Jack..."

He pushed hard into her. "What, baby?"

"Don't stop."

Laughing, he bent to kiss her. "No chance of that."

David was waiting for them when they came down to leave the next day.

Andi cast one last critical eye over the lobby, pleased to see everything where it belonged, even as her heart ached a little.

The bellman had already loaded the last of her bags into the car that would take them to the airport.

"Are you ready?" David asked.

"You didn't have to come in on a Saturday," Andi said.

"I wanted to see you off. Shall we?" David signed the last two words to include Eric, who rewarded him with a big grin.

Eric had a backpack filled with things to do on the plane and wore his Chicago Cubs ball cap as they went out through the hotel's revolving front door.

While David guided Eric into the car, Jack waited for Andi to take a last wistful look at the hotel.

"Ready?" he asked, putting an arm around her.

"Yeah. Let's go."

The ride to the airport seemed quicker than usual, and before she knew it, Jack and David were helping the driver load their bags onto a cart.

When Jack had put the last of the bags on the pile, he turned to David with his hand extended. "Thank you, David, for everything. I hope you and your family will come see us."

"Count on it." David shook Jack's hand and folded Eric into a long hug. "Take good care of these guys."

"I will." Jack took Eric's hand. "We'll wait for you inside, Andi."

David held out his arms to Andi. "I guess this is it."

She hugged him hard and then stepped back to look at him. "I can never thank you enough for everything. I'll do a good job for you in Newport."

"I have no doubt. But there's something far more important you can do for me."

"What's that?"

"Be happy, Andi." He kissed her cheek and hugged her again. "I'll miss you."

"Me, too." Tears rolled down her face as she watched him get back in the limo. When the car had driven out of sight, she went to find Jack and Eric.

They arrived at home in two cars overflowing with people and luggage. Andi was delighted that Frannie, Maggie, and Kate had come to the airport with Jamie. She had been amused by Maggie's sign, which had Welcome Home ERIC in big bold letters and her name added almost as an afterthought. Still, she was thrilled to know her son would be well loved in his new home. She could tell that Jack had been disappointed that Jill hadn't come to the airport.

After Jack and Jamie had lugged the bags into the house, they went into the kitchen, stopping short when they saw balloons and a large cake on the table, with "Welcome Andi and Eric" written on it.

"I thought you might be hungry," Jill said with a shy smile.

"You did this, Jill?" Jack asked, clearly stunned.

She walked over to him. "I'm sorry, Dad," she whispered as she hugged him. "I know I've been awful. I'm willing to try this for you."

"Thank you."

Overwhelmed with relief, Andi caught his eye and sent him a warm smile. "That cake looks fabulous to me, Jill," Andi said. "How about I help you serve it?"

Once they had consumed the cake, they gave considerable discussion to what they should have for dinner and agreed on pizza.

"Can I do anything to help you get settled, Andi?" Frannie asked after dinner.

"I just have to make Eric's bed and find his pajamas, but that's all I'm doing today."

"Maggie and I made his bed yesterday after it was delivered."

"Thank you, Frannie."

"I knew you'd be tired tonight. I was glad to be able to help."

"I'm going to like having you around," Andi said.

"We'll be spending a lot of time together since you'll be working at home for the next few months, and I'm still using my studio here while our house is being built."

"I wonder if we'll get anything done?" Andi asked as she topped off their wineglasses.

"You'd better hope so, since most of what I'm doing right now is for your commission," Frannie said with a grin.

She and Jamie got ready to leave a short time later.

"Thanks for all the help today," Jack said as he and Andi walked them to the door.

"It was our pleasure," Jamie said. "We're all glad to have you here to stay, Andi, especially him." He poked Jack. "I don't know that we could've stood him for much longer."

"What? I wasn't that bad!"

Frannie and Jamie shared a look.

"I was not!"

Andi laughed and put her arm around Jack. "I'll take it from here, guys. Thanks for the help."

Shutting the door behind them, Jack turned to hug Andi. "I feel like a kid on Christmas."

"Speaking of kids, let's go find mine and get him to bed. He's got to be exhausted after staying out late last night and all the excitement today."

Eric was delighted by his new room, which had been painted the same pale blue as his room in Chicago. He was also surprised to find his bed from home waiting for him. They all laughed when he asked if it'd been on the airplane with them.

"Whew," Jack said on the way downstairs with Andi. "I hope they're not going to be that wound up every night."

"They might be for a while."

"Maggie's so thrilled to have him here. Don't get me wrong, I'm glad she's happy, but it kind of surprises me, since she's always loved being the baby of the family—and played the part to the hilt."

"She's never had anyone to take orders from her before," Andi said.

"True. What else do you need for tonight?" he asked, gesturing to the pile of luggage in the foyer that they planned to deal with in the morning.

She pointed to a small bag. "Just that one."

"Give me five minutes and come on up." He kissed her and took her bag with him.

"What're you up to?"

He held up a hand on his way upstairs. "Five minutes."

She locked the back door and flipped the front light on for Jill and Kate, who were babysitting. On her way upstairs, she stopped to check on Eric. He'd fallen asleep right away and was on his back with both arms thrown over his head. She covered him, picked up his stuffed dog off the floor, and put it back in bed with him. When she looked in on Maggie, Andi found her also fast asleep and uncovered. She tucked the girl back in and went up the spiral stairs to Jack.

On the way upstairs, Andi felt some of the tension she'd been carrying for weeks drain from her shoulders. Now that she and Eric were finally here and the move was behind them, she gave herself permission to start hoping that everything might just be okay.

The newfound hope in her heart grew and expanded when she entered their bedroom, which was alight with candles. He'd also lit the fire, and Andi felt its warmth when she entered the room. The furniture she'd sent from Chicago was arranged in a way she would've done herself, and the room had taken on an entirely different atmosphere than it had the only other time she'd been up there.

"Hello?"

Jack came out of the master bathroom wearing just jeans and a big smile. "Hi there."

The sight of him in the candlelight sent a wave of desire charging through her. She ran her hands over his chest and leaned into him, still wanting to pinch herself to believe she now *lived with* the love of her life.

He hugged her. "How about a soak in the Jacuzzi?"

"I'd love that."

He led her into the spacious bathroom, and she gasped at the two-dozen red roses he'd left on the counter for her.

"I was going to put a card with them, but I figured I'd just tell you what it would've said."

She breathed in the fragrant roses. "And what's that?"

"Something like, 'Welcome home. I'm so glad you're here.'" He stole a lingering kiss and bent to start the tub.

"They're wonderful, thank you."

"I have something else for you." He reached into his pocket and pulled out a ring of keys. "The three silver ones are for the house. The others are my office, the boat, and Haven Hill. Oh, and this one's for my car."

"The keys to your kingdom," she said, touched by the gesture.

He handed her the ring. "Everything I have."

She put the keys on the counter. "Thank you."

"Let's soak."

The pulsing water soothed away the strain of the last few weeks. "Jill was so sweet to get the cake and the balloons," Andi said as she relaxed against his chest.

"I couldn't believe it. She really surprised me."

Andi closed her eyes and sighed with contentment. To finally be with him without a time limit was nothing short of a dream come true. After they'd soaked a long while in silence, she said, "I'm turning into a noodle."

"That sounds serious." He helped her out and wrapped her in a huge white towel and tied another around his waist. He picked her up so fast, she never saw it coming.

Lowering her to their bed, he leaned in to kiss her. "Don't move." He reached down to where he'd hidden a cold bottle of champagne and two glasses. "I thought we needed to celebrate tonight."

"I couldn't agree more."

He popped the cork, poured the foaming bubbly, and handed a glass to her. "Here's to you and me and the rest of our lives together."

She touched her glass to his. "I'll drink to that."

PART III

The Butterfly: To burst forward through the water by the simultaneous up and down movement of the arms and legs.

CHAPTER 21

Andi made good use of her two weeks off to unpack and get settled. She was careful to make changes only to the room she shared with Jack and left everything else in the house just the way it was, which she felt would be important to the girls.

She made them a fancy, candlelight dinner for Valentine's Day. The kids enjoyed the dinner and the silly gifts she got each of them. Jack surprised her with a pair of enormous diamond earrings that sat in a box on her pillow at bedtime. She gave him a new watch to replace the one he'd broken the week before.

The next weekend, he took her to shop for a car and talked her into a midnight blue convertible BMW, the four-door version of his. When he tried to buy it for her, she protested and let him know she was capable of buying her own car. He put up an argument—and even created a bit of a scene in the dealership—until he finally got that he couldn't win this one.

"Andi…" He reached for her hand as they drove home in his car. Hers would be delivered the next day.

She tugged her hand away and looked out the passenger window.

"What did I do?"

"You know what you did."

He pulled the car off the road. "Look at me." Using his finger to turn her chin, he seemed shocked to find tears in her eyes. "Talk to me. What's wrong?"

She looked down to study her hands. "I totally overreacted. You were just being generous, like you always are. I'm not used to that. No one has ever wanted to take care of me the way you do."

"I *do* want to take care of you—and Eric."

"Since Alec left us—and even before then—it's been up to me to take care of us. I can't stop that now. I make plenty of money, and I want us to have an equal partnership."

"I make plenty of money, too," he said with a pained expression. "In fact, I *have* plenty of money. Well, tons of it actually, and that doesn't even include the money from my father, which I've never touched. It's been years since I've worked because I had to. I want be able to do things for you and Eric without upsetting you."

She knew he was successful, but to hear him use the words "tons of money" made her laugh. "Tons, huh?"

He winced. "You don't even want to know. What can I say? The business does well. Really well."

He was so embarrassed that she loved him all the more for his humility.

"Can we compromise?" he asked.

She thought about it for a moment. "I'll allow the occasional indulgence, but I pay for the big things—my car, Eric's school, anything he needs. I don't want to spoil him. And my salary goes into the household pot. Fair?"

"We'll go to the bank tomorrow and open a joint account. We'll pay for everything out of that, okay?"

She nodded. "Will you do something else for me?"

He kissed her hand. "There's absolutely nothing I wouldn't do for you."

"Don't get mad when I won't let you pay for something."

"I'll try."

She raised a skeptical eyebrow.

"What? I *will* try."

"I'll believe it when I see it."

Grinning, he leaned over to kiss her. "Did we just have our first fight?"

Laughing, she said, "When we fight, buddy, you won't have to ask."

On her first day back to work in early March, she drove Eric's carpool and stopped for coffee on her way home to her new office in Jack's study. He'd made room for her to work from home during the final months of construction when she would oversee hiring, publicity, and the opening gala.

Frannie worked every day in her studio while she waited for construction to be completed on their new home. Andi looked forward to their daily chats and often walked with her to pick up Maggie at school. They'd begun to notice crocuses nudging their way through the still-frozen ground, a sure sign that spring was on its way.

One afternoon, Frannie came in from the studio looking frazzled.

"What's wrong?" Andi asked.

"My stomach has been a mess all day."

Andi took a closer look. "You're kind of green."

"Ugh! I can't afford to be sick right now with so much left to do on your commission."

"Are you sure it's a bug and not something else?"

"Like what?"

Andi made a pregnant-belly gesture.

"No way. That ship has sailed for me. I'm sure of it."

"How sure?"

"Sure enough that I haven't been doing anything to stop it." Frannie's face went slack with shock. "You don't think… I mean really…"

Andi roared with laughter. "You are *so* pregnant. I hope it's not triplets."

"That's not *even* funny! I've got to go get a test. Do you mind going for Maggie?"

"Not at all. Are you coming back here?"

"I guess so. I'll need reinforcements if it's positive."

"I'll be here," Andi said, laughing again at the shell-shocked look on Frannie's face.

Andi walked to Maggie's school and arrived just as the students poured out the front door of the elementary wing. She waved to Maggie when she saw her come running out.

"Hi, Andi. Where's Frannie?"

"She had something she had to do, so you're stuck with me."

"That's okay."

Andi smiled at her. She still sometimes felt that Maggie put up with her because she was part of the package that came with Eric. But Andi was making a concerted effort not to push herself on the girls, hoping a relationship would develop over time.

"Did you have a good day?" she asked Maggie.

"It was okay. Bobby Denton puked at lunch. It was *so* gross." Maggie shuddered with fifth-grade revulsion.

"That poor kid, I'm sure it was embarrassing for him."

"It probably was. I hadn't thought about it that way. There's Hailey Harper." She nodded at a girl across the street. "I don't like her."

"Why not?"

"She thinks she's so fancy with her funky French braids."

"Guess who knows how to braid like that?"

"You do?" Maggie's eyes lit up. "Could you do it for me?"

"Sure, we'll do it tomorrow."

They chatted all the way home, and Andi celebrated her first breakthrough. One down, two to go.

Andi stifled a laugh at the loud moan from the master bathroom.

"Oh my God!" Frannie flung open the door and held up the stick with the large pink cross. "I'm almost forty-four. I *can't* be pregnant!"

Andi hugged her. "You can, and you are."

Tears spilled from Frannie's eyes. "Jamie will *freak*," she moaned. "We're both too old!"

"He'll be thrilled," Andi assured her.

Frannie sat on the sofa and dropped her head into her hands.

Andi did and said everything she could think of to comfort Frannie, but nothing seemed to work. "I'll be right back." She went downstairs to use the phone in Kate's room, so Frannie wouldn't hear her. "Hi, Jamie, it's Andi."

"Hey, Andi, what's up?"

"Everything's fine, so don't worry, but can you come over to the house… um…now?"

"Is something wrong?"

"No, it's Frannie, she's—"

"I'll be right there."

Jamie bounded up the stairs fifteen minutes later and stopped short at the doorway when he saw Frannie crying.

"Frannie, honey, what's wrong?"

"I'll leave you two alone." Andi closed the door and went downstairs. A few minutes later, she smiled at the loud whoop that came from upstairs.

Jack came in a few minutes later looking worried. "What's wrong, Andi? Quinn told me you called and Jamie went running out of the office."

Andi kissed him. "Nothing's wrong."

"Then why did Jamie come over here like that? It scared the hell out of me."

"I'm sorry it scared you, but you'll have to let them tell you," she said with a mysterious smile.

He seemed to get that whatever was going on wasn't bad news, so he picked her up. "Tell me what you know, woman!"

"Put me down!"

But instead he flung her over his shoulder and pretended he'd drop her if she didn't tell him.

"What'll we do if our kid turns out like him rather than me?" Jamie asked as he and Frannie came into the kitchen.

Jack gasped as he set Andi down. "Your *kid?*"

The others nodded.

Jack let out a whoop of his own and hugged them both. "Congratulations! What a surprise!"

"No kidding," Frannie muttered.

Glowing with delight, Jamie put an arm around his wife.

Jill came into the kitchen. "What's all the yelling about?"

"Your aunt and uncle have some wonderful news," Jack said.

"We're having a baby!" Jamie said.

Jill squealed and called her sisters downstairs.

Eric trailed along with Maggie, and Andi signed the news to him.

Everyone was talking at once when Frannie turned green again and ran for the bathroom.

Frannie was sick for weeks, until Jamie couldn't take it anymore and called her doctor. She was admitted to the hospital and put on intravenous fluids. An ultrasound done the first day she was in the hospital confirmed what the doctor thought she'd heard on the fetal heart monitor—two heartbeats.

Frannie was asleep when Andi stopped to visit later that day after Jamie called to tell them about the twins.

She woke up when Andi sat down next to her bed. "I blame you, you know."

"Oh, really? I can't wait to hear this."

"Everyone you buy paintings from ends up with all these kids—first triplets and now twins. You're some sort of fertility witch."

Andi snorted with laughter. "You keep thinking that, but I'll tell you exactly what got you in this boat—two weeks in a hut in Fiji."

"It was a very nice bungalow, and we saw no reason to leave it," Frannie said with a spark of life back in her eyes. "I'm thinking now that maybe we should've done some sightseeing."

"I'll bet you are," Andi said with a chuckle.

"My mother was here earlier, telling me how twins run in her family. Mine will be the fifth set she knows of. Her great-grandmother was a twin. I never knew that. I was like, thanks a lot, Mother, but it's a little late now to tell me I was playing with fire."

"No kidding! Are you feeling any better?"

"Yeah. At least I'm not puking constantly anymore."

Andi winced. She could think of nothing worse. After an easy pregnancy with Eric, the delivery had been chaotic and ended in an emergency cesarean. She often wondered if the problems during delivery had somehow caused his hearing impairment, but she would never know for certain. "Well, I'll let you get some rest. I'm sure the girls will be by, and Jack will want to come in later, so I'll see you then, okay?"

"I still blame you."

After a spell of rainy days that Andi thought would never end, May dawned warm and sunny. The tulips were in bloom, and a few days were nice enough for her to finally try out her new convertible. She picked Jack up at his office one day and took him for a ride on Ocean Drive. They stopped to inspect the hotel, which was now framed and crawling with construction workers. Jack had been there earlier in the day and said he was pleased with the progress.

A week later, he and the girls noted the second anniversary of Clare's accident by visiting her and having dinner out. They asked Andi and Eric to join them for dinner, but Andi thought they needed to be alone together and took the opportunity to spend some time with Eric.

She was in bed reading when Jack came home looking exhausted. "How is everyone?"

He unbuttoned his shirt and sat next to her on the bed. "They did very well. They handle seeing her much better than they used to."

Andi reached out to him. "How about you?"

He laced his fingers through hers. "It never gets any easier to see her like that. I can't believe it's already been two years."

"Can I do anything for you?"

"You already have. I was anxious to get home to you."

She gave their joined hands a tug to bring him close enough to kiss. What she intended to be a quick kiss turned into a lingering embrace, and before long, her hands were under his shirt, caressing his back.

He shivered from her touch and kissed his way up her neck. "You make me crazy with wanting you, Andrea."

"You have me, love. I'm right here."

CHAPTER 22

As Jillian Frances Harrington's name was called at graduation, Jack held on tight to Andi's hand and fought the urge to bawl his head off.

Jill walked across the stage in her red cap and gown to shake hands with the principal. She wore gold cords around her neck, signifying her acceptance into multiple honor societies, and Jack thought he would burst with pride.

When she reached the end of the stage, she moved her tassel to the other side and blew them a kiss.

To his right sat Andi, his parents, Clare's mother, Frannie and Jamie, Neil and Mary Booth, Kate, Maggie, and Eric. The adults wept as they watched the girl they loved leap into adulthood.

Jack wished Clare could have been there to see it. He'd thought of her often in the weeks leading up to the ceremony and knew she was also on Jill's mind that day. The time with his first-born daughter had gone by in an instant, and he was sad to think about her leaving them at the end of the summer. When the last of the graduates had been called, he went to find his girl.

Jack took them all out to dinner and invited everyone back to the house to swim and have cake. They were throwing a party for Jill and her friends the next day, but this night was for family.

Jill glowed with excitement as she opened cards and gifts. She was delighted with Andi's gift—a certificate for professional decorating services for her dorm room at Brown University. Jack thought it was a great gift, and Andi seemed relieved that Jill liked the idea.

When Jill had opened all her gifts, Jack handed her a black key and pointed to the front door.

Shrieking, she flew out the door to find a lime-green Volkswagen Beetle with a large yellow bow on top sitting in the driveway.

Jill let out another shriek and launched herself into his arms when he followed her out the door. The others were right behind him.

Her eyes widened with excitement. "Is it really mine?"

"All yours, with only one string attached—you have to come home to us often."

"I will, Dad. I promise." She hugged him again. "Come with me. You get the first ride."

He slid the bow off and handed it to Andi.

Jill almost jumped out of her skin with delight as she beeped at the family on her way around the circular driveway. She hit the gas, and the gravel went flying.

He groaned. How many times had he talked to her and Kate about blasting in and out of the driveway? He was forever raking the gravel back into place.

Jill drove around the block to the beach. "This was the best day of my whole life."

"You'll always remember it." His right foot shot out looking for brakes that weren't there. "Slow down, Jill!"

She flashed him a saucy grin that reminded him of her mother. "Thank you for the car. I love it."

Willing his heart back to a normal rate, Jack said, "I had a feeling you would."

She pulled into a parking space at the beach, where the surf was up, and people were enjoying the end of one of the year's longest days.

They sat on the sand to watch the surfers riding the waves.

"I was so proud of you today, and your mother would've been, too. She'd be thrilled to know you're going to Brown."

"I hope so."

He slipped an arm around her. "I know so. I love that you're staying right here in Rhode Island but still going Ivy League. That gives me *lots* of bragging rights."

She groaned and laughed.

"You're a good girl, Jill, and a wonderful daughter. I hope you'll never forget where your home is or that you can come back any time you want to or need to. I'll always be right here for you."

She leaned into him. "Thank you, Dad," she whispered. "For everything."

Overcome, he kissed the top of her head and held on tight, wishing he could hold on forever.

"We'd better get back to the party," he said.

They got up, brushed off the sand, and walked hand in hand back to her new car.

With Jack in New York for a few days of client meetings, Andi sent the kids to the beach and buckled down to write a recruitment ad for an executive chef. After working for several hours, she pushed back from the computer and stretched.

She wandered into the kitchen for a glass of juice and to watch the surf for a few moments before she used the last of the juice to refill her glass. Looking around for a piece of paper to make a grocery list, she noticed the dry erase board that no one seemed to use on the side of the refrigerator. Taking a wet paper towel to wipe off the old writing, she started a new grocery list and then went back to the window to finish her juice. She never grew tired of such ready access to the ocean and had come to depend on the roar of it to lull her to sleep at night.

Andi was back in her office when the garage door opened. Checking her watch, she couldn't believe it was so late and went out to greet the kids.

"Hi," Kate said as she came into the kitchen with Jill right behind her.

They made a beeline to the fridge.

Jill stopped short, let out a cry, and looked at Andi. "*Did you erase that?*"

Taken aback, Andi said, "We needed a new list."

"*Nooooo*," Jill wailed and flew from the room.

Andi turned to Kate, who seemed stricken as she studied the board.

"What's wrong? I don't understand."

Kate shrugged. "My mom wrote that."

Andi's stomach dropped. "Oh my God, Kate. I had no idea. I'm so sorry." The note had been there for more than two years, and she'd wiped it away in a careless instant. She'd hardly even noticed it before.

"You couldn't have known," Kate said.

Andi wondered how many more times she would hear that phrase.

"What's wrong?" Maggie asked when she came in with Eric. She let out a short gasp when Kate pointed to the dry erase board.

"I'm sorry, girls. I didn't know it meant something to you." Andi signed to Eric that she would be right back and went upstairs to find Jill stretched out on her bed. Andi sat next to her. "I'm sorry, Jill."

"I overreacted. It was just this dumb thing I looked at every day."

"It's not dumb. I'm sorry, honey. I really am."

"Sometimes I get through a whole day without thinking about what happened to my mother, and then other times it still hurts so much."

Andi reached out to Jill and held her for a long time.

Jill pulled back and gave Andi a shy smile. "I'm sorry I freaked."

"Don't be. I understand." As she smoothed the silky dark hair back from Jill's face, Andi's heart swelled with love for the young girl who'd lost so much. "No one can ever take the place of your mother, Jill, but I hope you know I'm right here for you, and I care for you very much."

"I know. I like having you here."

Touched, Andi said, "Will you be okay now?"

Jill nodded.

"Why don't we go out tonight so no one has to cook?" Andi had been taking turns making dinner with Jill and Kate, and it was Jill's night.

"Sounds good to me," Jill said with a grin. "I'm going to take a shower."

When Andi went back downstairs, she found Frannie waiting for her.

"Everything okay up there?" Frannie asked.

"Seems to be. I messed up pretty badly today," Andi said with a gesture at the innocuous-looking dry erase board that had set off a firestorm in the house.

"You need to give yourself a break. You had no idea. We just left it. It's kind of silly, when you think about it."

"It's more sweet than silly. Are there other landmines around here I should know about? I'm terrified of doing or saying something that'll upset them."

"I can't think of anything, but if I do, you'll be the first to know," Frannie assured her.

"Figures it happens when Jack is away."

"Trial by fire for you," Frannie said with a wry grin.

"I'm taking the kids out to dinner tonight. Why don't you guys join us?"

"We'd love to."

Andi treated them all to lobster at a seaside restaurant, and by the time they returned home, the girls were in better spirits. Frannie and Jamie's company had helped to improve their mood. After Andi tucked in Maggie and Eric and said good night to Jill, she heard Kate playing her guitar by the pool. The full moon hung over the ocean as Andi walked outside.

She perched on the end of Kate's lounge. "That sounds lovely, Kate."

"Thanks."

"You didn't say too much about what happened earlier. I'm sorry it upset you all so much."

"It's okay. You didn't mean to hurt us."

"I'd never do anything to hurt you."

"I know."

"May I listen to you play for a while?"

"Sure."

The kids were at the beach again, and Andi was working the next morning when she heard the front door open. She figured it was Frannie and knew she would wander in to say hello on her way to the studio. Construction on Frannie's studio at their house was almost done, and Andi would miss having her around every day.

Andi went back to answering an email from the director of the new hotel division in Chicago and was absorbed in her reply when Jack sneaked up behind her and kissed her neck.

Letting out a surprised shriek, she jumped out of the chair into his arms. "What're you doing home two days early?"

"I missed you. Where're the kids?"

"Beach," she said, reaching for him.

"Mmm. Good." He captured her mouth in a deep, passionate kiss as he lifted her and carried her out of the study. On the way upstairs, she wrapped her legs around his waist and kissed his face, wallowing in his familiar scent. "I missed you so much. You can't go away anymore."

"Or you have to come with me." He put her down next to the bed and pulled off her shorts and T-shirt.

She unbuttoned his shirt, pushed it off his broad shoulders, and yanked at the waistband of his khakis.

"Hurry, Jack," she sighed against his lips.

He eased her onto the bed and thrust into her.

With her arms tight around him, she hooked her legs over his hips and took him deep.

He rocked against her. "It's like half of me is missing when I'm away from you."

She cradled his face in her hands and brought him down for a soulful kiss that sent desire darting through her. Her toes curled as she lifted her hips to give him more.

"I need to move," he said with a gasp.

She let her legs drop and fall open.

His back was slick with sweat as he pounded into her.

Andi had no choice but to go along for the ride until he sucked her nipple deep into his mouth and sent her into a climax that she felt from her toes to the tips of her fingers.

Suddenly, he went still. "*Andi*," he moaned. "Oh, *God*, I love you."

She kissed his brow, his closed eyes, his cheek, the end of his nose, and finally his lips. "I love you, too. So, so much. I don't know what I'd ever do without you, without this."

"You'll never have to find out." He held her close to him as he tried to catch his breath. "I don't ever want to be away from you again."

"Good, because I'm not letting you go anymore. All hell breaks loose when you're not here."

"Jamie told me what happened with the girls." He kissed her and shifted to his side, bringing her with him. "I'm sorry you had to deal with that by yourself."

She smoothed a hand over his chest, stopping to linger when his nipple pebbled under her finger. "I felt bad about upsetting them. I had no idea Clare wrote the note on that board."

"They know that." He reached for her dallying hand and brought it to his lips. "I'm sorry I never mentioned it. I heard Jill took it hard."

"She did, but we had a good talk, and she even let me comfort her."

"She's matured a lot this year."

"She told me she's happy I'm here," Andi offered with a smile.

His grin lit up his face. "Did she? I'm so glad to hear that."

"I was, too."

"See? It's all working out. We're becoming a family, one small step at a time."

The phone rang, and he reached for the bedside extension. He told the caller that Kate was at the beach. "Yes, I'll tell her." Jack hung up and rolled his eyes. "That was *Ryan*."

"So I gathered."

"Kate's not answering her cell, and he wants to make sure she knows he's picking her up at seven thirty rather than seven. Oh, the *joy*."

She laughed at him. "You're lucky it took this long for one of them to have a boyfriend."

"That doesn't mean I have to like it," he grumbled.

Andi settled herself on top of him. "I can see for Kate's sake, I need to get your mind off her love life and back on your own."

He raised a crooked eyebrow. "Oh, yeah? What do you have in mind?"

"You'll see," she whispered in his ear.

They spent two blissful weeks on Block Island at the beginning of August, relaxing on the beach, sailing in Block Island sound, and taking long walks into town for ice cream.

Late on their last night on the island, Jack sat with Andi on Haven Hill's back porch long after the kids had gone to bed.

"I can't believe this is our last week with Jill at home."

"The summer went by so fast."

"I never really went home again after I left for college. In fact, I didn't spend a night in my parents' house for ten years."

"That was different, Jack. Your father was so hard on you. You know Jill will be home for weekends all the time."

"It won't be the same."

"No, it won't. We're all going to miss her, but she'll be fine. She's smart and clever, just like you. And I know it'll be such a difficult transition for you, but she's so excited. Don't take anything away from her joy by letting her see how sad you are, okay? It'll be much harder for her to leave you if she thinks you're sad."

"You know me so well." He lifted their joined hands to kiss hers. "And you're right. I need to keep that in mind over the next week. I can be sad later, and you'll take good care of me, right?"

"Of course I will."

He released her hand to run his fingers through her long hair. "Are you happy here with us? Do you miss the city—"

She put her fingers on his lips to silence him. "I'm thrilled to be here with you. I've never known anything like what we have."

He hugged her, grateful for the second chance at love she had given him.

The family celebrated Jill's eighteenth birthday a week early, since she'd be in the midst of freshman orientation on her actual birthday. Jack's parents came for the party and to see Jill off to school. There were tearful good-byes at the house when Jack, Andi, and Jill left for Providence in two cars packed full of Jill's belongings.

"Thanks again for this, Andi," Jill said later that afternoon.

Andi had created an away-from-home sanctuary for Jill by using a combination of the girl's favorite colors: lime green, purple, and blue.

"My pleasure, honey. We'll sure miss you at home." Andi hugged Jill one last time. To Jack, she said, "I'll wait for you downstairs, okay?"

"I'll be right there." He appreciated that she understood his need for a last moment alone with his daughter. "You're sure you have enough money and everything?" he asked Jill for the third time.

"I'm sure, Dad. I have everything I need. You don't need to worry about me."

"No chance of *that*," he said with a grin. "You've got your cell phone and charger, right?"

"Yes, and I'll use it to call you—often."

"I'll be waiting." He hugged her. "I want you to enjoy every minute of this, but use your good judgment and stay away from things you know you shouldn't be doing. There'll be lots of temptation—"

"You don't have to worry. I'd never do anything to disappoint you."

He hugged her again. "I love you." His throat tightened with emotion, but he maintained a smile for her. In one instant, he saw her dancing at five in a pink tutu, walking over the bridge to Girl Scouts, flying down the lacrosse field with her long hair in a ponytail, jumping off the boat into cool blue water, and skipping across the stage in her cap and gown. How fast it all had happened.

"I love you, too. You can go. I promise I'll be okay."

With a deceptively jaunty wave, he finally left her.

Andi waited for him in the driver's seat of his car.

He got in next to her and sank into her loving embrace as he struggled to compose himself. "You know what I can't stop thinking about?" he asked after several quiet minutes.

"What's that?"

"I have to do this *again* next year."

Andi laughed. "Yes, you do. Why don't we go have a nice dinner, and I'll buy you a bottle of good wine so you can drown your sorrows?"

"I like the way you think." He was up for anything that would postpone going home to a house where Jill no longer lived.

They went to an Italian restaurant in the city's Federal Hill section, where he did his best to put away a bottle of wine, but rather than helping him forget, it only made him sadder. They held hands as she drove home.

"Thanks for everything you did to help out today." He looked over at her. "Jill's room is amazing. She'll be the envy of all the freshmen."

"I'm glad she liked it. It was a lot of fun to do."

"We're all lucky to have you." He leaned over to kiss her cheek and rested against her as they crossed the Newport Bridge.

Jack arranged for the kids to spend the night at Frannie and Jamie's on the twenty-fourth of August—the one-year anniversary of the day he met Andi. Planning a special night for them had helped to take his mind off Jill being gone, and he'd told Andi to be ready at six.

"Ready to go, hon?"

"Ready when you are."

"You look beautiful." He drew her in close to him and gave her a lingering kiss. "Happy anniversary."

Andi curled her arms around his neck. "Same to you. With Jill leaving and everything, I wondered if you'd remember."

"Of course I remembered."

She laughed. "I should've known better."

With his arm around her shoulder, he walked her to his car. "Yes, you should have."

"Where're we going?"

"I thought we'd spend the night on the boat like we did that weekend you came to visit," he said as they drove to the marina.

"There's nothing I'd rather do tonight, but I didn't bring anything to stay."

He kissed her hand. "I took care of it."

She sighed. "I'll never get used to being with a man who thinks of everything."

"You'd better get used to it. You're stuck with me."

"Yes, I'm just *so* stuck," she said with a smile. "So *blissfully* stuck."

He'd been to the boat earlier in the day, and everything was ready for them when they arrived.

They motored toward the bay to see the hotel's progress from the water. The exterior was just about shingled, the roof was on, and the contractors were putting up the interior walls. They'd had a lucky run with the weather all year, which had kept things right on schedule.

"It looks wonderful, Jack. I can't believe how close to done it seems from here."

They lingered for a moment longer to look at the hotel that had brought them together. Then he steered the boat across the bay to anchor in Mackerel Cove for the night.

The same Sinatra CD they'd listened to last time played on the stereo as they dove into the dinner he'd brought.

As Andi polished off the last brownie, she said, "I'm so full, and yet still I eat."

"I can't move." He groaned as he reclined on the other side of the boat's comfortable rear cockpit. The night air was heavy with humidity, and water lapped gently against the hull.

She gazed up at the spectacular show of stars. "What a lovely evening."

He looked over at her. "What a lovely year."

She brought her eyes down from the heavens to meet his. "The loveliest year ever."

"No regrets?"

"Are you waiting for me to have regrets, Jack?"

"I keep hoping you won't."

"I won't. Not today, not tomorrow, not ever, so don't spend one more minute worrying about that."

"You know me so well—better than anyone ever has."

The gravity of that statement hung in the air between them.

"I feel so disloyal to Clare even saying that, but it's true."

"Jack," she sighed. "I hate the terrible pain I still see in your eyes once in a while."

"It's better than it was, but it still gets to me every now and then."

"Of course it does."

When their song came on, he sat up and held out a hand to her. "Dance with me?"

She got up to take his hand.

"We might need a new song," he whispered as he drew her in close to him.

"How come?"

"Since we're together every day now, I don't have to remember the way you look tonight to hold me over during the lonely times."

"I remember how I felt the last time we were right here, knowing I had to leave you in a few days and how hopeless it all seemed. We wouldn't be here now if you hadn't had enough hope for both of us."

"Hope was the only thing I had left then. I don't even like to think about how differently things could've turned out if you hadn't had the courage to give it a try."

She reached up to kiss him. "I'm so glad I did."

"So am I."

Jack awoke the next morning to his cell phone vibrating on the table where he'd left it the night before. He jumped out of bed to grab it.

"Dad!"

"Kate, what is it? What's wrong?"

"Frannie had the babies! I've been trying to call you all night."

"The phone was on vibrate. I didn't hear it. Is everything okay?"

"It is now, but she had a C-section. I guess there was some bleeding or something."

"You're sure Frannie's okay?" he asked as he went in to wake Andi.

"I'm sure. Uncle Jamie just called a few minutes ago. They had a boy and a girl. Owen and Olivia."

"I can't believe we slept through all the excitement."

"Come home! We want to go to the hospital."

"We're on our way."

Maggie Harrington thought the arrival of Olivia and Owen Booth was the most exciting thing that'd ever happened. She'd never seen fingers and toes so tiny as she gazed at them in their bassinettes.

Across the room, Eric signed to his mother, "She likes them better than me now." He watched Maggie stare at the twins.

"Oh, no, sweetie, she's just excited about the new babies. She won't forget you," Andi assured him.

"I hope not," he signed, casting another worried glance at Maggie.

"We're going home soon," Andi told him.

The new parents took in the chaos from Frannie's hospital bed.

"Are you tired, hon?" Jamie asked his wife.

"Getting there. You can shoo them out in a few minutes."

Neil leaned over to take another look at his first grandchildren. He'd handed out pink and blue cigars to everyone he encountered since leaving Palm Beach that morning.

Jack came into the room with a pizza for Jamie and found his daughters holding their new baby cousins. Jill had been in earlier for a brief visit before going back to school. "Hey, Kate, why don't you think about taking the kids home? It's getting late."

"Five more minutes, Dad," Maggie said as she held Olivia.

After the kids left, Jack wandered over to Frannie's bed. "How're you feeling, Fran?"

"Like I got sliced in half by a speeding train." She shifted, trying to get comfortable.

Jack winced. "Sounds awful."

"It was pretty scary, but look at those babies."

"They're beautiful," Jack said. They had a dusting of her auburn hair, and Jamie had joked earlier about being stuck in a house full of hot-tempered redheads. "I love their names, too."

"Thanks. I still can't believe I'm finally a mom."

"It'll become real at three in the morning when they're both awake and hungry."

She grimaced. "I can't wait. We'd like you and Andi to be their godparents."

He kissed her forehead. "We'd be honored. We're going now so you can get some rest. Call if you need anything."

Jack and Andi left the new family and walked to his car. The stifling heat of the late August day still clung to the blacktop.

"What a day," Jack said as he held the car door for Andi. "Did we really wake up on the boat, or was that a month ago?"

She chuckled. "The babies are adorable. They're so lucky to have one of each."

"A ready-made family. They want us to be the godparents."

"Frannie told me. It's so sweet of them to include me."

"Do you ever think about having more kids?"

Amazed by the question, she looked over at him. "Do *you*?"

"Not really, but I have three. You only have one, and you're younger than I am."

"Only seven years."

"I wouldn't be opposed to one more if you had the urge."

"With your kids so close to being grown?"

"Eric's only six, so we've got a lot of years of parenthood left. What's a few more?"

She shook her head. "You never cease to amaze me, Jack. Just when I think I have you figured out…"

He glanced over at her. "So what do you think? Want to have one of our own?"

She thought about it for a moment. "I'd love to have a child with you, but we have a very nice family the way it is now, and with the twins coming into our lives, I think we'll be set for kids. We can always borrow them when we feel the hankering for babies."

"Are you sure?"

She leaned over to kiss his cheek. "I am. But I love you for asking."

"I love you, too." He held her hand as he drove them home.

CHAPTER 23

Other than a quick trip to Chicago in late September so Eric could see his grandmother, Jack and Andi were occupied with finishing the hotel in time for the December opening. By mid-October construction was almost done, and the Chicago-based interior-design team arrived to put the suites and guest rooms together. Andi settled into her office at the hotel in late October and was busy hiring and training staff while making final plans for the gala opening on December twentieth.

Eric moved to first grade at the girls' school and was doing well with his sign-language aide. Jack and Andi had talked about hiring a housekeeper to help with the kids in the afternoons, but Kate said she would do it, and they agreed to pay her. She usually made dinner for the family and helped the two younger children with their homework.

Their lovely arrangement came to an ugly end the week after Thanksgiving when Jack came home from work early and caught Kate in a passionate embrace with her boyfriend, Ryan.

"*Are you kidding me, Kate?*" Jack asked after he showed Ryan the door.

"With two kids in the house who, I'd like to remind you, you're being *paid* to watch? You know my rule about having boys here when we're not home."

She didn't answer him, which made him even angrier. "You're grounded. No Ryan, no car, no cell phone, no nothing for one month."

"You can't do that!"

"I can and I did. You've betrayed my trust and Andi's. We were counting on you to watch Maggie and Eric, and this is what you're doing? I just can't believe it, Kate. I'm so disappointed."

"Maggie and Eric were fine. They were watching a movie! You can't keep me from seeing Ryan! I love him."

"You might think you love him, but I won't stand by and watch you mess up your future for a boy. You're grounded, and that's the end of it."

She bolted through the kitchen on her way to the stairs.

Andi had arrived home in the midst of the screaming match and was waiting for him in the kitchen. "What's going on? I've never heard you yell like that."

"I came home early and found Kate and Ryan going at it. If I hadn't come in when I did, I think they would've had sex right there in the study."

"She wouldn't do that."

"You didn't see what I did. I still can't believe it."

Andi stayed home the next morning to participate in a conference call from Chicago without the noise at the hotel. After the meeting, she was in the kitchen making coffee when Kate wandered in, still in her pajamas.

"Why aren't you in school?"

"Teacher training day," Kate muttered.

"Are you all right, Kate?"

Kate shrugged and poured a cup of coffee. In a rush of words, she said, "Dad doesn't understand anything."

"He's upset that Ryan was here when we weren't home. We're really counting on you, especially in the next month."

"I'm sorry. I never wanted to let anyone down. I take good care of the kids, and that was the first time Ryan's been here when you guys weren't home. He stopped by to bring me some books I left in his car. I know you don't believe me."

"I do believe you. You're not a liar, Kate."

She seemed to brighten a bit at that. "Could I ask you something?"

"Of course." Andi sat next to her at the table.

"How old were you, the first time you, you know, went all the way?" Kate's cheeks colored with embarrassment.

Startled by the question, Andi released a ragged deep breath. "Well, let's see, I was in college, so I must've been nineteen or twenty. Why?"

Kate studied her coffee cup. "I was just wondering."

"Are you thinking about that with Ryan?"

"Dad doesn't believe me, but I love him, and I know he loves me, too."

Andi fought to stay calm as her heart raced and her palms went damp. She was in *way* over her head here. "I'm sure you do, but you're both still so young. You'll be in college next year, and who knows if you'll even be at the same school? Are you sure you want to let things get so serious?"

"I'm not going to college."

"*What?*" Jack would *freak out* when he heard this. "What do you mean? Of course you're going to college."

"I'm going to pursue my music. I'm not wasting four years in college. It's not for me. I'm not a straight-A student like Jill."

"You don't have to be like Jill. No one expects that."

"Dad does."

"He knows you each have different strengths. You need to talk to him about this."

"He's going to flip, though. I know it."

"You still have to talk to him. You can't just drop this on him later."

"You won't tell him about the other thing, will you?"

Andi thought about that for a moment. "I just hope you'll really think about it before you take a step you may not be ready for. And what about protection? Have you thought of that?"

"I'm probably going on the pill, just in case."

Andi let out another long breath. It was better not to think about what Jack would have to say about *that*. "The pill won't protect you from disease," Andi reminded her, wondering where the normally quiet, reserved Kate had gone.

"He's never done it before, either, so we're both safe."

"It sounds like you've given it some serious thought. I hope you know what you're doing. Sex changes a relationship—not always for the better."

"It's not happening this month, because I can't even see him." Kate turned her stunning blue eyes on Andi. "But if I wanted to be protected, just in case, would you help me? Get on the pill I mean?"

Andi thought about that, her head spinning. "There's almost nothing I wouldn't do for you, Kate, but you can't ask me to go behind your father's back on something like this. I won't do that to him. But I'll make you a deal. If you can get him to agree to it, I'll take you."

Kate rolled her eyes. "Like that's *ever* going to happen. He almost passed out when he saw me *kissing* Ryan."

"You won't know if you don't talk to him," Andi said, even though she wasn't optimistic, either.

"You won't say anything?"

Andi shook her head, even though she had serious reservations about making such a promise. "Please don't let me down by doing something foolish. Talk to your father." She got up, kissed the girl's forehead, and walked over to put her coffee cup in the dishwasher. "You're all set to get the kids at three today?"

"I'll be there," Kate said. "Andi?"

Andi stopped on her way to the garage. "Yes?"

"Thanks."

"Any time."

Andi couldn't focus on the mountain of work on her desk as she replayed the conversation with Kate. All she could think about was how upset Jack would be to hear that Kate didn't want to go to college, not to mention she was thinking about having sex with her high school boyfriend and wanted to go on the pill. Imagining the scene, Andi shuddered.

Jack appeared at her office door, carrying his hardhat and wearing jeans, a thermal shirt, and work boots. His cheeks were red from being out in the cold all morning with the stonemasons who were installing the south veranda. Somehow he managed to look as sexy in work clothes as he did in a tuxedo. He'd told her this would be his last week of work at the hotel, which made her sad. She'd miss having him around during the day.

"What planet were you visiting?" he asked. "You were a million miles away."

Andi caressed his cold face when he bent to kiss her. "I was just taking a quick trip to Pluto, but I'm back now."

"What's on your mind?"

She wanted so badly to tell him everything Kate had told her. "Nothing special. Are you having a good day?"

Seeming exhausted and troubled, he dropped into a chair. "The stone guys don't speak a word of English, so it seems my job is to stand back and let them do what they want. Since the veranda is coming out only slightly different than I'd planned, I've chosen not to do battle with them. Yet."

"I'm sure it'll be fine," she said as she studied him.

"I also can't stop thinking about what happened with Kate last night."

"You should talk to her—when you're not mad."

"Do you think I was too hard on her?"

"Not at all. She knows she's not allowed to have boys there when we're not home. You absolutely did the right thing."

"That helps, thanks. I'm on unfamiliar ground with this whole Ryan situation. She says she loves him, but what does she know about love? She's just a kid."

"Jack, think about it. You've told me boys have been asking her out for years, and she's never said yes until now. Why do you think that is? She probably *does* love him, and you can't just blow it off and wish it wasn't true." Andi hoped he would take the initiative to talk to Kate—and soon. She didn't like keeping things from him.

"You're right, and I'll talk to her. Well, I'd better let you get back to work and go see how much damage they've done to my design." Leaning over to kiss her again, he said, "I'll see you at home."

"I might be late."

"Take your time." He waved as he walked away.

Andi ached for him, knowing he would be upset by what Kate had to tell him. With a deep breath to clear her mind, she forced herself to focus on work. She picked up the phone to dial Bill's direct line in Chicago to update her replacement on their progress. Since she'd been so involved with the initial planning for the Newport property, she'd overseen much of the installation work herself.

Jen Brooks, her former assistant, answered Bill's line. "Hi, Andi, how are you? Is it crazy there?"

"It's like a war zone. I have trouble imagining we'll be ready in just twenty-five days. My office is still in boxes, and all I do is sit in interviews and meetings, but I love it. How are you?"

"Okay, I guess."

"You don't sound okay. What's wrong? Are you enjoying working for Bill?"

"He's great—not as great as you, of course."

Andi laughed. "Of course. So what's going on? You sound so down."

"Mark and I broke up two weeks ago."

"Oh, no! What happened?" Andi knew that Jen had hoped to marry the handsome attorney she'd dated for a couple of years.

"You know we'd been talking about getting married, but he's always said he doesn't want kids. I hoped he'd change his mind, but he's not going to. I can't imagine never having kids."

"I'm sorry, Jen. I know how happy you were with him."

"Other than that one big sticking point."

"You did the right thing. You don't want to miss out on being a mom some-day if it's that important to you."

"I just hate being here. I keep worrying about running into him in the city. We have all the same friends. It's awful."

"I have an idea."

"What's that?"

"How'd you like to come here and be my assistant manager? It'd be a big pro-motion for you, and we'd get to work together again. You could use the change of scenery. I could use the help—"

"I'll take it."

"Are you sure? Have you ever even been here?"

"No, but I'm dying to get away from this city, and I'd love to work with you again."

"We could try it for a year, and if you wanted to go home after that, I'd totally understand."

"When do I start?"

"How soon can you get here? We'll pay for your move, and I'll help you find a great apartment. You'll love it here. It's the most beautiful place to live."

"I'll be there in a week. I can come back after the opening to move for good."

"Bill's gonna kill me."

Jen laughed. "Yes, he is, but you've made my day, Andi. Thank you so much."

"Thank *you*. You're saving my life. So where is he?"

"In a meeting. Do you want me to have him call you?"

"Yes, please, and send me your flight information. I'll pick you up at the airport."

"Will do, thanks again."

Andi walked in just after seven to the smell of something that made her mouth water. "What're you cooking, Jack?"

He stirred the pot with one hand and reached out to hug her with the other. "Pesto, but I can't take credit."

She kissed his cheek and peered into the pot.

"Kate made it. I'm just supposed to stir."

"I'm impressed and starving. Where are they?"

"Kate had some homework to finish. Maggie and Eric are in her room. They visited the twins this afternoon."

"We need to get over there, too. I haven't seen them in three days. Did you get a chance to talk to Kate?"

"Not yet, but I will after dinner." He kissed her nose and went to call the kids for dinner.

The pesto tasted as good as it smelled, and Kate's meal was a big hit.

"I'll clean up, guys," Andi offered. "Maggie, will you run Eric's bath, please?"

"Sure, come on, Eric," Maggie signed.

"Kate, can I talk to you in the study?" Jack asked.

"Okay." As Kate followed her father, she cast a nervous glance at Andi.

"Talk to him," Andi whispered as she bit her thumbnail, worried about how he would take what he was about to hear.

"I hope you understand why I was so upset last night," Jack said, working to keep his emotions in check and his tone civil.

"I shouldn't have let Ryan in, but he came over to bring me some stuff I left in his car—"

"You're right—you shouldn't have let him in. I know you have good judgment, and I've never had any reason to question it before now. It's so important that I can trust you—especially when you're supposed to be watching Maggie and Eric."

"You *can* trust me, Dad."

"I have to apologize for one thing I said last night."

"Really?" she asked, looking surprised.

"I shouldn't have been so dismissive when you said you love Ryan. Maybe you do. I don't know, but it's not fair for me to tell you how you feel."

"I *do* love him. I know we're young and all that, but we love each other."

He knew he had to ask, but, *God*, he really didn't want to. "Tell me you're not, you know…"

She looked him right in the eye. "Having sex with him?"

His heart stopped. "Are you?"

"I'm thinking about it."

"You're too young to even think about it."

"Half the girls in my class have already done it."

Shocked to hear that, he forced himself to focus on his daughter. "Look, so you love him. You still have to think about the big picture. What if you get pregnant? You can't go to college if you're pregnant or have a baby to take care of."

"Andi said the same thing, and I told her I'm not going to college."

"What do you mean you're not going to college? You talked to Andi about this? When?"

"This morning. I want a career in music. Why do I have to sit through four years of college to do that?"

He put up a hand to stop her. "That's crazy. You're going to college. We're not even talking about that."

"I'm not going. And you may as well know, I want to go on the pill." She swallowed hard. "Just in case."

Jack's head was going to explode. Any second now… "Is Ryan pressuring you to have sex?"

"Not at all," she said, looking offended. "I know you can't imagine *I* might *want* to do it. I want to be safe about it. I wish you could understand that. Andi did."

"Did she?" He couldn't believe Andi had kept this from him.

"You know how I feel, and I've been honest with you about what I want to do. I hope you'll respect that." She got up and left the room.

He sat there fuming for several minutes before he went to find Andi.

CHAPTER 24

"*You knew this all day and never said anything?* I was in your office, for Christ's sake!"

"She confided in me, Jack. I couldn't just come running to you."

He followed her into their bathroom. "She's thinking about having sex! You should've told me that."

"No, I shouldn't have. I've been walking on eggshells around here for almost a year, especially with Kate and Jill. Don't you see what a big deal it was that she came to me with this? I told her to talk to you, and I pushed you to talk to her. That's all I could do. I couldn't betray her."

"Instead, you betrayed me." He stormed out of the bathroom and slammed the door, needing to get the hell out of there before he said something else he'd regret.

Since it was too dark to run on the beach, Jack stayed on the quiet street and watched for patches of ice. Running without music or a destination, he couldn't believe Andi had kept something this important from him, even for just a few hours.

After a while, he looked up to discover he'd run three miles and was approaching Frannie and Jamie's new house, a contemporary Jamie had designed and built overlooking the water. He'd drawn the plans for the house years ago and put them away when it seemed like he wouldn't be having a family. Jack saw the lights were still on, so he decided to stop to see them. He walked in to find Frannie curled up on the sofa, feeding one of the babies.

"Hey," he said. "I didn't want to ring the bell and wake someone up."

"You don't have to ring the bell here. You know that. What're you doing out so late?"

"Just taking a run. Who do you have there?" he asked as he wiped the sweat off his face with a gloved hand.

"Owen. He's insatiable." She smiled when the baby wrapped his tiny fingers around hers as he breastfed under a light blanket.

Jack dropped into the chair across from Frannie and pulled off his gloves. "Enjoy them while they're that age."

"What's the matter?"

He told her about finding Kate with Ryan and the fight he'd had with her. "She wants to go on the pill, and she's not going to college. Other than that, everything's groovy."

"Wow, she put it right out there, huh? Don't you want her on the pill if things with him have gone that far?"

He struggled not to raise his voice as the baby dozed on Frannie's shoulder. "*No*, I *do not* want her on the pill. I'm not giving her permission to have sex."

"Jack, she's seventeen. She doesn't need your permission. If she wants to do it, she will. Wouldn't it be better to make sure she doesn't get pregnant?"

"I can't believe we're even having this conversation. Oh, and get this—Kate talked to Andi about all this earlier, and she never said a word to me. I mean my daughter is talking about having *sex*, and Andi doesn't think I need to know that?"

"So you expect Andi to tell you everything the girls confide in her?"

"Stuff like this—yes."

"I didn't."

"What do you mean?"

"There were lots of times the girls told me things and made me promise not to tell you because it was embarrassing or it was just girl stuff. Sometimes I told you, and other times I didn't. It depended on what it was. Don't you think it's great that Kate went to Andi with this? It shows what a good job she's done getting the girls to trust her. If Andi had gone blabbing to you, Kate would never tell her anything again."

Jack hated to admit Frannie might have a point. "Andi could've cued me in so I wouldn't have been totally blindsided."

"I know it's hard to see the girls growing up. It's hard for me, and I'm only their aunt."

"You're much more than that to all of them, and you know it."

"Get her on the pill so a year from now you aren't wishing you had."

"I'll think about it, but I hate the idea of it."

"Weigh it against how you'd feel about being a grandfather, and you'll start to feel a whole lot better about it," she said with a grin.

Jack grimaced at the word *grandfather*. "What'll you do when Olivia tells you she wants to be on the pill at seventeen?"

"Olivia won't be allowed to date until she's thirty. That's where you made your mistake—letting her go out with him in the first place."

He smiled. "I hope I'm around for that fight."

"So she says she's not going to college? What's that all about?"

"She wants to pursue music, and 'why should I waste four years in school?'"

"Who's wasting four years in school?" Jamie asked as he came into the room.

"Kate. She's got a big idea about a career in music." Jack rolled his eyes.

Jamie leaned down to take the sleeping Owen from Frannie. "She's good enough."

"Make sure you tell her that," Jack said dryly. "You'll really help my cause."

"Well, she is," Jamie insisted. "She's got a real talent. Maybe you should let her see where it takes her."

"Clare would have a shit fit over this. She pounded college into their heads from the day they were old enough to know what school was. She'd never go for it."

"Aren't you doing to Kate the same thing your father did to you?" As he spoke, Jamie rubbed Owen's back. "Do you want Kate to resent you the way you resented him all those years for not understanding you well enough to let you go your own way?"

"So I just say 'good luck, honey, hope it works out. Call home every now and then?'"

"Maybe you do," Frannie said softly. "If that's what it takes to prevent what happened between you and Dad from happening again, maybe that's exactly what you do."

Jack shook his head as he got up. "I can't see myself doing that, Fran. I'm sorry I barged in on you guys. Thanks for letting me vent." He gave Owen a pat on his well-padded bum.

"It's too cold to take the babies out, so we're always home these days," Frannie said.

"Come by any time," Jamie added. "We like the company."

Jack jogged home thinking about what Frannie and Jamie had said. He knew they were probably right, but he had no idea how to let Kate follow her dream and keep her safe at the same time.

He took a shower and lay awake next to Andi for a long time. As he stewed about Kate, he found himself longing for Clare. She'd know exactly what to do.

Jack woke up to a note from Andi, asking him to come see her when he got to the hotel.

He dropped Maggie and Eric off at school and was at the hotel by nine. Sleep deprived and cranky, he was hit right away with a slew of new issues with the stubborn stonemasons. He finally blew up at the Portuguese crew chief, the only one who spoke English.

"*Do it the way it's drawn, or I'll find someone else who will!*" Jack left the man speechless in his wake as he stormed into the hotel, went to Andi's office, and slammed the door.

"What's wrong?" she asked.

"They're making a goddamned mess of that veranda." He ran a hand through his hair in frustration. "I'm giving them one last chance to follow the plans, or I'll replace them."

"We don't have time to get another crew. I've had a disaster a minute myself since I got here at seven, and I don't have the patience for another one."

"If you don't care if it's done right, then I don't either. You're the client."

She got up and walked around the desk to face him. "Is that what I am now, Jack? The client?"

"You know what I mean."

"You're mad I didn't tell you about Kate, but I'd do the same thing if I had it to do over again."

"I just wish you'd warned me or something."

"Would that have made it easier to hear? Any of it?"

"Probably not, but I don't want us keeping things from each other. I don't operate that way, and I didn't think you did either."

"You're being very unfair, and I don't deserve it." Her normally soft brown eyes flashed with fury. "I'm living in your wife's house, eating off her dishes, and using her towels while trying to be a friend to her daughters. I'm doing the best I can. For God's sake, Jack, *what else do you want from me?*"

"Andi—" he said, stunned by her outburst.

She held up a hand to stop him. "Forget it. I don't have time for this now. I'll be here until ten o'clock tonight at this rate. Thank you for driving Eric this morning and for pitching in with him while I'm so busy."

"You don't have to thank me. I'm happy to take care of him."

"I'll see you tonight."

With a sick feeling in his stomach, he went back to work.

They didn't see much of each other over the next few weeks as Andi worked long hours, usually crawling into bed long after midnight.

Two days before the opening, the executive team from Chicago completed its inspection and declared the hotel ready to go. Andi's reservations director told her they were sold out for the first month, and the front desk manager reported her group was ready to begin receiving the VIPs invited to the gala opening.

Andi had supervised every detail of the gala and was tending to final preparations the day before the opening as she walked through the lobby, where the house staff was decorating a huge Christmas tree.

The first thing guests would see upon entrance through the main door was an enormous staircase with the registration desk on one side and the concierge and bellman's stations on the other. The staircase divided the two sides of the hotel and served as the symbolic center of the building. Guests choosing to take the stairs would be rewarded at the top with a full-length window view of the lawn and the bay. Andi loved the night view when she could see the Newport Bridge lit up in the distance.

Jen Brooks had arrived two weeks earlier and was already indispensable to Andi. Jen had taken on the housekeeping and food service staff. Louis Jacard, the executive chef Andi had hired away from a top New York restaurant, was temperamental, but Jen assured Andi she could handle him.

"Everything looks wonderful, Andi," her colleague, Bill, said as they toured the suites in the west wing. "It came together beautifully."

"It really did," Andi agreed.

"And the art is superb. Frannie Booth did an outstanding job. We'll have to use her again."

"She's busy with the twins right now, but she might be interested in some work down the road."

He scowled playfully at her. "I shouldn't even be speaking to you after the way you poached Jen right out from under me."

Andi laughed. "It was truly awful of me, but it had to be done. I'd never have gotten everything finished in time if she hadn't shown up when she did."

"I saw her battling with Louis earlier, and she was holding her own. It was a good move for her. She was in bad shape after she ended it with Mark."

"She already seems better after just a few weeks. I'm thrilled to have her with me, but I'm sorry I stole her from you," Andi said, full of mock contrition.

"You are not!" he said, and they laughed.

They were in the America's Cup suite when Jack appeared at the door.

"Hi, there." Andi was surprised—and thrilled—to see him. He'd made himself scarce around the hotel since they'd argued about Kate. Repairing their rift was her top priority after the opening.

Jack shook Bill's hand. "Hi there, Bill. How are you?"

"Nice to see you. You guys did an outstanding job."

"So did you. The suites are amazing."

"Andi deserves most of the credit for that. Would you two excuse me? I need to get over to the east wing where the rest of my people are handling the finishing touches."

"I'll see you later, Bill." Andi was hosting a dinner that evening for her former coworkers as a thank you for their hard work over the last few months.

"How're you holding up?" Jack asked, studying her. "You look tired."

"I'll be glad to get through tomorrow. Is everyone all set to come?"

"We're looking forward to it. I bought Eric a tux yesterday. Wait until you see how cute he is."

He looked delighted, and she felt her heart soften toward him for the first time in far too long. "I can't wait. Thanks for taking him."

"It was fun."

She looked up at him, her heart aching. "I miss you."

"I miss you, too." He held out his arms to her.

Taking a step to meet him halfway, she released a deep sigh of relief at being back in his arms and engulfed in his familiar scent. "I'm scared, Jack. I never would've thought we could drift so far from each other so quickly."

"We'll work it out, honey. After the opening, we should get away for a few days. Just the two of us."

"I'd love that." She reached up to kiss him and lingered longer than she'd intended when the old thrill chased through her the moment their lips touched.

He seemed reluctant to let her go. "I'll make some plans for us. Any preferences?"

"Surprise me." She kissed him again. "I've got to get back downstairs. Jen and Louis were going at it pretty hard earlier. I need to make sure they didn't kill each other."

"Sounds like fun." He kissed her one last time before he walked her back to the lobby.

She saw him out the door and went to find Jen.

Andi didn't get home until almost two the next morning. She set her alarm for six so she'd have time to pack what she needed to stay at the hotel after the gala. When she got into bed, Jack reached for her and pulled her close to him in his sleep.

She smiled in the dark. It had been weeks since she'd slept in his arms, and she hoped they'd taken a small step back to each other.

CHAPTER 25

Andi wouldn't have changed a thing about the opening of Infinity Newport, from the Mayor of Newport presenting David with the key to the city, to the food, the music, and the holiday décor. The highlight for her was when Jack and Eric arrived in their tuxedos. Eric loved his cool suit, and Andi got to dance with him several times before Jack's parents took him and Maggie home. Frannie and Jamie enjoyed their first night out since the twins were born, but they left early to get home to the babies.

Andi looked for Kate in the crowd and found her sitting with Jill at the table reserved for the family.

"Are you guys having a good time?" Andi asked. She wore a midnight blue velvet gown and had contained her hair in a high twist.

"It's great, and the hotel is beautiful," Jill said. With her first semester behind her, she was home for a month.

"Your dad's company did a wonderful job," Andi said. "Kate, may I talk to you for a minute?"

"Sure." Kate got up to walk with Andi to the bar.

Andi ordered a glass of wine for herself and a soda for Kate. "I'm sorry I haven't had a chance to check in with you before now. How is everything? Did you talk to your dad again?"

"Briefly. He said if I feel the need to be on the pill, he won't stand in my way, but he doesn't approve. He wants me to wait, and he thinks I'll be sorry if I don't."

"That sounds fair to me. Don't forget I promised I'd take you to the doctor if you want me to."

"I'm not sure anymore. Ryan and I haven't seen each other much since I was grounded. He was really embarrassed when Dad caught us, you know…" Her cheeks lit up. "I don't know if he loves me anymore."

Andi slipped an arm around Kate. "I'm sorry. It may not seem like it now, but you've got so much ahead of you and so many people to meet."

"I know. I'm okay about it."

"Good." Andi hugged her. "You know where I am if anything changes."

"Thanks, Andi. I know Dad was mad at you, and I'm sorry about that, but I appreciate you keeping my secrets."

"Don't worry about it. Come to me any time, you hear?"

"I will," she said, returning Andi's hug.

The gang from Chicago was entertaining Jack when Andi asked if she could borrow him.

"What's up?" he asked when she led him away.

"I'm about to drop. Am I allowed to leave my own party before it's over?"

"I don't see why not. Wait right here. I'll let the girls know we're going, and I'll tell David and Jen they're in charge for the rest of the evening."

David hugged Andi and told her to get some well-deserved rest. She and Jack kissed Jill and Kate good night and climbed the stairs in the lobby.

Andi stopped him at the top. "This is my favorite spot in the hotel."

He put an arm around her. "I'll let you in on a secret."

"What's that?"

"I added that window to the plans the week I met you. They'd put a wall of Newport memorabilia here. I nixed it and went for the view."

"Good call." She smiled up at him. "Have I told you how hot you look in a tux?"

He crooked an amused eyebrow at her. "Are you coming on to me?" he asked, relieved to feel some of the old magic returning between them. He, too, had worried they'd crossed a point of no return over the last month. "I thought you were tired."

"I'm not *that* tired."

Running his hand up and down her back, he pressed a light kiss to her lips. "In that case, have I told *you* how hot you look in velvet?"

"Hey! You're stealing my line!" She opened the door to the Kennedy suite, which was dominated by Frannie's painting of Hammersmith Farm and another of the dashing young president at the helm of his sailboat.

Jack studied the portrait as Andi slipped off her heels and asked him to help with her zipper. He unzipped her, took her hair down, and kissed her neck when he was finished.

Turning to remove his bow tie, she nodded to the painting of Hammersmith Farm. "I fell in love with you that day, Jack, and I've loved you every day since then."

"Even on days I didn't deserve it?"

She looked up at him with surprise.

"I've had some time to think about everything that happened, and I can see now that you did the right thing with Kate." He reached for her hands. "That doesn't mean I liked being kept in the dark, but she needed a woman's advice. I'm grateful she turned to you and even more grateful you were there for her. I'm sorry I acted like such an ass." He leaned in to kiss her. "I've loved you from the first instant I ever saw you, and I always will."

Sighing, she wrapped her arms around him.

"What you said that day about living in Clare's house…" He pulled back to look at her. "I've thought a lot about that, too."

"I don't know why I said that. I honestly hadn't been thinking about it. Chalk it up to heat of the moment."

"We can make some changes around the house."

"We don't have to."

"But maybe we should."

"Maybe. Hey, I have some news that'll make your day," she said, removing the black onyx studs from his tuxedo shirt.

"What's that?"

"Kate and Ryan have cooled it."

His eyes lit up with delight. "That's the best news I've had in weeks."

"You may've dodged a bullet this time, but you've only postponed the inevitable."

"I don't have to think about it now." He swept her off her feet, swung her around, and lowered her to the bed with a serious expression on his face. "Right now, I'm thinking only of you."

"Is that so?" She ran her fingers through his thick dark hair. "And what're you thinking?"

"That it feels like I haven't made love to you in ages."

"That's because you haven't," she said with a playful pout.

"What do you say we fix that immediately?"

"I say hurry up and get naked."

Laughing, he did as directed and slid into bed beside her, sighing with relief at the feel of her soft skin against his.

Andi snuggled into him, pressing her lips to his throat.

"Let's not allow this to happen again, Andi. No matter what."

"I hated feeling estranged from you."

"I hated it, too." He captured her mouth in a deep, searching kiss as he cupped her breast and rolled her nipple between his fingers. Steeped in the scent that had driven him wild since the day he met her, Jack breathed her in. He hadn't realized he'd been starved for her until she was back in his arms.

A tremble rippled through her, and she shifted onto her back, bringing him with her. "Now, Jack. I want you so badly."

"Mmm, I'm here." He dipped his head to kiss her as he entered her slowly. "You mean everything to me. I hope you know that."

She gasped and raised her hips to meet his thrusts. "I do. I know that. You're everything to me, too."

He held her tight against him, filled with love and relief as he drove them both to an explosive finish.

Jack woke before dawn and was unable to go back to sleep. Since Andi was still asleep, he moved carefully so he wouldn't disturb her. He closed the bedroom door, hoping she would sleep awhile longer. All the plans she'd made and staff she'd hired would shift into gear today when the hotel opened to the public.

He called room service to order breakfast, asking them to send coffee and a paper now, and the rest in an hour. Looking around the elegant room, he was deeply satisfied with the way the hotel had turned out—it was everything they'd hoped it would be and so much more.

By the time he took breakfast in to Andi, he'd already finished a small pot of coffee, read the paper, and called home to check on the kids.

He bent down to kiss her awake. "Good morning."

"Hey," she said sleepily. "What time is it?"

"Almost ten."

She sat straight up. "For real? I need to get to work."

"You can take another hour, babe. You're the boss. Have some breakfast." He poured her a cup of coffee, brought an envelope from behind his back, and handed it to her.

"What's this?"

"Open it."

Her face lit up with delight when she pulled out two plane tickets to the Virgin Islands and a brochure for a resort on St. John.

"It's all-inclusive, so we can eat, sleep, and soak up the sun."

"That's it?" she asked with a sexy smile.

"Well, maybe a few other things, too," he said, leaning in to nibble on her bottom lip.

"It's just what we need. When are we going?"

"I left the tickets open-ended so you could check your schedule, but I was hoping to go in February since we'll have another anniversary to celebrate."

"Yes, we will. I can't believe we've already been living together for almost a year." She kissed him and lay back against the pillows. "Thank you," she said, caressing his face. "I don't know if I can wait until February to spend a week alone with you."

He kissed the palm of her hand. "I figured you'd want some time to make sure everything is running smoothly here before we go."

"You figured right." She took a bite of toast and reached out to coax him into bed with her. "I'm only working a few hours today and then you know what we *have* to do?"

"I'm almost afraid to ask…"

"Christmas shopping. I haven't bought a thing for anyone."

He groaned. "Do we have to? The stores will be mobbed today."

"Yes, we have to."

They returned home weary but with their shopping finished. The first day at the hotel had gone smoothly, and Jen was in charge for the weekend with orders to call Andi if anything arose that she couldn't handle.

Andi trudged upstairs while Jack went for a run. All she wanted was a long soak in the Jacuzzi and eight hours of sleep. She peeled off her clothes, opened the medicine cabinet, and reached for her birth control pills. Opening the container, she did a double take.

The pack was almost full.

When was the last time I remembered to take it?

Dazed, she pulled on a robe and sat on the edge of the big tub with the pack of pills in her hand, trying frantically to piece together the last few weeks. Judging by the pills still in the package, it'd been more than two weeks since she'd taken one. She had never missed a day, let alone two weeks.

"Oh my God," she gasped when she remembered making love with Jack twice the night before and again that morning after weeks of hardly seeing each other. "Oh *God*," she moaned as she quickly did the math.

The timing was ideal.

Knowing she shouldn't take them if there was a chance she could be pregnant, she got up to put the pills back in the cabinet.

"Pregnant."

She had to say the word out loud to get it to register as she tried to remember how long she had to wait to take a test.

Andi got through Christmas by willing herself not to think about the possibility that she could be pregnant. The kids were on vacation, and Jack and Jamie had closed HBA for the holiday week as a thank you to the staff for their hard work on the hotel. Andi and Jen were working alternating days so they could each have some time off during the holidays.

On New Year's Eve morning, Andi finally took a pregnancy test. Afterward, she stared at the pink plus sign for a long time before she walked out of the bathroom and got back in bed. Suddenly, cold all over, she began to tremble as the shock set in.

"Everything all right, hon?" Jack asked.

"I thought you were still asleep."

"I'm programmed to get up for work." He put an arm around her. "You're shivering. Come over here." He drew her closer to warm her up. "Better?"

She squeezed her eyes closed and a tear leaked from one of them. "Much."

He kissed her cheek and discovered dampness. "Hey! What's wrong?"

Taking a moment to pull herself together, she turned to him. "How do you feel about his, hers, and ours?"

"I don't get it."

"We have yours, we have mine, and now it looks like we're going to have one of our own." She watched the comprehension light up his face.

"*Really?*"

She nodded.

He hugged her tightly. "Andi," he whispered.

"I'm such an idiot. During the hotel chaos, I stopped taking my pill, and I discovered it after the opening. We agreed we weren't going to—"

"Who cares what we agreed?"

"I can't believe how stupid I was."

He chuckled and cuffed her chin. "I'm so glad you were stupid."

She looked over at him. "What if..."

"What, honey?"

"What if this baby is deaf, too?" The worry had been on her mind for days.

Jack raised himself up on one elbow and caressed her face. "If that happens, we'll deal with it together, and we'll love him or her as much as we love all the others. I'd never leave you alone like he did."

"I know."

"The only thing you need to be worried about is taking care of yourself and the baby." He kissed her cheek and then her lips. "I love you, and I'll love our baby. You can count on that."

She felt the last of her reservations evaporate as he held her tight against him.

"A baby!" he said. "What a great way to end the year! I can't wait."

"It takes a few months, you know," she said, amused by his delight.

"When can I tell the world?"

"Can we keep it our secret for a while? I'm superstitious."

"*Do I have to?*"

"You can do it."

"I can do it for you," he said, kissing her, "but it won't be easy."

CHAPTER 26

Jamie surprised them with lobsters to celebrate New Year's Eve and his first anniversary with Frannie. Jack and Andi had offered to babysit so they could go out for their anniversary, but they preferred to stay home with the babies.

After dinner the kids went off to watch a movie until the midnight festivities. Jack followed Jamie upstairs to check on the sleeping twins while Andi helped Frannie clean up from dinner.

"No wine for you tonight, Andi?" Frannie asked.

"Not in the mood." Andi avoided Frannie's probing stare as she dumped lobster shells into the trash. She hadn't had any wine in more than a week, but in all the holiday craziness, no one had noticed.

"Since when are you not in the mood for wine?"

"My stomach was bothering me earlier."

"Kind of like my stomach was bothering me that day at your house when you thought the same thing I'm thinking?"

Andi's heart began to race. "What's that?"

"You're pregnant, aren't you?"

"Who's pregnant?" Jamie asked as he returned with Jack right behind him.

Jack laughed. "I don't believe it! You didn't even last a day!"

Andi wondered how she'd ever expected to keep a secret in this group.

"And you thought *I'd* be the weak link," Jack added.

"I didn't say a word." Andi tossed a look at Frannie. "She guessed."

Frannie clapped her hands. "I knew it!"

Andi shushed her. "I'm only like five minutes pregnant, so we aren't saying anything for a while…or we weren't going to."

Frannie hugged her. "We won't tell, will we, Jamie? I'm so glad our kids will have a cousin almost the same age. Congratulations, Jack," she said, hugging her brother.

"Bit of a surprise, old man?" Jamie asked Jack.

"Just a bit, but a good one." Jack put his arm around Andi. "The best kind of surprise."

"God, I hope you're not sick like I was," Frannie said with a shudder.

"I wasn't with Eric, so I probably won't be this time, either."

That turned out to be wishful thinking. Andi was so sick one day that Jack stayed home from work because he was afraid to leave her alone. He called Jen to let her know Andi wouldn't be into work. They'd had no choice but to bring Jen in on the secret. Fortunately, her assistant was happy to cover for her. They'd told the kids she had a stomach bug but would have to tell them the truth if it kept up much longer.

Jack ran a cold cloth over her face after she was sick again. "Let me call the doctor."

"No." Even her voice was weak. "I don't want to end up in the hospital."

"But you can't keep anything down. I can't stand this. It can't be good for you or the baby."

She started to get up from where they sat on the bathroom floor. "It's stopped now. I want to go back to bed."

"Wait." Scooping her up, he was alarmed by how light she was. He carried her back to bed and tucked her in with an extra blanket since she was shivering. She was asleep the moment her head hit the pillow, and he prayed the vomiting had passed—for now.

Except for Frannie, he'd never heard of pregnancy making anyone as sick as Andi had been for weeks now. Clare was never sick with the girls, and Andi hadn't been with Eric, either. While she slept, he went downstairs to call Frannie.

"How's she doing?" Frannie asked.

"Not so good. I don't know how much longer this can go on."

"Months, I'm afraid."

Jack groaned. "I can't imagine that."

"Try to get her to eat—anything. Just a few crackers and some ginger ale or something like that. I found it helped to feed it, as odd as that sounds."

"I don't think she could keep it down."

"It might be time to call Dr. Abbott."

"She's afraid she'll end up in the hospital."

"I felt better after. Maybe you should call her anyway."

"I think I will."

"Let me know if you need anything. I know how miserable this is."

"Thanks, Fran."

He hung up and stared at the phone for a minute before he picked it up again to call the doctor. Andi wouldn't be happy, but he wasn't risking her or the baby.

Jack went back upstairs and found her awake but still in bed. He brushed her hair back from her face. "How you doing?"

"I've been better."

"I called the doctor."

She whimpered. "I told you not to."

"I'm worried, Andi. You have to be dehydrated by now. Dr. Abbott wants me to bring you in."

She began to cry. "I don't want to."

"Honey, think of the baby. Frannie was much better after she was in the hospital. Let them help you. *Please*. I can't stand seeing you so sick. It's scaring me."

A sob hiccupped through her. "Okay."

Jack got her dressed and into the car without her doing a thing, which was just as well since she couldn't have anyway.

Dr. Abbott took one look at Andi and ordered IV fluids.

Frannie had recommended the doctor to Andi, who was now almost through her sixth week. They'd postponed their trip to the Virgin Islands until she felt better, and the one-year anniversary of the day she moved in with Jack had passed without fanfare earlier in the month.

"Not feeling too hot, Andi?" Dr. Abbott asked after the nurses had settled Andi into a bed.

"No," Andi said.

"We'll do what we can to help you, but you've got another few weeks to go before you'll start to feel a lot better."

Andi groaned.

"*Weeks?*" Jack asked.

"I'm afraid so. Moms who're this sick are often stuck with it for the first trimester. But we'll get you some fluids to help you get your strength back. I also want to do a quick ultrasound to check on your little one. Nothing to worry about, though. Be right back."

Andi reached for Jack's hand. "I hope the baby's okay."

"I'm sure he's fine."

"You're quite sure it's a *he*."

"There's *no way* it can be another girl."

"Actually, there's a fifty-percent chance."

"That much?" He brought their joined hands to his lips. "I'm so sorry you're going through this, honey."

"This is what I get for being stupid."

He chuckled as a nurse wheeled in the ultrasound machine.

The doctor came back a few minutes later to take a look. She tilted her head and moved closer to the screen.

Jack never had seen anything resembling a baby on those screens, and this time was no different, but he could make out a strong heartbeat. And then he saw another one. He looked up at the doctor just as she looked down at him.

"So Frannie tells me twins run in your family," she said with a smile.

"That's what my mother says," Jack stammered.

"Looks like she's right." The doctor pointed to the screen so Andi could see. "One heart there, another there."

Andi let out a gasp and tightened her grip on Jack's hand. "*Two?*"

Amused by their shock, the doctor held up two fingers. "Although, if they're identical, it's sheer luck, not heredity."

Jack let out a long deep breath he hadn't realized he was holding.

Andi eyes were riveted to the screen. "Can you tell whether they're boys or girls?"

"It's still early—you're right at six weeks. This one here could be a boy." She pointed to the screen. "But don't buy anything blue just yet. They look great. Their heart rates are very strong, and they seem to be growing, despite how sick Mom's been. That means we have to make sure you're getting what you need, Andi, because they'll take what they need from you."

"She can't keep anything down," Jack said, still trying to comprehend that there were two babies.

"We'll do what we can for you while you're here. In about four or five weeks, you should start to feel much better."

"I hope so," Andi said, her eyes still glued to the monitor.

"Will she be able to carry twins?" Jack worried that Andi's willowy frame wouldn't be able to withstand the weight of two babies.

"The last couple of months will be tough, but she'll be fine."

The doctor left them, and Andi turned to Jack, her eyes wide with disbelief. "First Jamie and Frannie and now us," she marveled. "What're the odds?"

"I can't believe it. We had no idea how strong the twin gene is in our family."

"Oh my God, Jack! We're going to have *six* children!"

"Two are technically adults," he reminded her. "I was all set for five. What's one more?"

"It must've happened the night of the gala."

"Which is entirely fitting, since the hotel brought us together, and now it's brought us the twins."

They told the kids the news when Andi ended up in the hospital for several days to treat the dehydration. Like Frannie, Andi felt much better after she was released and soon turned a corner where she was sick in the morning but better by noon. By April she finally felt well enough to go on their long-postponed trip to the Virgin Islands.

The night before they left, Andi called her mother to tell her about the babies.

"*Twins?*"

"That's what they tell me, Mother. Apparently, they run in Jack's family. Remember last summer when his sister had twins? Ours will be born just about a year after theirs."

"You'll sure have your hands full."

"I hope you'll come be part of it. I'll need your help."

"I'll be there, Andi, and I'll bring Auntie Lou with me. Will you still send Eric out this summer?"

"Jack will probably bring him. I'll be disappointed to not get to see you, but I won't be going too far from home by then." Eric planned to spend two weeks with his grandmother in July, and Andi had promised him he'd be home long before the babies were born in late September—if she made it that far.

"We're looking forward to it."

"So is he. Well, I'd better go. Jack and I are leaving tomorrow for a week in the Virgin Islands we've had planned since December. I've been so sick with this pregnancy we couldn't go until now." She hadn't told her mother she'd been in the hospital, knowing how she'd worry. "But I'm much better now and looking forward to lounging in the sun."

"Send me a postcard, honey. Enjoy yourself."

"I will. You take care, Mom. Give Auntie Lou a hug from me," Andi said and ended the call.

"How'd she take it?" Jack asked.

"Amazingly well. I think she's totally stunned."

He put his arms around Andi from behind and patted her belly, which had begun to pop out. "These guys were a big surprise to all of us."

"I need to go to bed if we're going to make that flight." They were flying out of Boston at noon, and since the airport was almost two hours away, a limo would pick them up at eight. Jack's parents had driven up from Connecticut earlier in the day to stay with the kids while they were gone.

"Let's go." He swept her up and carried her through the house, pretending to be staggered by the weight of her.

"You'd better knock it off, buddy. That will *not* be funny in a few months."

"You'll have to get your own ride then." He tried to kiss her, but she wouldn't let him after that crack.

They flew to St. Thomas and took a short ferry ride across the sound to St. John.

The resort had every imaginable amenity, but they were content to do nothing after the nonstop activity since their last vacation on Block Island the summer before.

Andi sipped a virgin piña colada late one afternoon as they reclined on a double lounge at the beach. Thankfully, there'd been no nausea or vomiting during their vacation. "I'm in heaven," she said.

"Me, too. We should just move here." He took in the sleek black one-piece bathing suit that covered the bump in her once flat belly. Her breasts spilled out the top.

"Oh, yeah, right, I can see it now—living with our *six kids* on the beach." She glanced over at him and caught him checking out her newly voluptuous figure. "Quit ogling, Jack!" She tugged at the top of her suit.

He laughed at her. "Why can't I enjoy the best part of getting you pregnant?"

She rolled her eyes. "Just don't get used to them. They're temporary."

"That doesn't mean I can't enjoy them while they're here, does it?"

"Do you think about anything else?"

"Not lately." He stretched and yawned. "As a matter of fact, I'm getting very sleepy. I need you to take me in for a nap."

"You just had a 'nap,'" she reminded him.

"That was hours ago, and I need my rest." He got up to offer her a hand. "Plus, I'm starting to freckle in this sun."

She snorted with laughter and let him help her up. "We can't have that now, can we?"

The moment they were in their room, Jack nudged the straps to her bathing suit off her shoulders.

When her breasts sprang free, Andi folded her arms over her chest self-consciously.

He moved them aside. "Don't. I want to see you."

"They're ridiculous," she said, her face burning with embarrassment.

"No, they're not." He skimmed her suit down over her hips and rested his hand and then his lips on the baby bump. "I didn't think it was possible for you to be more beautiful, but seeing you pregnant with my babies... You're so incredibly sexy, and I want you all the time." He sat her down on the edge of the bed and knelt in front of her. Cupping her breasts, he captured an extra-sensitive nipple between his lips and skimmed his tongue over it.

Her head rolled back as she grasped his hair and moaned.

He eased her back so she was lying down, and still he kept up the tugging, sucking, and licking until she writhed beneath him. His lips were hot on her belly as he coasted over the bump and then went lower. Propping her legs on the edge of the bed, he nuzzled at her and teased her with his tongue. His fingers found her slick and ready for him, and as he slid them gently into her, he brought his tongue down hard against the spot that pulsed with desire.

Andi cried out when the orgasm blasted through her. She was still coming when he shed his bathing suit and entered her. Struggling to accommodate him, Andi moved her legs farther apart to take him deeper.

He was careful not to rest too much weight on her. "I need to keep you pregnant from now on," he whispered against her lips.

Her arms tightened around him. "Is that so?"

"I didn't think there could be any more between us, but lately…"

"Mmm, I know." She arched into his thrusts. "Jack…"

"What, honey?"

Her eyes fluttered closed. "I think I'm going to…again…"

He reached down to where their bodies were joined and sent her soaring.

Clutching him tightly from within, she took him with her.

They flew home tanned, rested, and relaxed after a week on St. John. Spring had sprung in their absence, and bright yellow forsythia bushes were in full bloom when they arrived late on Sunday afternoon.

The car dropped them off at home, and Jack gathered up their bags. He wouldn't let Andi carry anything heavier than her purse.

They were surprised when Jamie came out of the house to help with the bags. "Hey, guys. How was it?"

"Fabulous," Jack said. "We only came back because the law says we have to take care of our kids. What're you doing here?"

"Come in, and I'll tell you."

Jack sent Andi a questioning look.

She shrugged.

"What's going on?" Jack asked, beginning to sense something was wrong. "Where is everyone?"

"Jack, Clare's in the hospital. She's developed an infection. They've got her on high-dose antibiotics, but she's not doing too well."

Andi reached out to Jack.

"What kind of infection?" Jack asked, his heart in his throat. "How long has she been there?"

"They think it's a blood infection. She spiked a high fever yesterday, and they took her in last night."

"Why didn't you call me? I would've come home."

"We figured you probably wouldn't get here that much sooner if we called you last night."

"I need to get over there."

Andi hugged him. "Of course, Jack, you should go to her."

"Will you be all right?"

"I'm fine. Go on ahead. Jamie, will you take him?"

"Yeah. I stayed here with Eric while Jack's parents took the girls to the hospital. He's upstairs playing in his room, but he's waiting for you."

"Thanks, Jamie," Andi said.

"I'll call you," Jack said. He gave her a distracted kiss on the cheek and followed Jamie out the door.

Jack's parents brought the girls home just after midnight.

"How is she?" Andi asked Madeline after the girls had gone upstairs to bed.

"Not good. The fever hasn't broken, despite massive doses of antibiotics." Madeline's shoulders slumped. "I'm afraid we're losing her."

"I'm so sorry." Andi hugged the older woman. "Can I do anything for you?"

"I don't think so, honey. I need to get to bed and so do you. You need your rest."

"I was hoping to hear from Jack. How's he holding up?"

"He's upset but resigned. He knows Clare might be better off dead than living the way she has for the last three years."

"Is anyone with him?"

"Frannie was in earlier, and she took Clare's mother home with her, but Jamie stayed. He won't leave Jack, honey. Don't worry. Why don't you get some sleep?"

"I'll try," Andi promised as she kissed Madeline good night.

Jack never came home that night, and she didn't see him again until ten the next night, when he came in looking like he was about to drop.

"Hey." She got out of bed to go to him.

"Hi." He hugged her and kissed her cheek. "Don't get too close. I need a shower." He was still wearing the same clothes he'd worn home from St. John.

"I don't care." She held him for a long time. "Why don't you let me draw you a bath?"

"That sounds good, thanks." He sat on the bed to take off his shoes.

She turned on the water in the Jacuzzi, went back to sit next to him and brushed the hair off his tanned forehead. St. John already seemed like a long time ago. "Are you hungry?"

He shook his head. "Jamie made me eat earlier. He was with me the whole time. I kept trying to get him to go home, but he wouldn't."

Andi had never seen Jack looking more exhausted. "I'm glad he was there. How is she?"

"Still the same. They can't figure out why she's not responding to the antibiotics." He rested his head on her shoulder and ran a hand over her pregnant belly. "How are you, hon?"

"I'm fine, Jack. Don't worry about me."

"I do worry about you. And them." He bent to press a kiss to the bump.

She ran her fingers through his hair, her heart aching for the pain she felt coming from him. "We're fine, sweetheart."

"I'm going to soak for a bit."

"I'll be right here."

"Good." He kissed her and went into the bathroom.

Clare's fever lasted twelve days. Just when Jack was certain he was losing her for good this time, she opened her eyes and looked at him.

PART IV

Backstroke: Swimming forward while
appearing to go backward.

CHAPTER 27

When Clare opened her eyes and focused on him, Jack jumped to his feet. He could see right away that the vacant look she'd worn in her eyes for the last three years was gone, and she was alert. "Clare? Oh my God! Can you hear me?"

"Mmm."

He ran to the door yelling for a doctor.

"What's wrong?" she whispered when he returned to her bedside and took her hand. "Why am I here?" Her voice was weak and rough, but it was Clare. Until that moment, he hadn't realized how much he'd missed the sound of her voice.

He leaned over the bed rail to kiss her forehead. "You've had a bad fever." Tears rolled unchecked down his face.

"Why are you so upset? Was I sick for a long time?"

"Yes," he said hoarsely.

"I'm thirsty."

The doctor came in, followed by two of the nurses who'd been caring for her in the hospital. Jack asked one of them to go get Kate, Maggie, Clare's mother Anna, and her nurse Sally in the cafeteria.

"Clare, how're you feeling?" the doctor asked.

"Weak," she replied in a raspy whisper. "And very thirsty."

"She can have some water," the doctor told the nurse.

The door opened, and Kate flew into the room ahead of the others, who were close behind. She took one look at her mother and burst into tears.

Clare attempted to hold a weak hand out to her middle daughter. "Kate, honey, come here."

Kate fell sobbing across her mother's chest.

Clare struggled to get her hand up to comfort Kate, but the years of inactivity had rendered her muscles almost useless, despite the physical therapy she'd received nearly every day.

Maggie stood frozen in place.

Sobbing softly, Anna moved to the other side of the bed and kissed her daughter's forehead. "It's so good to hear your voice."

As the surreal scene unfolded before him, Jack couldn't believe what they'd spent three years hoping for had finally happened. Then he remembered he needed to call Jill at school, so he stepped into the hallway.

"Hi, Dad. What's up?"

"Honey…"

"Did Mom die?" she asked in a tiny voice.

"Quite the opposite. She's awake. Really awake."

"*What?*"

"I want you to come home, but if you don't think you can concentrate on driving, get someone to bring you. Do you hear me?"

"I'm leaving right now. I'll be careful," she assured him. "She's really awake?"

"Honest to God."

"I can't believe this. I'll be right there."

"See you soon, honey."

He ended the call, went back into Clare's room, and approached Maggie. "Honey, do you want to see Mommy?"

Maggie's eyes were glassy with shock, and Jack cast a worried look at Sally, who kept an arm around Maggie.

"Sweetie?" He took Maggie's hand to lead her to Clare's bedside.

Clare inhaled sharply. "Maggie! *You're so big!* How long have I been here, Jack? I don't remember being sick."

Maggie stared at her mother while Kate sobbed quietly.

"Guys, can you give me a few minutes with Mom?" Jack asked. "Just a few, and then I'll bring you right back in, okay?" He helped Kate up and gave her Maggie's hand. "Will you call Frannie and Jamie?"

Kate wiped her face and nodded.

Anna ushered her granddaughters into the hallway.

When they were alone, Jack took Clare's hand again and perched on the edge of the bed. He had no idea how to tell her what she needed to hear.

"Jack, what's wrong with me? Why is everyone so upset?"

He rested his forehead on their joined hands for a moment trying to collect himself and then looked up at her. "Almost three years ago, you were hit by a car."

She gasped when he told her the date. "*Three years?*"

"You suffered a massive head injury, and they said you probably wouldn't recover. But you have, and it's a miracle."

"That can't be. I was with the girls…"

"It happened in the mall parking lot. Do you remember anything about it?"

"Nothing." She looked away from him to process what he'd told her. "Where's Jill?"

"In college at Brown. She's been here, but she had to go back yesterday."

She turned back to him, eyes wide. "She's in *college?* Oh my God."

"I called her. She'll be here soon." His emotions again overwhelmed him, and his voice broke. "So much has happened, Clare." For the first time in an hour, he thought of Andi at home, pregnant with his babies, while he talked to the wife he'd thought lost to him forever. The magnitude of it all settled like a block of ice in his gut.

"The girls are so grown up."

"You'd have been so proud of them. We visited you often."

"Where was I?"

He pushed the button on her bed to help her sit up a bit. "We had you at home with us for more than a year. After a while, when we'd accepted you weren't coming back to us—or we thought you weren't—I bought a place for you. I hired nurses to take care of you. I didn't know what else to do."

She hung on his every word.

"I'll tell you something else that's new," he said with a smile. "Frannie married Jamie more than a year ago, and they had twins last summer."

She gasped. "They did not."

As if on cue, they walked into the room. Frannie put a hand over her mouth and shook her head in disbelief when she heard Clare talking.

"Oh, it's true!" she cried as she moved to Clare's bedside. "Oh, thank God!"

"You guys are *married*?"

Blinking back tears, Jamie showed Clare his wedding ring. "Married with eight-month-old twins, Owen and Olivia." He took a photo out of his wallet and held it up for her.

As she gazed at the picture of the babies, tears leaked from Clare's eyes.

"Frannie saved my life," Jack said. "She lived with us for the first year and a half and took care of the girls. I don't know what I would've done without her."

"Thank you," Clare whispered to Frannie, who gripped her hand.

Kate stuck her head into the room. "Dad? Can we come back in?"

"Of course."

Maggie still looked shocked, but this time she walked right over to her mother's bedside.

"It's okay, Maggie," Clare whispered.

"Are you going away again?"

Heartbroken for her, Jack put his arm around his daughter.

"Not if I can help it," Clare said.

Maggie reached for her mother's hand. "I missed you so much."

"I'm sorry, baby. I'm so terribly sorry."

The door burst open again, and Jill came flying in, stopping short when she saw her mother talking to Maggie.

"Jill," Clare whispered. "Oh, you're all grown up! Come here so I can see you."

Jill took a few steps forward, and Jack moved to let her in. She leaned down to kiss her mother's cheek and shook with sobs.

Jack ran his hand over Jill's back.

The doctor on call returned with the neurologist who'd treated Clare early on.

"Mr. Harrington, I'm Dr. Blake. I consulted on your wife's case."

Recalling their grim meeting weeks after the accident, Jack shook his hand. "I remember."

"This is quite a development." Dr. Blake smiled and nodded toward Clare, who was absorbed in the girls' excitement. "It's nothing short of a miracle."

"Indeed," Jack said, his stomach aching at the implications.

"As you can imagine, we're anxious to fully examine her," Dr. Blake said. "But I can see this isn't the time."

"She's been through a lot, especially over the last twelve days," the attending physician added. "We don't want to wear her out."

"I'll clear the girls out soon, and the rest of us will go, too, so she can get some rest," Jack assured the doctors.

He let the girls visit with their mother for another half hour before he sent them home. Frannie and Jamie took Anna home with them for the night, and they promised to come back the next day.

After everyone left, Jack returned his attention to Clare. "Are you tired?"

She nodded, and her eyes filled again. "I can't stand that I missed three years of their lives, *our* lives."

"I can't imagine how that must feel." He paused and debated, not sure if it might be too soon... "Clare, there was something kind of odd about your accident."

"How so?"

He hesitated again, but three years of horrible uncertainty won out against his better judgment. "When the car hit you, it seemed like you didn't really try to get out of the way."

"I don't understand."

"The girls said you seemed to let the car hit you. I didn't believe you'd do something like that until I saw the video—"

"What video?"

"From mall security."

"I want to see it."

"That's not a good idea. It's very upsetting."

"I want to see it," she insisted.

Reluctantly, he said, "I'll bring it with me tomorrow."

She had a faraway look on her face as she tried to think back. "I remember shopping with the girls, but nothing else from around that time. It's all fuzzy."

"Don't worry too much about it tonight, okay?" He smoothed her blonde hair back from her brow and kissed her forehead. "We'll figure it all out. You need some rest." He stood up and reached for his jacket. "I'll be back in the morning."

"Jack?"

He turned to her.

"What else did I miss?" she asked, her brows knitted with worry.

Swallowing hard, he said, "Nothing that won't keep until tomorrow."

On his way upstairs, Jack checked on each of the girls, who were euphoric to have their mother back, but he could tell they were still processing it, as he was himself. He walked up the spiral stairs to find Andi packing a small bag. Eric sat on the bed with his backpack next to him. His eyes were red from crying.

"What are you doing?" Jack asked.

Andi kept her head down. "I'm taking what we need for a couple of days. I'll send for the rest later."

He put his hand over hers to stop her. "A couple of days? Where're you going?"

Eric watched them intently.

"To the hotel until we find something more permanent," Andi said. She still hadn't looked at him.

"You aren't leaving, Andi. This is ridiculous. You're pregnant. This is your home," he said desperately. He signed to Eric, asking him to please take his bag and wait for them in his room. "Everything's all right, buddy. I'll be down in a minute, okay?"

Eric nodded and did as Jack asked.

Jack turned back to Andi as she zipped the small black bag. He took her hand and tugged her down next to him on the bed.

"Look at me." He used his finger on her chin to compel her to meet his gaze. Her eyes were broken, and he wanted nothing more than to wrap his arms around her. "I don't want you to go."

"This is her home, and she'll want it back now. It was on loan to me, just as you were."

"*No*, Andi. I was never on loan to you. I *love* you. I want you to stay." He tried to embrace her, but she moved out of his reach. "I need you."

"You're married, Jack. My mother was right all along."

When she stood, he took hold of her arm.

"Your wife will need you, and she won't want to share you. Please don't make this any harder than it already is." She tugged her arm free and picked up her bag.

"So that's it? You're just leaving? What about Eric? What about our babies?"

"Eric will want to see you, but that'll be up to you. We'll work something out when the babies are born. Please, Jack. Let me go now."

Brushing past him, she took her bag and went downstairs to Eric's room, where she put his backpack on him and took his hand.

"Honey, listen to me," Jack said. "Let's talk about this. We don't have to decide anything tonight." He followed her through the darkened house to the front door. He caught up to her and put a hand on the door so she couldn't open it. "Please."

She reached for the door handle, and when she pulled to open it, he removed his hand to let her.

Eric looked up at Jack with big blue eyes. "I love you," he signed.

"I love you, too. I always will." Jack felt like his heart had been ripped out and run over as they walked to her car.

Andi opened the back door for Eric, helped him into his booster seat, and got into the driver's seat.

Jack walked up to the door before she could close it. "Andi, honey. Please don't go. I love you so much."

"Bye, Jack." She closed the door and drove off without looking back.

He watched her taillights fade out of sight and then took off running. He ran for miles without paying any attention to where he was or where he was going, emerging from his daze to discover he was on the beach. Exhausted, he fell to his knees on the sand and screamed, with agony and joy at war inside of him.

When he had screamed himself hoarse, he wept.

Andi got Eric settled in bed and tried again to explain why they'd had to leave Jack's house.

"He loves you," she reminded her son as she brushed tears off his cheeks. "He'll be in touch with you. I know he will."

"It won't be the same as when we lived there."

"No, baby, it won't."

After he'd nodded off, still sobbing in his sleep, she tucked the covers up around him and walked out of his room. Swiping at fresh tears of her own, she blamed herself for his heartbreak. She'd allowed him to love a man and a family that didn't really belong to them.

They were staying in the suite Infinity provided to each of its property managers so they could live at the hotel if they wished to. Since she hadn't needed the suite before now, it'd been available to guests. Fortunately, it wasn't booked that night. They could stay there as long as they needed to, but she hoped to find more of a real home for Eric and the babies when she caught her breath.

Andi sat on the sofa and put her feet up on the coffee table, seeking relief for her swollen ankles. When she ran her hand along her burgeoning waistline she felt a first flutter and recognized it as a baby moving. In that moment, the dam broke, and her gut-wrenching sobs would've woken Eric if he could've heard them. She cried until there was nothing left, and then she slept on the sofa, dreaming of Jack. But when she reached out to him in her sleep, she couldn't get to him. Suddenly awake and forced to absorb the blow all over again, she dragged herself to bed and drifted back into a fitful sleep. This time she dreamed of two beautiful babies with dark hair and gray eyes.

Jack spent a sleepless night worrying about Clare as well as Andi and Eric. In the morning, when he tried to reach Andi at the hotel, she refused his call.

Despite their protests, he sent the girls to school. They'd missed enough days since Clare had been in the hospital, and he promised they could see their mother right after school.

Jill wondered how she'd ever concentrate on her classes, but he encouraged her to try.

"Where're Andi and Eric?" Maggie asked over breakfast.

"They went to stay at the hotel for a few days."

"They can't live with us anymore, can they?" she asked sadly.

The pain must've shown on his face, because Kate intervened.

"Let's go, Maggie," Kate said. "I'll drop her off, Dad."

"Thanks." He kissed them good-bye. "I'll see you after school."

Feeling as though he were trudging through quicksand, Jack walked into the hospital and took the elevator to the seventh floor, where Clare had been moved from the intensive care unit after her fever broke.

Propped up in bed, she lit up when he came in.

"Good morning. Did you sleep well?" He kissed her cheek and set a dozen yellow roses in a crystal vase on the table. Her dazzling blue eyes were filled with life, the way he remembered them, and he was once again so grateful to have her back. But when he thought about what he had to tell her, his stomach ached and his heart raced.

"The flowers are gorgeous. You look exhausted. Didn't you sleep?"

"I'm fine. Have the doctors been in yet?"

"I talked to the neurologist, but I couldn't tell him much." Her voice was already stronger than it'd been the day before. "The psychiatrist will be in later this morning to talk about the accident."

"What about rehab?"

"They're arranging for me to go to a facility here in the hospital to help me regain my mobility. I'll probably have to be there for quite a while, maybe even six months. And it's still possible I may never walk again." She looked down at her hands. "I'll have to relearn everything, from the simplest of tasks to the more complicated," she continued. "They said the physical therapy you made sure I got is the only reason I have a chance to fully recover."

"They told me that at the very beginning, so I always insisted you be cared for as if your condition were temporary. I'm glad now that I did."

"You had hope, Jack. Even in what must've seemed like a hopeless situation."

"Not always." He dropped into the chair by her bed. "I did for the first year. After that I had to stop hoping. The girls were a mess. I was a mess. I had to get back to taking care of them. I couldn't rely on Frannie to fill in for me anymore."

"I can't imagine what it was like for you."

"It was the worst thing that's ever happened to me, Clare. There're no words to describe how helpless I felt." He'd felt almost as helpless the night before watching Andi leave with Eric and his babies.

Clare tried to move her hand to take his. "I'm sorry."

He reached out to save her the trouble. "Don't be sorry. Nothing about this is your fault."

"Did you bring the video?"

"I did, but are you sure you want to see it? It haunted me for months after I first saw it. I'm not sure that showing it to you is the right thing to do. Maybe we should ask the psychiatrist."

"I want to see it. Please."

He got up to put the disk into the DVD player that was part of the hospital TV. After he turned it on, he went back to Clare's bedside and took her hand. The whole thing happened quickly, but there was no denying she'd had time to get out of the way.

"Play it again."

"Clare—"

"Please, I need to see it again."

Jack released her hand and got up to replay it.

Her eyes were riveted to the screen until the moment of impact when she was forced to look away. "Did I have other injuries?" she asked in a small voice.

"You broke your left arm and leg, your liver was lacerated, and your spleen had to be removed."

"I don't understand. Why didn't I move?"

"I don't know, honey. I've asked myself that question over and over again for three years."

"What in the world was I thinking? The girls must've been so traumatized."

"I got them into counseling as soon as I saw the video. I felt so bad because I didn't believe them when they first told me how it happened."

"I don't remember anything about it. I've been racking my brain trying to think of a reason why I'd do something so foolish."

"I'm sure you'll remember in time." He took a deep breath, knowing he couldn't put this off any longer. "Listen, there's...um...more I need to tell you— things I don't want you to hear from anyone else."

"What things?"

He struggled to find the words to tell her about his life without her, the choices he'd made, and the other woman he loved. "After I'd had you at home for a year, Frannie talked to me. She helped me see that having you in the house in that condition was hurting the girls, and me, too. The hospital bed, the equipment, the nurses in and out. Our home was like a hospital. We couldn't go on any longer the way we were. So we moved you to your own place. That was the lowest point for me. I felt like I'd failed you so completely." Battling the overwhelming emotions that came with revisiting the darkest time in his life, he glanced down at the floor.

"Jack," she said softly. "You didn't fail me."

"Frannie and Jamie helped me so much, and I'm so grateful to them. I guess by helping me, they found each other after all those years of being friends. In a way, you can take some of the credit for them being married."

"That's something I still can't get over."

"Sometimes I still can't believe it myself, and I was there." He smiled and forced himself to continue. "I finally went back to work. I'd been gone fourteen months by then. Can you imagine that?"

"You never even wanted to take two weeks at a time for a vacation."

"I proved I'm totally dispensable."

"Did you feel better when you went back to work?"

"It was good to get back to some sense of normalcy. We'd been hired to design and build an Infinity hotel on Ocean Drive. I took over that project, and it gave me something positive to focus on. Of course, I had the girls, too, and they gave me a reason to get up and keep moving every day." He hesitated and must have looked pained, because she tuned right into his dismay.

"What is it?"

His heart beat frantically, and his hands were suddenly damp. "The hotel project moved forward, and through our work with Infinity, I met someone, Clare."

"What do you mean?"

"I met a woman in their Chicago office, and we…I fell in love with her."

Clare closed her eyes and sucked in a sharp deep breath.

Jack had to force himself to press on. "I hadn't been dating or anything like that, so this wasn't something I was out there hoping to find. It found me, and I struggled with it, believe me. Everyone was pushing me to get on with my life. They told me I had to live, that you'd want me to be happy."

"This woman," Clare said haltingly.

"Her name is Andi."

"Do you still love her?"

"Yes."

Clare turned away. "Where is she now?"

"She and her son have lived with us for more than a year."

Her gaze whipped back around to him. "In my house? You brought her into *my* house? The house you built for *me*?"

He had to remind himself that to her it was like five minutes had passed, not three years. "I thought about moving when they came to live with us, but we didn't think it would be good for the girls to leave their home after they'd already lost you. So we stayed there."

"Are we divorced?"

"No." He held up the hand where he still wore her ring. "It never crossed my mind, Clare. I never would've done that. Ever."

"So my return from the near-dead must not have been an entirely pleasant surprise for you," she said with a bitter edge to her voice.

"That's not true! I'm thrilled to have you back, and the girls are, too. It's what we've wanted for three long years. But we had to stop spending every day hoping it would happen so we could find a way to live without you."

"Does she plan to continue living in my house when I get home from the hospital?"

"She left last night."

"No wonder why you look so devastated and exhausted," she said in an accusatory tone.

He couldn't deny that, so he said nothing.

"Is there anything else the rest of the world already knows?"

The look on his face must have told her there was more—much more.

She gasped. "Do you have children with her?"

"Her son is important to me. And we're expecting twins in September." He looked her in the eye as he said it. He refused to be ashamed of his relationship with Andi or of the children they were having together.

"Please go."

"Clare…"

"Please. Just leave me alone." She turned to look out the window.

"We need to talk about this.

"Not today."

Jack stood there for a long moment before he turned and left the room.

CHAPTER 28

Frannie stepped off the elevator on the seventh floor and found her brother in the waiting room, hunched over, elbows on knees.

"Jack? What's wrong?"

"Hey, Fran."

"Why aren't you in with Clare?"

"She asked me to leave."

She sat next to him. "Oh. You told her."

"I keep telling myself that to her everything's the same as it was three years ago. It's like time stopped for her. But it didn't stop for us."

"Let me talk to her. Why don't you get out of here for a while? Mother and Dad are with the twins, but they want to come in later to see Clare, so someone will be here."

"The girls will be in after school, too."

"You can spend some time with Andi. How's she coping?"

"She left," he said, still unable to believe all that had happened.

"Where'd she go?"

"To the hotel, for now anyway." He sighed. "She won't see me, won't take my calls."

"Damn."

"My thoughts exactly."

"What'll you do now?"

"Go to work, I guess. I don't want to be at home without Andi, and I'm not welcome here right now. I'll come back later. Hopefully, Clare will cool off."

"I'll talk to her, and then I'll take a ride over to see Andi, just to make sure she's okay."

He brightened. "Oh good. Thanks, Fran."

"Go on ahead. It'll all work out. Don't worry."

"You have a lot more faith than I do. It's a goddamned mess, and I have no one to blame but myself."

She rested a hand on his arm. "Don't do this. You did the best you could every step of the way during this whole thing. You never made promises you couldn't keep to anyone, especially not to Andi."

"I promised I'd never leave her alone with the babies."

"And you won't. Don't drive yourself crazy second-guessing every decision you've made over the last three years. I know it seems awful right now, but you'll figure something out."

"I wish I could be as optimistic."

"I'll call you later." She kissed his cheek and pushed him toward the elevator.

As she walked into Clare's room and saw that her sister-in-law had been crying, Frannie wasn't sure if she'd be welcome, either. "Hi."

"Hey."

"I hear you're having a rough day."

Clare shrugged and played with her fingers but didn't look at Frannie.

Frannie sat next to Clare's bed. "Could I tell you something? And will you listen to me as someone who loves you?"

"I guess."

"I've never seen anyone suffer the way my brother did after your accident. There were times when I feared he'd die of a broken heart. He was a wreck, for a long, long time. Even after all the doctors told him there was nothing they could do for you, he continued to hope. It was only after he finally gave up hoping that he allowed himself to grieve for you, and that's when I worried we'd lose him, too."

"I get he's a man with needs, and three years is a long time, but did he have to bring her to live in *my* house? With *my* children? What kind of woman moves into another woman's home and family like that?"

"The loveliest kind of woman," Frannie said with a sigh. "She was nice to your girls, cared for them as best she could, and never once tried to take your place with them. She left everything in your home just as you had it, except for the room she shared with Jack."

"That's *my* room! I can see you love her, and I suppose I'll have to hear my own children tell me they love her, too. You say she didn't try to replace me with them, but she's probably managed to do a good job of it anyway."

"You're way off, and you're being terribly unfair to Jack."

"Unfair to *Jack*? While I was lying in a hospital bed, he was off starting a new life with someone else, and *I'm* the one being unfair?"

"Yes, Clare, you are," Anna said from the doorway.

"Even my own mother doesn't see how wrong this is? My husband has another family! Another family with another woman!"

"I love you, Clare, and I'm so glad you've come back to us," Frannie said. "But he's my brother, and I love him, too. I can't stay here and listen to you talk about him like this after witnessing the way he suffered over you. I hope you'll think long and hard before you judge him too harshly on choices he made in an unbearable situation. You know he'd never have hurt you on purpose. Not in a million years."

Frannie squeezed Anna's arm on her way out the door.

Anna moved to her daughter's bedside. "She's right, you know. You can't imagine what this was like for him. Where is he anyway?"

Clare turned away from her mother. "I asked him to leave."

"You're making a terrible mistake, Clare. He wants to be here with you. He hardly left your side for two weeks when you had that terrible fever."

"Have you met her?" Clare asked, turning back to look at her mother.

"A couple of times."

"And you just sat idly by while he moved another woman into *my* house—the house he built for *me*—and said nothing about it?"

"It wasn't up to me to tell him how to live his life, Clare. He'd done everything he could to find help for you and to make sure you were well cared for. By the time he told me about her, I was almost relieved to see him getting on with his life. He'd suffered so terribly. It was painful to watch, for all of us." She reached for Clare's hand. "He never forgot he had a wife. He was there all the time to see you, and if you don't believe me, ask Sally. She's been your nurse for years. She'll tell you."

Clare continued to stare out the window.

"I know this is a terrible shock, but it's just not possible for you to know what it was like for him, for me, for everyone."

"He has another family, Mom." Clare's voice caught on a sob. "My Jack has someone else."

"I'm so sorry, sweetheart." Anna hugged her daughter. "I wish there was something I could say."

Shaken by the scene in Clare's room, Frannie left the hospital. She tried to put herself in Clare's place to understand what a shock it would be to wake up after three years to find out the whole world had gone on without you. But that didn't give her the right to speak so harshly about Jack.

On the way to the hotel, Frannie decided she'd check in with Jack after she'd seen Andi. She parked at the hotel, hoping this visit would go better than the last one.

Frannie spotted Jen Brooks across the lobby and went over to her.

"Hi, Jen, I'm not sure if you remember me. I'm Jack Harrington's sister, Frannie Booth. We met at the gala."

Jen shook Frannie's extended hand. "Nice to see you again. Do you know what's going on with Andi? She and Eric are staying here, and she asked me to drive him to school today for her. She sent him out to meet me, but I haven't seen her."

"She left Jack last night."

"Why?" Jen asked, her face slack with shock.

"His wife has recovered."

Jen gasped. "That's amazing. But God, Andi…"

"Could I see her?"

"She's in the manager's apartment. I tried to get her to talk to me about an hour ago, but she didn't answer. Maybe you'll have more luck." Jen pointed t he way.

"Thanks, Jen."

Frannie made her way across the lobby and up the stairs to the manager's apartment at the far end of the east wing. She knocked on the door. "Andi, it's Frannie. Open the door, honey." She knocked some more, and when the door finally opened, Frannie was shocked by Andi's shattered expression.

"What are you doing here?" Andi tied her silk robe tighter across her rounded middle.

"I wanted to check on you. May I come in?"

Andi stepped aside to let her in.

"Are you all right?"

"I will be."

"Jack's worried about you."

"He needs to focus on his family right now."

"You're his family, too, Andi. You and Eric and the babies."

"His wife needs him." Her voice, like her eyes, was dull and lifeless. "That's where he should be."

"What'll you do?"

"I'll stay here and work and take care of Eric while I wait for the babies."

"Can I do anything for you? Anything at all?"

"You've been such a good friend to me, Frannie. There's one thing I need."

"Anything."

"I can't see you. I can't see any of you. I have to make a clean break if I'm going to get through this. Please tell the girls, too. I love them, but I can't see them. Try to make them understand. They need to be thinking of their mother, and they don't need to be worried about me."

"What about the babies? And Eric?"

"I'd never keep the babies from their father, and Eric is counting on seeing Jack. But I won't. Please tell him that. I won't see him, and I won't take his calls. Not now. I'll contact him after the babies are born."

"You can't just cut him off this way."

"I have no right to him. I probably never did. His wife won't understand that he has another family waiting in the wings, so I'll make it easy for him— and for her."

Frannie couldn't believe how Andi had summed up Clare's exact sentiments.

"Please ask him, ask everyone, to respect my feelings."

"If you're sure that's what you want."

"I am."

Nothing in Andi's firm tone betrayed the terrible pain she must've felt as she said the words, but Frannie saw it in her eyes. "I'm sorry. I know this must be awful for you."

"I'm not sorry those beautiful girls have their mother back or that Clare has her life back. And I'll never be sorry for the time I spent loving your brother and living with him. It was the highlight of my life." Her voice finally broke.

Frannie took a step toward her, wanting to offer comfort, but Andi held up a hand to stop her.

"Don't. Please. I appreciate you coming, Frannie, but you have to go now."

Frannie opened the door. "We love you and Eric very much. I'm just a phone call away if you ever need me."

With tears in her eyes, Andi nodded but said nothing more as Frannie let the door close softly behind her.

CHAPTER 29

Clare was transferred to the rehabilitation center at Newport Hospital, and the doctors marveled at her speedy progress. She was eating solid food and beginning to regain some of the strength she'd lost, although it would be months before they'd know for sure about any limitations. Until then she was confined to a wheelchair and worked for hours each day with physical and occupational therapists.

The girls spent as much time as they could with her and even participated in her therapy. Clare allowed Jack to visit with the girls, since they were so delighted to have their family back together, but she'd yet to speak to him again about Andi. In the meantime, she tried to cope with the fact that he'd brought another woman into his life and had two children on the way with her.

She'd had several sessions with her psychiatrist and discussed some of her feelings about her husband with him. While the doctor was sympathetic to her plight, he urged her to remember how much can happen in three years' time.

The psychiatrist wanted to try hypnosis to jog her memory of the accident and the months leading up it, hoping to find something that might explain why she'd failed to act on the most human of impulses—to get out of the way of imminent danger. Clare promised to think about it, but for some reason, the idea frightened her.

After a few weeks in rehab, she asked to see Jill and Kate alone, and they came in together on a Sunday afternoon—the one day off she had from the grueling physical therapy sessions.

"Why did you want to see us, Mom?" Jill asked.

"I want to know more about what happened when I was…sick. I don't know who else to ask, so I'm asking you."

Kate and Jill exchanged glances.

"I want to know about Andi."

Kate shifted in her seat. "What about her?"

Clare felt guilty for putting them through this, but she had to know more. "What does she look like?"

"Um, she's tall and has long, dark, curly hair, and brown eyes." Jill described a woman who was her mother's physical opposite in every possible way.

"She sounds very pretty."

"She is," Kate said. "And she's nice, too. She was nice to us."

"I'm sure she was. She wanted your father, and the three of you came with the package," Clare said in a bitter tone that stunned her daughters.

"It wasn't like that," Kate said in a whisper.

"What was it like, then?"

"I'm not sure what you want us to say," Jill said, glancing at her sister. "We liked her, she was nice to us, she was good to Dad, and her son's adorable. He's deaf, and we learned sign language so we could talk to him."

Clare's heart broke all over again as she listened to Jill describe the family they'd created—with someone else playing the starring role. "Where're they now?"

"We haven't seen them," Kate said. "Andi moved to the hotel. She's the manager there, and she told Frannie she doesn't want to see us."

"She said that?" Clare asked, amazed by the other woman's gall. First she moved in with her children and then she rejected them?

"She wants us to focus on you," Jill said. "She never took your place, Mom. We wouldn't have let her, and besides, she never tried."

"She took my place with Dad," Clare said sadly. "Does he love her? Really love her?"

The girls exchanged nervous glances again, and Clare realized she'd put them in an awful position. She could also see the answer to her question on their faces. "Never mind. Don't answer that."

Jack walked into the room and was surprised to see the girls. He'd hoped to find Clare alone. He hadn't had the chance to talk to her alone since the day she asked him to leave her room. She'd only been civil to him since then because of their daughters.

"Hi there," he said as the girls got up to leave. He noticed how uncomfortable they seemed when they kissed their mother and told him they would see him later at home.

"I feel like I interrupted something," he said to Clare when they were alone.

"We were just talking. What're you doing here?"

"I came to see my wife. Is that all right?"

She shrugged. "Free country."

He sighed. "How long are we going to do this?"

"Well, let's see, your lover hasn't even had your twins yet, and you'll have eighteen years to raise them, so maybe by then I'll be used to the idea."

"I haven't seen or talked to her in weeks."

"Where's your heart, Jack? Is it here with your sick and broken wife? Or is it with your beautiful mistress who's pregnant with your twins?"

She'd caught him off guard with the question, and he had no easy answer. How could he explain his heart was in both places?

"I can tell just by looking at you where your heart is, and it isn't here. Why don't you go to her and leave me alone? I'm sorry I ruined all your plans by waking up."

Jack fought to control the burst of anger that blazed through him. "I'd do anything to change what happened to you, but I can't. I couldn't then, and I can't now. I waited *years* for you to come back to me. I'm here with you because it's where I want to be, and it's where I belong. But I won't be here for long if you keep this up."

"That'd be a nice easy way out for you, wouldn't it? You could tell people your wife was different after her long coma. She didn't want you anymore."

"It doesn't seem like you *do* want me anymore, Clare. Andi's gone. She's moved out of our home." He paused to absorb the burst of pain that came with that statement. "I'll play an active role in the lives of her son and our babies when they're born. If you can accept that, we have a chance to move forward together. I don't want to throw away more than twenty years of marriage like it meant nothing to me, because it did. You know it did."

"Does it still?"

"Of course it does. But you have to decide if you can live with everything that happened while you were sick and the fact that those three children are in my life to stay, no matter what."

"I don't know if I can do that. I just don't know if I can."

"Be sure to let me know when you decide."

"Would you go back to her if things don't work out between us?"

"I don't know that she'd have me."

"But you'd try?"

"I'm not thinking about that right now. I'm focused on helping you get well and trying to save our marriage."

"I need some time to process it all."

Hands on his hips, he studied her. "I'm so sorry I hurt you, Clare. I wish there was some way to convey to you how very lost I was without you."

"Until you met her."

"Even then... I never stopped missing you or thinking about you or wishing for your wisdom with our girls."

"I have a lot to think about."

"No matter what happens between us, we have three amazing kids to consider. I understand you're angry with me and hurt by the choices I made, but they've been through so much. Can we please try to be civil to each other for their sake?"

"Yes," she said softly. "Of course."

"Whenever you're ready to talk about what's next for us, I'm here."

"Okay."

Andi threw herself into her work and taking care of Eric. She kept her days long and busy so she'd drop into bed exhausted every night. More often than not, though, the pain she'd run from all day would catch up to her at night when her yearning for Jack would leave her breathless.

As she moved into her sixth month of pregnancy, the babies were more active than ever, and she knew she needed to take it easy. But she couldn't imagine having all that free time to think about how badly her life had gone off course. So she kept up the frenetic pace. She also needed to find a permanent place for them to live, but she and Eric had settled into a routine at the hotel, and she was too tired at the end of every day to even think about house hunting.

Eric lived for his weekly visits with Jack. Andi set up the visits by email and arranged it so she didn't have to see him when he picked up Eric or dropped him off. Until one day, about a month after she moved out, she wandered upstairs to the window in her suite to watch the parking lot when she knew Jack would be leaving with Eric. She was hungry for just a glimpse of him, and her heart raced when she saw him holding hands with her son on the way to the car.

Jack opened the passenger-side door for Eric and helped him into the backseat. He shut the door and then looked up, as if drawn to the window.

She gasped when he caught her watching him. Frozen, she couldn't bring herself to move and was startled to feel the overwhelming connection to him even from a distance. The pain of losing him sucked the air from her lungs, as fresh as it'd been the day she left him. Unable to bear the sadness she saw on his face, she moved away from the window and let the drapes fall back into place.

Still rattled by the encounter, she returned to her office off the lobby. She was walking fast and not paying attention to anything around her until she heard her name. She spun around and suppressed a groan when she saw her mother and Aunt Lou.

"Mom! Auntie Lou! What are you doing here?" *Oh, dear God.* She hadn't told her mother about leaving Jack or anything that'd happened.

"We decided to surprise you," Betty said.

"Well, you did." Andi forced herself to be cheerful as she hugged and kissed them.

Betty stood back to pat Andi's pregnant belly. "Let me get a look at you. You're so *big!*"

"Gee, thanks," Andi said with a dry chuckle. "There *are* two of them you know."

"Should you still be working?" Lou asked as she took in the hustle of the busy hotel lobby.

"I'm fine for another month or so. Why don't you come on back to my office so we can catch up?" Andi's stomach churned with anxiety. *How will I ever tell her that she was right all along?*

They followed Andi into the office where she offered them coffee or sodas. They both chose diet sodas, and Andi opened the cans for them. "I can't believe you guys are here."

"We wanted to see where you're living, dear," Betty said. "I hope you don't mind."

"Of course I don't. You're staying here I hope."

"We are," Lou said. "We wanted to check out your new hotel, too. It's so lovely."

"Where's Eric?" Betty asked.

"With Jack." Andi felt a pang at the sound of his name rolling so easily off her tongue, as if everything were normal. "He'll be dropping him off here in a while." She paused before she added, "There's something I need to tell you…"

"Is something wrong, honey?" Betty asked. "I knew you didn't look quite right. Is it the babies?"

"Everything's fine with the babies." She took a moment to summon the courage to tell her mother the truth. "I'm not with Jack anymore." It hurt to say the words.

Betty gasped. "Since when? *Why?*"

"His wife's medical situation improved. She's recovering, actually. I moved out about a month ago."

"Oh, honey. Oh God, I'm sorry—not that his wife is better, but what it means for you…"

"You tried to tell me," Andi said with a shrug that did nothing to betray her true feelings. "I didn't listen."

"You followed your heart."

Andi looked at her mother with surprise.

"I have to give you credit for that. But what'll you do? You'll have three children!"

"I'll keep doing what I've always done. I'll work and take care of my kids and do the best I can. That's all I can do." She still found it hard to believe she'd be doing it all without Jack and the girls. She missed them almost as much as she missed him.

"Will you come home to Chicago?" Lou asked.

Andi shook her head. "My children's father is here, and he'll want to be involved with them—all of them."

"He still sees Eric?" Betty asked.

"Every week. He won't let Eric down, and he won't let these children down, either." Andi ran a hand over her pregnant belly. "That's the one thing I'm sure of."

Betty reached out to caress Andi's face. "Are *you* all right, honey?"

The loving gesture put a lump in Andi's throat. "I'm better than I was. I miss them all so much. But sometimes I think I'll die from missing him." Tears spilled down her cheeks, and she swiped at them, refusing to give in to the helpless grief again.

Betty hugged her daughter. "I'm so sorry."

"It's such a mess, and you told me it would be."

"Not another word about that," Betty said. "We'll get through this together. Don't you worry."

Andi spent a lovely week with her mother and aunt. Eric was thrilled to see them. They spoiled him rotten and insisted on pampering Andi, too.

They left promising to be back to help when the babies arrived. Andi appreciated that her mother offered only support and never came close to saying, "I told you so," even though Andi wouldn't have blamed her if she had. Who could've predicted just how big of a mess she'd find herself in?

Andi was working in her office the day after her mother and aunt went back to Chicago when the front desk called to tell her she had a visitor. She walked out to the lobby and was surprised and thrilled to find Kate waiting for her.

"What're you doing here?" Andi asked as she hugged the girl.

Kate gaped at the round bulge under Andi's black dress.

Andi laughed at her reaction. "I know. I'm explosive." The babies seemed to get bigger by the day, and she found herself frequently out of breath as they squeezed closer to her lungs. "Come on back."

"I know you told Frannie you don't want to see us," Kate said as she followed Andi to her office.

"Oh, sweetie, it's not that I don't *want* to see you. I just think it's better for you to focus on your mother. But I'm so glad you're here." Andi patted the sofa. "Come, have a seat."

"I'm glad I came. I've missed you. We all have."

"I've missed you, too. But I'm so happy for you girls that your mother's getting better. You must be thrilled to have her back."

"I guess," Kate said with a shrug. "I mean, we are, don't get me wrong. It's just that she's…well… She's different. She seems mad a lot of the time."

"I'm sure she's very angry to have lost so much time with you all. I can't imagine how that must feel." Andi didn't mention the far more obvious reason for Clare's anger.

"I wanted to tell you that Dad has agreed to give me a year to pursue my music. He'll even pay for me to have an apartment in Nashville. I have to wait until I'm eighteen in November, and then I've got a year to get a recording contract. If I can't do it in that time, I have to go to college."

Andi was proud of Jack and knew how far he'd had to bend to reach such a compromise with Kate. He'd never have the animosity with his daughter that he'd experienced with his own father. "That sounds very fair. Are you happy with it?"

"It was hard for him, I get that, but I can do it. I know I can."

"I have no doubt. You certainly have the talent. What'll you do until November?"

"That's what I wanted to talk to you about. I was wondering if I could work here. I know you planned on outdoor entertainment in the summer, and it'd give me a great chance to practice before a live audience and to try out some of my own songs."

"Have you talked to your father about this?"

Kate nodded. "He said I have to ask you, that it's your decision."

So he put the ball in my court, Andi thought. Kate would be a terrific draw on the verandas, each of which had outdoor bars in the summer. She decided to hire her to work during the day when the crowds at the bar were less likely to be rowdy, since she was still only seventeen. However, Andi wanted Kate to believe in her talent and not see the job as a favor.

"My assistant manager, Jen Brooks, is in charge of hiring the entertainment. You'd have to try out for her. Is that okay?"

Kate's eyes widened. "Now? I have my guitar in the car."

"Do you have something ready?"

"I've been working on a few new things—well, really they're old things, but you know how I love the old stuff."

Smiling at Kate's enthusiasm, Andi walked around her desk to open the door. "Let me find Jen and see if she can do it now. Go get your guitar and meet me back here."

She surprised Andi with a hug. "Thanks, Andi."

Kate went to get her guitar, leaving Andi staggered for a moment by intense longing for Kate, her sisters, and their father. She shook it off and went to find Jen, who was happy to be brought in on Andi's plan to hire Kate but to make it look like it was Jen's decision.

"Wait until you hear her play," Andi said. "It won't be any decision at all."

They escorted Kate into the deserted lobby lounge, which wasn't due to open for another hour. Kate set up her guitar and plugged it into the amplifier on the small stage while Jen flipped on the power to the microphone.

Watching Kate tune her guitar and do a quick sound check on the microphone, Andi was startled by her professionalism. She hoped Jack was prepared for his daughter's success.

"This was originally done by Carole King," Kate told them.

As Kate began to play, Jen looked at Andi as if to confirm she'd been right about the young girl with the powerful talent. She played "Now and Forever," a song about a perfect love that had gotten away and the memories it left behind.

As Kate played the last notes of the song, Andi stood, muttered an apology, and rushed from the room. The song had pushed its way past her stiff resolve and punctured her broken heart by summing up exactly how she felt without Jack.

She ran through the crowded lobby where one employee after another called out to her with concern. Pushing through the large double doors leading to one of Jack's stone verandas, she hurried across the lawn. Andi knew she shouldn't be running in her condition but was unable to stop herself until the grass met the rocky shore. There she sank to the grassy lawn and sobbed.

That's where Kate found her.

She sat next to Andi. "I'm so sorry. I didn't even think before I played that song. I was so excited to have the chance to try out."

Andi reached out to hug her. "I'm sorry I reacted that way. At least you don't have to wonder if your music touches people."

Laughing softly, Kate said, "If it helps at all, I don't think my dad is in much better shape."

Strangely comforted to hear that, Andi held Kate close to her for a moment longer. "You got the job."

Kate's eyes lit up. "I did?"

"You're going to knock 'em dead, Kate, here and anywhere you go. I have no doubt. Someday when you're rich and famous, remember who gave you your first job."

"I'll never forget," Kate said softly. "I'll never forget any of it."

"I won't, either." For however long it had lasted, they'd been a family, and neither of them would ever forget it.

"You can start on Sunday at two. Wear whatever you're comfortable in."

Kate hugged her again. "Thank you so much, Andi. Walk you back inside?"

"I think I'll stay out here for a few more minutes." Andi looked out over the vivid blue waters of the bay where a few sailors enjoyed one of the first warm spring days. "I'll see you soon."

After Kate walked away, Andi reclined on the grass and let the sun warm her face. The babies moved relentlessly, reminding her that life went on even when it seemed the world had ended.

CHAPTER 30

Clare's heart beat fast, so fast she couldn't catch her breath. He grabbed her, and she shrieked.

The car was hurtling at her, offering relief, blessed relief.

Big, blond, handsome, vicious. He was going to hurt her. Then she was on the floor. He was on top of her, tearing at her clothes.

Clare screamed when he forced his way inside her, but there was no one there to hear her. It went on forever, or so it seemed. The red-hot pain tearing through her took her breath away. Then he was done. Somehow, though, he managed to do it again, but this time she blacked out when his crushing weight stole the air from her lungs.

The car came at her—a blue sedan, the driver hunched over the wheel. *Take me away. Make it all go away.*

The monster dragged her to her feet, ordered her to get dressed. Her clothes were torn, but she put them on anyway. He made her drive him back to his car. Before he got out, he grabbed a handful of her hair and pulled her so close his spit hit her face. "If you tell *anyone*, I'll kill one of your kids. You won't know when, and it won't matter to me which one, but I'll do it. Breathe a word of this to anyone and one of your girls is dead, you got me?"

Mute with shock and fear, Clare nodded.

322 | MARIE FORCE

"Try to get me locked up," the monster continued, his once handsome face now twisted and ugly, "I'll get someone to do it. Don't fuck with me."

Clare nodded again, desperate to be rid of him.

He released her abruptly and was gone.

The car came at her faster this time. *Not in front of the girls. Don't do this to them. I'm so tired. I can't move. He can't hurt them if I'm dead. Take me. Take me away. Make it all go away.* She saw Jack's handsome, smiling face, and then blackness—beautiful, peaceful nothingness.

Clare woke up screaming and crying.

Nurses came running into her room.

"Clare, honey, what is it?" one of them asked, brushing the hair off her sweat-soaked forehead.

On the verge of hysteria, Clare fought for every breath.

"I'll get the doctor," the other nurse said. "She'll give you something to settle you."

"*No!*" Clare shrieked. "I want to remember." She'd had the dream before. The car was new, but she remembered dreaming about the attack for months afterward. She'd been haunted by it but had suffered even the nightmare in silence to protect her children.

"What do you remember, Clare?" the doctor asked.

Clare forced herself to take a deep breath in an attempt to calm down but couldn't stop the shaking of her hands or the hard, relentless beating of her heart. "I want Jack," she whispered. "Will you please call my husband?"

Jack ran through the dark hospital parking lot. His first thought when the phone rang in the middle of the night was that Andi had gone into labor early.

The nurses were waiting for him when he reached Clare's floor in the rehabilitation facility.

"What happened?"

"She had a nightmare and woke up screaming and crying. She's asking for you."

He ran past the nurse's station to Clare's room. She wept quietly while one of the nurses held her hand and tried to comfort her. When Jack stepped in, the nurse got up and left the room.

"Clare, honey, what's wrong?" he asked, taking the hand the nurse had been holding.

"I remember," she whispered. "The car... I did it on purpose."

"No. You wouldn't have done that to the girls."

"I should've told you then." She shook her head as fresh tears spilled down her cheeks. "Maybe none of this would've happened if I had."

Confused, he said, "Told me what, honey?"

"I was raped. By a client in an empty house I was showing him."

Stunned, Jack stared at her.

"I didn't tell you or anyone because he told me he'd kill one of the girls if I did. I believed him." She choked on a sob. "His name was Sam Turner, and all the girls in my office were jealous because he was so handsome, and I got to work with him."

Jack moved onto the bed and put his arms around her. "I would've killed him, Clare. Before he could've harmed anyone else in my family." He struggled to contain the rage that threatened to consume him. "I would've killed him."

"I wanted so badly to tell you," she whispered against his chest. It was the first time she'd let him hold her in all the weeks since she'd come back to them. "But all I could think about day after day was what I'd do without one of my girls. One day I'd imagine Maggie was gone. The next day it would be Jill and then Kate. The way he said it, I know he would've done it."

"I never would've let that happen."

"I was so afraid, Jack. That day, in the parking lot when the car was coming at me, all I saw was a way out."

"Clare…" He gasped, stunned by her admission. "But the girls, they were standing right there. How could you do that to them?"

"I thought of them. I thought of you. But I couldn't make myself move. I just knew if I were gone, they'd be safe. They'd all be safe."

"Had you been thinking about that?" He chose his words carefully. "About taking your own life?"

"It never crossed my mind until that car was coming at me."

"I don't know what to do for you. What do you want me to do?"

"Call the police, Jack. I want to report a rape."

"Are you sure?"

She nodded. Her tears were gone, and in their place was anger and determination.

Jack asked for Sergeant Curtis, the officer who'd investigated the accident, and he arrived thirty minutes later.

"Good to see you, Jack." Curtis shook his hand. "I was delighted to hear about your wife's recovery."

Jack introduced him to Clare, and she told him her story, gave a description of the man, and the approximate address of the house where the attack had occurred. She said her office kept logs of agents' appointments, and they'd have the exact address and be able to confirm the dates she'd worked with Sam Turner.

"I'll be honest with you, Clare," the officer said. "I believe you. I believe your story. I want you to know that." He paused before adding, "But there's no physical evidence to tie him to the crime." Curtis had cringed when she said she threw away the clothes she'd been wearing. "The crime scene itself was long ago compromised. *If*—and that's a very big *if*—we're ever able to bring this case to trial, it'd be your word against his. An entirely circumstantial case."

Jack stared at him, incredulous. "So you're saying this guy can rape my wife, terrorize her by threatening the lives of our children, and he could get *away* with it?"

"We'll do our very best for you," Curtis said. "I'll have his name run through all the databases, and I hope we'll find he's in the system somewhere. If we can nail him, Clare, we'll do it."

"Thank you, Sergeant," Clare said as she clutched Jack's hand.

"I want your guarantee that my daughters will be safe," Jack said, mentioning that Jill was at Brown. "If he finds out we told the police—"

"We'll have people everywhere they are. I'll contact the Brown University police, too. Nothing will happen to them," Curtis assured them as he got up to leave. He promised to keep them informed.

After he left, Clare's psychiatrist, Dr. Baker, came in to talk to her. Clare told her story yet again, and when she was finished, she had only one question for the doctor.

"Did I try to commit suicide?" she asked in a small voice.

"I think it might've been more of a post-traumatic stress reaction."

Clare was relieved to hear that.

"We'll need to spend a lot of time talking about this," Dr. Baker said. "But right now, you need rest more than anything. I'll be back in later to check on you."

When they were alone, Jack said, "I need to talk to the girls so they'll know why the police are around."

"I should tell them myself," Clare said.

"I'll take care of it. I don't want you to worry about anything."

"Thank you for coming when they called you. I appreciate it."

Jack sat back down on the bed and took her hand. "Of course I came. There's nothing I wouldn't do for you."

"I haven't been very nice to you, and I'm sorry for that." She reached up to caress his face. "Jamie was in the other day. Did you know that?"

Surprised by the loving gesture, Jack shook his head. Jamie hadn't told him.

"We had a long talk. He said a lot of what everyone else has said, but he also told me how worried you were that people would think you'd forgotten about me if you pursued a relationship with Andi. It helps to know you thought of me."

"I never stopped thinking of you."

"But you had a life with her," Clare said sadly. "You're in love with her. I don't know where I fit into that."

"We don't need to talk about it now. You've had a tough night. Why don't you try to get some sleep while I go talk to the girls about the police?" He pulled the covers up around her and leaned down to kiss her. "I'll be back."

"She was *raped?*" When his legs seemed to fail him, Jamie dropped into a chair.

Jack had stopped by Frannie and Jamie's house on his way back from seeing Jill in Providence. The girls had been stunned to hear what'd happened to their mother. He'd glossed over some of the details to keep them from being terrified. As much as it pained him, he'd had to tell them they'd been threatened so they would be vigilant and ask for help if they needed it. Maggie was still afraid the bad man would make good on his threats, but after Jack pointed out the police car in the driveway, she felt better.

"Why didn't Clare say anything?" Frannie asked, shocked by the news.

"He threatened the girls." Jack told them about Turner's threat.

"*Son of a bitch,*" Jamie swore under his breath.

Jack relayed what Sergeant Curtis said about the lack of evidence and how they should be prepared for Turner to possibly get away with what he'd done to Clare.

"No way," Frannie said. "There's no way we can let that happen. All the pain and grief… He can't get away with it."

"I just keep asking myself, where was I when this was happening to her?" Jack asked. "What was I doing?"

"Quinn could tell you if you wanted to know that badly," Jamie replied warily.

"You might be better off not knowing," Frannie said.

Jack ran his hands through his hair, pacing the room as the rage he'd kept under control all morning came to a boil. "I never thought I'd be capable of killing someone, but if you put him in this room right now—"

"I'd help you," Jamie said.

Sergeant Curtis was in Clare's room when Jack arrived the next morning.

"Did you find him?" Jack asked as he sat next to Clare and took her hand.

"He's in prison in California. Apparently, he did almost the same thing again. He was convicted of raping a Realtor in San Diego about a year after he attacked you. The case is eerily similar to what you described yesterday, Clare."

"At least he's locked up," Jack said, relieved.

"He's serving a life sentence with no chance of parole for aggravated assault and first-degree sexual assault." Curtis explained that with convictions in two prior felonies in California, Turner had been put away for life under the state's three strikes law. He'd been on parole and running from the law when he raped Clare.

"We can file new charges in your case, and we'd have a better chance of securing a conviction since we're dealing with a pattern."

"Why do I hear a 'but' in there?" Clare asked.

Curtis paused for a moment before he continued, appearing to choose his words carefully. "Your family has already been through a terrible ordeal. A trial would be ugly. You'd have to recount the assault in open court, and his lawyer would do a number on the fact that you remembered it in a dream. He's in prison for life, and he'll never be paroled. You have to weigh whether adding another conviction to his rap sheet is worth the toll on you and your family."

"It isn't," she said without hesitation. "He's in prison, and he's not getting out, so there's no way he can do this to someone else. If I pressed charges, I'd have to worry that he'd make good on getting someone else to hurt my kids. I won't take that risk."

"If you're sure," Curtis said.

"I'm sure," Clare said, tightening her hold on Jack's hand.

"For what it's worth, I think you're doing the right thing. A rape victim is often put on trial herself, and I'd hate to see that happen to you when you've already been through so much."

"Thank you, Sergeant, for believing my story yesterday, for moving so quickly to protect my family, and to find Turner," Clare said. "I appreciate it."

"I'm just glad we were able to find him."

"Could you keep this out of the papers? My family has been through enough without this being splashed all over the news. We'll tell the people we want to know."

"Consider it done," Curtis said as he got up to leave. "I admire your courage, Clare. Good luck to both of you."

Jack stood to shake the detective's hand. When Curtis had gone, Jack turned to her. "I'm proud of you. I'm sure you want your own justice, but you made the right decision."

"He's taken enough from me—from all of us. I'm ready to get back to living. I could never do that with a trial and his threats hanging over my head. I want to put it behind me."

"Then that's what we'll do." Jack squeezed her hand and kissed her cheek, hoping he could do it for her.

Andi groaned and rolled over, dropping her feet down to propel herself out of bed. Now in her seventh month, she couldn't imagine being any bigger than she was already. *It'll get worse before it's over*, she reminded herself. Her back screamed from the weight of the babies, and Dr. Abbott had threatened to put her on bed rest if she didn't slow down on her own. She hadn't seen Jack in three months and still found that continuous activity was the only thing that kept her mind from wandering back in time.

Eric was in Chicago for a longer-than-expected stay, since Andi was either working or exhausted and was almost too big to fit behind the wheel of her car to take him anywhere. Betty had flown to Rhode Island right after school ended to pick up her grandson for a month-long visit. Andi figured it was his best hope for a fun summer and was grateful for her mother's help.

Kate had been a big hit from her first day at the hotel, and the bar manager reported there were now regulars who showed up on the days she was working just to hear her play. Andi enjoyed having her around, and Kate usually stopped in to see her before her shifts.

Andi waddled back downstairs after a brief rest, knowing Kate would be coming by soon. She'd just made it back to her office when Kate came in looking all grown up in a white blouse, black skirt, and high-heeled sandals.

"Hey, how's it going?" Kate studied her with concern.

Andi knew her face was probably devoid of color and, as usual, she was out of breath. "Just had a nap to get me through the afternoon. How are you?"

"Good." Kate cast a nervous glance over her shoulder. "Um, listen, my car's in the shop having the new stereo put in so my dad brought me to work today. He was wondering if he could talk to you. Just for a minute…"

Andi's heart fluttered. "I don't think that's such a good idea."

"Please, Andi. He needs to see for himself that you're okay."

Andi didn't have the strength to argue. "Fine. Send him in. I'll see you later?"

"I'll come by before I leave." Kate went to get her father.

Andi's heart went from fluttering to hammering as she sat behind her desk and waited for him. When he came in, she experienced the familiar surge of love that'd left her breathless long before twin babies were squeezing all the air from her lungs.

He leaned against the door frame as if he was afraid to step inside. "Hi."

She drank in the sight of him, hungry for as much as she could get. "Hi."

"Thanks for seeing me. How are you?"

She pushed back from her desk so he could see her huge belly. "Enormous and getting bigger every day."

His eyes almost popped out of his head. "Does it *hurt*?"

She smiled at his reaction. "Just my back, which is killing me, and I have the lungs of a three-pack-a-day smoker since these guys are taking up all the room." She patted her belly and told him the doctor had said everything was great at her last appointment. She didn't add that she'd chosen not to find out the babies' sexes, since she couldn't bear to hear that news without him with her.

"You've never been more beautiful. You're glowing."

"Like a nuclear reactor," she said with a dry chuckle.

He laughed.

"Do you want to sit for a minute?" She gestured to the chair next to her desk, and he came in, bringing his achingly familiar scent with him. "How are *you*?" Something about him was different, but she couldn't say what.

"I'm hanging in there." He told her what Clare had remembered.

"Oh, Jack. God… I'm so sorry. Poor Clare. What a terrible burden she carried all alone."

"She was too afraid to tell anyone, even me. I felt so helpless and enraged when I heard it that I realized I could kill him if I had the chance."

The hint of rage she'd seen in his eyes was the difference. "I don't doubt it." She wanted so badly to reach out to him that it took every ounce of willpower she had not to. "How is she now?"

"She's working really hard on her therapy—all of it. Knowing what happened seems to have fueled her desire to get better and to not let him win."

"Good for her. Kate told me Clare was able to attend her graduation."

"It was her first time out of the hospital. Kate's class asked her to sing, and Clare couldn't believe how good she was."

"Kate showed me her car, too," Andi said with a smile. Kate had received a yellow Beetle.

He chuckled. "Maggie put in an order for a red one when her time comes."

"Kate has become a big star around here. The guests love her."

"She's enjoying it so much. Thanks for giving her the opportunity."

"I should be thanking her. My bar receipts are way up since she started." Andi leaned her elbows on the desk to take some pressure off her back. "She told me what you agreed to let her do. It's a wise move, Jack."

"I hope so. The whole thing still freaks me out, but I guess I have to let her try it. I also have to work up the nerve to break the news to Clare that Kate's not going to college."

"If she's heard Kate sing, I'm sure she'll understand."

After a moment of awkward silence, he looked up at her with those potent gray eyes. "What'll we do about the babies, Andi? It's all I think about. I promised you I'd never leave you alone, and now…"

His tortured expression almost undid her cool composure. "Can we talk about it later? I just can't think about that right now." It overwhelmed her to imagine being alone with three young children. Even though she knew he would help as much as he could, it wouldn't be like they'd planned.

"I miss you so much."

His words and the emotion behind them pierced her heart. "Don't," she said softly. "You'd better go."

He stood to leave. "Will you promise to call me if you need anything? You have all my numbers."

"I will." She told him what he needed to hear but knew she never would.

CHAPTER 31

Andi was reviewing final plans for an upcoming wedding at the hotel when the phone rang. "Andrea Walsh," she answered as she looked over the menu the bride had chosen.

"Yes, hello, this is Clare Harrington."

The contract fluttered from Andi's fingers and landed on the desktop. "Hello," she said when she'd recovered her senses.

"I'm sorry to call you out of the blue this way, but I was wondering, could you maybe come by here to see me? I'd come there, but they're not letting me venture out on my own yet."

As her heart raced, Andi hesitated. "Of course. When would you like me to come?"

"The sadists they call therapists are done with me by three. Would four work?"

"Sure, that's fine. I'll be there."

"Thank you," Clare said and ended the call.

Andi sat back in her chair and wondered why Jack's wife would want to see her, of all people.

"I guess I'll find out soon enough," she said and went back to the contract but gave up a few minutes later when she'd read the same sentence for the fourth time.

Andi enlisted one of the hotel's drivers to take her into town. She'd given up driving when she couldn't push the seat back any farther and still reach the pedals.

The driver pulled up to the front door of the rehabilitation center and promised to wait for her in the parking lot.

"Thank you, Tom."

He held the door and gave her a hand out of the car. "My pleasure, Ms. Walsh. You take your time now."

"Don't have much choice there."

Inside she asked for Clare at the reception desk.

The nurse pointed the way down a long hallway. "Last room on the right."

"Figures," Andi muttered as she waddled to the room and knocked on the door.

Clare called for her to come in.

On first glance, Andi decided Clare looked just as she had in the pictures around the house but seemed more fragile after everything she'd been through. Her hair was longer than in the photographs and was still a rich blonde. But it was her eyes that caught Andi's attention. They were the same dazzling blue as Maggie's and Kate's. And just as Andi had been taken aback by Jill's striking resemblance to Jack, she could see Kate just as plainly in her mother.

"Thank you for coming," Clare said.

As Andi sat across from Clare, she hoped she'd be able to get herself out of the low chair. "It was no trouble."

"Somehow I doubt that."

Andi laughed in spite of the tension in the room. "I'm like a hot-air balloon these days."

"When are you due?"

"September twentieth. Two months to go."

"I'm sorry to drag you away from your work, but I wanted to meet you. I needed to meet you." Clare looked down at her hands as if she were nervous after summoning the other woman in her husband's life.

"I understand."

"My daughters speak highly of you."

"They're wonderful girls. You should be very proud of them."

"Maggie showed me some of her sign language. It's impressive."

Andi nodded in agreement. "She's as good at it as I am. She's been so great with my son, Eric. They all have."

"My recovery has left you in a terrible spot, and for that I'm sorry."

Astounded by Clare's generosity, Andi said, "You have nothing to apologize for, Clare. I heard about what happened to you. I can't imagine someone threatening my son like that. I'm glad to see you're doing so well now."

"I was up on crutches earlier today and even took a few steps."

"That's wonderful." Andi paused, choosing her words carefully. "I know it must've been awfully difficult for you to hear about me and the babies. I want you to know you don't need to worry about me. I won't interfere with your family."

"Jack will want to see the babies and your son."

"I'd never stand in the way of that, but I won't be lurking on the sidelines."

Clare crooked an eyebrow. "Won't you?"

"I'm afraid I don't understand."

"You're in his heart, Andi. I can see that in his stricken expression whenever your name is mentioned. You won't be on the sidelines. You'll be right in the middle of our lives." Clare spoke frankly and apparently without malice.

"I've seen him once in three months, and it was for ten minutes. He wanted to know how I was feeling. I haven't spoken to him other than to coordinate his visits with Eric. I'm hardly in the middle of his life."

"You underestimate him if you think he can walk away from you and your children and go back to the life we had together like you never happened. That's not who he is, but I probably don't have to tell you that. Besides, the life we had is gone now anyway."

"You don't know that yet. You have to give it some time. Your family's been through so much." Andi didn't know why she was trying to convince Clare to give her marriage a chance. It seemed like the right thing to do.

"I could give it from now until the end of time, but he won't stop loving you, and every time he leaves my house to see your children, I'll have to wonder if he's coming home to me because he wants to or because he has to. I don't want a husband who's so loyal he'll spend the rest of his life living with me because he promised he would when he's in love with someone else. After all that's happened to me, I want more out of the rest of my life than that."

Andi's racing heart slowed to a crawl. "What're you saying, Clare?"

"I want what I had. But since I can't have that now, I'm letting him go. Maybe you two will work things out. Maybe you won't." Clare shrugged. "I'm getting out of here in another month or two and going home. I have my girls, and someday maybe I'll go back to work. I don't know. I'll be all right, though."

"I don't know what to say," Andi said, flabbergasted.

"I'm glad you came and we had the chance to meet."

"I am, too." Andi struggled to her feet, overwhelmed by their conversation and Clare's strength. "I wish we'd met under different circumstances. We might've been friends." She extended a hand to Clare.

Clare took her hand and squeezed it before letting go. "Maybe someday we will be."

"Take care of yourself, Clare."

"You, too. Good luck with the delivery. I hope it goes smoothly for you."

"Thank you." Andi waved good-bye from the door and replayed their conversation on the long walk back to the car. Clare's generosity had been astounding. Andi had expected Clare to insist she never see Jack again, and she would've understood that. The one thing she never could've imagined was Jack's wife stepping aside. Andi's heart gave a happy flutter at the thought that maybe, just maybe, there might still be a chance for her and Jack after all.

Clare was working on a simple needlepoint sampler the occupational thera-pist had given her when Jack arrived at her room. He stood in the doorway for a minute and watched her. "Look at you go," he finally said.

"Oh, hi. Come in. I'm making a mess out of this." Seeming frustrated, Clare pushed the needlepoint aside.

"You'll get the hang of it again."

"I was standing up on crutches today."

"That's so great. I can't believe how far you've come in such a short time."

"I'm feeling every muscle, believe me."

"I'm sure you are. I got your message. I'm sorry I couldn't get here sooner. I was working in Boston today and then got stuck in traffic on the way home. You said you wanted to see me?" He came to see her just about every evening lately, but she'd called to make sure he came that night.

"Have a seat." She invited him to sit next to her on the small sofa and reached for his hand. "I have a theory," she said with a smile.

"And what's that?" He was relieved to see the Clare he'd once known reemerg-ing little by little.

"Do you know why we stayed together all those years when it seemed like everyone we knew was splitting up?"

"I always thought it was because we loved each other," he said, not sure what she was getting at.

"Yes, but it was also because neither of us ever wanted anyone or anything else. We were completely content with each other. That's not the case anymore, is it?"

As her words sank in, he looked down at the floor. He couldn't deny that when he lay awake, night after night, it wasn't his wife he longed for but the dark-haired beauty who'd stolen his heart the first time he ever saw her.

"I met her today."

His gaze whipped up to meet Clare's. "You *did*? How?"

"I called her and asked her to come see me. I like her. I didn't want to, but I do."

As he tried to imagine Andi and Clare engaged in a civilized conversation, he remembered Jill once saying almost the same thing about Andi.

Clare took a deep breath. "It's over for us, Jack."

"But—"

She held up a hand to quiet him. "You aren't to blame, and neither is she. The man who attacked me is the one to blame. I see that now. But we can't change the simple truth that you love someone else, and since I won't ask you to choose, I'm deciding for both of us. I've already contacted Coop and asked him to start the process," she said, referring to their friend and attorney. "I'll file, so no one can ever accuse you of leaving me for her. I won't have anyone belittling what we had together by dragging you through the mud."

"You had a busy day while I was in Boston," he said, astounded. "So that's it? That simple?"

"Not simple at all. It hurts like hell, but it's the only thing I can do. I can't spend the rest of my life with someone who wants to be somewhere else, even if you'd spend every day pretending otherwise if that's what it took to do the right thing. I know you'd never leave me, so I'm leaving you."

"Without even giving me a chance?"

"Would it matter? A year from now, will you feel differently about her?"

He shook his head as he realized she'd made up her mind. "What'll we tell the girls?"

"The truth—that too much time has gone by, too much has happened, and we couldn't go back. They'll understand. They lived it."

"I'll take care of you. You know that, don't you?"

"I know you will. All I want is the house and enough to pay the bills until I can get back to work. Jill and Kate will be in college. We can figure something out so Maggie spends time with both of us."

"None of that's a problem, but about Kate and college…" He'd put this conversation off long enough. "She's not going this year."

"What do you mean? Of course she is."

"I've given her a year to focus on her music. She's enormously talented. You saw for yourself at her graduation. She has one year from her eighteenth birthday to land a recording contract. If she doesn't, she has to come home and go to college."

"Come home from where?"

"Nashville."

"I can't believe you agreed to this! You know how I feel about them going to college!"

"Which is why I fought this at first. Then Jamie reminded me of what caused the terrible rift between my father and me. I didn't speak to him for years because he didn't understand that I needed to go my own way. I couldn't let history repeat itself. I wouldn't have been able to stand that with one of my kids. You weren't here, and I had to decide. I hope you'll respect my decision. She hasn't applied anywhere, so it's too late for September, anyway."

"I guess we can give her a year," she said, surprising him. "I'm not thrilled about it, but I remember how much your father hurt you. I don't want that for our children any more than you do."

"I appreciate that, and I know she will, too."

"You should know that when I talked to Coop today, I told him everything— about Sam Turner and Andi and the babies. While I don't care if anyone else does, I wanted him to understand why I'm doing this and why I want it done quickly." She paused and looked up at him. "You'll want to marry her before the babies are born."

"Clare—"

She took his hand again. "Thank you for all you did to care for me while I was sick, for making sure I had the therapy that's given me a chance to reclaim my life, for visiting and bringing flowers, and all the times you brought my girls to see me."

She'd obviously been talking to Sally and the other nurses who'd cared for her.

"Thank you for all the wonderful years we had together. Let's not have any regrets. We had a good run, but it's over now."

Filled with nothing but regret, he shook his head. "I never wanted us to end up this way, Clare."

"I know."

He reached out to hug her. "We'll talk to the girls together tomorrow?"

She nodded.

"I'll see you then." He stood to leave. "You know where I am if you need anything, right? Ever?"

"Yes."

Lingering at the door, he couldn't bring himself to leave.

"It's okay, Jack," she said softly. "Go."

When they gathered in Clare's room the next day to break the news to the girls, Maggie was sad, but Jill and Kate were resigned. They were old enough to understand how much had happened while their mother was sick and could see how it was impossible for their parents to get back what they'd lost.

"Will you marry Andi, Dad?" Maggie asked, and all eyes turned to him.

"Would you mind if I did?"

"Would *you*, Mom?" Kate asked.

"If that's what Dad wants, I wouldn't object, honey. The one thing you have to remember is that even after everything our family's been through, and now that Dad and I aren't going to live together anymore, we'll always love you guys. Nothing could ever change that."

"Where will I live?" Maggie asked in a small voice.

"You and I will still live in our house, and I'm sure you'll spend lots of time at Dad's house, too," Clare said.

"Where will you live, Dad?" Jill asked.

"I don't know yet, but wherever I end up, there'll be plenty of room for all of you," he assured them, and they were satisfied.

Drained after the emotional conversation, Jack went back to the office while the girls stayed with their mother to help at her afternoon physical therapy session.

Jamie and Frannie were returning from lunch when he pulled into the HBA parking lot.

"Do you guys have a few minutes? There's something I need your help with," Jack said as he walked in with them.

"Sure," Frannie said. "Jamie's parents are with the twins, so I've got the day off."

"Great, thanks," Jack said. "I have to make a phone call, and then I'll find you in Jamie's office."

After asking Quinn to join them, he went into his office and closed the door. He dialed Cooper Hayes's number.

"Jack, how are you?"

"Holding up, Coop. How are you? The family's well?"

"We're all doing fine. We were so happy to hear Clare's on the mend."

"She's making amazing progress. I heard she called you yesterday."

"She did, and it's a damned shame. I'm sorry for both of you. What happened to her... I guess I don't have to tell you."

"No, you don't." Jack still had trouble even thinking about it, but the white-hot rage he'd felt initially had abated somewhat as he tried to follow Clare's lead by putting it behind him.

"I was over to the hospital this morning, and she's filed the initial paperwork," Coop said. "Seems pretty straightforward. She's asked for the house, temporary spousal support, child support, and joint custody for Maggie and Kate, until Kate turns eighteen in November. That's about it."

"Not a problem. I'd also like to provide a cash settlement to ensure she's financially independent." Jack named a seven-figure sum that elicited a low whistle from Coop.

"That's very generous. I'll get the papers moving today. I understand there's a need for expediency."

"Yes," Jack said but didn't elaborate, knowing Clare had already told him the whole story. "I'd like to get the paperwork by the tenth. Does three weeks give you enough time?"

"No problem. I'll get it moving for you."

"Thanks, Coop. Before I let you go, can you recommend a good private investigator?"

CHAPTER 32

Andi awoke early on the twenty-fourth of August and moved to take some of the pressure off her aching back. The pain in her lower back had become almost unbearable overnight, but it was nothing compared to the pain in her heart as she waited weeks without a word from Jack.

Surely by now Clare had told him she was leaving him. Had she changed her mind? Had he changed his? Why hadn't he come to her? Andi jumped out of her skin every time the phone rang, went giddy with anticipation at every knock on the door, and spent big chunks of time looking out the window, waiting for his car to pull into the lot. It took all her willpower not to pump Kate for information during their regular visits, but she never gave anything away.

As one long summer day faded into another Andi began to accept he wasn't coming and felt like she'd lost him all over again. Now here it was, August twenty-fourth, and she was left to mark the second anniversary of the day they met alone, with only his babies moving around inside her to remind her that they'd ever been together at all.

Eric came out of his room and peeked in to check on her. While he couldn't wait to be a big brother, she knew he was grossed out by the size of her belly. He'd told her he hoped the babies would come soon so she could stop being so fat.

She crooked a finger at him.

He jumped up on the bed with her.

She lifted the covers and snuggled him in next to her. They must've dozed off, because the next thing she knew, the phone was ringing, and she was startled to see it was after nine. She reached for the phone.

"Good morning," Jen said. "How are you feeling today?"

"Like I'm eight months pregnant and overslept," Andi grumbled.

"Why don't you stay there for a while longer? I'll send up some breakfast for you and Eric. I can cover this morning. Take a break, Andi."

"I just might do that. My back is on fire." Andi reached down to massage it. The pain in her back had gotten worse since yesterday, which had been a chaotic day at the hotel. Among several smaller disasters, Jen had closed the south veranda after cracks were discovered in the still-new patio. Jen arranged to have it repaired, and Andi left it in her capable hands.

"Don't forget, you have the meeting with that distributor at noon, but otherwise, I can handle everything else," Jen said. "Bring Eric down with you when you come. He can hang out with me while you're in your meeting."

The rep from the liquor distributor had left so many messages that Andi finally agreed to let Jen set up a meeting to discuss stocking his brands at Infinity Newport.

"Sounds good, thanks," Andi said and hung up. "Well, buddy, looks like we have some time to hang out and relax," she signed to Eric.

He grinned. "Good."

Just before noon, Andi and Eric walked hand in hand through the lobby to her office, where Jen waited for them.

She looked up from Andi's desk. "Hey, guys." Jen signed to include Eric. She'd insisted her boss slow down over the last few weeks and had taken on many of Andi's duties.

"Thanks again for the morning in bed. It did wonders for my disposition," Andi said with a grin. "Is the liquor guy here yet?"

"He came in a few minutes ago. For some reason, he wants to meet with you upstairs, so I'll walk you up and then I'll take this guy outside for a while," Jen said, reaching out to ruffle Eric's hair.

He dodged her hand with a giggle.

"Why upstairs?" Andi asked, annoyed by the pesky salesman. "We have a perfectly good conference room down here."

"I don't know," Jen said with a shrug. "He said he'd be up there when you were ready, so let's go."

Since Andi avoided the stairs these days, they took the elevator to the second floor. Jen and Eric walked out ahead of her, and when Andi stepped off the elevator, Jack was waiting for her.

She gasped and drank in the sight of him. He wore a navy polo shirt with khaki shorts, and even though he looked tired, he had never been more handsome. "What're you doing here?"

He held out one hand to her and the other to Eric as Jen stepped into the elevator and left them alone.

Andi looked back as the elevator doors closed. "What's going on?"

"Come with me." Jack led them to the top of the stairway, to the spot she'd once told him was her favorite place in the hotel, and gestured for her to have a seat in the chair he'd put there for her.

Standing next to her, Eric put an arm around her shoulders.

Jack knelt in front of her to rest his face against her pregnant belly and was rewarded with a solid kick to the cheek from one of the babies. He laughed as his eyes met hers.

The look on his face stopped her heart.

"Andrea, two years ago today you walked into my life and changed it forever." Jack signed as he spoke to include Eric.

Andi looked down at Jack, still shocked to see him and not sure yet why he was there.

"I asked you to take an enormous leap of faith by coming into my life, and you did it so willingly. A lot's happened since then, but one thing has never changed. I've loved you from the first instant I saw you, and I always will. I'm here today because, for the first time since we met two years ago, I'm completely free to love you, free to make a life with you and our children, and free to marry you if you'll have me." He held up a large diamond ring.

Andi's hand flew to her mouth. Tears rolled down her face as his words registered, and she finally got exactly what he was doing.

He slid the ring onto her left hand. "Andi, will you please, *please* marry me?"

Unable to get a word past the huge lump in her throat, she nodded and glanced at Eric, who didn't seem as surprised by this as she was. She held out her arms to Jack, and he wrapped her and Eric in a tight embrace. Andi breathed in the scent she'd recognize anywhere as his.

He held them both for a long time before he leaned back to kiss her and wipe the tears from her cheeks.

"I thought you weren't coming," she whispered when she could speak again.

"I wasn't coming until I could offer you everything." The weariness she saw in him told her what it had cost him to stay away.

Reaching into his pocket, he retrieved two folded pieces of paper. The first one he handed her was a marriage license.

She sucked in a sharp deep breath when she saw the date. "*Today?*"

He smiled and signed. "It had to be today. And do you really think there're cracks on *my* veranda?"

Eric giggled at the face she made when she realized she'd been had.

"Were you in on this?" she signed to her son.

Eric nodded with glee.

"He gave me his permission to marry you a week ago and was a very big boy to keep it a secret. I have something for you, too, Eric." Jack handed the second piece of paper to the boy.

Eric unfolded it and passed it to his mother when he didn't understand what it said.

"It's a petition for adoption," Andi signed for Eric. Alec Walsh's signature relinquished all claims to his son. Stunned, she looked up at Jack. "How did you do this?"

"I hired an investigator to find him, and he signed it two days ago," Jack said, but he didn't sign that part to spare Eric.

"He wouldn't have done that unless there was something in it for him," Andi said softly.

"Don't worry about that."

"He'll be back for more."

"No, he won't."

Eric looked confused, so Jack turned to him.

"I love you, Eric, and I want you to be my son," he signed. "I want more than just to have you living in my house. I want you to have my name, too. I'd like to adopt you, and that's what the paper says. Will you have me as your father, Eric Harrington?"

Eric nodded eagerly. "Can I call you Dad now?"

"Yes, buddy," Jack signed, his voice hoarse with emotion.

He hugged them both as a loud cheer erupted from downstairs.

Their family and friends started up the stairs, dressed for a Tuesday afternoon wedding. Jill, Kate, and Maggie were first in line. Andi's mother and Aunt Lou followed the girls. David, Lauren, and their girls were there, as were Frannie, Jamie, and the twins, Jack's parents, and Jamie's parents. Standing behind them were Andi's former coworkers from Chicago, Jack's colleagues from HBA, and most of the Infinity Newport staff.

Jen gave Quinn a high five and a delighted smile that they'd managed to pull off Jack's best surprise yet.

Jack took Andi's hand to help her up to greet their guests. "We have a wedding to get to," he said.

"I can't go looking like this." She gestured to her casual summer dress as she received hugs from the girls. Seeing Jill and Maggie for the first time in months brought new tears to her eyes.

"Not to worry, Andi, I've got you covered there." Frannie handed Olivia to Jamie. "Let's go. He's giving us thirty minutes, and that's it."

"Don't be late," Jack said, watching her be swept up by Frannie and the girls.

Almost afraid to walk away, Andi glanced back at him. What if she'd imagined the whole thing? "How in the world did he do all this?" she whispered to Frannie.

"He enlisted the help of all of us to throw together a wedding on short notice. I hope you don't mind that I designated myself your matron of honor," Frannie said as she hustled Andi into the suite that had been set aside to get her ready.

"Of course not. You'd be my first choice. But Frannie, how did he get divorced so fast? I don't get it." She kept her voice low so the girls wouldn't hear her.

"He went to the Dominican Republic."

Andi had heard of the expedited Dominican divorce, but had never known of anyone who'd done it.

"He's been divorced for more than a week, but he was waiting for the adoption matter to be resolved and then, of course, the date today was significant."

"I still can't believe it." Andi looked down at her gorgeous engagement ring. On her other hand, she still wore the sapphire he'd given her on their first Christmas together.

"He didn't want the babies coming into the world without their father married to their mother. When it became possible for him to prevent that, he did. He's been like a cat on a hot tin roof hoping you wouldn't deliver early."

Andi smiled at the image, knowing patience wasn't Jack's strong suit.

"We'll run out of time if we keep gabbing. Let's get you dressed and ready."

Andi put her hand on her soon-to-be sister-in-law's arm. "I have no doubt you moved heaven and earth to help him like you always do. Thank you for everything."

"It was my pleasure. Come see the dress I found for you—they won't even be able to tell you're pregnant."

Andi howled with laughter.

She floated through a dream as she married Jack on the south veranda, which had been converted to a magical setting for the wedding. Jamie once again served as Jack's best man, and Frannie stood with Andi. Before they took their vows, they asked the girls to come up next to Andi, and Jack extended a hand to Eric, who'd put on a tie for the occasion. The only thing that detracted from an otherwise spectacular day was the grinding pain in Andi's back, which was becoming harder to ignore.

After the ceremony, the band Jack had hired called Kate up to sing with them. Jack sat with an arm around Andi to watch Kate perform with a live band. She sang "Bless the Broken Road," and by the time she reached the chorus, the bride and groom were mopping up tears.

The wedding guests cheered as the band played the final notes of the song. Kate was so polished and professional when she turned to applaud the band that Andi clutched Jack's hand when she saw him watching in amazement.

He told Andi he would ask for only one dance that day and sang along to "The Way You Look Tonight," changing "tonight" to "today."

When she reached up to kiss him a gush of wetness between her legs made her gasp.

"Honey, what is it?"

"I think my water broke."

"Are you sure?"

She looked down at the puddle around her feet and then back up at him, nodding.

"Okay, come on, I'll tell Jamie to keep things going here. No need to break up the party," Jack said as he spirited her off the dance floor.

But before they could make their getaway, Andi bent in half with a contraction that left her unable to move or breathe. She'd no sooner gotten through that one when another hit her.

"Jack," she panted, already resisting the urge to push. "I don't think we have time to get to the hospital."

Frannie helped Jack get Andi upstairs while Jamie asked everyone to continue enjoying the party.

"Looks like we might be offering two events for the price of one today," Jamie said to nervous laughter from the wedding guests.

"Oh my God, I need to push," Andi said, overwhelmed by the sensation.

Jack gave Frannie a panicked look.

"Maybe there's a doctor in the hotel," Frannie said.

The minute they got Andi into bed, Jack called down to the front desk and asked them to see if they could find a doctor. He also called Dr. Abbott, who assured him she was on her way but would be thirty minutes or more.

"Hurry," Jack said and turned back to Andi, who cried out as another contraction ripped through her. Between contractions, Jack and Frannie helped her out of her wedding dress and into a nightgown.

"I'm so sorry, Jack," Andi said, blinking back tears. "I ruined our wedding."

"Don't be sorry, honey. I'm just glad we got the first part taken care of in time." He kissed her as another contraction hit.

She bit back the urge to push. "I can't wait any longer."

A knock on the door sent Frannie flying across the room. She returned with a young couple. "We're in luck." Frannie introduced Mark and Julie Patterson.

"I'm a cardiology resident, and my wife is a labor and delivery nurse," Mark said, shaking hands with Jack, who was weak with relief to be getting some qualified assistance. "We're here on our honeymoon and heard you could use some help."

Andi nodded when Julie asked if she could examine her.

"You're crowning, Andi. Are you ready to push?"

"I've been trying not to for half an hour. I should tell you I had a C-section seven years ago."

"Looks like we don't have time for anything other than the good old-fashioned way, so on the next contraction, let's give it a push." Julie gave Frannie and Jack instructions on how they could help.

John Joseph Harrington IV came into the world ten minutes later, followed eight minutes later by his identical twin brother, Robert Franklin Harrington. They named the boys for their father and grandfathers but would call them Johnny and Robby.

Both babies let out lusty cries, and Julie estimated them to be a very healthy six pounds each, even though they'd arrived a month early.

Dr. Abbott rushed into the room five minutes after Robby was born, shocked to see the babies had already arrived and everyone seemed to be doing fine. "I missed it?"

"We work fast around here," Jack said as he held Andi and brushed at tears.

Mark and Julie left promising to check on the new family later. Jack and Andi thanked them profusely for their help, and Andi promised to comp their stay at the hotel.

When Dr. Abbott cleared everyone from the room so she could examine Andi, Jack took the babies to the hallway, where an anxious group of grandparents and siblings waited to meet their new family members.

A few minutes later, Dr. Abbott came out to tell Jack he could take the babies to their mother.

Andi rested against the pile of pillows, her eyes bright with excitement.

Jack sat next to her, handed Johnny to her, and kept Robby for himself.

"Dr. Abbott said I was probably in labor all night and didn't recognize it because the pain was in my back," she said with a sheepish grin. "The back pain was nothing new, so I ignored it."

"No wonder it happened so fast. But I'm glad we didn't have time to get you to the hospital and our sons were born in *our* hotel, which, I might add, is home sweet home until we find a house for this brood of ours." He leaned over to kiss her. "You were amazing, Andi. I'm so proud of you."

Caressing his face, she was flooded with relief that he was back to stay and hers to keep. She had two new rings on her left hand and two new babies to prove it.

"I woke up today with three kids, and now I have *six*," he said, gazing down at Robby. Both babies had caps of shiny black hair.

"I had *one,* and now I have *six.*"

"Okay, you win," he said, and they laughed. "I have *sons.*"

"Three of them. Do you remember what Dr. Abbott said about identical twins?"

"A stroke of sheer luck," he recalled. "You hear that, boys? You're a stroke of sheer luck—just like your mother was for me."

She tugged him close enough to kiss. "I love you, Jack."

"I love you, too, but I have one question for you," he said with a devilish gleam in his eye.

"What's that?" she asked, amused by him.

"How will we *ever* explain to these boys that they were born on our wedding day?"

"As soon as I figure out how it all happened, I'll be sure to let you know."

They laughed while the babies slept in their arms.

The story begun in "Treading Water" continues in "Marking Time." Clare's story picks up on Jack and Andi's wedding day as she begins to put her life back together. We also follow Kate as she sets out to find fame and fortune in Nashville. And then read "Starting Over" and "Coming Home."

Turn the age for a sneak peek of, Marking Time!

MARKING TIME
CHAPTER 1

Clare checked her watch again. One thirty. *It must be done by now. My husband—or I should say ex-husband—is remarried.*

"Ex-husband," she said with a shudder. Unimaginable. Divorced... Such an ugly word.

She wheeled her chair across her room in the rehabilitation center and gazed out at the steamy August day. Somewhere along the Ten Mile Ocean Drive in historic Newport, Jack had exchanged vows with Andi. *He has a new family now.* Clare had known this day was coming and had set the whole thing in motion by letting him go, but that didn't make it any easier to imagine her Jack married to someone else. "Not my Jack anymore," she said to herself.

The door opened. "Mrs. Harrington?"

Clare didn't correct the nurse. She wasn't "Mrs." any longer. "Yes?"

"They're ready for you in PT."

Taking another long look at the City by the Sea, Clare wondered what Jack was doing right at that moment. Was he kissing his bride? Making a toast? Dancing with one of their daughters? She shook her head, angry to have allowed herself even a brief trip down that road. What did it matter now?

"Let's go." She wheeled herself to the door to let the nurse push her through the long hallways to physical therapy.

After dinner, Clare worked her way into lightweight pajamas. She was proud of her ability to do things for herself, even small things like changing her clothes. Each little victory added up. Rolling the wheelchair across the room she'd called home for the last four months, she eased herself from her chair to the sofa on her own—another recent accomplishment. Her recovery was coming along slowly but surely.

That she had recovered at all was a miracle, or so they all said. No one had expected her to ever emerge from the coma she'd been in for three years after being hit by a car. But four months ago, she'd defied the odds and awakened after a fever doctors had feared would finally end her life. Yep, a real miracle. Everything that happened since then had been somewhat less than miraculous: her twenty-year marriage had disintegrated, and her days were now marked by the struggle to regain her health.

Clare knew she was lucky, but she'd grown tired of hearing that word. Doctors had told her she would most likely be confronted with physical challenges for the rest of her life, including chronic urinary tract infections, a propensity toward pneumonia, fatigue, muscle spasms, and other fallout from three years of inactivity. Oh yeah, what a miracle.

A tearjerker movie on TV caught her attention, and it was a relief to be absorbed into someone else's drama for a change. When someone knocked at her door, Clare muted the television. "Come in," she called and was surprised to see Jack's sister, Frannie Booth.

"May I come in?"

"Of course," Clare said to her former sister-in-law. "Come sit."

Frannie crossed the room to sit next to Clare on the sofa. She wore her auburn hair in an elegant twist left over from her brother's wedding.

"I didn't expect to see you, especially tonight," Clare said, admiring the yellow floral silk dress Frannie had worn to the wedding. "You look fabulous."

"Thanks. I was thinking of you and thought I'd stop by to see how you're doing."

"I'm fine, but you didn't have to come."

"I wanted to."

"How was it?" Clare tried to sound casual as she twirled a lock of her unruly blonde hair around a finger.

"It was lovely but a little more exciting than we'd planned. Andi's water broke during the reception. They had twin boys right there at the hotel. The doctor said they appear to be identical."

"Oh." Clare struggled to hide the surge of emotion. Jack had sons.

"It all happened so fast." Frannie shook her head and smiled. "Apparently, she'd been in labor all night and didn't realize it because she'd had back pain."

Clare worked at keeping her expression neutral as she absorbed the news that the babies had arrived a month early. "They're all fine?"

"Yes."

"The girls must've been excited," Clare said, referring to her daughters.

"They were."

"What're their names?"

"They named them for Jack and the grandfathers, John Joseph Harrington the fourth, and Robert Franklin Harrington. Johnny and Robby."

Despite her best efforts, Clare's eyes flooded with tears. "Johnny and Robby," she whispered.

"I'm sorry to upset you."

Clare wiped her eyes. "It's okay."

"I've wanted to come for weeks to say…what you did…letting him go…" Frannie had a look of awe on her face. "It was so selfless."

"It was the only thing I could do. It was selfish more than anything."

"No, it wasn't. It was amazing. I don't know that I could've done it."

A stab of pain hit Clare just below her broken heart. "I don't want to talk about that anymore. It's over and done with. But I'm glad you're here for another reason."

"What's that?"

"I've had lots of time to think," Clare said with a small grin. "I don't know if I ever adequately thanked you for what you did while I was sick. I mean for you to give up a year and a half of your life to take care of my kids—"

"Taking care of your girls was a pleasure. You don't have to thank me. You'd have done the same for me. So you're really doing okay?"

Clare raised a suspicious eyebrow. "Did Jack send you to check on me?"

"Not this time. I think he's so stunned by the babies arriving in the middle of his wedding, he doesn't even know his own name right now."

They shared a laugh.

"I'm sure," Clare said. "I'm doing fine. Don't worry about me."

"I also came because I have something for you." Frannie reached into her bag for a leather-bound book. She held it against her chest for a moment as she collected her thoughts. "Shortly after I moved in with Jack and the girls, I started keeping a journal. It was odd because I'd never had one before, but I suddenly had a need to write things down. Anyway, I debated for a long time about whether I should share it with you. And then I realized that most of the time I was keeping it, I was doing it for you. I was writing it for you."

"Did you think I'd recover? No one seemed to think I would."

"No, I didn't think so. But for some reason I started writing things down, and when I read it over recently, I understood I'd done it for you, like I was talking to you. I didn't consciously set out to do that. Oh, I'm not explaining it well."

"No, you are. Can I see it?"

She handed the book to Clare. "I know you'll be so happy to get back some of the time you lost with the girls by reading about their lives, but there're other things in there that'll cause you pain. I wish I could spare you that. I didn't give it to you before now because of that."

"You wrote about them, too, didn't you? About Jack and Andi?" Clare asked as she brushed a hand over the leather cover.

"Yes, and I don't know if you should read those parts."

"Maybe I'll skip them. You have no idea how much this means to me."

"I think maybe I do. I'm a mom now, too, remember? If you want to talk about it—any of it—you only have to ask."

"Thank you." Feeling as if she'd been given a priceless gift, Clare reached out to squeeze Frannie's hand. "Thank you so much."

"I hope you'll still be thanking me after you've read it," Frannie said with a grin. "Have you made any plans?"

Clare shrugged. "Not really. They're saying I have maybe another month of rehab, and then I can go home. I'm not sure what's next for me." She twisted her face into an ironic smile. "I find myself at loose ends for the first time in more than twenty years."

"I'm sure you'll figure it out. I know the girls are looking forward to having you at home. Do you need anything?"

"Your brother made sure I'd never want for anything. I got my bank statement the other day, and my eyes almost popped out of my head."

"He doesn't want you to worry about supporting yourself."

"With that kind of money, I'll never have to worry again, that's for sure. He didn't have to do that."

"Yes, he did."

Clare smiled. "I'm glad you came, Frannie. Will you come again and bring your babies? I'd love to see them."

"You bet."

"Come on, Clare, give me one more step. Just one more."

Sweat rolled down her face as she struggled against the crutches. "You're a sadist, Jeffrey."

"You love me. You know you do."

Clare put her last bit of energy into that final step and then rested against his outstretched arms.

"Right," she panted. "Just keep reminding me."

Behind them, someone applauded.

Clare turned to find her doctor watching. "Great, an audience," she grumbled and swiped at the sweat on her face.

Dr. Paul Langston came across the room. "That was outstanding. I counted at least fifty steps."

"I counted fifty-five," Jeffrey said.

"I don't remember sending you an invite, Dr. Paul. What're you doing here?" Clare thanked Jeffrey when he eased her into her wheelchair.

"I came to check on my star patient. Do I need an invitation?"

She took a long drink from her water bottle. "Not if you're going to charm me."

Dr. Langston tapped a toe against the chair. "I'm thinking we're just about ready to kiss this baby good-bye and talk about sending you home."

Her stomach clenched with anxiety. "Already? I thought you said another month?"

"You've gotten used to us, huh? Can't live without me?"

"Yeah, something like that," she said with a grin. He was a dreamboat with close-cropped blond hair and mischievous blue eyes. Too bad he was also ten years younger than her. "You're easy enough on the eyes, I guess."

He hooted. "Such flattery! It's going straight to my head. I'll take Miss Congeniality back to her room," he told Jeffrey.

"See you tomorrow, Clare," Jeffrey said.

"Can't wait."

"You've been doing so well," Dr. Langston said as they rolled along the corridor. "The nurses tell me you're showering and dressing on your own and relying on them less every day." He stopped next to a bench in the hallway and sat to bring himself to her eye level. "I thought you were busting to get out of here. What gives?"

She shrugged.

"Is it what's waiting for you at home?"

She raised an eyebrow. "Don't you mean what's not waiting for me?"

"Have you talked to Dr. Baker about it?" he asked, referring to Clare's psychiatrist.

"Here and there, but we've been more focused on the attack and all that. I haven't wanted to talk about the untimely demise of my marriage. I'm just a bundle of unresolved issues," she said with the good-natured grin that had made her a favorite among the medical team that had cared for her over the last four months.

"I think we should set a date." Dr. Langston folded his arms over his white coat. "Two weeks from today?"

"Are you sure? That's awfully soon."

"Your daughters are waiting for you. Don't you want to get home to them?"

"They're happy living with their father right now."

"They'll be thrilled to have you home again. They've waited a long time."

"I'm sure they're more than used to being without me. How do I get back three years with them?" She bit back the urge to weep.

"You can't. All you can do is go forward from here. I'm going to be honest with you, Clare. None of us imagined you'd get this far. You've defied the odds. Don't let yourself down by giving up now."

She smiled. "You're tossing me out, huh?"

"I'm afraid so."

"You've all been so great. I'll miss you."

He got up from the bench. "Nah, you'll be too busy enjoying your fabulous new life to give us a thought."

"Somehow I doubt that." She twisted her hands in her lap. The idea of going home filled her with apprehension.

He squatted down so she could see him. "Talk to Dr. Baker. Tell him how you feel about going home. Let him help you."

"I will. Thanks, Paul."

An item in the *Newport Daily News* caught Clare's eye the next day:

Prominent City Architect Welcomes Double Delivery

NEWPORT—(August 27) It's not every day that twins interrupt their parents' wedding, but that's what happened Tuesday.

Jack Harrington, co-owner of the Newport architectural firm Harrington Booth Associates, and his wife Andi welcomed twin sons, John Joseph Harrington IV and Robert Franklin Harrington. The twins arrived in the midst of their parents' wedding at the Infinity Newport Hotel where their mother is the general manager. The hotel, which opened in December, was designed and built by Harrington Booth Associates.

"We thought we were just having a wedding, but I guess the babies didn't want to miss it," said Jamie Booth, Mr. Harrington's business partner and brother-in-law. Mr. Booth is married to Mr. Harrington's sister, Frannie. The Booths are also the parents of twins, one-year-old Owen and Olivia. "Andi and the babies are doing great," Mr. Booth reported.

The new twins are the grandsons of John and Madeline Harrington of Greenwich, Conn., Betty Franklin of Chicago, Ill., and the late Robert Franklin. They join sisters Jill, Kate, and Maggie, and a brother, Eric.

Clare read it a second time. It was still so hard to believe that Jack was now married to someone else and had twin babies with her—twin sons, no less. And it was splashed all over the news. Anyone who didn't already know she and Jack had recently gotten divorced did now.

Knowing how much her daughters loved babies, she could imagine their delight with their new brothers. No doubt she would hear all about it when they came to visit. Thinking back to the girls being born brought a smile to Clare's face. Jill had just turned nineteen and was beginning her sophomore year at Brown University in Providence. Kate would be eighteen in November, and they had agreed to let her go to Nashville for a year after her birthday to pursue a career in country music. And Clare's "baby," Maggie, would be thirteen in December.

Clare reached over to the table next to the sofa to pick up the book Frannie had left. She had spent a few days working up the courage to look at it, and now the curiosity was overwhelming. Opening the book, she flipped to the first page, taking comfort in the familiarity of Frannie's precise penmanship. The first item was dated June 20.

It's late and the girls are finally in bed. They were wound up today—the last day of school. We now have an 11th grader, a 10th grader, and a 4th grader. I'm thrilled to see them excited and happy for a change. It's been a while.

July 26

Jack sits by Clare's bedside hour after hour, day after day. He talks to her until he's hoarse and weak with fatigue. I look at him and wonder how he'll ever live without her. But he's not ready to think about that. I don't know if he'll ever be.

Clare brushed a tear from her cheek and read several entries about the girls' activities that summer. Jill had babysat for a neighborhood family, and Kate had gone to sleepaway camp for the first time. They went to the beach a lot, and Jamie took them out on the sailboat he owned with Jack.

August 19

Jill is sweet sixteen today, and it's her first birthday without her mom. She was weepy during the day but enjoyed the party we had for her after dinner. The nurses who care for Clare have become part of the family, and Jill invited them to have cake with us.

Enough, Clare thought as she closed the book and wiped her tears. That's enough for today.

Get *Starting Over* now. Order a signed copy from Marie's Store at *marieforce.com/store*.

ABOUT THE AUTHOR

Marie Force is the *New York Times* bestselling author of more than 50 contemporary romances, including the Gansett Island Series, which has sold nearly 3 million books, and the Fatal Series from Harlequin Books, which has sold 1.5 million books. In addition, she is the author of the Butler, Vermont Series, the Green Mountain Series and the erotic romance Quantum Series, written under the slightly modified name of M.S. Force. All together, her books have sold more than 5.5 million copies worldwide!

Her goals in life are simple—to finish raising two happy, healthy, productive young adults, to keep writing books for as long as she possibly can and to never be on a flight that makes the news.

Join Marie's mailing list for news about new books and upcoming appearances in your area. Follow her on Facebook at https://www.facebook.com/MarieForceAuthor, Twitter @marieforce and on Instagram at https://instagram.com/marieforceauthor/. Join one of Marie's many reader groups. Contact Marie at *marie@marieforce.com*.

OTHER TITLES BY MARIE FORCE

Other Contemporary Romances Available from Marie Force:

The Treading Water Series

Book 1: Treading Water

Book 2: Marking Time

Book 3: Starting Over

Book 4: Coming Home

The Gansett Island Series

Book 1: Maid for Love

Book 2: Fool for Love

Book 3: Ready for Love

Book 4: Falling for Love

Book 5: Hoping for Love

Book 6: Season for Love

Book 7: Longing for Love

Book 8: Waiting for Love

Book 9: Time for Love

Book 10: Meant for Love

Book 10.5: Chance for Love, *A Gansett Island Novella*

Book 11: Gansett After Dark

Book 12: Kisses After Dark

Book 13: Love After Dark

Book 14: Celebration After Dark

Book 15: Desire After Dark

Book 16: Light After Dark

Gansett Island Episodes, Episode 1: Victoria & Shannon

The Green Mountain Series

Book 1: All You Need Is Love

Book 2: I Want to Hold Your Hand

Book 4: And I Love Her

Novella: You'll Be Mine

Book 5: It's Only Love

Book 6: Ain't She Sweet

The Butler Vermont Series
(Continuation of the Green Mountain Series)

Book 1: Every Little Thing

Single Titles

Sex Machine

Sex God

Georgia on My Mind

True North

The Fall

Everyone Loves a Hero

Love at First Flight

Line of Scrimmage

Made in the USA
Middletown, DE
27 July 2018